HEARTBEAT

HEARTBEAT

EUGENE DONG, MD.
SPYROS ANDREOPOULOS

Coward, McCann & Geoghegan, Inc.
New York

Acknowledgments

We want to express our gratitude to Alfred Coppel, John Gofman, M.D., Janet Lewis, Milton Schemm, and Edward Stinson, M.D. for their kindness and helpfulness in our work.

E.D.
S.A.

Published on the same day in Canada by Longman Canada Limited, Toronto.

SBN: 698-10875-2

Library of Congress Cataloging in Publication Data

Dong, Eugene.
Heartbeat.

I. Andreopoulos, Spyros, 1929- joint author.
II. Title.
PZ4.D6815He [PS3554.04694] 813'.5'4 77-10720

PRINTED IN THE UNITED STATES OF AMERICA

"I submit that as scientists we have no business asking what the truth may lead to . . ."

From Bertolt Brecht's "Galileo"

To those who work to protect us
from our own folly.

HEARTBEAT

Chapter 1

The blue princess telephone rang gently. It was 5:30 A.M. Not that the hour mattered. He was wide awake anyway. He reached for the receiver in one swift motion, as he had done so many times before. His wife didn't even stir.

"Hello, Dr. Bradfield?" The early caller did not need to identify himself. His greeting was more of a grunt than a hello, and unique. Bradfield knew instantly it belonged to Buchanan, his senior resident.

"Yes, Don. What's up?"

"We have just the case you wanted. . . . "

As Buchanan spoke on, Bradfield could picture him: a straight six feet, three inches tall, weighing 200 pounds, broad-shouldered, thick-handed. The face with the narrow-set brown eyes was adorned by long Civil War-style sideburns and a short, well-cropped mustache. The voice went on, clearly, professionally.

"The patient is a forty-three-year-old white engineer. He suffered a massive myocardial infarct two months ago and has been hospitalized at Stanford Hospital ever since—"

Bradfield cut in. "Did they evaluate him as a candidate for a heart transplant?"

"Yes, they did. As I understand the situation, his left ventricle is compromised severely."

Buchanan carefully described his assessment of the angiogram and other tests. They showed the important coronary artery to be critically blocked. The heart chamber was mostly dead tissue and overly large, with its pumping function diminished. It all added up: the patient was a prime candidate for heart replacement and he needed it right away.

"What's his clinical status?" Bradfield asked.

"He's conscious, alert, but breathing rapidly. Blood pressure is low, heartbeat is ninety to a hundred per minute and the lungs are congested. His liver is enlarged and kidneys aren't producing much urine."

"How is it he wasn't transplanted?"

"He's a poor tissue match."

"Right. How did we learn about him?"

"His fiancée is a nurse. She's familiar with our work on the artificial heart. When the Stanford people told her he couldn't be transplanted, she called us."

"Have the shrinks seen them?"

"Yes. Both are solid as the Rock of Gibraltar."

"How about . . . um, I'm blanking on the name. You know, Miss Goody Twoshoes, the social worker—oh, yes, Louella Commons."

"I couldn't get hold of her last night. But the Stanford case worker thinks their social situation is good: short illness, intelligent, both professionals, good insurance. You can collect a fee and plug in the pump."

Buchanan's flip remark annoyed Bradfield, but he ignored it.

"Good work, Don. Have the patient transferred over by ambulance. Send one of the junior residents—say Jack Johnson—to make sure everything gets well organized. I'll see the patient in the Intensive Care Unit after the first case this morning. The pump is sterile in the lab and ready to go. Call Allen Ridley, the health physicist. Tell him tonight's the night and we'll need the plutonium this evening."

"Okay. Anything else? How about the O.R.?"

"Right. We'll need the shielded operating room for 7:30 P.M. Make sure Mrs. Donald is notified so we can keep the transients out of the room."

"Okay. Shall I notify anybody in administration?"

"No, I'll do that. Oh, what's the patient's name?"

"Henry Gray."

It was nine o'clock in Bethesda, Maryland. Harris was sitting at his cluttered desk on a gray metal Naugahyde swivel chair reading a letter. A thick, gray paper card was folded on the desk top, with RONALD HARRIS, PH. D. embossed on it in yellow letters. The overhead fluorescent light hummed at sixty cycles per second. The cold outdoor light entered his windowless domain through the opened door of the receptionist's office. Along the left wall was a carefully lettered oversize poster. It showed the stages of the artificial heart development, with the subcontractors named, the amounts of the contracts and estimated date of completion. Red pins were placed as each task was finished: "new power supply," "control system miniaturization," "thermal engine test."

Wanda Narewski was standing by his desk, pencil and pen in hand, her eyes staring blankly at the wall. Harris's secretary wasn't thinking of her work at the moment, but of the tall, handsome athlete with whom she had planned the evening.

The telephone broke into her concentration. She lifted the receiver. "Artificial Heart Branch, may I help you?"

"Yes. Is Mr. Harris available?"

"May I tell him who's calling?"

"This is Dr. Bill Bradfield from California."

She handed Harris the receiver after he said he would take the call.

"Hello, Ron."

"Hi. How are you? Isn't it a bit early there? I just this minute came into my office."

"Early! You ought to know by now that a surgeon's day is long and hard."

"Yes, of course. What's happening?"

"I've just received word from my senior resident. We have a

patient who meets our criteria for artificial heart replacement. He was evaluated at Stanford and he's unsuitable for a transplant. I believe the time is propitious for us to act."

Ronald Harris lowered his voice and a significant degree of concern crept into his words.

"Now, Bill. This is pretty short notice. The forms have not been fully evaluated by the task force."

Bradfield thought, damn, he's backing out. He's one of those people who's pestering you and pushing for results, then when the time comes to act he warns you he can't approve your decision. But almost immediately Bradfield dismissed the thought. He understood that if Harris was perplexed, it was for substantial reasons.

The subcontracts for an artificial heart had been let four years earlier. At the time no one thought that permanent installation, even experimentally, to replace somebody's hopelessly diseased heart, was in sight for at least ten years. But Bradfield's work was ahead of schedule. Six calves had had their hearts quietly and efficiently replaced by Bradfield's device for up to six months without difficulty. And, without Harris's knowledge, Bradfield had built one unit for implantation in humans. He had listed it as a "prototype small working model."

This was the heart Bradfield now referred to, causing Harris to shuffle in anxiety, making his hands cold and moist as he realized what it meant. If Harris was anything, he was orthodox. On one wall of his office, next to his impressive work charts, was a map of the world, the kind in which the United States was squarely at the center. Behind him was a photograph of the White House and underneath that, the well-known pictures of George Washington and Abraham Lincoln. What he was hearing over the telephone was decidedly unorthodox.

But Bradfield's skill in reading people was uncanny.

"Look, Ron. How many years have you been in the government—twenty-five, thirty? How long has it taken you to get this program where it is—eight or nine? If we put this pump in the guy now, you'll finally make it big!"

Harris thought of Bradfield's word "propitious." If Bradfield only knew how propitious it was! Just the evening before, the director of the National Heart Institute had resigned in an internal political dispute. He had almost completed a report establishing stricter standards for the use of nuclear materials in artificial organs. The action would have required major modifications in the device and delayed a clinical trial for months, even years. Now the report would be shelved until a new director was appointed. In the interim the implantation in a human could proceed.

Harris still hesitated. "We're really up the creek if the surgery goes wrong?"

"Ron, we haven't failed once. The power supply works. The surgery is duck soup. You need us to do it now. I say, let's go!"

"Oh, all right. You win."

"That's it?"

"Yes."

"Okay. See you in Sweden!"

As Bradfield hung up softly, he took a deep breath and let it out slowly. He looked over at the sleeping figure beside him. Charlotte had not stirred. She needed the sleep and he wanted to shave, dress, and clear out without awakening her. Bradfield's relationship with his wife was not what one might call "intense." Their couplings were satisfying, but only in a physiological sense. His passion was reserved for his surgery. Charlotte had been trained from childhood to be cool and serene. Still, it was a mutually enjoyable partnership. They gave each other enough of themselves to make the marriage work. They had agreed before marriage not to have children. She had concentrated on social functions and volunteer work to further his career. He worked hard on climbing the academic ladder. It was all very rational of them both.

In Bethesda, Harris's eyelid twitched several times as he replaced the receiver on its cradle. His pulse was fast, and he asked himself, "Why did I let myself be talked into that?" Then, out loud, "Miss Narewski, get me a round-trip ticket to San Francisco. There should be a flight at noon. And hurry."

Chapter 2

At dawn the sky was overcast and the wind increased steadily as a predicted Pacific storm blew in from the west. Rain began at nine and came down intermittently in sheets and drizzle.

The artificial heart laboratory of Aspermont University's School of Medicine on the San Francisco peninsula was situated seven hundred yards from the main complex. The lab lay in the backyard of a brownstone building, the former home of the Anatomy Department. A six-foot hurricane fence surrounded the area of the laboratory, an untended field out of direct sight of the futuristic high-rise hospital. Weeds rose two and three feet high except in two areas: a path from the gate to the door of the first building, and the wooden, fenced-in preoperation corral for the domestic animals used in the experiments. Within the corral, the calves had eaten and trodden down the plant life, making a hard brown patch in the summer, a muddy quagmire in the winter. So it was today.

Experimental programs brought luster to medical schools, but however much lip service was given to surgical research, the facilities actually provided by the medical school at Aspermont for the artificial heart project consisted only of the plot of land. Everything else was funded by government contracts. The intellectual projects, smaller and more esthetic, were housed in the main building.

For Bradfield's work, however, the location could not have been better, despite its bleakness. The further removed he was physically from the school administrators, the less they knew and the less control they exerted over his activities.

In one small building were two stalls, each containing a calf with a functioning artificial heart. The animals stood peacefully, chewing their cud, drinking water from troughs six inches in front of their muzzles. The whirring of the ventilation system, the beeping of the monitoring system broke the sterile quiet. Today the wind and rain added to the sound. Six closed circuit TV cameras were panning slowly over the animals. A complex system of electronic gear transmitted the TV pictures, the heart beat, the electrocardiogram to a control room. The data now being analyzed indicated no malfunctions.

Another building, connected to the first one by a covered wooden walkway, was the surgical suite where the implants were carried out. On this day, the respirators, the operating table, the anesthesia machine, the suction apparatus—all movable equipment—were stacked along the left-hand wall. Incandescent surgical lights cut through the outer gloom. In the center of the room was a simple two-by-four stainless steel table with ballbearing roller feet. Right next to it was a tall black drum, three feet in diameter. The drum was lined with eight inches of lead. Bright yellow stickers with three spokes and the words CAUTION—NUCLEAR MATERIALS were plastered across the surface. The drum was used to transport the plutonium energy source, but at this moment it was empty.

In the laboratory Elizabeth Browning and Richard Wheeler were in the process of preparing the artificial heart for sterilization. Elizabeth wore a blue cotton surgical gown that could only be termed "suitable to the occasion." Her surgical dress looked like pajamas. The absence of darts, the straight cut, without elastic or drawstrings, made the garments simple to launder, easy to repair.

But Browning's natural sensuality, despite years in operating-room work, would not permit her to appear in unbecoming clothing, so she had tucked her long, brown-blond hair in a full cap made of high-grade Dan River material patterned with yellow flowers. Her silver eye makeup was simple but attractive. Slight wrinkles showed around her eyes when she smiled. To define her neat waistline, she folded in the material and fastened it with adhesive tape. A fine perfume permeated the laboratory when she moved. Her feminine, rather tinkling laugh was frequently heard.

On this day and at this time, however, the activity was strictly professional. Don Buchanan had called her at 6 A.M. and informed her of the impending operation. She remembered his greeting.

"Hullo? Is this the Alviso-Boston cooperative redevelopment agency?"

"Listen, Buchanan, cut the crap!" she had replied. "Six in the morning is no time for jokes."

"Sorry about that. Right, listen!"

Browning could visualize Buchanan, standing bone-tired at the hospital desk, speaking without moving a hair in his mustache. "You know that dinky pump that's in the lab? Well, Bradfield says it's ready and we're going to give it a go for real."

"Wow! How long do we have to get the stuff together?"

"Until tonight."

"Right. We'll have it ready."

In this day of job descriptions, group responsibility, and a forty-hour week, Browning was a refreshing breeze in more ways than one. She had the "I can get it done for you" attitude, instead of the whining "why don't you give me more time" response. Thus it was that Liz Browning leaped out of bed on that blustery gray morning, made toast and coffee, washed and did her eyes up carefully, applied a light pink lipstick, wrote a short note to her still sleeping twelve-year-old daughter, and drove off to the laboratory. The cold wind bit into her as she left the house, and she shivered. Momentarily, she longed for the warmth and comfort of a loving man, felt the pain of loneliness after a very early divorce. Then, resolutely, she brought her mind to bear on the important tasks before her. She pushed the painful thoughts down and drove off.

Richard Wheeler was tall, gangly, black, and wore an Afro cut which always stuck out from under his surgical cap. He arrived at the laboratory as usual, anywhere from fifteen to twenty minutes late. He was the bane of Browning's existence. He would bump into the sterile operating field, or bring the wrong medication, or break a bottle when pressured or flustered. But despite his faults and his frequent clashes with Browning, he stuck to his laboratory job tenaciously, progressing from cleaning floors and washing instruments to his present task of senior laboratory technician. He had spent the last two years working with the bovine model of the artificial heart. He knew its working parts by rote, but understood little of the physics, engineering, metallurgy, or ethics of the machine. At twenty-two, he was naïve and gullible. Everything Bradfield told him he accepted in wonderment. He didn't know, for example, that the little 100-gram block of material he often handled was worth a fortune in the open market.

Liz Browning had hoped that Bradfield would see that Wheeler was a problem and fire him. Indeed, Bradfield had intimated once that someone else would be involved in working on the human model, but in the foreshortened developmental phase, this replacement had been put off. So it was that on this day two unlikely teammates were assembling a small but complicated machine on which a man's life would soon be totally dependent.

Jack Johnson entered Aspermont Medical Center at 6:15 A.M. The youthful assistant resident in heart surgery had not been on duty the night before and he felt refreshed as he considered what his work for the day might entail. The corridors at this time were in half darkness, and the paging system was turned to a low level. He passed an occasional orderly sleeping on a chair during a break, but otherwise the entrances to the hospital appeared deserted. It was a peaceful start to a day.

Johnson entered the locker and dressing room on the second floor adjacent to the operating room suite and intensive care units. He stripped off his motorcycle helmet, Levis, well-worn ski jacket and sports shirt, and donned the pressed greeny-blue surgical scrub suit. He then pulled on his long white coat. A stethoscope and reflex hammer peeked up over the edge of a hip-level pocket, and the indispensable notebook for keeping track of his work weighted the front. Thus transformed, Jack Johnson, M.D., passed out of the dressing room with an air of authority and strode toward the I.C.U. A pot of freshly brewed coffee sat in the "conference" room next to the nursing station. He poured himself a generous cup and opened the solid maple door leading to the unit proper.

On the left of the long hallway were sixteen rooms in which patients were being cared for by a hierarchy of nurses and respiratory therapy technicians. On the right of the hallway were two nursing stations, both brightly lit with fluorescent lighting. Medications, charts, and oscilloscopes were distributed efficiently in these areas. The bustle of intense and dedicated men and women inside these rooms was in marked contrast to other hospital areas.

Dr. Sasha Romanoff stood in his rumpled surgeon's suit in the hallway. He was Jack's co-resident and had had the night duty. Johnson approached the desk, where he saw Buchanan holding the tiny telephone and engaged in animated conversation. Something must be happening, Johnson thought. The pattern of early morning work was disturbed. Romanoff's eyes sparkled, belying the fatigue in his drooping face.

"Big news, man!" he said to Johnson.

"What's up, Sasha?"

Sasha drew lightly on the extra-length cigarette he indulged himself in, tilted his head back, and exhaled away from Jack.

"We're going to do it!"

Several nurses looked up and shook their heads at this childish exuberance. To them, heart surgery was a routine miracle.

"Bradfield has given Don the go-ahead on the heart replacement for tonight."

Buchanan looked up from the phone. "Cut the chatter, Sasha. Jack, there is a patient by the name of Henry Gray at Stanford. Arrange to get over there and transfer him here. Sasha and I will do the first patient this morning. You clean up the ward and then ride the ambulance over for the patient. I'll notify the cardiologists and social worker that he's coming. Right?"

Johnson was as eager as any of the junior staff to follow Bradfield's charismatic leadership. Like other surgical residents at Aspermont, Johnson came from a medical family, and had scored high in medical school and impressed his teachers with his altruism, maturity, and academic achievements. He had scrubbed with Liz Browning on a couple of the calf operations, but he was unaware that the project was so close to human trial. Some faculty members had expressed misgivings to Johnson about the use of the device in human beings, not only on technical grounds, but also because of the problems of an unsecured quantity of plutonium circulating in an open society. Johnson was thinking briefly of inquiring who would actually take part in the operation, when the appearance of two medical students and an intern signaled the formal start of patient rounds.

Buchanan moved off rapidly with his entourage trailing after him in a ragtag fashion. Patients seeing this motley group for the first time often said they felt a part of a poor man's version of the Roman games with themselves as the victims. With thirty-five patients to see in the forty-five minutes left before the start of the first operation in the surgery unit, it was easy to see the pressure the senior resident was under. Yet he pressed on with grace and good humor.

"What's the foot's name?" he asked, as he entered the second room looking for a patient whose left leg had been operated on two days before. Buchanan reached the first bed, lifted off the covers to reveal the perfectly normal feet of a wide-eyed patient. "Left or right?" he said. Romanoff replied, "Left."

"Not a bad job, eh?" Buchanan slyly asked the medical student right next to him, who nodded his agreement.

"Well, this is the wrong patient!" Pointing to the name on the chart, Buchanan suddenly whirled around and left the room, leaving Romanoff to explain the confusion as best as he could.

Out in the corridor Buchanan assumed an expression of mock bewilderment. "When things are so similar, like 'right foot' and 'left foot,' I get confused," he said out loud to no one in particular, and strode on. He came upon a three-year-old boy who had had an atrial septal defect repaired the day before. The child was standing with his diaper at half-mast, arms hanging over the edge of the crib. His nurse, a pleasant, first-year graduate, rose to greet Buchanan.

"Hello, punkins!" Buchanan said to both. With children and young nurses, he virtually melted. Buchanan poked playfully at the little boy's protruding stomach while the intern, the students, and Johnson looked on. The child, shrieking with laughter, took careful aim at Buchanan's left ear and let fly with a haymaker.

"Looks like he passes the test," said Buchanan. "He can return to the regular pediatrics ward."

This happy byplay was interrupted as the ward clerk entered with a message for Buchanan from Stanford Hospital. The doctor's face and demeanor changed as he listened to the clerk. He looked over at Johnson.

"It looks bad with Henry Gray," he said. "Get him over here pronto and keep him alive until tonight."

With that, Johnson, no questions asked, left the group at a run, weighing the responsibilities suddenly thrust on his shoulders alone.

Chapter 3

Johnson and staff nurse Sue Myers accompanied the patient and his fiancée, Janet Chen, in the ambulance. In the cramped compartment only the most essential equipment was available. Going south on Highway 101 from Stanford to Aspermont was difficult because of heavy commuter traffic. Red lights and sirens gave little headway as every lane was jammed with cars.

Gray's precarious condition was termed "cardiac cachexia." The heart had been badly damaged by his earlier heart attack. The amount of oxygen being delivered to the tissue was borderline in keeping the kidneys and other organs functioning. Thus, he retained more salt and water. His legs had become swollen, the liver was enlarged and processed bile pigments inadequately. The difficulty in breathing was increased by the excess fluid in his lungs. Normally light, thin, and fluffy, the lungs were now stiff and unyielding. Oxygen was not being transferred to the blood expeditiously. His fat stores and muscle mass had gradually melted away. Now, he was pale and jaundiced, with a fine, cold sweat on forehead and palms. The hollows of his cheeks moved with each straining breath.

His legs and abdomen, swollen with fluid, were covered by thick red blankets tucked neatly into the stretcher.

Gray gazed at his new physician, but made no effort to speak. A moist mist of oxygen flowed into his mouth and nose. A bottle of sterile electrolyte solution dripped slowly into one of a set of prominently distended veins on the back of his hand. A new catheter for measuring blood pressure, neatly covered with tape and white gauze, was sutured into an artery in his left wrist. The reading of the arterial pressure was continuously available to Johnson.

Johnson checked the position of the artificial respiration equipment and the portable heart defibrillator. He might need them to shock Gray's heart out of abnormal rhythm, which could very easily occur. A portable electrocardiograph indicated that the patient's heartbeat was indeed irregular.

Gray had been relatively stable in the Stanford Coronary Care Unit. But there, every drop of drug infused, every drop of urine excreted, each heartbeat had been monitored on computers by a crew of nurses and adjustments made accordingly. Here, in the midst of a traffic-congested highway, the basic senses of the trained physician were extended only slightly by technology. Here, the balances one could achieve were less exact, and the physician had to fall back upon experience and intuition.

After a while, Johnson sensed a major change in his patient's condition. "Miss Chen," he said. "I think Mr. Gray has been deteriorating since we took him from the C.C.U. I'm going to increase the concentration of the cardiac stimulant, dopamine, and give 80 milligrams more of furosemide to eliminate fluid from his lungs. Also, he should have a quarter grain of morphine. I can't measure his potassium level, but I'll give him a dose over the next fifteen minutes."

"Go ahead, please," she replied. Janet, having spent virtually all of her working hours in a C.C.U., recognized the deteriorating condition of her fiancée, and the heavy responsibility on this young surgeon.

Johnson was now immersed in the balances, the doses, the

rate and rhythm of his failing patient. The uncertainty in taking action was replaced by intense concentration in carrying out the diagnostic and therapeutic tasks in sequence. By the time the ambulance jockey had cleared the traffic and was screaming along Fremont Expressway at seventy-five miles per hour, Gray had again been stabilized. Still, they sat wondering if that old, weak heart would last long enough to be replaced by the device now being prepared at Aspermont. Johnson's orders, via Buchanan from Bradfield, were to bring this guy back alive.

It must have been quite a sight to the orderly on duty when Johnson finally opened the rear door of the ambulance at the Aspermont emergency entrance—a lean, handsome, black man in a white physician's coat leaping out of the cramped interior crying out to no one in particular, "Get this man out of here!" Swiftly, efficiently, Gray's stretcher was hauled out and Johnson and Myers moved it rapidly through the corridors to the Intensive Care Unit.

Bradfield turned away from the patient on the operating table. The operation had been an aortic valve replacement.

"Nice job, Don. Gray ought to be in by now, so can Romanoff help you finish?"

"Sure. Thanks, Dr. Bradfield."

"Thank you, one and all."

Bradfield stripped off the flexible, snug-fitting rubber gloves from his hands. A comfortable feeling of coolness spread over the skin as the moisture trapped for two hours within the gloves evaporated. His face mask would stay in place until he had stepped outside the operating room. The circulating nurse quickly moved up behind him and untied the knots in the tapes of his gown. He murmured his thanks. His thoughts had already turned away from the present operation to the challenge ahead of him. He automatically acknowledged the "good mornings" from admiring nurses and students as he headed to the Operating Room Director's office. Mrs. Helen Donald greeted him at the door.

"Dr. Bradfield, Don Buchanan has told me you have special needs this evening. Something about a new artificial heart?" There was concern and a note of pique in Mrs. Donald's voice.

As with most top-flight administrators, Mrs. Donald thought it essential that she be told about everything that was to happen within her domain before it actually happened. Unexpected occurrences were strictly *verboten*. In her world, even emergencies were thoroughly planned for, and so there was a mild degree of annoyance on her pale, silvered face as she confronted Bradfield. He had failed to communicate with her in advance about the planned operation tonight. The ultimate relationship between the surgeon and the operating room nurse, in her view, was achieved if the nurse handed the surgeon every stitch, clamp, and needle in the proper sequence with nary a word passing between them during the procedure. In her younger days, she had always quietly observed the surgeons she worked with whenever she had time. At home, copies of the surgeons' instrument lists were painstakingly memorized. She knew each doctor's idiosyncracies, whether right- or left-handed, whether he worked with silk or nylon sutures, and so on. Indeed, house officers were awed at her single-minded dedication to the chief surgeon, and had been more than once embarrassed by her telling them, with complete assurance, what instrument to use in the next step of the operation and what instrument was not what they had asked for. Now, with a staff of fifty-six female and two male nurses, sixteen orderlies and six technicians, the interpersonal relationships were as sterile as the filtered atmosphere of the O.R. itself. The operating room reflected her image—very efficient, very cold. To look at her was to wonder if humor, charm, and sex were ever on her agenda. To the patients of Aspermont, it made no difference. To the surgeons, her efficiency represented financial rewards. But to Bradfield, she was only an obstacle to be dealt with.

"You, of all people," she was saying, "must know how embarrassed I am in not being prepared for your little procedure." It was evident she had decided to use her "I'm injured" routine.

"Mrs. Donald, I'm sorry to have put you in such an awkward position." Bradfield spoke with a broad grin, moving close to her in a conspiratorial attitude.

"Yes, perhaps." She refused to be mollified so easily. "You know, of course, that our schedule is full through ten o'clock." She took a half step backwards and continued in a single breath. "I will, of necessity, have to use the staff on second call, and that will be double pay. They have not worked with you before, either, which will make it unpleasant for them. And what is meant by a 'shielded room,' and why is it needed?" She drew a breath at last. "Do you have the necessary permission to do this operation? And—"

Bradfield cut in. "It doesn't appear as if you're completely in the dark, does it?" He looked down directly into her eyes.

"If I had to depend for my information on surgeons like you, the O.R. would be a shambles," she said curtly.

Bradfield considered the incongruity of the situation. He was about to make or break his own reputation. If unsuccessful, he might just finish the day by killing a man. If successful, he might usher in a revolution in the practice of medicine. Yet here he was dodging and weaving with a bleached, prune-like female done up in a sack, arguing about overtime pay, an operating schedule probably full of nose jobs, and being questioned about his right as chief of cardiovascular surgery to carry out an experimental procedure.

"Why don't we move into your office where we can speak more freely, Mrs. Donald," he said, placing a firm hand under her right elbow. She turned under his pressure and they completed the journey into her office together. To her, the sudden contact was electric, and she furtively looked around over halfglasses to see if anyone had noticed the little intimacy. Bradfield's expression was unchanged.

Closing the door behind them, Bradfield waited until Helen Donald took her place in the swivel chair. He glanced at the recovery room through the wall window. It was filling up as the first operations of the day were finished. He took in the scene and reflected that other doctors could treat chronic diseases for years on end, some could look at people impersonally as mere statistics, preventing disease by chlorinating water or inoculating masses of children. But surgeons cured by dint of individual effort, each case a challenge to their talent and each patient also a threat to their ego. It was a singularly personal relationship they developed with their patients.

Mrs. Donald interrupted his thoughts as she said suddenly, "There has been gossip that the use of atomic fuel is too risky. My own concern relates to the hazards to my nurses, and of course to the patients, too. You remember the problem of miscarriages and cancer in woman anesthesiologists and nurses? The unsuspected cause was contamination of the O.R. atmosphere by what we thought were safe levels of anesthetic gases exhaled by patients. The patients were exposed only a short time individually, but we breathed the air all the time."

"Yes, I remember. But this is a quite different situation. The atomic fuel is Plutonium 238. If the material itself gets out, it would be hazardous. But it can't. It's in a shockproof container."

"How about radiation? Doesn't it escape from the container? We have to shield the walls of our orthopedic surgery rooms with lead. They take a lot of X-ray pictures there."

"True. But those are X rays. To shield them, you need dense material. The stuff we plan to use is pure medical-grade plutonium. It gives off alpha rays mostly."

"So we don't need a truly shielded room?"

"No. But we'll need to take precautions. When we transfer the plutonium from the storage container to the heart capsule, we will show you that simple distance is the best protection."

"Okay. Are there any special instruments needed?"

"Rib-cutting shears in addition to the sternum saw."

"What for?"

"One problem with the design of the pump had been bulk.

How to put the plastic heart, the electronic control unit, and the power supply into the space previously occupied by the natural heart. This space is confined by the sternum in front, the lungs to the sides, and the esophagus behind. Many researchers tried to design experimental hearts that would fit this space. They failed. It was my idea to remove the sternum altogether to create a generous space. We designed the power supply and control unit of the machine in the shape of a slightly convex breastbone. This replaces the patient's sternum."

At that moment, a small darting figure scooted past outside the office, then suddenly wheeled around, came close to the window, and peeked in. Her lacquered fair hair quivered as she burst through the door upon finding Bradfield. It was Louella Commons, the social worker assigned to the surgery service.

"I'd hoped I'd find you, Dr. Bradfield. Did you want me to talk to the family? I hope I'm not interrupting, but I'm sure you're discussing the case. . . . " Her voice rose in inquiry.

"No, Louella, no problem. Mrs. Donald and I were in fact reviewing the project."

"Super," the woman from Missoula, Montana, replied. "That Janet Chen, Mr. Gray's fiancée, is—well, just terrific. She has great emotional strength." She stood looking at Bradfield expectantly, but then she always seemed to have that look on her face. She was slim, indeed virtually underdeveloped. Her hair was always precisely in place. She had a large wardrobe of matching coordinates, and on this day she had on a gray pleated dress with long sleeves. A red scarf round her neck added a touch of brilliant color. She carried her ever-present notebook close to her bosom. One could tell this thirty-four-year-old spinster suffered from being so easily identifiable as "hickish." She sprinkled her conversation with Anglo-Saxon words in the oddest situations in the belief they added sophistication to her image.

"I was just about to run over to see them," Bradfield said. "Would you mind waiting for me at I.C.U.?"

"Well, I've just gotten this shitty assignment in the O.P.D.," Louella said and smiled nonchalantly. "Why don't you page me when you need me, and I'll be right over?"

"Fine."

Louella scooted out, oblivious to the disruption she had just created.

"I'm really fascinated by these developments," Helen Donald remarked, a tinge of warmth creeping into her voice.

"I must run over to the I.C.U. to meet the patient," said Bradfield. "Before I go, let me make a couple of specific surgical points. First, Elizabeth Browning from my lab will be bringing over the sterile unfueled heart later this afternoon. I hope by five o'clock. Let's see, it's ten o'clock now, about six hours from now. The plutonium is in a large drum, also in the lab area."

"How will I sterilize the plutonium?"

"The material is hot, both in temperature and radioactivity. It's naturally sterile."

"I believe I can have the schedule rearranged for you, Dr. Bradfield. And I'll be here tonight also."

"Thank you. It'll be good to have you in the operating room again—especially on such a historic occasion."

As he walked swiftly out of the O.R. suite, Bradfield thought how progress was impeded only rarely by actual physical barriers. The intangible roadblocks he was encountering now were just as real as the walls of Jericho. Would he be able to blow the walls down? Certainly, if enough delays accumulated, he might just not have sufficient time to get things organized. He increased his pace as he made for the Intensive Care Unit.

Chapter 4

Ronald Harris left his office in a hurry and headed north for Dulles International Airport. It was a forty-minute drive and he had barely enough time to catch United's Flight 110 non-stop to San Francisco. Harris had commuted to Dulles frequently in his travels to visit subcontractors in Houston, Ann Arbor, Menlo Park, and Berkeley. In his Chevrolet Vega he carried two old briefcases. One contained the file on the Aspermont artificial heart project, the other a change of clothes and his toilet kit.

Harris swept to the west on Loop 410 until he reached the Dulles turnoff. The early March sunlight was cold and the landscape had yet to blossom. The trees still branched out bare and forlorn, although the sap was beginning to run. Harris felt uneasy, afraid of the events now passing beyond his control to a place out of his immediate reach. As a physicist-administrator, he had dealt with technical and money decisions only from afar. He had viewed the statistics of life and death as impersonally as a pilot dropping bombs from 40,000 feet by plotted targets visualized on a radar screen. But now Bradfield had trapped him, enmeshed him in a real flesh-and-blood situation. If the operation succeeded, the potential for good and the rewards for both of them would be incalculable. If it failed, Harris would have to share some of the blame. He wished that Bradfield had gone ahead without telling him. It would have been so much easier!

It was 11:30 A.M. and Harris was just passing Reston, Virginia. He pressed on the accelerator. He wanted very much to get to a phone and put a call through to the West Coast.

That same morning, in Portola Valley, California, another physicist was just finishing his breakfast. Normally, Allen Ridley would be on his way to work, but the morning paper contained two items which caught his eye. They applied to his job as a radiation safety officer.

The first news item was a story of yet another leak in the radioactive waste tanks at Hanford, Washington. The second item concerned the use of a nuclear explosive in Colorado to recover oil from shale. He clipped the information to file later, and left the table.

Ridley was married to Cynthia, a childhood sweetheart. He was thirty-one and she twenty-nine. They had two children, who at this moment were still asleep.

Cynthia stood in the kitchen pouring coffee. She heard him getting ready to leave and turned around to the door to see him off. She was barefoot, her red hair falling over the shoulders of a white sweatshirt.

"Why, Allen, what's the matter with you? You're looking awfully glum."

"Oh, it's nothing, love."

He smiled, kissed her goodbye, and walked to the garage to pick up his bicycle. He slipped on his orange parka against the light rain. Perched firmly on his light Peugeot touring bicycle, he started down the two-lane Alpine Road that passed in front of his home. After eight miles, it joined Junipero Serra Expressway and then he would need to thread his way through the morning urban traffic all the way to the medical center. But his mind was still on the news items.

Ridley's problem was his job. Since World War II radioactivity had become a big help in medicine. Very small doses of a radioactive isotope could be injected into a patient and special counters used to trace the passage of the material through the body. Pictures of an internal organ such as the kidney could be obtained "noninvasively," or without surgical incision. These advances had created special responsibilities for Ridley. He took care of the disposal of radioactive wastes. He taught scientists and technicians who used isotopes in their daily work. He served on radiation hazard committees and studied radiation accidents. But recently he also had become a nuclear policeman and a nuclear banker, and that was the trouble.

The radioactive material used in artificial heart research was in a different class from what Ridley had dealt with previously. It was fissile and in gross quantities. Plutonium had strategic significance far beyond the boundaries of the medical center in the fields of weaponry and energy production. At $1,000 per gram, it was about a thousand times the value of gold. At the present time Aspermont had a hundred grams in each of two calves, and another hundred grams in a thick vault—a total value of $300,000 on the legal market, undoubtedly much more under the counter.

Protection of the stuff in power plants and industries involved complex physical barriers, computerized systems, sophisticated monitors, and tough trained guards. The money to develop this kind of protection was not available to Ridley. Prevention of theft at Aspermont depended on discretion, and the unusual hiding place of the nuclear fuel in the chest cavities of domesticated animals.

As Ridley wheeled under the telephone lines which paralleled Alpine Road, Cynthia was speaking to Elizabeth Browning about his whereabouts.

"I'm sorry, Miss Browning, he isn't home."

"Is it possible," Browning insisted, "to get a hold of him. It's an emergency!"

"Has there been an accident?"

"No, no. Dr. Bradfield—" She spoke the name with a slightly exaggerated sense of importance,—"must have the remaining plutonium for surgery tonight. I'm just making sure that preparation goes smoothly."

"Well, I'm afraid there's no way to contact him now. He should be in the office in about a half-hour. By the way, Miss Browning, I really think discussion about this project should be restricted to Allen and Dr. Bradfield. You're taking too much upon yourself."

Browning retorted instantly. "Well, that's the difference between administrators and those who take care of patients. Thank you. Goodbye!"

Cynthia hung up the phone with a bang. My God, she thought, what arrogance!

At Dulles, Harris parked in the long-term lot. He transferred his clothes into the suitcase with the Aspermont file, walked across to the lower level entrance, passing the waiting buses for downtown Washington, and moved up the sloping ramp to the second floor of the airport terminal. He went to United's counter and picked up his ticket. It was twelve o'clock. Passengers were already queuing at Gate 4 for the short bus trip from the Saarinen-designed, futuristic passenger terminal to the waiting planes out on the apron. He found a telephone in a remote corner with a view of the line at the gate and dialed a Berkeley, California, number directly, then counted out the correct change. A feminine voice answered.

"Hello?"

"Sylvia?"

"Yes."

"This is Harris. They're going ahead with implantation at Aspermont. Please withdraw $10,000. Put in a buy order in the morning with Scheinblum and Company to purchase ATOCOR on twenty-five percent margin at three."

"Okay."

"I'll call you after it's all over."

Harris hung up and rapidly joined the embarking passengers.

* * *

Ridley adjusted his position on the leather saddleseat. He hunched down low, switched to the highest gear, and swept onto Junipero Serra. He blinked frequently as the cool rain pattered onto his face and ungoggled eyes with the increased speed.

With all the uncomfortable realities he had to cope with, Ridley was actually not the kind of man who would shade the truth when nuclear materials had been used safely. The possibilities for misuse were real enough without clouding the issue with false alarms.

A case in point was that of a nuclear technician at the university's cyclotron laboratory. The man's name escaped him for the moment, but Ridley remembered him as pale and thin, with a peculiar disposition. The word was that he was very bright, but had had a nervous breakdown as a result of some war experience. Whatever it was, he had been sent to the laboratory from the Veterans Hospital on a work-release program. The man seemed to blend well with the highly regimented environment of the nuclear laboratory, and Ridley noticed him as he inspected the facility for radiation hazards. Ridley was cordial, but the man kept everyone at arm's length. He left the job and Ridley lost track of him until he was called to testify at a Workman's Compensation hearing for the university.

The man had a black spot in his lung. It was cancer. He claimed it was caused by exposure to radioactive materials shipped through the laboratory, like plutonium for the projects of the medical center.

Ridley testified but he was of no help to the man. First, for lung cancer there had to be a release of the radioactive stuff into the air. There had been no such accident. Second, safety precautions in the lab had been excellent and stray radiation extremely low. Ridley could remember clearly, even now, the way he had questioned the man at the hearing.

"Sir, do you recognize this ledger sheet?"

"Yes, of course."

"Is it not the weekly log of the film badge recordings?"

"That is correct, Mr. Ridley."

"Is it true that you initialed every entry, beginning from the first day you came to work? The initials are yours, are they not?"

"Uh, yes."

"It appears you never missed a single required inspection?"

"That's right."

The man, like everyone else at the plant, wore a film badge attached to his uniform. Ridley knew the badges were handed in and the films checked for radiation exposure at regular intervals. Each worker initialed the ledger. Blood and urine samples were also checked. This fellow had meticulously initialed every entry. Inspection of the badges indicated he had received a lower exposure than workers in less shielded, ordinary buildings. In addition, background radioactivity was not associated with deep organ disease. Ridley had told the hearing there was a resort on the Black Sea for Russian nuclear submariners. The radiation shielding in their submarines was often so poor that sailors had become bald, sterile, and afflicted with leukemia. "So the Soviet government had provided for them for the rest of their days," Ridley said. "Those are the kinds of problems one runs into with stray radiation, not lung cancer."

Ridley knew his testimony was correct because there were no such problems at the cyclotron. Physicists, having worked in nuclear research for years, seemed to have great respect for the dangers of radiation. He was considerably less assured, however, with the cavalier way the medical people approached the use of these materials. Some day there might be a very significant problem.

As he swung onto the Aspermont campus thinking about the many facets of his job, he remembered the name, Daniel Cooper. He wondered where Cooper was. He had lost his case. Ridley was sorry for him, cancer and all that, but the basis of his claim was just wrong. Ridley thought that probably no more would be heard of Cooper again.

Chapter 5

Bradfield wore a white, knee-length coat with a single stethoscope peeking out of his right-hand pocket. He was still in his scrub clothes. Louella was as animated as always. Her head bounced back and forth with every phrase. She was telling Bradfield the social history of the patient. Jack Johnson joined them as she finished.

Bradfield summarized. "Essentially then, Mr. Gray is forty-three, is engaged to a nurse, is an engineer in partnership in an electronics research and development business, lives in Menlo Park, and is supposed to be well off financially."

Stanley Axelrod, a general surgeon, stopped briefly, attracted by the small, animated group. "Hi, there!"

Louella smiled brightly. Axelrod turned to Bradfield. "Very exciting news, Bill. Good luck to you."

"Thanks, Stan. We'll need all the luck we can get!"

After Axelrod had left, Bradfield said, "Word is getting around already. I think we should try to keep the lid on without really being secretive. Louella, please coordinate with the hospital P.R. office, will you? Protect the privacy of the patient."

"Right," she nodded vigorously. "I'll do that right away."

"Now," Bradfield said. "Tell me about the fiancée. Will she be helpful?"

"She's very interesting. She was born in New York. Her parents were Chinese immigrants. Both died when she was young. The family was raised in the Lower East Side by the oldest sister. She spent a fair amount of time in the Bellevue Hospital clinics as a child. I guess she drifted naturally into nursing and got her B.S. and R.N. together at the old Bellevue nursing school."

"Bellevue is one of the oldest nursing schools in the United States," interjected Bradfield. "The hospital is truly a great public institution."

"Well, she came to San Francisco three years ago," Louella went on. "She and Gray met at the hospital where she was working. They were serious about marriage, but that was before he became deathly ill. She's a very industrious woman—and so sweet. I think it's shitty that this should happen to her."

Bradfield turned to Johnson. "I expect you've talked to them about the radiation problem?"

"My goodness," said Louella. "I sort of pushed for—eh—, discussed it with them, mostly with her, that is, because he wasn't quite alert when I was there earlier." Her downward sloping eyes widened. "He's really sick, I mean. Aren't you going a little slow with this?"

"What did you tell them about radiation?" Bradfield asked firmly.

"Well, I really laid it out on the line to them in no uncertain terms. I told them the radiation level is safe if they use separate beds, that there might be unknown genetic damage so that they shouldn't have children, and that over the long haul the low radiation will make him sterile."

"If he should survive that long," Johnson quipped. Commons gave him a sharp glance.

"Jack, would you please check with anesthesia to see if they can shake a man loose for tonight?"

"Yes, sir."

"Dr. Bradfield, Dr. William Bradfield, extension 7-5776." The flat, mechanical voice of the paging system interrupted the informal patient conference.

"That's your office, Bill."

"Yes, I'll run over there. Louella, talk to them some more." Bradfield strode off rapidly.

Johnson turned to Louella. "Maybe it's because I don't have the experience, but this thing is coming off as if it were just another operation. No advance planning, little communication, and a lot of scurrying around."

"Yes, it may appear that way. But Bill Bradfield—well, we all believe in him."

"It's not really a matter of belief. For instance, the anesthesiologist isn't the only one who has been overlooked. There's no forewarning for the other supporting services. The blood bank, the hematology service are still in the dark. What if we had coagulation problems?"

"Well, Bill hates decisions by committee. I think he's afraid that once the medical schools' debating societies get involved with the pros and cons of the nuclear heart, he might never get to do one. Better do it now and talk later."

"I still think we should have a protocol. All of us . . . we should know our duties in advance. I'd be more comfortable. You know how much that plutonium costs, don't you? One hundred thousand smackers! Some dude just might . . ."

"Let's not discuss that publicly," Louella said severely. "It'll work out all right, you'll see." And with that she walked into the I.C.U.

United's Flight 110 was now two hours into its journey. The jet engines could hardly be heard, but the desiccated warm air circulating through nozzles had its usual distinctive sound. The stewardesses went about their business like mechanical dolls programmed to dispense services, trays, and smiles as cold as the *boeuf Bourguignon* being served. But Harris felt comfortable. A couple of sherries had reduced his anxiety. He reached into his suitcase and took out the large Aspermont file. It was an excellent record of success. No doubt about it, Bradfield could bring it off. He acted incisively and was rarely wrong technically. He was energetic and aggressive, perhaps a little rash. Harris reviewed the technical specifications of the energy source. Six and a half pounds, 50 watts output, 45 watts heat rejection, 10 percent efficiency; not really bad for the first human trial.

Ridley sat behind his desk in his office in the radiology wing. The cancer-treating X-ray, cobalt and pi-meson machines had all been installed on this floor, so the wing was shielded. Pedestrian traffic was light. In general, it was peaceful because of its location. But conflict was boiling over in this small basement office as Ridley looked up into Buchanan's eyes.

"Don, I'd love to help you fellows out, but you must be nuts if you think you can put that heart in a human being."

"Al, look at it this way. This man was examined at Stanford. He's sick enough to do a plant. He almost died in the ambulance coming over here. We've seen him, he won't last the night."

As Ridley listened to Buchanan's pleas, the anguish in his face was plain. He raised himself up to adjust his chair. "Okay, Don. Let me say this. You're a surgeon. You deal with life and death every day. Your duties are as old as the history of man. You've sworn to uphold the Hippocratic oath. But I'm a physicist, an ordinary safety officer. The field I belong to was created because people died from radiation exposure, because bombs were dropped. It's an offspring of death with a capital 'D.' The goal is to prevent death caused accidentally or by the foolish use of radioactive materials. I have just as important a responsibility as you do."

It had already been a long day for Buchanan. He was faced with yet another operation in the afternoon in addition to the now questionable heart replacement. He was emotionally and physically drained. As he listened with respect to Ridley's argument, he knew he just didn't have the mental keenness required to debate this profound issue. It was not, however, just an oath to which he had to be faithful, not just an abstract morality to preserve life as he saw it. It was a fundamental tenet of his own conscience, acquired long before the formalities of medical education. The two adversaries doggedly continued their search for an honest compromise.

"I don't want to hear any more. The picture is very clear to me," Ridley said quietly, staring at Buchanan.

"I think you'd better hear just a little more. Bradfield has had several animals survive for up to six months. He has two going right now. No radiation damage to them. You've seen them, Allen."

Ridley nodded. "But those radiation fields are high, perhaps higher than I'd like to see in humans."

Buchanan walked to the door, paused, and turned round dejectedly again. "Surely that risk—the radiation damage versus the death of the patient—is a medical decision. Surely it's reserved to the patient, his family, and his physician. Don't you agree?"

"Don, that stuff is dangerous not only to the patient but to many people. The society we live in is turning upside down. I just cannot open the vault."

"I'll make a deal, Allen. You open the vault, and I'm going to get Bradfield and the Dean. They can, I'm sure, provide enough armed guards or whatever the law requires for protection to move the plutonium just three floors! After that, it will be in a can inside this fellow until he dies. There just has to be a compromise."

"Don, there may be room to debate on moral grounds. But, legally, I hold the license for the use of this plutonium. I say it does not leave this vault except under the terms of the contract—which does not specify human use. I'm sorry."

"I am, too."

Buchanan left, the bounce in his step perceptibly less resilient. The poor guy isn't going to make it, he thought. No way, if this doesn't get straightened out soon.

Ridley turned around on his swivel chair. He shuffled some papers on his desk without reading them. He waited for the visitors he was sure would soon be bursting through his office door.

Two floors above, a young man was entering Room 202, the room where Henry Gray lay in the Intensive Care Unit. The Reverend Milton Kastenmeyer was dressed simply in his short-sleeved, black uniform with a white clerical collar. His congregation was a significant challenge to him because it included many classes of people—professionals from the university, as well as blue-collar workers from the aerospace and electronics industries that abounded on the San Francisco peninsula. His dynamic sermons were well received by both. Gray and Janet were active and devout members of his congregation.

Gray's illness had personal significance to many of the church members, although presently they were in the dark about his fate and the drama unfolding behind the hospital walls. Janet, however, had called Kastenmeyer the night before to say that a heart transplant had been ruled out, and she needed his advice. The replacement of a diseased heart by a machine was an extraordinary new concept, even for Kastenmeyer, who was generally quite knowledgeable about things medical, a knowledge due to his natural curiosity and interest in the fundamental interweaving of medicine and religion in the human life-cycle.

Janet turned her head and saw him come in. "Hello, Reverend Kastenmeyer. I should apologize for calling you so often."

"God's grace on you, Janet," he said in a polished, yet sincere voice.

"Thank you, pastor."

"The congregation has asked me to tell you they're remembering you and Henry in their prayers. What is the situation?"

"We haven't seen Dr. Bradfield yet. We rode over with a resident, Dr. Johnson. We've talked with Miss Commons.

The cardiologist has been consulted and concurs. We have to be interviewed by their psychiatrist, and I really don't know who else. I can only see that Henry is slipping rapidly. They have now added epinephrine to the drug infusion into his veins."

She spoke in a soft voice edged with a note of desperation. "While I realize there are risks ahead, we may finally just be overwhelmed. So many people are involved. Even I feel the impersonality of it all; medical technology lacks any kind of human reassurance."

Janet's stomach flip-flopped and turned queasy when she thought Gray might not even make it through another night. She turned away to avoid showing the pastor the salty tears welling up in her tired brown eyes. He reached for her hand to reassure her, to transfer to her some of his own spiritual strength.

"Janet, let me share this with you. The sermon I'll be preaching this Sunday is providential. It may be appropriate for you and Henry. The text is from Matthew: 'But straightway Jesus spake unto them, saying, Be of good cheer, be not afraid.' It is the account of Christ stilling the tempest. After a day of teaching and healing the sick, he directed his disciples to cross to the other side of the Sea of Galilee. The moon reflected on placid waters, until a violent storm blew in. The disciples could not control their boat and were driven away from the shore. They were 'sore afraid' until they saw Christ beckoning to them. Peter, fixing his eye on the face of Christ, left the boat and walked on the surface of the sea. The wind howled round him, the cold spray dashed in his face. Fear stole into his heart. In an instant he began to sink and, looking to Jesus, cried 'Lord, save me.' Jesus caught him up, saying, 'O thou of little faith, wherefore didst thou doubt?' and when they were come into the boat, the wind ceased.

"So it is with *faith.* Faith secures courage and the will to live."

Kastenmeyer spoke in powerful phrases. "Lord, grant us faith, that peace in the sea of life which is seldom calm and which often pulls us down into a trough of despair. Let us heed the voice of the Savior, saying, 'Be of good cheer, it is I.' So let us toil on. After a time we shall reach the other shore, and when we do we shall be done with the storms and there will be a great calm, the calm of undisturbed happiness and blessedness."

His voice fell silent and in the quiet that followed, their thoughts turned to the skill of the physicians, the warmth and talent of the nurses, and the inner strength of Gray's spirit.

Chapter 6

The paging system began early in the morning, built to a crescendo in the afternoon, plateaued through the evening, and died off rapidly during the night, mirroring the cycle of human activity. If one were to remove the hospital roof during the day and observe from above, it would appear like an active anthill, the ants scurrying around first in one direction, then in another, as the calls came out of the loudspeakers.

Bradfield walked quickly to his office in the adjoining building in response to his page. The office was a picture of frugality. Small and closetlike, it was carpeted in dark blue, with a walnut desk, a couple of bookshelves, and a swivel chair. Pipes carrying the gas, water, and sewage of the floor above were exposed below the ceiling. Overhead and inside the door was a large, coarse chain attached to a chrome shower head, a remnant from the conversion of this former laboratory to an office. The shower had been placed there for safety in case any corrosive liquid spilled on clothing or caught on fire. Bradfield liked to tell of the time when Buchanan, then a new intern, was driven by an irresistible urge to pull the chain. Unfortunately, he had pulled a little too hard and the valve stuck. Water cascaded down in torrents over him and out into the hallway until it was shut off from a central control. It was the first time that Buchanan came to his chief's attention. The shower-head caper made a great conversation piece for visitors, most of whom looked about the room with astonishment, unwilling to believe that this was the office of a chief of cardiac surgery. Bradfield never made any excuses for this spartan setting, but it was no secret that the hospital complex had been built with too many functional defects, due to the ineptness of the planners. To save ten percent in building costs, they had changed the room sizes from twenty-four- to twenty-foot modules. The savings were obtained at the cost of cramped patient rooms and insufficient space. When these deficiencies interfered with the care of patients, Bradfield's anger rose. Technicians and staff would go around whispering, "Wooee, was he fit to be tied!"

On entering the office Bradfield gleefully put his hands to his mouth, forming a resonating chamber, and blew hard twice, the honking sound making his presence known to his staff.

"You called?" he said to Valerie Rigg, his secretary.

"Bob Clever wants to talk to you about Mr. Stanley. He says there are no beds available and he has to cancel his reservation."

Bob Clever was the department of surgery's business manager. He had the thankless job of admitting patients at times when the hospital was crowded and beds in short supply.

"Tell me about Mr. Stanley."

Valerie read off details from the card she had pulled from the file. "He's forty-six and has coronary artery disease. He's to be admitted for bypass surgery only. No workup necessary. Outside angiograms done two months ago. His condition is stable. He's coming from Eureka."

"Hmm, that's five hundred miles away from here. Tell Clever this guy is an emergency. See what he says."

Valerie realized that Clever, although quite independent, would never contradict a cardiac surgeon's judgment. Some other surgeon would be discomfited, but Clever would have to take the heat, not Bradfield. To Bradfield, "emergency" meant getting his patients into the hospital. So much for the "quota."

"Anything else, Valerie?"

"Yes, Dr. Tanaka and his entourage." Valerie rolled her eyes to the ceiling in mock despair.

"Oh, yes, I forgot. The visiting group from Japan."

"They'll be here tomorrow morning at nine o'clock."

Bradfield laughed. "Well, won't they have something to talk about!" He spun around merrily in his swivel chair.

Valerie continued. "There'll be Tanaka, two nurses, three residents, five other surgeons, one cardiologist, one administrator, and an interpreter. Fourteen people! The Japanese are replacing the Ugly American!"

"I wonder how they'll react to the nuclear heart in view of their war experience. Verrrry interesting!" and he rolled the *r*'s broadly.

Valerie went on. "Gloria Lasser, the Dean's secretary, called. Dean Geld and Dr. Holborn are meeting right now in the Dean's office. I tried to put her off by telling her you were in surgery, but apparently she knew you were out."

"Did the secretary say what they wanted?"

"She mentioned the Dean was concerned about permission to do your new operation. They would like to talk to you."

"Ah, yes, the kingmaker beckons!" Bradfield said. "This is the first time they've requested my presence. I'm more used to tippy-toeing down there with my hand out. Perhaps I should let them cool their heels for a while, Val."

"Well, Dr. B., I'd get it over with. From what I've heard, you have a real 'sickie' for a patient."

"Practical, as usual. I suppose you're right."

There was a comfortable relationship between the surgeon and his secretary. Valerie Rigg was an attractive young woman with poise, good manners, and intelligence. She had been raised in Sandusky, Ohio and, like so many educated women, she had met a stone wall in job opportunities; so she had

turned to secretarial work and had come to California. Typing pools were too impersonal, particularly for the skimpy pay, and work in the business world too apt to end in lechery. So she felt fortunate in finding a job in Bradfield's office.

With a little smile on his face, Bradfield walked briskly out of the building to the meeting with Dean Geld and Frances Holborn, Chief of Surgery. No thought entered his mind that they could influence his decision in any way.

Meanwhile, in Room 202, Gray's heartbeat began to falter, and the computer was calculating new decision matrices.

Flight 110 was now crossing over Colorado. The atmosphere was so clear that the ski resort of Breckenridge could easily be picked out. Harris was in conversation with Detective Simus Twomey of the San Francisco Police Department, a veteran of twenty years on the force who was returning from Washington after a brief bomb-explosives study course at the FBI Academy.

"Now, that's real interesting," Twomey remarked, showing all his dentures in a dazzling smile. "You fellas are real clever. You're telling me that you can put a mechanical heart in an animal and it'll run for months without recharging? I never would have believed it."

"Not only that," said Harris, "but I hope by this time tomorrow it'll be inside a human being."

"That's *real* interesting. That's why you're going out to the Coast?"

"Yes, I hope you'll keep this confidential until it breaks in the newspapers. The operating itself is chancy. It may be premature to let the news out before the operation is finished."

"Sure, Doc. I'm full of confidential information."

"What's your field?"

"Well, Doc, like I say, I'm on the bomb squad in San Francisco. Just coming back from D.C. Had a two-week intensive course on the new bomb materials being used in crime. It's getting pretty rough, let me tell you. The instructor touched on nuclear bombs. That's why I got interested in your heart when you mentioned it's fueled by plutonium."

Harris was quick to reply. "You needn't worry about that. The stuff that might get out and fall into the wrong hands is from large nuclear power plants."

Twomey's eyes narrowed as he looked at his slightly tipsy traveling companion. "In my business, Doc, I worry about everything. I've seen it all. If you don't think somebody might not just make a bomb out of the plutonium stuff, you're pretty naive."

"I don't think I'm being naive. We've looked at this problem for a long time. First, you need about one to two kilograms of pure stuff to make a bomb. The power supply of our nuclear heart contains only a hundred grams. You'd have to round up a convention of twenty patients to get enough."

"Would be pretty hot in that room! Eh, Doc?" Twomey quipped.

Harris's eyelid began to twitch as he tried to make some telling points. "It would take some pretty elegant technology to put a bomb together."

"An unfriendly country might just have the technology."

"Yeah, but they won't be going around swiping one hundred-gram dribbles."

"Single terrorists might." Twomey continued to probe.

"Well, it goes back to technology again. Basically, the atom bomb idea is simple. You take two subcritical masses of fissionable material. With a controlled high explosive, you drive the two together so they are held for a long time in a critical mass. The decaying atoms give off enough particles to split other atoms and presto—the atomic bomb! But for a hundred grams you wouldn't have enough high explosive to do the job anyway, so why bother?"

"You sound pretty convinced."

"The Rand Corporation has been playing computer games with all sorts of possibilities. Basically, they say the bomb hypothesis is gamed out."

"Doc, I wish you'd told me something else. I know computers are good for adding numbers in the bank, and you can't beat them for getting stolen car data from license plates." Twomey paused and lit a cigar. "But people behavior? Nope," he said with finality, shaking his head. "In my business, Doc, I've seen it all. Unpredictable? How about the Patty Hearst case? How about the airline highjacks, the Munich massacre, the Charles Manson gang? The world is full of nuts."

"Well, you have a point."

"So I don't believe in computer games."

"But there isn't enough plutonium in an artificial heart."

"Well, my point dealt only with behavior. You're the expert on the Big Bang."

"Sir," the stewardess leaned over Harris. Her tailored bosom hung over his face and her thigh pressed his knee as she talked to Twomey. "Sir, the passenger in back of you has requested that you not smoke a cigar. Would you mind terribly?" she asked with charm in her voice.

Detective Twomey stood up and looked pointedly behind him. "Well, Doc, if you don't mind I'll just step over you and go to the bar."

Harris nodded and moved his legs to the side, a little disturbed. The girl's perfume and nearness had aroused him. He was momentarily lost in frankly sexual thoughts.

Early afternoon. The computer monitoring Gray's vital signs worked at the limit of its speed and capacity. A bell rang. The red warning light began to wink, calling attention to a new message that flashed on the luminous oscilloscope screen. Nurse Sue Myers saw it. The letters were printed in milliseconds, using a five-by-eight dot matrix.

CONDITION: SERIOUS
VITAL SIGNS: BP 80/76 , VP 20 cm, HR 102, RHYTHM IRREGULAR
DX: AF WITH PVCS
ESTIMATED CARDIAC OUTPUT: 1.2 l/min/M²
URINE VOLUME: 25 cc/min
RESPIRATION: 18, SHALLOW
PO2 76; PCO2 36; pH 7.32; TEMP 36.9 ° C
WARNING: IMMINENT CARDIAC ARREST
INSTITUTE PROTOCOL A

SECOND MESSAGE:

PROTOCOL A:
1) CHECK SENSORS
2) FLUSH ARTERIAL LINE
3) DRAW BLOOD FOR ELECTROLYTES
4) PWR ON DEFIBRILLATOR
5) CALL PHYSICIAN
6) CONSIDER: POTASSIUM CHLORIDE: 5 mq IV STAT
LIDOCAINE 100 mg IV STAT
ISOPROTERENOL—DECREASE MECHANICAL SUPPORT

Then the first message reappeared.

Sue Myers began to institute Protocol A. She took a sterile syringe with 10 cc of clear saline and an anticoagulant. She injected it into the three-way stopcock connecting the radial artery line to the blood pressure manometer. The line was clear of clot and obstructions. She inspected the electrodes attached to Gray's chest. The white dots of silver and electricity conducting salt gel were firmly in place. The electrical waves of the dying heart had been faithfully conducted to the computer's diagnostic programs. They were not spurious signals confusing the complex machinery. A blood sample was drawn from a plastic tube inserted into the internal jugular vein. The sample was immediately taken to the chemistry laboratories to determine the potassium and sodium levels, two important elements for the normal electrical activity of the heart. She reached over and turned on the power to the defibrillator, a device able to shoot a brief, concentrated high voltage shock. In the event of heart fibrillation the current shocks the heart cells into a single state of readiness. Then the heart resumes its normal beat.

Johnson looked at the electrocardiogram to analyze it directly, to compare his diagnosis with the imperturbable machine. Sue was near the drug cabinet completing the preparation of the suggested medications. Both were absorbed in their tasks when a sudden stillness crashed upon their consciousness simultaneously.

“Jack, would you check Mr. Gray,” Myers asked urgently.

He put down the ECG and stepped quickly to the apparently sleeping patient. He glanced at the monitor screen. The red light was no longer winking. It was now constant. The ECG screen showed a wildly chaotic pattern. Gray took a breath in with a loud sigh.

“Mr. Gray.”

No answer.

“Mr. Gray!” Johnson looked at his patient in helpless despair. He wished that Gray’s heart was pounding as hard as his own.

“Jesus Christ! Not again! Sue!”

“God, Jack! Push on his chest!”

“Call Buchanan. Call Bradfield.”

Sue Myers pushed a yellow-and-black fixture on the wall. The cardiac arrest bell rang in the corridor. Johnson got onto the bed above Gray and began to push desperately on the sternum, applying external cardiac massage.

Chapter 7

"Doctor Geld's expecting you." It was the voice of the receptionist in the Dean's office.

Bradfield smiled at the slim young black woman with the Afro hairdo and headed for the executive suite. It was tucked away in a corner of a long hallway lined with rich walnut paneling.

Dean Geld sat on a black leather chair behind a rosewood desk. Frances Holborn was seated on a couch set against the wall. In front was a round glass and walnut coffee table holding a silver coffee service, complete with blue English porcelain cups. The floor was covered with a golden wool carpet, except where the desk and executive chair stood. (These were set on brown oak parquet.) As was his habit, the Dean kept the desktop clear of papers. Only a calendar, a lamp, and a pipe rack disturbed the smooth surface.

Bradfield hesitated before stepping into the room. His rumpled surgical garb—white coat and green sneakers—seemed inappropriate. However, Dr. Holborn wore similar working clothes.

"Come in, Bill." Geld beckoned with a quick, extravagant gesture and stood up. He was short but certainly dapper: gray custom-tailored suit, light-blue pima cotton shirt, and red silk bow tie.

Irwin Geld, M.D., was the holder of an endowed professorship in medicine and psychiatry. As a child he grew up in the world of New York's Lower East Side where his stern, rabbinical father hawked used clothes from the back of an old Ford pickup truck. He made the boy study the Torah and shouted at him if he had too much time at play. Blond and pretty classmates persecuted Geld with taunts of "Jew boy!" and "Kike!" and Irwin willed that one day he would be different, not like his family. He held fast to a faith in his future, and had made it come true. He had come a long, long way.

"So how are you, Bill?" Geld came around his desk and offered his hand. It was a firm, warm handshake. His voice was soft, but his eyes reflected the decades-old inner conflict with a tyrannical God.

"Really pretty good, Irv."

"Good, good. Sit down over there with Franny. We were just going to have coffee. Would you care for some? Brewed from fresh ground beans by my secretary. Franny will pour, won't you, Fran?"

"Yes, of course."

"So, how's the wife, Bill? I haven't seen you two for quite some time. Have to have you over some time." Geld took the offensive in leading the discussion. He had learned to use noncontroversial, positive observations and questions to settle his mind down until he was ready to get to the heart of the matter.

"Charlotte's fine." Bradfield took a sip of the delicately aromatic coffee. The porcelain cup rim lay lightly on his lip.

Dean Geld went on in his mellifluous voice. "Franny was briefing me about the development of our cardiac surgery program. Your accomplishments are certainly impressive."

"Well, we try."

"Billy." The Dean's tone of voice was now serious. "Franny tells me you've developed an atomic heart?"

Bradfield thought, Nobody has called me "Billy" since grade school. "Yes, that's right, Irv. We've had two six-month implantations in calves. We have two more calves living at present. Absolutely smooth implantations and only a minor hitch or two in each one."

Geld was back in his swivel chair, luxuriating in its comfort, cleaning his Dunhill pipe. "Franny also tells me that you want to put one in a human today?"

Bradfield nodded.

"That's great! You're leading the way again, Billy. You know the Dean's office will be supportive, and what little we can do for you we will. You know how I wish I were back seeing patients again instead of all this dull administrative work and fund-raising."

"You're welcome to come and observe tonight, of course."

"Tell me, will there be any surgical problems? I know you guys are good, but what are the risks when you translate the animal experience to a human patient?"

"No problems. At least, we don't expect any."

"You seem pretty certain. You feel you have the technical problems solved, I presume?"

"That's a safe presumption, Irv." A note of impatience crept into Bradfield's voice.

"How about the other issues—cost, legal, moral, ethical, and so on?" Geld said. "Have you or any medical center committee reviewed these concerns?"

"In my view, this is a legitimate clinical trial. We've been very careful about publicity for reasons you're well aware of."

"Yes, I've been aware for some time of the care you've taken in that respect. I emphasize that I hope there won't be a circuslike atmosphere."

"Of course not. As for the morality aspect, we can't identify any issue ourselves. Replacement by a machine should be no different from human heart transplantation. And the religious experts have pretty well clarified the views of the various faiths with respect to the former." Bradfield continued, listing his points on his fingers. "Legally, the risks of radiation damage, sterilization, and malfunction have been explained to the patient. So we think that the informed consent legalities have been met."

"What's the environmental impact?" Geld asked. "What happens if two or more of these patients get in the same room?"

Bradfield was taken aback. The question implied that the combination of two or more patients with atomic hearts in a room could cause an explosion. This worked against Geld's reputation as a "quick study." "To have an accident," he said finally, "two plutonium masses from two hypothetical patients have to be intimately joined. By that I mean you have to have a high explosive to shoot one mass at a high speed at the other mass. Therefore, the mere proximity of two patients in a closed space cannot cause an accident."

"But a Federal panel has questioned this problem," Geld persisted. "If you remember, Bill, one of the members was our Dean of Religion. His and their fear was that if a number of recipients were brought together, say at a party, they might start a nuclear chain reaction."

"I thought I answered the question satisfactorily, but I'll go over it again," Bradfield replied quickly. "I remember the group you mention. It was formed to study the several nontechnical implications of the artificial heart. None of its members was professionally qualified to evaluate this problem. The AEC, however, has looked into it. Its analysis shows that even an infinite number of patients could be assembled in a room without any risk."

"What about accidents?"

"The plutonium is encapsulated in a T-111 pressure vessel designed to withstand any credible accident. The shearing resistance is 10,000 pounds for one hour, the incineration temperature is 2,310° F for four hours, the puncture resistance is 44 FBS into one-eighth of an inch diameter pin, crush resistance 20,000 pounds for one hour."

"Sounds well designed! Looks like you really have something."

Bradfield had not finished. "The proof of the pudding is in the eating. The experimental animals are the biological tests, and they're really successful. Now we're prepared to try our first in a human." He looked steadily at Geld.

The Dean returned the gaze. "How much is this going to cost us?"

"Virtually nothing need come out of medical center funds."

"Fine! We don't have anything to pass out anyway!"

"The plutonium is the most expensive item—$100,000."

"What?" Geld said in astonishment. "This will be amortized over the life of the patient, I suppose?"

"Yes. We figure the material is reusable to eighty-seven years, so only finance charges for use of the money would be handled by the patient's insurance company."

"I see. Good!"

"We're using the plutonium already bought on our government contract. The patient has major medical insurance for hospitalization. I won't be charging a fee, of course."

"You're going to have some trouble getting the insurance to pay for experimental research. You may nick us for a big sum there, Bill. Who's building the heart?"

"Two companies. ATOCOR, a small R. & D. company in Berkeley, is building the heart itself. The Menlo Institute holds the patent on the control unit. They've farmed out the manufacturing to Zee Electronics."

"How do you spell the names?"

"A-T-O-C-O-R; Z-E-E."

Geld made a note on a slip of paper. "Anything I can do?"

"There remains the problem of the Human Experimentation Committee clearance. This case has come up rather suddenly. I haven't had the time to work up a report for their perusal."

A buzz interrupted the conversation. "Dr. Bradfield is wanted in I.C.U. immediately."

"Well, if that's what I think it is, we might not get to do the operation today at all."

"Call me if I can help, Bill."

Bradfield left, walking rapidly out of the office. Holborn got up and also left. Geld picked up his telephone.

"Get Andy Workman in here with the Bradfield file."

* * *

He arrived in Geld's office almost immediately.

"Andy, come on in. Sit down," Geld said.

Andrew Workman was the Associate Dean for Administration. He affected the new-man appearance: wire rim glasses, bold shirts, aggressive personality, BMW car. It had been the hope of Aspermont's trustees that Workman's experience in systems analysis would make the medical center more efficient and sound financially.

"Andy, review for me the bottom-line figures for cardiovascular surgery," said Geld.

Workman opened Bradfield's file and read from a yellow sheet of paper. "Total medical school budget is $27 million. Professional income from 912 open heart operations was $1.4 million. Personnel costs, including Bradfield's salary, was $257,000, a net overage of $1,143,000."

"And his research grants and contracts?"

"That's another $800,000. The school got an additional $376,000 for overhead costs. And gifts directly to cardiovascular surgery totaled $47,385 this year, but we can't touch that."

"Well, Andy, I can't agree with that. We get, let's see, $1,519,000 for discretionary use. Watch that heart implantation, though. I have a feeling Bradfield may pull something. The hospital bill, for example. If the insurance doesn't cover it, make sure the patient is billed."

"Or his estate," Workman snickered.

"Or his estate. Right."

"If the operation goes well tonight, make sure our public relations office is on top of it. I'm certain a press conference will have to be called."

"I'll see to it that Jerry Cibelli is informed."

"This could be big—financially, I mean."

"You think it's worth betting some money on the market?"

"Of course. ATOCOR is the company involved in development and marketing of the artificial heart. I can guarantee that after the news breaks their stock will go up."

"Irv, I didn't know you were interested in the stock market?"

"I wasn't until I read an article about it in a recent medical journal."

"What did it say?"

"It documented how large profits can be made by betting against the value of medical breakthroughs in the lay press."

"Does the idea work?"

"Like a charm. You buy on bad news, sell on good news. The authors figured that most items reported as medical breakthroughs by the press are inaccurate. So any stock that rises as a result of the publicity will plunge to its lowest value when people realize that a cure has not been discovered."

"Clever," Workman said. "I'm sure the short sales in each instance generate a handsome profit."

"Right," Geld said. "But most physicians are ignorant of the basic rules of the stock market. That's why we are the butt of jokes in the financial community. By the way, who's on the Human Experimentation Committee?"

"Professor Applebaum in sociology, Professor Lindstrom in psychiatry, Professor Rosenthal in genetics, yourself, and Dr. Holborn."

"Okay. Take this down. 'Due to the emergency nature of this case, a telephone poll of the available members of the Human Experimentation Committee was taken. After thorough discussion, approval was obtained for clinical trial of a prototype artificial heart. Approval is for one time only. Further protocols for implantation will have to be taken up for consideration one at a time. Signed, Irwin Geld, M.D.' Fill in the gaps and have copies sent to Ridley and members of the committee. Okay, Andy, beat it now. I have some private calls to make."

After Workman left, Geld picked up the phone.

"Get me Fred Hull of E. L. Gerard." He drummed his fingers on the desk for a moment. "Hello, Fred? Irwin Geld here."

"Yes. How are you, Dr. Geld?"

"How's the market today?"

"Changing."

"You say that all the time."
"How's my favorite customer?"
"Not bad. Got some tips."
"Oh ho! Good! What you got?"
"Just like the last time. Remember ComputMed?"
"Yep. That's the company that uses a mass spectrometer and a giant computer to analyze complicated molecules?"
"They made it big, because the costly development work was done here on campus with Federal basic science research money. They took the public with unpublished information and went to work for themselves before anybody else knew the stunt. I got you in on the ground floor."
"I never forget my friends."
"Okay. ATOCOR makes an artificial heart. Our surgeons are going to put one in tonight. Should get a big play in the media next few weeks."
"Let me look it up." Pause. "Yes, ATOCOR traded over the counter: two million shares outstanding. Bid one-and-a-half, asked one and seven-eighths. High ten-and-a-half last year. Record earnings. Listed here as making atomic powered pacemakers."
"That's the company."
"Crashed this year when GE announced a new ten-year battery for use in pacemakers."
"Great. New low then?"
"Yes."
"Okay. This stock is to be played. Only one heart is going to be put in. My guess is the damn thing is going to cost too much money to be of practical use, and a lot of do-gooders in Washington are going to get very mad about the publicity. Buy fifty thousand shares at market on margin. Sell twenty-five percent at five, fifty at seven, and the rest at ten."
"Right, doctor. Think I should buy myself?"
"In and out, Fred. It's going to bust. Goodbye."
"Thanks a lot, Doc."

Chapter 8

Sasha Romanoff assisted anesthesiologist James Takaoka with the first heart patient of the day, pushing the bed down the corridor from the O.R. to the I.C.U. An orderly carried the A-size oxygen tank and hung it on to the corner of the bed frame. Takaoka stood on a rung built into the head of the bed, squeezing rhythmically on the Amber bag. The patient's chest rose and fell with each artificial breath.

Nurse Ginger Brown, young, attractive, and Romanoff's current objective, watched as they approached down the corridor. It was crowded with laundry carts, breakfast trays, and medical equipment. The O.R. nurse had carefully covered the patient with a white cotton blanket up to the neck to camouflage the wounds of surgery from curious eyes, but there was no way of concealing his condition. A dark bag of blood hung above the bed on its holder, and the blood dripped down slowly through a thin plastic tube into a large neck vein. A plastic breathing tube extended out of the nostril and was taped tightly to the patient's nose. The plastic "Pleurevac" hung below the patient on the side of the bed. It collected the ooze of unclotted blood still leaking slowly from cut capillaries and suture lines.

It was slow going, moving the bed around obstructions, and it was worse during visiting hours with patients' families waiting right in the hallway. The move from the O.R. to the I.C.U. had to be carried out expeditiously for nursing care to start, for monitoring to be set up, for the drugs and blood replacement to be accurately charted. Ginger thought wryly that on TV or in the movies, this part of the patient's saga was never displayed. Emergency stretchers always had a clear hallway; oxygen was always ready. But then, nobody thought it dramatic that outwardly beautiful, newly built hospitals were often so poorly designed that nurses and doctors were hindered in the performance of their duties.

"He belongs here, Sasha," Ginger called, but her voice was drowned out by the clanging cardiac arrest bell. The nurses in the unit momentarily froze in their tracks. The yellow-painted globe above Room 202 shone brightly, and the red light at the nursing station flashed on at two-second intervals.

Romanoff sensed instantly that the distress signal originated in Gray's room. He had planned to look in on him as soon as he had finished his present chore. He stopped pushing the bed and turned to rush to Room 202. The pocket of his white coat caught on the corner of the bed frame, knocking his stethoscope with a clatter on the floor. The material tore suddenly, releasing him, but he overlooked a rubber tube that stretched between the orderly's oxygen tank, the Ambu bag, and the patient.

"Hey!" the orderly and Takaoka shouted simultaneously as the lifeline stretched out like a giant slingshot, and snapped off where it joined the patient's airway. The tube, hissing pure oxygen, snaked about the floor of the hallway until the orderly trapped it. Takaoka grabbed the end and reattached it one-handedly, while his other hand continued to ventilate the patient.

"Damn it, Romanoff!" Takaoka shouted. "Get your ass back in here. Let's get this patient settled in his room first."

The bed and medical team partially obstructed the hallway. Others were responding to the alarm, muttering about the nitwits holding up traffic. Romanoff took Takaoka's command to heart and settled down. Chasing two objectives jeopardized both. As Ginger helped Romanoff swing the bed into the room, she couldn't help but tease him.

"Is young Doctor Kildare requested to take charge of an emergency?"

Romanoff, sheepish at being caught wanting, quietly went about writing the postoperative orders and visually checking the patient. Ginger Brown was immediately sorry she had taunted him. Sasha was an okay guy in her opinion. Keeping an eye on the patient, while putting the ECG electrodes and attaching the "Pleurevac" to negative suction, she sidled up to Romanoff.

"Hey, man," she said softly. "How about meeting this evening for dinner?"

Romanoff's spirits lifted. "With you, sweetheart, any time."

Dr. Isaac Stearns, the anesthesiologist, responded to the emergency call. He was a gaunt, elderly man with thirty-two years of clinical and academic experience. He surveyed the scene at a glance on entering Gray's room. Jack Johnson was up on the bed kneeling over the patient. He was pushing heavily and steadily on the sternum. Sweat dampened his brow and the front of his shirt. Sue Myers was feeling for a pulse to gauge the effectiveness of Johnson's effort. Another nurse and an orderly were waiting to assist. The respiratory therapist placed a black rubber breathing mask over the nose and mouth of the gasping patient. Green bile trickled from Gray's mouth onto the pillow with each push on his chest. It was necessary to stop the artificial respiration for a second to suck out the acid fluid surging back into the mouth so that it would not sear the delicate cells of the lungs. In doing so, the patient became more dusky in color.

It was an ugly scene, a seemingly disorganized crowd fighting in all directions under the imminence of death. One could smell it.

Professor Stearns made his presence known immediately.

"Oh, Dr. Stearns." Johnson was gasping a bit. "This is the patient scheduled for a mechanical heart. He just fibrillated."

"Are you the resident in charge?"

"Yes, sir."

Dr. Stearns put a comforting hand on Johnson's back and said, "Then why don't you get one of those medical students standing over there to do the pushing. You can get a better handle on the overall management back here."

Johnson nodded. "Belknap, you know how to do this?"

The junior medical student, anxious to participate, replied, "Yes, sixty times a minute, hand crossed over the lower half of the sternum, pause for respiration."

"Okay. Hop up here and go to work!"

Stearns signaled to the float nurse. She brought the tray of emergency equipment over. "I would establish airway, wouldn't you, Jack?" Stearns continued in his soft midwestern voice. "I believe I can do it. May I?"

"By all means, Dr. Stearns."

"While I do, perhaps we might reduce the crowd a bit."

Johnson pointed to all idle bystanders with an imperious finger. They reluctantly drifted out. The noise and extraneous activity faded away.

The lesson Professor Stearns had skillfully imparted to young Johnson and the students was that even in critical conditions in medicine, there must be a single leader. Johnson now directed the preparation of drugs to be injected, unconsciously emulating the Professor's soft, yet incisive tone of voice.

"Amp bicarb, please." "Hundred of lidocaine." "Five milliequivalents potassium chloride into the IV bottle."

While Sue Myers drew up the clear solution from the color-coded bottles, Johnson directed yet another student to look over Dr. Stearns's shoulder as he prepared to insert an endotracheal tube into the windpipe. The tube allowed direct movement of oxygen into the lungs of the patient and also prevented stomach acids from surging back into the trachea. The virgorous heart massage and ventilation had to cease during the insertion. Speed without injuring the vocal cords was important.

Stearns said, "Remove the face mask and stop massage."

The sounds from the patient ceased, and a tense silence fell. Two seconds went by, then another as Stearns, standing over the head of the bed, reached for the dying man's slack jaw and opened the mouth. Death was not a pretty sight. Another two seconds passed. In his other hand Stearns held the L-shaped, hard-steel chrome laryngoscope. He inserted it to move the tongue up and out of the visual path so that he could look at the vocal cords. But the route was obscured by white foamy secretions. Another few seconds went by. To a very experienced eye, the color of the patient was becoming more dusky.

"Suction, please."

Instantly, a blue plastic suction catheter was in Stearns's free hand. The tip of the thin plastic tube was guided expertly over the protruding epiglottis, the light on the end of the scope illuminating the field. The opaque obscuring material was removed. The vocal cords were pale, tough, and wide apart. It was black beyond.

"Belknap, Jones, Schwartz!"

Each medical student took his precious moment to observe the position of Stearns's hands, the angle of the laryngoscope, the attitude of Gray's head in relationship to the bed, the clear view of the cords. Another five seconds passed.

"Schwartz, slip it to him!" and Stearns, still exposing the field, leaned his body far over to one side.

Johnson held his breath as the student directed the plastic breathing tube into the cavity. The tip of the tube shook a little, amplifying the frail tremor of the student's moist hand. With a single swift motion, the tube was slipped between the cords and into the windpipe. Stearns removed the laryngoscope and Schwartz stood up and held the tube in place. The respiratory therapist gave the student the ventilatory connection. The gas pressure built up in the conduit with a hissing flowing sound. Gray's chest rose, filling with life-sustaining oxygen. The inflow stopped, the chest full, washing out the buildup of acidic waste carbon dioxide.

A scant thirty seconds had gone by since the face mask was removed. Belknap leaped back onto the bed and resumed his heart massage as the endotracheal tube was fastened in place with wide adhesive tape.

"He's pinking up!"

"I feel a pulse."

"He's still fibrillating!"

"Epinephrine, Dr. Stearns?" It was Johnson's voice.

"You're the doctor, Jack. I would."

Sue Myers handed Johnson the long intracardiac needle with 10 cc of epinephrine already drawn up in it. Johnson, now calm and confident, proceeded to administer the injection.

The landmarks for injecting the epinephrine directly into the heart were the bottom tip of the breastbone, the xiphoid, and the left shoulder. Belknap stopped massaging. Johnson wiped the skin surface with cold alcohol, and rivulets of the antiseptic dripped down onto the bed. Deftly, the sharp point of the long hypodermic needle was pushed through the skin over the xiphoid. There was no response from the patient. He pointed the shiny, liquid assembly toward the left shoulder and the back, and pushed hard. The needle entered to three inches. With an educated sensitivity in the tips of his fingers, he could feel a slight give as each layer—skin, pericardium, and heart—was penetrated. A tentative one-handed pull on the plunger of the syringe and the welcome sight of dark blood appeared, swirling slowly into the clear epinephrine solution. The needle was in the ventricle. He pushed carefully on the plunger, releasing 3 cc of the powerful drug directly into the heart and bloodstream. Belknap resumed the massage after the syringe was withdrawn.

Johnson looked over at the oscilloscope screen. The waveform was still chaotic but was much larger in amplitude.

"Time to defibrillate," he said out loud. He grasped the high dielectric plastic handles of the defibrillator. The paddles were placed on the chest over the heart.

"Everybody away from the bed!"

There was a momentary wait to make sure the aides were no longer in contact with bed or patient. "Hit it!"

The electric jolt was so strong that the ECG on the scope immediately went blank. A fraction of a second later, Gray's nerves and muscles twitched in one great spasm. The heart cells, contracting in a wild disorganized frenzy, were put to a resting state at once by the 1,000-volt shock. All eyes in the room turned toward the ECG screen anxiously. The trace returned. It was a straight line—no activity. Belknap again took over the pumping action, massaging in desperation. After two seconds, a beat appeared, then another and another. A rapid, but regular rhythm returned. Inquisitive hands went quickly to the patient's groin to feel the femoral pulse. It was weak and collapsing but present. The arterial pulse trace on the oscilloscope face was increasing with each beat. Johnson motioned to Belknap to come off the bed. The almost tangible tension relaxed noticeably as the patient began to breathe spontaneously. The red warning light blinked off and all was quiet except for the living sounds made by Gray, returning from death's doorway.

"Okay," said Johnson. "Let's clean up the room."

"Good job, Jack," said Stearns. "Call me if you need any more assistance. Looks like you should keep the ventilation going for a good while."

"Thank you very much, Dr. Stearns. Thank you."

Sue Myers, watching the patient carefully, saw his eyelids flutter. She leaned over him.

"Mr. Gray, it's all right," she whispered. "You have a tube in your windpipe to help you breathe. Your heart skipped a few beats. Don't try to talk."

Romanoff walked carefully into the room. Most of the bystanders had left so he knew that either there was nothing more to see or the patient had died.

"Well, Jack, what happened?"

"Christ, we just got the lab work back. His potassium got too low. He developed ventricular extrasystoles on top of atrial fibrillation. Look at the ECG tracing: an R wave on a T and bang—fibrillation!"

"Is he okay?"

"Well, he's on epinephrine, artificial respiration, and has been defibrillated once. His B.P. is low and he's not making much urine. Otherwise, Mrs. Lincoln, he's fine!"

"Gotcha!"

"I've got a feeling that we've only saved him from one death so he can jump in the box tonight!"

"Well, he has one foot in it now."

Bradfield entered, a worried, hurried man. "Jack, Sasha, you guys get the situation fixed up?"

"Jack took care of it, Dr. Bradfield."

"Okay. Looks good now. Eh, Jack?"

"I'd say it's pretty grim."

"Well, it won't be long now. Seven-thirty is the time. The heart and the O.R. are ready. So stick with it. Get Sasha to help you if you need to. Where's Don?"

"He's looking for you."

Bradfield walked over to the patient. He pulled the white bedsheet down to get an overall impression. He saw the wasted chest muscles, the swollen pale belly, the thick waterlogged ankles and feet, the various tubes, electrodes, and catheters attached to his body.

"Not very promising," he said quietly, looking up at the concerned young woman still cleaning up the mess of the successful resuscitation effort. "Is he alert?" he asked as he bent down to talk to the patient. "Ah, Mr. . . ."

"Gray." Myers filled in.

"Mr. Gray." The eyelids fluttered in semirecognition of his name, but the eyes were unseeing.

Johnson said, "He wasn't that with it this morning, but I don't think he's got squash rot. We resuscitated him pretty quickly. Doesn't make much difference anyway, does it?"

Bradfield turned to Johnson and Romanoff. "What do you mean, Jack?"

Johnson was uncomfortable. Romanoff felt Johnson had just made a real faux pas.

Johnson cleared his throat nervously. "I figure the first case is a 'free cut.' You need the kind of patient who has little chance of making it in any case. Then if it fails, you don't look so bad. In fact, you'd be a hero for attempting the impossible!"

Romanoff thought, Bye-bye, baby, Johnson!

Bradfield was thinking briefly how to respond to Johnson's remark.

"Jack," he said suddenly, "I like your forthrightness. You're expressing the viewpoint some of the old doctors out in practice have about university surgeons. But it's really just the reverse. For any new operation you want the best possible condition because early success is politically important—technical success for the operation, success for patient rehabilitation. If the patient dies, nobody will refer another patient to you. An operation has its indications and contraindications. It isn't a last resort procedure, and it isn't an exercise. You want to be successful, and you want the product of your effort to be useful to society. It's a social judgment, to be sure, but one we can make. Okay? And I don't mean we'd pick a white manufacturer over a black janitor. I do mean that when we get through, the patient should be healthy enough to do his thing, be he mighty or humble."

Johnson asked, "What about *this* patient?"

Bradfield replied, reassuringly, "He'll be okay when he gets some circulation. His pupils react and his reflexes are intact, aren't they?"

"Yes."

"I'm going to find Buchanan. Romanoff, get ready for the second case."

After Bradfield left, Romanoff stayed to examine Gray himself and to talk with Johnson.

"Well, Jack, he could have raised the roof."

"He didn't, Sasha. I guess that's why he's the Professor!"

There was silence, except for the rain falling steadily on the manicured grounds outside.

Chapter 9

2:30 P.M. The second open-heart surgery case was over earlier than usual. Bradfield dropped out of the O.R. to recheck Gray's condition before returning to his office, where Buchanan awaited him.

"The O.R. has been set up," Buchanan said. "Mrs. Donald cancelled the elective plastic surgery scheduled after six o'clock. She moved our case to Room Thirteen."

"Good."

"Ray Evans will be here to run the pump. We have six units of fresh blood ordered, two to prime the pump and four to replace the postoperative loss. Takaoka will be the anesthesiologist. The cardiologists have seen Gray. They want to talk to you about why he wasn't admitted on their service rather than ours."

"Because they'd kill him with their herbs. Did you tell them that?"

"I would have, but no point in getting them agitated."

"Did they agree or not?"

"Sure."

"Couldn't argue with you! That's why I picked you, Don. You're so big, you intimidate them!" Bradfield said slyly.

"The operation permit was signed."
"Before or after the cardiac arrest?"
"Early this morning. His fiancée signed as a witness."
"He certainly is in no condition to give informed consent now."
"Louella and Jack talked to both of them."
"Okay. How about the heart?"
"I just called the calf lab. Liz Browning says the heart's in the exhaust phase of the gas sterilization."
"That was a mistake on my part. I thought she was keeping it sterilized. We could have hurried the O.R. schedule, but we can't hurry that."
The artificial heart was a delicate instrument requiring cold sterilization instead of steam. Hot steam under pressure could easily melt the heart's solid-state control unit and the lightweight superstructure of silicon rubber sacs. Instead, pressurized gas, ethylene oxide, was used to kill common bacteria and spores with tough, resistant shells. But gas sterilization had a drawback because plastics absorb toxic gas. After sterilization, the heart had to be placed in a vacuum to allow the gas to diffuse slowly out of the chambers. The process took a slow four hours. If the heart were to be placed in the body too early, the gas would seep gradually and lethally into the patient. Thus, the present long wait.
"We'll start the operation at six-thirty, then the patient will be open and on the pump," Bradfield said. "When the heart comes out of the sterilizer, we can go right ahead."
"The remaining problem," Buchanan added, "is the release of the plutonium by Ridley."
"That's no problem. I spoke with the Dean earlier. It's all set. In fact, he polled the Human Experimentation Committee by phone to help us along."
"Well, I just talked to Ridley in his office. He says 'No dice! No plutonium for human use.' "
"Doesn't he know that this patient is about to croak? That he's interfering with patient care? Valerie, get Ridley on the phone!"
"Better talk to him face to face," Buchanan suggested.

"For crying out loud! This place is going to hell! Valerie!" Bradfield shouted through the door, "Have him come up. We'll get him straightened out."

Quickly, Valerie Rigg dialed the number of Ridley's office.

"That son of a bitch," Bradfield continued, anger lighting his narrowed brown eyes. "This is just lovely. This puts us in a helluva tight spot."

Valerie interrupted. "Mr. Ridley's secretary says he's already left. She said he left early because he's bicycling home."

"You mean, in the rain?"

"Yes."

"Christ! Where does he live? Here, let me talk to her." Bradfield grabbed his telephone. "Hello, who's this?"

"I'm Marty Lane, Mr. Ridley's secretary. Can I help you, Dr. Bradfield?" The voice over the phone was young and anxious.

"Our problem is that we have scheduled an operation and we need the plutonium Mr. Ridley has locked up. Can you get the material?"

"No, sir. Only Mr. Ridley has the combination in this office."

"Okay. Did Dean Geld send a memo approving the plutonium release for our operation?"

"There was an envelope from the Dean's office delivered here, but I don't know what it contains."

"Did Ridley read it?"

"No, it just came in."

"God, that's three hours to get a piece of paper from one desk to another. You know, I just did an entire heart operation during this time. And you said Ridley has left already?"

"Yes, sir." Marty was beginning to feel badgered and flustered. Although it certainly was not her fault, the overpowering pressure of Bradfield's hammering at Ridley made her feel guilty.

"And he's bicycling home in the rain?"

"Yes, sir."

"He's crazier than I thought—a physical culture nut. What's his phone and home address?"

Marty gave the information to Bradfield. "But I'm sure Mr. Ridley won't be home yet," she said.

"If I drove over to find him, would you know what route he would be traveling?"

"Yes, I do." She replied almost gaily, happy to know she could at last give Bradfield some useful information. "I've driven out there with him. He takes the Campus Drive out to Junipero Serra, heads north, and on to Alpine Road out to his home."

"Okay. Thank you."

Bradfield hung up abruptly and turned to Buchanan. "I'm going out to find that guy. Start the case on time."

"I can go find him, if you like."

"You had your try with him already. It didn't work. When something needs to be done, better do it yourself. What's gotten into him, anyway?"

Buchanan sighed. "Well, it has to do with several things, really. First, he thinks the residual radioactivity escaping from the artificial heart is too high. Second, he believes strongly that plutonium is too toxic and shouldn't circulate in society, and third, you're taking shortcuts that violate his guidelines."

"That's really tough!"

Bradfield put on a light raincoat and walked with Buchanan to the I.C.U. "You manage the patient, and I'll see you when I get things straightened out." He headed quickly out to the reserved parking lot and his car.

Cold wind, rain—buckets of it. Ridley was engrossed in the demanding task of pedaling the light, swift bicycle through the bad weather. He was down low in a racing crouch to minimize wind resistance. The old country road was empty at this hour, but soon even the few commuters who lived in the valley would make bicycling hazardous. The road was narrow and rough, scheduled to be repaired, no doubt, in the summer. An occasional car had already blinked its headlights at him and passed, invariably splashing mud down his left side and over the orange parka. He thought of a hot shower and dry clothes. He was so engrossed in this comforting idea that it was a few seconds before he became aware of the blinking lights of another car behind him. He pulled over as far as he dared, but the road shoulder was badly pitted. Today he could see the oozing mud sliding gently down the cut edge of the hill, filling the potholes to a deceptive smoothness.

Ridley gestured with his left hand to signal the car to pass. The car was close behind him, but it did not pass. It paced him, the headlights still blinking. Was it a police car? The bicycle was licensed properly with the proper safety devices attached. Then the horn sounded briefly, curiously muffled as the wind blew the sound away. He glanced back quickly and saw the amber directional light indicating a right turn. An arm was waving out of the driver's window. Ridley braked the bicycle to a stop, then hopped off and wheeled it to the shoulder. The car stopped alongside him, lights blinking, windshield wipers surging rhythmically, the engine turning over quietly. The car was nothing fancy—a late model Plymouth Fury sedan, clean and tuned. The passenger window rolled down, the rain drifting in, as Bradfield thrust out his head.

"Allen, I've got to talk to you. Leave your bike and get in the car."

"Yes, sir." Ridley opened the door and settled on the front seat next to Bradfield. "You certainly have a knack for finding unusual places for a chat. Fire away."

"Buchanan tells me you've refused to give us the plutonium for our operation tonight."

"That's absolutely correct."

"You know, of course, that a patient who can use this heart is dying right now in the I.C.U.?" Bradfield spoke with careful intonation so there was no doubt that he would hold Ridley personally responsible for the patient's death.

"That's what Don told me, but my answer is still the same. Until I see a piece of paper that says this machine has been approved for human use, I must refuse. The rules exist to safeguard the public. You have no right to circumvent them unilaterally."

"This is a helluva time to argue morality, fella. The hospital isn't an assembly line with auto parts on a belt. It's a place with human lives on the line."

"But you've conveniently forgotten about your responsibility to live by the rules. Expediency is a bad thing in a hospital—taking things for granted, establishing your own rules of conduct, taking shortcuts. You've no right to do that."

"You're getting as bad as some of the nurses."

"I hate to argue this point as much as you do. But my hands are tied. And so are yours, may I add."

"So you think the radiation from the power source is high? I say that's not for you to decide. This patient will die. I know it without any doubt. I have the approval of the Dean and an authorized committee—although, to be frank, I'd have bypassed them if they had dragged their feet."

"As far as I'm concerned that piece of paper is worth just what you think of the committee. It says you can do experiments on human beings. It doesn't deal with the social consequences of this operation."

"Ridley, you've hit the nail right on the head. We deal with one problem at a time, and we solve it if we possibly can. I don't need to remind you that our hospital has the best heart surgery program in the world. It's recognized as such because we pay attention to the patient and his needs. Each of my residents is trained exactly the same way. They work up to thirty-six-hour stretches to care for patients if that's what's required. Nobody argues about the social consequences when these patients get well and return home to laughing children and a grateful spouse."

"I'm fully aware of your accomplishments, Dr. Bradfield. And by no stretch of the imagination do I doubt your sincerity. But unless I get some assurance that it's both legal and moral that I release this plutonium, I will not do it."

"Christ! You're not doubting my sincerity!" Bradfield yelled. "Would I be out here in the damn rain talking to a half-demented philosopher if you weren't? Have you ever killed a man by error, by mistaken judgment, by a slip of the hand? Have you ever seen death?"

"Not as dramatically as you put it. But, yes, I've seen death." Ridley's mind was suddenly several years back. He and Cynthia, both enthusiastic mountaineers, had taken part in an expedition to the Peruvian Andes during their honeymoon. In Peru they had visited the ancient capital of Cuzco, 11,000 feet up, and the old city of Machu Picchu. This isolated spot was the backdrop to a rustic government tourist hotel in which they had consummated their marriage. After an exhausting night, Allen had remarked that climbing Huascarán, the highest mountain in Peru at 22,201 feet, was going to be a snap. It was not. The adventure was cut short when an avalanche of snow and rock roared past the Ridleys, killing two members of the expedition.

"I've seen men die with their life rope slipping through my hands, then snapping, with the awful feeling of not being able to do anything about it, with their screams in my ears," said Ridley recalling the episode. "I don't want to experience that ever again. You say you speak for the patient. Who speaks for all of us?"

"Do you? A bearded little man with a ponytail pedaling through the mud?"

"Look, Bradfield. There's no need to get personal. I'm trying to be reasonable. All I want to know is that the consequences of this development have been evaluated by someone who has no vested interest."

"I have the project officer's concurrence."

"You mean, Harris approved a human trial?"

"Yes. And if you don't believe me, you can pedal on home. But be prepared to get your ass back to the hospital. We'll get Harris to phone you. The operation starts at six-thirty, and the plutonium better be ready!"

"Bradfield, you're crazy. Don't start the operation."

"It will start on schedule, Ridley. And I'm telling you, I'm going to call you in your nice comfy bed if that fuel capsule isn't out of the vault when I need it. Then, you can tell your story to the personnel office of another university, because I'll kick your ass right out of Aspermont. I'll hold you responsible for the patient's death and you'll learn to do things the right way."

"You're mad! Don't start that operation."

"Think about what I've said."

The confrontation between Bradfield and the radiation safety officer was over, although the conflict between them wasn't settled. Ridley got out of the car, slipped back onto the bicycle, looked for traffic, and pedaled off into the brisk wind and cold rain. Bradfield rolled up his window and started to make a turn, his headlights following Ridley until he disappeared from view. Bradfield noticed the roadbed was narrow, and it was not possible to make a U-turn at that spot. He drove slowly forward concentrating on finding a driveway or a wider area. He found one six hundred yards further on and turned the car quickly.

Neither Ridley nor Bradfield had noticed the continued oozing of mud on both sides of the roadway. On the roadbed where Bradfield's car had parked there were tire tracks two inches deep. The water was no longer being soaked up by the ground and the hill was a gooey mess.

Chapter 10

Bradfield returned from the dismal roadside meeting with Ridley. He was chilled, wet, and angry, with no time for pandering to his feelings. The complex undertaking begun four years earlier was coming to fruition. His goal now was to keep the operation on schedule.

Intuition plays a key role in a surgeon's practice. Unlike the scientist who follows a hunch and gets enough negative and positive results to indicate that his conclusion is not due to chance, the surgeon has to guess correctly from the start. To do so, he relies on past experience and quick insight. So it was that under no circumstances would Bradfield consider leaving Gray without benefit of surgery. He had a hunch he was right. It was now or never.

"Valerie, we've still got a problem with Ridley. I want you to get hold of Harris and have him talk directly to Ridley about Federal approval for this implanation. We need it quick. We start surgery at six-thirty sharp."

"Yes, of course." She looked at her bedraggled, dripping, and sneezing boss with maternal concern. "You look terrible! Why don't you get into some dry clothes? The house staff on-call quarters up on the ninth floor has showers and clean scrub suits. There's even a whirlpool tub you can soak in for a while. I'll page you when I connect with Dr. Harris."

"Fine, great idea, Valerie. I've never been up there."

"You'll need a key. You can have this one." She took the key from her desk drawer and handed it to Bradfield. "Sasha Romanoff has the other key, but he was on call last night and hasn't returned it to me yet. They'll wait for you, of course."

"Valerie, I don't want them to wait. Keep the momentum going!"

The secretary shook her head at her sometimes childlike hero. He walked down the hall, wet canvas shoes squishing with each step. His white coat and pants were soaked where the raincoat had not covered them. His wet hair had been pushed back roughly with his fingers.

There is a three-hour time difference between the East and West coasts. When Californians wind up the day's work, Easterners are well into their leisure-time activities. Mrs. Ronald Harris was the mother of three teenage daughters. Warm and friendly, she devoted her life to the care of her husband and children in their home in Silver Spring, Maryland. Mrs. Harris was finishing in the kitchen, and the girls were in their rooms busy with their homework.

Valerie Rigg was on the end of the telephone line that rang in the Harris household just after six o'clock.

"I'm sorry, Miss Rigg. Dr. Harris has not yet come home. He often works late. Sometimes he leaves in a hurry for out of town without calling me."

"Is there any way to get ahold of him? It's urgent!"

There was alarm in Valerie's voice. "I've already tried his office number. No answer. In fact, I had a security guard go over there. It took some doing, but I finally found out his office was closed."

"My goodness, let me think. There's Miss Narewski, his secretary. I have her phone number. Quite often she forgets to pass messages from my husband on to me. She's very nice, but a bit scatterbrained. Here it is: JK–5–4436. You have the area code?"

"Yes. Thank you very much, Mrs. Harris. If Dr. Harris should come in, please have him contact Dr. Bradfield's office immediately. It's very important!"

"I certainly will. Good luck!"

"Goodbye, and thanks again."

Wanda Narewski had just finished secretarial training when she went to work for Harris. Mrs. Harris had been generous in her estimation of Wanda as a "bit scatterbrained." She was disorganized about everything except the Washington Redskins and sex. At this moment she was preoccupied with both. And Jon Taylor was one young man who was glad of it. Jon passed himself off as a member of the Washington Redskins football team. In truth he was the assistant locker-room manager. It made little difference to Wanda, and when, purely by chance, she met Taylor, she lost her cool. He wasn't stupid and had eagerly accepted an invitation to have dinner at her apartment.

Their evening was proceeding according to plan. He was talking incessantly about the monstrous players, the infinitely wise coaching staff, the avaricious owners, the parasitic reporters, and the cruelly insatiable sports fans demanding meaner and rougher play. She was complaining of the excessive warmth of the apartment and, with his intermittent suggestions, shedding some of her clothing. Finally, with really no urging, she left the room to change into "something comfortable." Taylor couldn't have been more satisfied with his progress. She returned in a light, filmy peignoir that revealed rather than concealed a very shapely figure. It was a figure at that stage of life where youth had blossomed fully into maturity, and it was vibrant and receptive.

"Wow!" One word from Taylor only, but it seemed adequate enough to Wanda. He reached up and pulled her down against him. His blood was racing hot, and she was in a pleasurable state of anticipation when the telephone rang. They disengaged grudgingly and clumsily. Her voice was husky as she said "hello" into the phone.

The coolly efficient Valerie Rigg was on the other end. "Hello? Miss Narewski?"

"Yes, speaking."

"I'm sorry to disturb you at home."

"You don't know how sorry I am, too!" She winked at Jon who had taken the opportunity to remove his shirt and undershirt, revealing well-delineated pectoral and deltoid muscles. She turned her profile to him so that he could appreciate it more fully.

"Well, I do apologize," Valerie went on, "but something urgent has come up. We need to contact Dr. Harris as soon as possible."

"I'm sorry, Miss Rigg, but he left this afternoon for your place."

"He did! Which flight did he take?"

"Let's see. It was either Flight 110 at twelve o'clock or Flight 112 at one o'clock!"

"Do you remember the airline?"

"It was either TWA or United."

"Do you know when he's supposed to arrive?"

"Around two or three o'clock your time."

"Is he flying to San Francisco, San Jose, or Oakland?"

"Gosh, I really don't remember, but I think it's San Francisco."

"Do you know where he's going to stay?"

"No, he made his own motel reservation."

"Do you know in what city?"

"He wrote it down on his pad, but that's at the office."

"It's already after three o'clock here. Would it be at all possible for you to get that information?"

Wanda, standing during this exchange in a state of virtual undress, had goosebumps on her exposed parts. Although not very bright, she was conscientious.

"It'll take me some time to get over to the office, but I can get the information for you. Okay?"

"We would appreciate that very much. I'll try to catch Dr. Harris at the airports here. As soon as you find out where he's staying, please call me. I'll be in the office all evening. Goodbye, and thank you again."

"Bye." Wanda replaced the receiver on its cradle and looked at Taylor sadly. "Sorry this had to come up, Jonnie. Will you wait for me?"

Taylor looked on incredulously at this unexpected turn of events. She walked over to him and cuddled him to her soft comforting bosom. "There, there," she said. "I like you. It won't take long."

She bent over and gave him a quick kiss on his forehead. He could not avoid gazing at her breasts swaying under the peignoir. He protested plaintively, but she was adamant, and went to dress. He was still sitting on the couch in a daze, barechested, when she darted out of the apartment, blowing a kiss over her shoulder.

The flights into San Francisco had been held up by the bad late season storm, but Flight 110 had just been given the final okay to land. Harris and the other passengers welcomed the pilot's FASTEN YOUR SEAT BELTS sign and prepared for the final approach and touchdown at San Francisco airport.

It was four o'clock when Harris walked onto the long automatic ramp carrying passengers from the gates to the baggage areas. Since the news of the implantation would not break until tomorrow, he had decided to spend the evening in San Francisco. It was just the right escape city, he thought—escape from his measured workday, escape from a wife with whom life had gone stale, and escape from the tight, superficial social morality of big government and Washington. In San Francisco the specter of recognition was absent. He would be alone and anonymous. He was unaware that at this moment Valerie Rigg was frantically trying to find him.

Harris waited at the garish red-and-white Avis rental car booth. The uniformed buxom young clerk with the fixed smile explained the deductible insurance.

"May I see your driver's license, please? I will need a credit card. Please sign here."

She folded all the forms into a pocket envelope. "Your car will be in Stall Thirty-one at the end of the hallway in ten minutes." She handed him the keys and forms.

"Thank you."

She promptly forgot him and turned to the next customer. "May I see your driver's license, please? I will need a credit card. Please, sign here. . . ."

A few minutes later, the page system suddenly requested, "Mr. Ronald Harris, white courtesy telephone, please! Mr. Ronald Harris."

The young woman at the Avis booth showed no flicker of recognition as she served yet more customers disgorged from another plane.

Bradfield walked soggily to a back elevator which would take him up to the restricted ninth floor. The on-call quarters, where interns and residents on duty stayed, was a remodeled part of the hospital. Once it had housed the delivery rooms. Now it symbolized the decreasing birthrate in the United States, and the fundamental changes in medical training and mores. When Bradfield was in training, house staff doctors were not expected to be married. Like a priest, a young doctor was married to his profession. The intern was on call every other night and was expected to be in the hospital. Room and board were provided along with a paltry monthly stipend—$125 a month was generous. Rooms were assigned to the individual house officers and they became home for a year. But now internships in most hospitals were being dropped, residents belonged to a union, a goodly two-thirds were married, and getting home was an important factor in selecting residency positions. As a result, the on-call quarters now held a transient population, more like a motel for students, technicians, and house officers on Bradfield's service who worked a little harder and longer than the others.

"Bill Bradfield! What on earth are you doing up here, and

all wet, too? I haven't seen you in ages!" The voice was gravelly and unmistakable.

"Joanne, by golly. How are you?"

The thin, gray-haired woman held out her hand and Bradfield shook it. Joanne Schultz had an office on the ninth floor. She was sixty-two, a widow, and was in charge of non-academic house staff affairs. Every teaching hospital had someone like her. She registered the new doctors in, she kept lists of homes for rent or sale, she handled the paychecks and the supplies of clean white uniforms, she kept the records of training, and, most important, she listened to their problems. At the end of their training, she passed out the certificates, wished them well, and sent them on their way with a blessing.

"I got caught in the rain," Bradfield went on. "I've got another case to do. Valerie suggested I might get a shower. I haven't been up here since it was remodeled, so I thought I might try it."

"Sure, Bill. Make yourself at home. Nobody around here would complain. The sleeping quarters are down the hall on the left, showers and tubs over there. Round the corner is the TV, and there's a linen closet and a sitting room. I see you have a key. The cardiac surgery resident's room is 904. The key will open the sauna, whirlpool bathroom, and the warm room. I'll show you around after you change."

"Thanks a lot. It's very quiet up here."

"The rooms are soundproof for good sleeping and it's between shifts. On-call people are still eating and off-call people are going home."

Bradfield went off down the hall, still feeling a bit chilly. Unlocking the door, he found himself in a gymlike setting. A sauna and whirlpool bath were in the anteroom. The walls were white tiled and the floor terrazzo. At the far end there was a door leading to a second room with a couple of massage tables and built-in infrared heat lamps in the ceiling. Beyond that was the shower room. The facilities had been donated to the house staff by the hospital's auxiliary group.

Bradfield turned on the heat lamps. The warm red glow

penetrated comfortingly as he stripped off his cold wet clothes, which clung stickily to his goosefleshed skin. A hot shower, some rest under the warm lamps, and maybe some hot coffee later would relieve some of the pressure of the long night coming up.

He showered, rubbed himself briskly, and lay facedown on one of the massage tables. The room was now in a bright red glow and he reflected that a gentle warmth diffused over the body can be a most pleasurable and relaxing sensation. It was also clear to Bradfield that the current crop of house officers suffered little from the physical deprivations of just ten years ago. He recalled catching catnaps whenever he could. He hadn't lost the knack, although it certainly was easy enough today. As he lay in a naked torpor, he didn't hear the key opening the hallway entrance. It was not until a feminine voice from the outer room penetrated his consciousness that Bradfield realized he was exposed. While not exactly modest about his body, he was not an exhibitionist either; so he grabbed a towel, put it over his head, and turned his face away from the door. He hoped she would go away, if she happened to look into the warm room. He wanted a few more minutes of relaxation before the operation.

As the time passed, however, it became embarrassingly apparent to Bradfield that he was trapped in this little room, an unwilling third party to an amorous assignation progressing rapidly in the sauna room. There was a lower male voice and the sound of water flowing, accompanied by much laughing and giggling. Then he became aware of an unmistakable rhythm amplified by the splashing of the water and soft, animal-like cries.

Oh, for crying out loud, Bradfield thought, I've got more important things to do. He wrapped the towel about his waist and opened the door to stride rapidly through to the outer room. A white nurse's uniform hung neatly over the back of a chair. Lingerie was stacked carefully on the seat, with white shoes underneath. A white shirt and pants were hung on clothes-hooks on the wall. The man and woman were both in the whirlpool tub in such close proximity there was no doubt a pleasurable connection had been made. Bradfield's sudden appearance elicited a startled "What the hell!" from the man after he had stopped nibbling on the nipple of a beautifully rounded breast. The young woman, hair held dryly out of the water by a yellow bandana, was puzzled. Then, looking quickly over her shoulder, she recognized Bradfield and let out a shriek of dismay. Just as quickly, she turned her head and buried it against Romanoff's chest. She had been flushed and wet with exertion. She was now a bright crimson with embarrassment. It was nurse Ginger Brown.

Bradfield had intended to stride right through, ignoring the scene, but when he recognized Romanoff and vice versa, he stopped short in his tracks.

"What are you doing in there, Romanoff?" Bradfield could not suppress a smile.

Romanoff was cool in reply, though not in body temperature. "Well, sir, it's pretty obvious!"

Bradfield's lips spread into a wide grin. "So I see!" Then, falling back on his old medical training, he queried sharply, "Are you on call now?"

"No, sir."

"Are you scrubbing tonight?"

"No, sir. Buchanan and Johnson are. I'm scheduled to be off."

"Well, I see that the old saw 'When you're off, you're on!' applies to you, too, Romanoff. At least you have good taste. I'm terribly sorry to have interrupted!"

Bradfield exited gracefully to the cardiac surgery residents's room for clean greens. His body was relaxed, his mind calm, enjoying now the humorous situation. Fifteen years ago, being caught in flagrante delicto would have been grounds for instant dismissal. The mores of the young and with them of society in general had changed remarkably. Bradfield recalled that in his youth he had been wrapped up in his books and science. He had been awkward with girls. Small talk had frustrated him immensely. Later on, when he went to boot camp, he had had the overpowering fear he might die in the war a virgin, never having known the joys of sex.

As he was leaving, Bradfield stuck his head in Schultz's office. She had her coat on and was preparing to leave.

"Say, what are you running up here?" Bradfield asked slyly.

She smiled. "I can only guess what you're talking about. What happens up here is their own business. What I don't see, I don't know. If I do catch anybody in any hanky-panky, I just tell them to go someplace else. About as enlightened as I can get! I'll walk down with you."

It was 5:45 P.M.

Bradfield realized Valerie had not paged him. The operation was to start in forty-five minutes. Apparently Harris had not been located. It was getting a little too close for comfort, even for Bradfield.

Actually Valerie had received one phone call from Wanda Narewski. Harris's motel reservation was at the Holiday Inn in Palo Alto. A call to the Holiday Inn elicited the information that Harris was expected, but that he had put in a late arrival deposit to hold his room.

"When is he expected in?"

"After midnight," said the desk clerk.

"Oh, my God!"

"I beg your pardon?"

"Never mind. Please, leave a message for Mr. Harris to call Dr. Bradfield when he gets in. It's urgent. Goodbye."

Chapter 11

Bradfield was standing with Joanne Schultz when the elevator door opened on the second floor. Buchanan spotted him. "Here's where I get off," Bradfield said. "Goodbye, Joanne. Thanks for everything."

Buchanan greeted Bradfield impatiently. "What's the latest poop, Bill? Do we go? I heard Ridley hasn't come through yet."

"You bet your ass we're going ahead, Don. Get the patient into the O.R. and get the show on the road."

"But what if you don't hear from Harris?"

Bradfield said, "Go!"

"Okay." Buchanan rambled off and headed for the operating room.

James Takaoka, the anesthesiologist, was in Operating Room 13. He was busily checking the drugs, supplies, oxygen, and anesthetics he had on tap. The electronic monitors were warmed up. He checked with the scrub nurse. She was ready.

Buchanan dropped in through the wide automatic doors. "You ready, Tak? Would you call for the patient?"

"Yes, I'm ready and I will." With that, he nodded to the circulating nurse, who notified the communication clerk in the hallway.

Buchanan was glad that Takaoka was on this particular case. Tak was an intelligent, no-nonsense guy, able to perform in difficult situations. When a patient died on the table despite all efforts, Tak did not brood but would say, "That's the way it goes." If the same patient survived with a brilliant effort, Tak would still say, "That's the way it goes." Ritual, inner calm, and stoicism were prominent in his approach to medicine.

On Takaoka's signal, the communications nurse paged two orderlies to fetch the patient. Gray was awake, but his cerebral function was not sharp. Janet Chen kissed his cheek and held his hand until the very last second. Then two orderlies, with Sue Myers and Jack Johnson, pushed the cumbersome bed out of the I.C.U. The motley group with the semiconscious patient, the bottles of drugs hanging above the bed, moved noisily past the waiting room down the hallway and into the O.R. Johnson and the two orderlies put on paper gowns and booties over their "outside" clothes and moved Gray into Room 13. The time was 6:30 P.M.

The excited banter among the personnel hushed when Gray was pushed into the air-conditioned room. It was larger than the average operating suite, with more floor space, and contained all the apparatus necessary for modern heart surgery. The equipment included the bulky heart-lung perfusion machine, electronic monitoring systems, the anesthesia dispensing machine, the cardiac defibrillator, a small battery-operated pacemaker, and the electrocautery unit used to coagulate bleeding vessels. The personnel included Mrs. Donald and several nurses; the heart-lung machine operator, Ray Lower, and his assistant Ralph Gutierrez; and Bradfield's surgical team—Don Buchanan, the senior resident, Jack Johnson, junior resident, and Washington Belknap, a medical student.

Gray's wasted body was at a forty-five-degree angle to the bed. His heart was so weak that his lungs would have filled with fluid if he had been flat. Takaoka adjusted the O.R. table so that it was at the same angle. Then, assisted by the orderlies and the circulating nurse, he moved Gray gently from the bed to the table. The nurse checked the identification bracelet on Gray's wrist and read it aloud to Takaoka.

"Henry Gray, Hospital Number 035-75-42."

Takaoka checked this against the patient's chart and the charge-a-plate clipped to it.

"It checks." However, to make quite certain, Takaoka went over to the patient and impassively put his hand on Gray's forehead and shook him gently. Gray opened his eyes slowly.

"Are you Mr. Henry Gray? Blink your eyelids for 'yes.'" The patient complied. "Okay, Mr. Gray. I'm Dr. Takaoka. I spoke with you earlier. In just a few minutes I'll put you to sleep. Are you ready?"

Again Gray blinked his eyes. It was very quiet. Takaoka went through his ritual, checking the drugs, checking the equipment. There would be no delay with this patient. The monitoring lines were in place. He connected the electrocardiogram electrodes to the ECG monitor. A noise-free signal appeared on the screen immediately. He flushed the indwelling arterial cannula and then attached it to the pressure transducer. The pulsating arterial pressure showed immediately on the screen. He attached the venous pressure lines and checked the continuity of the intravenous line to make sure they were not leaking or obstructed. He then pressed several buttons on a console and the central computer began to operate off the hemodynamic data fed into it from patient No. 035-75-42.

Takaoka put a heavy steel stethoscope on the patient's chest and listened intently over both lungs. He could hear the patient's breathing. There were fine crackling sounds caused by fluid, which slowed the transfer of life-giving oxygen from the alveoli, the tiny air sacs of the lungs, to the bloodstream. Gray was blue. Increasing the concentration of oxygen in the inspiratory mixture would relieve this problem.

Takaoka attached a black rubber connector to the endotracheal tube that led to the anesthesia machine or "gas mixer." Under the machine a black rubber bag, now connected to the patient, inflated and deflated rhythmically in shallow, quick breaths. Tak turned a blue knob with a Vernier scale and the hissing oxygen flowed in, doubling the concentration from the natural 20 to 40 percent. Tak waited for a minute or two, watching while Gray became less dusky, finally almost pink in color.

"Ready?" Takaoka asked Buchanan. The big man nodded. Tak picked up his prepared syringe marked "morphine." He attached it to a three-way stopcock, turned it on, injected 10 mg, and opened the IV drip to flush the narcotic in. The clear glass bottle dripped furiously.

"You'll be asleep soon, Mr. Gray," Tak said.

Gray opened his eyes one more time. He saw Tak peering at him. Buchanan watched the dripping bottle. Johnson was at the foot of the table. The circulating nurse held his right hand gently and comfortingly. The scene was stark and in high contrast. Everything was hard without soft contours: the chromium lamp, the steel poles, the tiled ceiling. The colors were intense, the walls a lawn green, Johnson's skin an obsidian black, Takaoka's a brilliant wheat yellow, Belknap's beard under the mask a fiery red. The white-skinned people looked as though they were carved out of alabaster.

Gray's eyes became heavy and everything turned darker, softer. He closed his eyes and concentrated on his breathing. The tightness of his chest, the breathing difficulty which had been with him for months, seemed to be slipping away. Where was it going? He didn't have to breathe anymore. He vaguely heard his name echoing down a long dark corridor: "Gray, Gray, Gray." The pain was gone at last.

Johnson looked inquisitively at Tak. Wordlessly, he moved his lips—"Is he asleep?"—as the black rubber bag's motion became slower and the chest movement registered less excursion. Tak shook his head, but he made a gesture with both hands. "Go and scrub." Buchanan was the first to leave.

The respirations stopped completely. Tak reached for the

bag and squeezed it. The chest moved. He then switched to the artificial respiration, and with a rhythmical clicking sound, the patient was now breathing with the help of the machine.

"Mr. Gray?"

There was no response.

"Well, this dude didn't require much!" someone said.

"Ssshhh!" Tak's response came quickly. He turned on the halothane dial, and an anesthetic concentration of the gas flowed into the closed system. After a few moments Tak said, "Okay. Prep him."

Johnson checked the patient's position on the table, then put a folded Turkish towel under his back so that the chest would be convex toward the ceiling. He pulled the remaining white terry cloth sheet off Gray's inert warm body. A Foley catheter had already been placed through the penis into the bladder.

Tak asked Johnson to move the urine collecting bag from the foot to the head of the table so that he could visually monitor the function of the kidneys. There was one last check to see that the patient's arms were restrained under the table sheet, then the circulating nurse donned a pair of sterile gloves. With both hands she scrubbed the chest and abdomen of the patient with antiseptic iodine solution, starting in the middle and working out to the periphery. Gray's skin was now silky brown-yellow.

Belknap and Johnson had left the room to scrub their hands and arms. Buchanan returned, keeping his only slightly dripping hands out in front of him, allowing the water to flow off his elbows on to the dark terrazzo floor. After being gowned, he started to drape the patient. Sterile towels were dropped skillfully in place, covering the exposed skin except where the incision was to be made. He looked up briefly at the clock. It was 7:05 P.M.

"Please notify Dr. Bradfield that we're draping the patient," Buchanan said.

A large, clear, sterile plastic sheet was then unrolled and

held over the chest and abdomen. It was pressed down, sticking to drapes and skin, forming an impervious barrier. Finally, a large green-blue linen sheet was unfolded in the center over the patient, dropped to the floor, and pulled over the feet and the head, isolating the surgeons and nurses from the unprepared fields.

Bradfield and Johnson entered the O.R. almost simultaneously. As he was being gowned, Bradfield asked Tak, "Everything okay?"

"Yes," was the brief reply from the anesthesiologist.

"Ready to go, Don?"

"Well, everything's ready to come out, but what's going in?" Buchanan was a good soldier up to a point, but he was fast approaching that point. "Has Harris been reached yet?" he asked.

"No, he hasn't." Bradfield spoke with beneficent calm. "Couldn't find the son of a bitch." A silence fell over the operating room.

"What's up?" Takaoka interjected.

Buchanan replied, "Quite a problem. No fuel!"

Takaoka sat upright. "Wait a minute, fellows."

Bradfield was now standing at the table. "All right," he said. "Call Ridley at his home and put us on the loudspeaker." One knew that Bradfield did not expect failure.

Takaoka looked over the ether screen at Bradfield, but the surgeon had his attention turned to the circulating nurse dialing the telephone. Buchanan caught Takaoka's gaze and shook his massive head in disbelief. The anesthesiologist said clearly and with a sharp assertiveness, "We're not just playing games here. What's the situation?"

"Why, Tak? You're suddenly very talkative," Bradfield said sarcastically.

"Bill, I can wake this patient up and go home," Tak replied directly, without any tone of threat. He was absolutely sincere.

"Calm down, Tak." Bradfield's voice was soothing.

"I'm quite calm, but I don't think your team is."

This was true. From Belknap to Buchanan, the surgical team members were caught up in a vise of circumstances like mice in a trap. They were all junior to Bradfield with nowhere to go, yet believing it was murder to proceed with the operation without a replacement heart. The situation was not without analogy. A chimpanzee heart had once been implanted in a patient. The heart failed. The heart of a ram had once been transplanted, too, but it had failed immediately. Buchanan had heard Bradfield make disparaging remarks about the intelligence of the surgeons involved. Strangely, the public was rather tolerant of this aberrant conduct in surgeons; yet, to knowledgeable individuals, the hope of success had been zero.

Bradfield said, "Tak, let's see what our boy Ridley has to say."

The buzzing of the phone signal was interrupted and a "hello" was broadcast to every ear but Gray's in Operating Room 13.

Ridley had taken a hot shower and changed into warm, dry clothes. His home was a modest bungalow, situated at a cozy distance from the road and surrounded by a grove of pines and old gnarled oak trees. A small, crackling fire burned in the living room, which was decorated quietly with early American maple furniture. Outside the fury of the storm intensified.

After dinner, eaten in almost complete silence, Cynthia asked Allen what the problem was. He described the day's events, the argument with his old friend, Buchanan, the meeting in the rain with Bradfield, and the expected phone call from Harris that had not yet come through.

"Is there anyone who can influence Bradfield directly?" Cynthia asked.

"Yes, the Dean of the medical school. But it just happens that Dr. Geld is also the Vice Provost, so there's no real appeal. I don't want to be unfair, but I don't trust the guy. In the first place he denies his heritage."

"What do you mean?"
"Well, he's Jewish."
"What difference does that make?"
"None, but when a man trades in his cultural and religious heritage for a position of power, he doesn't exactly inspire confidence. One has to wonder why he would do that—an excellent doctor in a position of influence."
"That is sad. Wasn't it Robert Browning who said that every man has a fatal flaw of character?"
"Second problem is that academic medicine is big business today. The Dean, any dean, has to keep the enterprise going. He must raise money, and Bradfield is a valuable commodity. Why should he buck Bradfield for me? The answer is, he won't. It's down in black and white they have decided to go forward."
"It can't be that you're the only one in the whole world who believes this way, can it?"
"Well, sweetheart, it sure feels that way sometimes. Everybody at Aspermont seems to have his own little justification for going ahead. Bradfield says the patient is dying. Geld probably thinks of the money and glory that will come to his institution. The residents want spectacular medicine regardless of the consequences. The nurses are looking for something dramatically new for the care of the patient. The students want to be dazzled by the ingenuity of their professor. Harris probably allowed the clinical trial to go on to impress Congress at appropriations time. It's a discouraging situation."
The glow of the fire was dying down and Ridley got up from his easy chair to add another log. Cynthia, who had been sitting on the arm of his chair holding his hand, also got up and sat down on the divan.
"What about somebody outside the university?"
"It's so late," Ridley said slowly. "Actually, I thought of phoning Dr. Warren Coles. He was Bradfield's predecessor and has a reputation for integrity."
"What happened to him?"

"They forced him to resign."

"Any particular reason?"

"Coles didn't play the academic game. He criticized Holborn for allowing Bradfield to go on with development of the heart machine. At Aspermont criticism isn't exactly welcome. Loyalty is what is expected."

"Where's Coles now?"

"He has a private practice with the Mountain View Surgical Group."

"Why don't you phone him, Allen? He may have a different perspective."

Ridley got up and placed the call. The telephone answering service responded and took Ridley's name, number, and problem and told him they would have the doctor call back. When the phone did ring, Allen wondered whether it was Coles or Harris. It was Coles.

The blunt, strong voice boomed at him, "Allen, hello."

"Dr. Coles, I hope you remember me. . . ."

"Of course, I remember you. You're the health physicist at Aspermont. We talked at some length when Bradfield's atomic contract was being submitted. You were concerned about being involved in this plutonium business. What do you want from this old codger?"

Ridley again described the events of the day. Coles responded in his characteristic challenging manner. "Okay, what do you want from me?"

"I thought you might advise me on the matter."

"Sure, advice is free. First, let me say I'm not surprised. Bradfield is a first-rate surgeon, and I don't say that lightly. He is, as you know, a very bright, hard-driving, ambitious man who knows what he wants. He demands the most of himself and expects the same from everyone else. His only mistake in this case is overcommitment to a cause, and it sounds like you're caught in the middle. Frankly, I don't like him. He seems to belong to this new breed of whiz kids who have a different concept of humanity. He wasn't always like that. He's changed since I first recommended him for a position at Aspermont, but he's certainly one of the new breed now. You ask what you can do? There's not much you *can* do. You must realize that aligned against you are the big guns of cardiac surgery, the avarice of academic medicine, and the dollars of government-supported research. I'm a pragmatic guy. Do you have another job offer anywhere else?"

"No, I don't," Ridley said quietly.

"Well, then, here's what I would recommend. If Harris calls and confirms the okay, then do it. Don't butt your head against the wall. If he doesn't, then stick to your guns. Patients die every day without benefit of surgery. It may sound tough, but it's certainly true. Finally, Allen, in either event, get the hell out of there and find another job! Okay?"

"Thank you very much, Dr. Coles. Goodbye."

Harris walked the streets in San Francisco's North Beach with far more important things to him than Aspermont on his mind. Separated from Chinatown by Broadway, North Beach is owned largely by Chinese and Italian families. They live there, as do a sprinkling of young advertising executives, artists, homosexuals, and fun-loving young men and women. Here one finds the Italian, family-style restaurants, night clubs, art galleries, jazz places, massage parlors, and other visible aspects of Bohemia. Their signs were blinking their invitation to him. A raincoated barker stood under a marquee to avoid the pelting rain, moving his hands and legs to keep warm.

"Come on, man. Big Girls!" He pronounced the big as "beeg." "Hot action! Topless!"

The barker was accustomed to the fact that most passers-by ignored him. He couldn't have cared less. It was just a job. Then he noticed a respectable-looking businessman who showed nervous signs of interest. The barker's eyes lit up, and he began to work on Harris like a hunter circling ducks with a decoy call.

Ridley replaced the receiver and sat dumbly, trying to get his mind in order. Cynthia was putting their two children to bed when the phone rang again and broke the rural quiet.

The voice at the other end was distant and muffled, as if the caller were standing in a large echo chamber. There was a condenser hum in the background.

"Hello, this is Bradfield."

"Yes. I can barely make you out," Allen replied loudly. "We have a poor connection."

"I have this phone on the loudspeaker system because I'm standing at the operating table. The entire O.R. can hear your voice."

"Your man, Harris. He hasn't called yet. I hope you aren't going to start the operation."

"The patient is asleep and I have the scalpel in my hand!"

"I cannot . . ." In the operating room, Ridley's voice broke off in mid-sentence. It was followed by a steady hum. Ridley continued his sentence but he, too, heard the background noise suddenly disappear with a clicking sound. His phone became absolutely silent. He clicked several times on the cradle without result. The phone was dead.

In the O.R. the pall of uncertainty was almost tangible. Bradfield took the scalpel and made a long linear sternal incision all the way down through the periosteum to the bone. The darkish blood spurted out into the field. He had caught Takaoka off guard. The operation had started! The electrocautery machine buzzed and red bleeding points were charred into little black dry spots.

Bradfield motioned to Buchanan at the other side of the O.R. table. "Don, get an ambulance and the police and get Ridley here. Johnson, you're ready to assist? Someone dial Ridley's number again and see what happens. Sponge, please!"

The two scrub nurses instantly swung into action, passing clamps, ties, scissors in the proper sequence. Buchanan broke scrub and backed away from the table. He thought, Captain Queeg! But he wanted to have one more opportunity to talk to Ridley.

Ridley changed quickly after the telephone went dead. He thought the least he could do was to drive to his office and wait there until someone found Harris. Driving slowly along the rainswept Alpine Road to the narrow bend where he and Bradfield had met earlier, he saw the reason for the phone dysfunction. The rain-drenched topsoil, soaking up more water than its capacity, had sheared off the rocky base layer. A giant mudslide had oozed silently down the grassy hillside and obstructed the road completely. The river of mud must have been a hundred yards wide. The telephone pole on the right side of the road was angled crazily down the hill. It was supported only by the wires, which were nonfunctional. He got out of his car and tested the consistency of the mud. He sank immediately to his knees. It was impossible to get through either by car or on foot.

Neither Ridley nor Buchanan knew that they stood at the opposite ends of the wide obstruction. Ridley backed up a considerable distance before he was able to turn his car around. Buchanan, in an ambulance led by a police car with red lights circling and intermittently lighting up the dark road, looked helplessly at the mud. He cursed the weather, the road, and his luck. But most of all, he was concerned about Gray. It was he, Buchanan, who earlier on this day had started the cascade of events by accepting the fateful call from Janet Chen. Once started, there had seemed no way to stop the juggernaut of Bradfield's progress.

Chapter 12

7:30 P.M. Browning and Wheeler opened the door of the gas sterilizer. CORA III, the nickname of the artificial heart, was pulled out easily on its stainless steel roller-baseplate. The heart was triply protected in thick blue-green linen wrappers and was an irregularly shaped mass. At this point it was also fuelless.

"Come on, come on, Richard. Get it on the table," Browning said in her usual exasperated way. Wheeler slowly lifted the sterilized heart and placed it carefully in a plastic bag. Then he pulled the edges of the bag over the line. The object was to prevent the unsterile rain from wetting the linen and soaking through to the heart when it was carried over to the medical center.

"No, no, dammit, Richard. You left a hole on the top of the pack. The rain will fall right on it. Fold the edges down!"

"Oh, oh, you're right, Liz. Yes, I see," he said, nodding vigorously.

"Okay, let's go now. They're waiting. You carry it carefully and don't drop it. I'll open the door."

The two of them slowly paraded out of the door into the

stormy night. The pathway was unpaved, and the surface was muddy and slippery. A van was parked fifty yards away. Wheeler felt himself slipping with every step as Browning disappeared in front of him. He wanted to walk faster, but his feet kept on slipping. Through some premonition, Browning stopped and turned around to check her gangling charge.

"Jesus Christ, Richard!" she exclaimed as she watched, horrified, while he tried desperately to keep his balance. He finally managed, and she let out her breath in a gasp of relief. Browning ran over to him, her heart pounding, and said grimly, "Give me the pack."

"Don't worry, Liz. I can do it. Really."

"Don't argue!"

"Oh, come on. Let me alone." Wheeler was uncooperative in an uncharacteristic way. He knew it was a "big deal" and he intended to get some credit for his participation. The observers, he thought, would know he was important if he had been entrusted with the job of moving the heart to the O.R. He continued on, hugging the pack as he went. Elizabeth opened the back door to the van and Richard tried to get in still holding the device.

"Put it down in the van, for God's sake, and then crawl in."

"Okay, okay!"

He sat in the back watching the pack while Browning drove carefully to the hospital.

The news of the mudslide was still hanging over the crowded operating room when Wheeler and Browning arrived with the precious package. Buchanan had used the radiotelephone as soon as the police car had cleared the hills that formed an electromagnetic barrier to radio communication. Bradfield was incredulous that in this day, in a suburban area, a man could not travel at will—that a mudslide over which he had no control should appear suddenly to impede surgical progress. Just this morning, he felt that he only needed to motivate others to achieve his ends. Bradfield had finally come to a dead stop. He was worried now, and for the first time he was uncertain what to do. There was a faint tremor in his hands and a fine sweat broke out on his brow.

Wheeler stopped outside the O.R. door and put booties over his muddy shoes. He put his cap and mask on and a clean but unsterile surgical gown to cover his animal lab clothes. Browning held the door open as he walked proudly into the silent, tense room, then left hurriedly to change to operating room dress in the nurses' dressing room, unaware of the turn of events.

At first, only Belknap, the medical student, saw Wheeler through the crowd as he stood inside the door holding the fuelless artificial heart. Belknap said nothing, feeling it was not his place to break the pregnant silence. There were many people present already, but it didn't seem to make a difference. Unfamiliar with the etiquette of a human operating room, Wheeler just stood there, ignored. Although his load was not heavy, his disappointment at his unnoticed arrival was extreme, and his shoulders drooped. He felt an urge to cry. Finally, the circulating nurse motioned for him to come forward. Wheeler maneuvered the package through a narrow channel between the wall and the sterile nurse's table, while several of the onlookers now watched.

Bradfield looked up at the disturbance.

"Dr. Bradfield," said Richard, "the heart is sterile and ready."

"Okay, leave it there. We may have a problem. Stick around though. You may have to take it back again."

Wheeler noticed there was no note of congratulation, no "well done," no "swell," praise Bradfield had always given him freely before. The circulating nurse indicated that Wheeler should move to the head of the table and out of her way.

Bradfield said to Takaoka, "We're going ahead. We'll see if there's anything we can do short of replacement."

The anesthesiologist agreed. "Okay. He's a dead duck now anyway. His pressure and output are dropping again. His pulse rate is too fast, and I can't add any more epinephrine. A short ride on the heart-lung machine might tide him over the anesthesia insult."

The operation which had started with so much trouble and such great expectations proceeded quietly. With no history to be made, the curious onlookers rapidly drifted out of the room until Wheeler and Browning were the only bystanders left.

Bradfield thought out loud. "Someone should go out and prepare Miss Chen. Tell her things aren't so good. Goddamn Ridley anyway! No! On second thought wait until Buchanan gets back."

Takaoka asked Wheeler, who stood next to him, "Who are you?"

Wheeler responded with an air of self-importance. "I'm the chief animal technician."

Takaoka said, "Oh, yes. I thought you might be a medical student."

"No, not smart enough."

Takaoka was disarmed by Wheeler's artless yet accurate self-appraisal. Wheeler's problem wasn't simply a lack of brains. It was also an extreme reaction to criticism. Browning was always after him for mistakes. For example, when he dropped a vial of medicine, he would simply wash it up quietly instead of bringing its loss to her attention. Later, when the medication was needed, there would be great consternation. Now, however, Wheeler would score, and score big.

It happened as Tak continued his conversation with Richard. The patient's blood pressure was low, as would be expected in this situation. There was nothing more for Tak to do until Bradfield was ready to put Gray on the heart-lung machine.

"What do you do?" Tak asked Wheeler.

"I've been with Dr. Bradfield for a long time. I started as a lab assistant. I'm the man who puts the parts together for the artificial heart."

"So you put that one together?"

"Yes. The thing's made by this here company in Berkeley. I join the parts. I put the plutonium in. Then I cover the machine with silicone rubber. Then Dr. Bradfield and Liz Browning put it in. Works real good!"

"I heard you've had several calves go for six months or longer?"

"Yes, sir." Richard said proudly. "We have three altogether. That one and two cow models. After each experiment I clean the old pump and fix the worn parts. Mr. Ridley comes and gets the plutonium for safekeeping. Fact is, we have two animals over at the animal shelter . . ."

At that moment, subliminally, the conversation broke through to Bradfield's awareness.

"Christ, of course!" he exclaimed.

The team was startled by his outburst.

"Wheeler, you beautiful black bastard!"

Richard was pleased, even though he had been insulted. He was in the dark completely as to what Bradfield was shouting about. In fact, he was bewildered, and certainly Jack Johnson, also a black, wasn't pleased in the slightest.

"The cows! The cows have two hundred grams of plutonium in them." Bradfield's eyes blazed. His mind worked furiously, his normally well-controlled emotions boiling over. He turned to Johnson and Takaoka. "The fuel capsule is interchangeable! All we have to do is get it out of the calf and slip it into this engine. Richard, Liz, knock off the calf with the CORA II unit. Remove the fuel capsule and bring it right over. The hell with Ridley and Harris! And Liz, bring the loader over first so we can sterilize it here. You got all that?"

"Yes, Dr. Bradfield." They both answered together and left quickly, passing Buchanan in the corridor.

Browning briefly related the topsy-turvy turn of events to Buchanan, then she and Wheeler continued on their important mission. Patients in the hospital hallways were startled as the unlikely looking pair dashed joyously through the visitor-crowded area to their van.

Buchanan stuck his massive head through the O.R. door. "Hey, man! I hear you got the problem solved!"

"Don, get your ass in here. We've got a real operation to do!"

Buchanan left to scrub, while Bradfield scolded himself for

his shortsightedness. "I had all day! Why didn't I think of that earlier?"

Takaoka said, "That's what I want to know!"

Browning and Wheeler returned to the animal shelter after the short drive through the rain. The calf, kept alive by CORA II, stood in her stall quietly. Monitor cables coming out of a clean, protected wound between her scapulae were attached to a computer similar to the larger one in the hospital's I.C.U. Blood flow, pressure, and respiration were examined repeatedly every ten milliseconds. The function of the artificial heart was excellent. The calf chewed her cud peacefully and twitched her ear at an imaginary fly. The stalls were lined with once-sterilized straw, the floor with a rough, water-impervious material. She looked at the man and the woman in partial recognition.

"Too bad, Bossy," Wheeler said.

"Just hold the animal, Richard. Don't croon to it."

"Come on, Liz. You don't have to talk to me that way. You don't when Dr. Bradfield is around."

"Okay, okay. No time to argue. Just hold the animal."

Wheeler held the animal by its halter and tilted the neck up and back. The calf shuffled its hooves and then stayed in that position. A vein three centimeters in diameter popped into view along the left side of the neck muscle. Elizabeth hit it expertly with a large hypodermic needle and syringe containing 40 cc of euthanol, a high concentration of barbiturate. In fifteen seconds the slug circulated to the brain and the animal lost consciousness. It fell heavily on the straw. Five seconds later, it stopped breathing permanently.

In normal animals, when respiration ceases the heart continues to beat until the oxygen is used up, then slows gradually to a stop. In some instances the drug concentration is so high that both heart and breathing stop simultaneously. In this animal's case, the artificial heart did not respond to the lack of oxygen or to the barbiturate. It continued to pump and circulate the blood long after the brain of the calf had died. There was no way to shut off the machine fueled by atomic power, short of malfunction.

The two technicians dragged the limp beast onto a roller cart and moved the body into the animal operating room. There Wheeler prepared to perform the autopsy and remove the fuel capsule. For this he donned rubber gloves, a plastic apron, and rubber boots.

"Can you do this without screwing up?" Browning asked.

"Yes, I can."

"Okay. I'm going to take one of the loaders over to sterilize." It was a convenient excuse for Browning to leave the messy work to Wheeler.

The loader was a six-foot pole with a hinge in the middle so that it could be folded into three-foot sections and placed into the regular steam autoclave. At one end was a canlike device into which the plutonium fuel capsule fitted snugly. To load the fuel capsule into the heart's engine, the loader was pushed against the capsule by the technician holding the handle. This way, he could manipulate it a safe distance from the atomic radiation. He simply pushed the capsule into the fully shielded engine, removed the loader, and screwed the plate shut by hand. For removal the sequence was reversed.

Wheeler was left alone with the carcass. Using a sharp eight-inch knife, he cut expertly down through the hide to the engine lying between the fifth and eighth ribs. The heart was hot to the touch. He cut through the heavy scar tissue surrounding the capsule, and blood flowed down around his boots, congealing stickily. He found the knurled bolts which held the engine together and untwisted them with difficulty, as they had been in place for six months. He then unscrewed the engine, exposing half of the fuel capsule itself. Wheeler found the other loader. Standing six feet away from the calf, he removed the fuel capsule from the engine and carried it carefully over to a black oil drum. Inside the drum was an eight-inch thick lead cylinder suspended by a metal latticework. Between the lead cylinder and the drum side was a space to be filled with liquid, which absorbed the fast neutron particles not normally stopped by lead. Wheeler placed the fuel capsule in the lead cylinder and filled the drum with water. The heavy drum was mounted on six-inch wheels for easy transportation.

Wheeler removed his protective clothing and left the carcass on the floor to be cleaned later. He propped the lab door open and rolled the drum down the ramp into the rain. At the bottom of the ramp the wheels sank into the mud. The weight of the precious cargo anchored the drum firmly no matter how he struggled to go forward. He had to get to the O.R. After considering the situation, he tilted the assembly over on its side. The water barrier spilled out onto the ground. The drum could now be rolled on its side down the path to the waiting van. The hot fuel fell out of the latticework. Nonchalantly, Wheeler bent over, picked up the unshielded material, and put it in his pocket. It stayed there until he reached the van. With a tremendous effort, he lifted the drum and placed it behind the driver's seat. He replaced the fuel in the drum. He then got behind the wheel and drove slowly to the hospital's freight entrance. The area was deserted. Encircling the drum with his arms, he lifted it onto the freight dock and tilted it back upright on its wheels. He then looked for a hose, and finding one at hand, washed the muddy sides of the drum down, revealing the bright yellow decals warning of radioactivity. Then he refilled the drum with water and rolled it down the hall to the elevator, whistling in self-satisfaction.

Wheeler did not know he had been exposed to radiation in a way that a patient with an artificial heart normally would not be. In the patient the plutonium did not touch the tissues. The alpha radiation was shielded by the fuel container and the machinery and framework of the heart. Risk from alpha particles depends on distance from the source. They could be harmful if one touched the capsule for a long time. But a half-inch away from it the radioactivity level was remarkably low.

As Wheeler had handled the fuel, it was risky. The fuel used in animal experiments contained impurities and gave off

X rays and neutrons as well as alpha particles. Radiation kills white cells. Wheeler could become anemic and risk infection. Wheeler, of course, was not about to talk of the difficulties he had met in getting the plutonium over. Elizabeth Browning would have screamed at him again.

In Operating Room 13 the tubes which connected the patient to the heart-lung machine had just been inserted. For the next hour or so, the machine would take over the functions of the patient's heart and lungs.

The breastbone was held apart with retractors. Gray's huge, distended heart was now clearly exposed. However, it wasn't a pulsating, throbbing organ. This heart was sick and it just sat there with a terribly weak movement. It was no longer a vital red but pale yellow, filled with fat which had replaced the dead or dying muscle.

With disdain, Bradfield flicked the surface of the ventricle with his middle finger. That heart was his enemy. He had to get it out. The hearts he could fix, they were friendly and he repaired them. The patient? The patient was the container.

"Pressure?" said Bradfield.

Out of habit Takaoka glanced at the computer screen, although he knew what it was. He had just checked. "Eighty over seventy-five."

The sinusoidal arterial wave form was dampening out as more and more of the blood was diverted to the heart-lung machine and less and less moved through the heart itself. Actually, the pressure was higher than at any time in the past twenty-four hours, as the heart-lung machine now took over Gray's circulation. The heart finally quivered and remained in a slow fibrillation pattern.

Takaoka said blandly, "Fibrillated!"

The arterial pressure was now a straight line on the screen.

"Mean B.P., seventy."

"Fine. Ralph, flow rate?"

Ralph Guttierrez, monitoring the blood flow in the heart-lung machine, said, "Two thousand and going up."

"Flow at three thousand today."
"Three thousand—right."
"Pressure?"
"Eighty."
"Venous pressure?"
"Four."
"Okay, we'll go on total."
Bradfield took up the soft snares placed around the two large veins and cinched them down. All the venous blood was now diverted into the heart-lung machine. The large, flabby, distended heart collapsed slowly, much like a jack-o'-lantern at Halloween kept overly long through November.
"Aortic crossclamp."
The scrub nurse handed the instrument to Buchanan, who, standing on the patient's left and being right-handed, was in better position to apply the clamps. The instrument looked tiny in Buchanan's big hands. He closed the handle with the ratchets clicking loudly. The aorta was now obstructed and the heart excluded totally from circulation.
"Venous return okay?"
Guttierrez replied affirmatively.
"Okay, let's go. No turning back now!"
The patient's life was now supported by Ralph's inanimate machine.
Bradfield grasped the apex of the heart backhanded with his left hand and lifted it up into the open. It looked as if he were holding a chicken by the neck. The nurse handed him a pair of larger than ordinary Metzenbaum scissors. With little elegance, he cut the undermoorings of the heart. As he cut through the atrium, red blood flowed out into the field momentarily. Johnson, holding a pair of suction instruments, furiously aspirated the blood so that Bradfield's vision was not obscured. The heart, held now only by the outlet vessels, was so large Buchanan had to hold it with both hands while Bradfield finished the excision. He thought "large straight scissors," and they were placed in his outstretched right hand by the efficient nurse. The scissor blades stretched completely

across the pulmonary artery and Bradfield cut across it with one sure stroke. He repeated the stroke for the aorta, with immense satisfaction reflected in his eyes. Beautiful straight cuts were obtained for the attachment of CORA III.

Buchanan turned the excised heart upside down and shook it gently so as to conserve the small quantity of blood still in it. Then he dropped the heart into a waiting basin, making a short plopping sound. It was as flabby in feel as it had looked.

Bradfield and Buchanan both glanced at the gaping hole in Gray's chest where his heart had been. They looked at it with a surgical technician's eye, appreciating the area to be sutured, the size of the anastomoses to be made, and the space available to put in the power supply and control unit.

Johnson could only view the old heart with awe, aware of the enormity of the sight: a human heart, once living and beating in a person who talked and laughed and cried, and now it lay there, flaccid, assuming the form of its container, a stainless steel basin. The heart was to Johnson's left on a table, and the patient was to his right. He shook his head in amazement.

Belknap, the medical student, wondered when this would be over. He had suddenly developed a full bladder. It hurt him and he had to urinate, but squirming didn't help. He was ignored by all but Helen Donald, who thought, Serves him right for not preparing thoroughly for surgery.

Takaoka said, "Lots of sewing to do. Let's get the show on the road here." He turned off the mechanical ventilator. The lungs were bypassed in flow and function by the heart-lung machine until the circulation would be restored later in the operation. The only sounds now were the steady hum of the electrical pumps of the heart-lung machine and the hissing of bubbling oxygen in the plastic oxygenator. Browning, who in the meantime had returned from the animal shelter ahead of Wheeler, was standing on a stool to watch, shivering a little in the cold air conditioning.

Nurse Donald now had the artificial heart fully unwrapped and was moving it from the back table to the surgeon.

Bradfield said, "Let's sew it in."

Incredulous eyes were focused on the device—a self-contained package with pump and computer control all tightly compressed into a plastic box on a shiny stainless steel frame.

Bradfield took time to examine the device, turning it over and looking for any flaw. He handed it to Buchanan to hold it in place while Bradfield sewed and tied with both hands.

The engine was to be connected in a second step, and then the plutonium inserted.

Chapter 13

"I'm almost ready to connect the power fuel," Bradfield said. "Where's Richard?" He looked around the room. For a moment he debated whether he should ask Browning to check on the technician's whereabouts.

Suddenly, the doors opened accompanied by the sound of rolling metal grating against metal. Wheeler swung into the room with the large oil drum containing the plutonium. The noise jarred the people in the O.R. to attention. All eyes were fixed on the technician and the broad grin on his face.

Browning frantically signaled to him to put on his cap and mask. He nodded vigorously, recognizing his unintentional error, and, setting the drum upright with a bang, he went off to get dressed.

The timing was right. The atrial remnants of Gray's natural heart were sutured to the artificial atria. The aorta was connected to the crimped, woven Dacron tubular outlet of the artificial left ventricle. The back row of sutures was complete. The front row stitches were tied neatly, leaving the aorta open so that the pump could be emptied of trapped air and gas when the engine was fired up. The same was true of the pulmonary anastomosis.

The engine was unbolted. "In a short time it'll be ready to accept the fuel," said Bradfield. It was a crucial moment. His voice was calm as his gloved hand touched the machine for a final check.

"Liz, get ready!" Now Bradfield's voice had the sharp metallic ring of urgency.

Using an instrument resembling a long pair of right-angled pliers, Browning lifted the shiny capsule of plutonium out of the drum. With everyone at least six feet beyond range, she placed the source on the sterile table. Buchanan then held the six-foot loader and placed it over the four-inch wide capsule. Lifting the loader carefully, he aimed it into the fuel compartment of the cold engine. Bradfield, wearing a helmet and lead apron, held the compartment steady. All eyes were riveted on the target. Buchanan slipped the capsule right in on the first pass and removed the loader with a shaking, twisting motion. The end of the engine was bolted on. Liquid silicon was applied to seal the edges of the opening.

"That's it," Bradfield said. The entire assembly was ready to work. Tubes were attached to the inlets of the pump and connected to a reservoir of sterile saline placed one foot above the patient.

It was now a matter of waiting. The plutonium decayed at six hundred thousand disintegrations per second. Slow alpha particles bombarded the container. A lithium salt heat-storage layer slowly warmed up. At five hundred degrees the engine gave its first indication of operation. The drop of water inside the miniaturized steam engine vaporized at once, as intended. At twelve hundred degrees Fahrenheit the engine turned over regularly. A triple-fail vacuum layer, more sophisticated in design than the common thermos bottle, protected the patient from the heat. The engine's reciprocal action drove a fluid line in and out of the heart sac. The fluid became hot as it acted as a coolant for the waste heat. The heat was transferred to the artificial heart and removed as perspiration from the surface of the patient's body.

"Let's test it," Bradfield said. Saline fluid was circulated into the atrium. Air and salt water were flushed out through the gaps in the aortic and pulmonary artery sutures. Tension built as the heart rather weakly ejected this test solution.

Bradfield listened closely. A whooshing sound came from the device, followed by the click of the artificial disk valve opening. There was a weak, bubbling noise, then silence. The sequence was repeated until all the bubbles had been evacuated.

Bradfield asked Takaoka to expand the lungs so that small bubbles trapped in the left atrium could be expelled. One, two bubbles percolated out. Now CORA III sprayed salt water and blood mixture four inches into the air, but Bradfield was not ready to relax. Another critical point was reached—the switchover to real blood from the patient. The blood had to be pumped into the waiting aorta, but both outlets were leaking. Bradfield stopped the inflow to tie up the remaining sutures accurately. It had to be done quickly. The heat could not be transferred outward and would cause a temperature buildup.

"Clamp the inflow!"

Johnson and Buchanan clamped one tube, each with one hand while they held the aspirators to remove the salt water from the surgical field. The spray diminished with each stroke, then the whoosh and click were heard but no spray. CORA III was speeding up as it reacted to the information that pressure at the outlet was low.

Bradfield and Buchanan lifted separate sutures and pulled up, cinched, and tied the knots with rapid graceful motions. The blue-green suture material was made of fine braided Dacron for stretch, and coated with Teflon for inertness and smooth sliding through tissue. One knot, two knots, up to a minimum of six were tied to prevent unraveling. They were small square knots for optimal tensile strength.

"Cut!"

"Cut!"

Belknap was asked to cut the sutures as the surgeons picked up the lead of the next stitches to be tied.

"Too long. Half-inch tags, please, doctor."

"Cut!"

The student didn't move. "Belknap, wake up!" shouted Buchanan.

Belknap was not asleep, nor unmindful. It always fell to the medical student, the most inexperienced team member, to be the butt, the whipping boy. Like the plebe at West Point, he was teased, insulted, cajoled and, worst of all, ignored.

The rhythm of the team fell into a pattern—tie, cut, give the needle suture to the nurse, suck the field clean. The cycle was repeated. The circulating nurse carefully counted the needles on the sutures as they were passed to her. If she lost one there would be hell to pay. A missing needle was always assumed to be in the patient. X rays would be required to locate it.

"Unclamp the aorta!"

Buchanan unclamped the empty aorta and it distended. Bradfield and Buchanan released the snares around the great vessels. Ralph Guttierrez had to know that the blood volume returning to the heart-lung machine would fall off suddenly.

"Okay," said Ralph, as he slowed down the outflow of the heart-lung machine. Balancing the input and output of blood was a delicate procedure. It prevented the most disastrous of all perfusion accidents—the pumping of air from an empty oxygenator directly into the patient's arteries. This accident was called the "strawberry soda syndrome." A low-level detector could shut off the pump, but prevention was better achieved by human attention.

CORA III functioned. The pressure tracing was deformed with each beat. Monitoring of CORA's function was not done by an EKG machine but by auditory means. Takaoka listened through an esophageal stethoscope.

"Sounds like 'Show Boat'!" The sounds were not analyzable yet by ear. "All right, let's give it a go. Come down to five hundred cc a minute."

Guttierrez slowed the pump rate so that only 500 cc of blood flowed through the oxygenator. He did this by tightening a screw clamp on the venous line to prevent the reverse of the soda syndrome, exsanguinating the patient. A stitch hole needed repair where a tiny blood geyser jetted into the air.

"Pressure, Tak?"

"One hundred three on eight-five. How does it look down there?"

It was obvious Bradfield's eyes were now smiling.

"Okay. Double-armed five-zero suture with T-three needles, please." One deft stitch and the field was essentially dry. "Come off, Ralph, please."

"Five hundred . . . four hundred . . . three hundred. Power off, tubes clamped!"

"Pressure?"

"One hundred twelve on eight. The venous is twelve cm. Lung compliance improved. Some fluid must have already seeped out."

"Kidneys?"

Takaoka pulled aside the drapes obscuring the urine bag under the table. "The flow has doubled. It's pale and less concentrated. I'll send a spot out for sodium and potassium levels."

The room was hushed. The pumps of the heart-lung machine were stilled. The oxygen no longer hissed. Only the sound of the respirator helping Gray breathe could be heard clearly. But now, faintly, the steam engine inside Gray's chest could be discerned. It had a faint musical sound pitched about middle A. It was a reassuring sound. The clicking of the plastic and metal heart valves followed in sequence.

The medical technicians stepped back from the table to consider the sight of a patient with the first artificial heart. All the years, the fights, the worries, the scraping for funds had focused down to this one moment. It seemed fantastic. It was fantastic. To the scientist working daily in the laboratory in terms of an idea or theory, such things become a familiar reality. He develops a piece here or there, and either he or a colleague elsewhere tests it and finds it practical or unworkable. He watches his idea grow. The whole thing gradually assumes a kind of certainty that, to the outsider who has not followed its development, seems wholly visionary and a little mad.

It was Don Buchanan, amateur comedian, surgical resident, just three months short of going out into the world of medicine on his own, who broke the silence. He stuck his massive, bloodied gloved hand across the table over Gray's split chest and shook Bradfield's hand.

"Goddamnit, Dr. Bradfield, congratulations!"

"Thank you very much." Bradfield paused. "I think we can say that tonight we made history, and I thank you all for your help. Don, would you close, please?"

Bradfield left the table, allowing Buchanan to move into the number one slot. The others shifted accordingly. It was one illustration of the fact that it had taken the efforts of many people to reach this climax. But Bradfield knew that the accolades and the uproar would soon descend on him and virtually him alone. Left unsaid was his concern about the unknowns to be faced by Gray in his postoperative period.

10:30 P.M.

Social worker Louella Commons looked as neat as always. Not a hair out of place. She darted here and there like a hummingbird, but her posture was slightly backward, as if her feet were moving her too quickly, leaving her head and body trying to catch up. She had stayed up on this night to be available if needed. She had kept Janet Chen company through the early evening and looked on herself as a liaison between Bradfield and the patient's fiancée. Bradfield actually preferred to deal with the family directly. He did not delegate that physician's prerogative to anyone. But in an age when government or private insurance paid the bills for health care, and doctors' decisions to hospitalize were evaluated by review committees, it was handy to have someone like Commons to cut through the red tape. Bradfield and Louella met in the open foyer of the operating room suite.

"Boy, that was fast!" she said with an expectant expression.

"Hi, Louella. Where's Miss Chen?"

"It must have gone well—the operation, I mean. Didn't it?"

"Like a charm. Couldn't have been better planned."

"How's Mr. Gray doing?"

"Fine. I'd like to talk with Miss Chen."

"She's in the I.C.U. waiting room."

"Okay. Do you have anything to do?"

"Gee, no. I was going to go with you. Are you going to tell her about the problem with Ridley?"

"Oh, you know about that. Christ, you can't keep anything secret around here!"

"Everybody's talking about it."

"But we aren't going to discuss it when we talk to Miss Chen, are we?" Bradfield said sweetly, arching his eyebrows.

"No, we aren't, unless she brings it up."

The halls were deserted. The night shift was not yet on duty and visiting hours were long over. The medical staff had retired to await the night's emergencies. Janet Chen sat primly on the outer edge of a row of chairs, trying to read a book. She looked up and saw a tired, unsmiling Bradfield coming toward her. Her heart began to pound. She rose quickly and tensed as Bradfield spoke.

"Miss Chen, I think it's going to be all right."

"Ooooh . . . How is he?"

"He'll be just fine. Surgery's been nice and quiet. We haven't had any postop hassles. Dr. Buchanan, my associate, is still finishing the operation. It should be another hour before Mr. Gray leaves the O.R. I needn't discuss with you arrangements for his care, need I?"

She shook her head.

Bradfield went on. "As far as we can tell, the heart's working well. Based on our animal work, we don't expect any malfunction. However, there are always surgical problems and complications—delayed bleeding, lung collapse, kidney failure. But I believe we're on top of all that right now. So keep your chin up. I'm very hopeful." He put his hand gently on her shoulder. "I suggest you go home after you've seen Mr. Gray in the I.C.U. You need the rest."

A tremulous smile appeared on her face. "Yes, thank you. I'm feeling much better now! I think I'll stay on."

"All right. You do as you want. Miss Commons here can help you if you need anything." Bradfield patted her shoulder and walked on to the I.C.U.

The Intensive Care Unit, usually a hive of activity, was quiet at night. Bradfield headed for the nursing station and asked the desk clerk, "Who's the charge nurse tonight?"

"Ginger Brown," she replied.

"Hmm, I thought she was on this afternoon."

"She's working a double shift today."

Bradfield thought, Lady, you don't know how busy she's been.

"Sue Myers is on duty, too," the desk clerk volunteered. "The unit is quite excited."

Bradfield smiled. Despite the dedication with which these young women carried out their routine nursing duties, Bradfield thought a little dramatic excitement was a plus for hospital morale. Undoubtedly, Mrs. Donald would be rushing to the next Nursing Association convention to lecture on the nursing management of atomic-fueled heart patients. Nurses gave just that little bit more when they were proud of their unit.

"Would you get Nurse Brown out here, please?" Bradfield asked.

"She'll be right out. At the moment she's receiving the report."

"Report" is an almost sacrosanct ritual in the nursing profession. The head nurse of one shift sits down with the head nurse of the next shift and methodically covers each patient's nursing plan. It was a method developed over the decades and it worked. Doctors trying to interrupt a "report session" had better have a real emergency on their hands.

Ginger Brown was the assistant head nurse on the swing shift and would be the head nurse on the night shift. The information was passed quickly between her and the head nurse. As Ginger came out to meet him, Bradfield noted there was not a hint of embarrassment at the earlier meeting in the residents' quarters. He realized that she was indeed a lovely young woman despite her severe-looking uniform.

"Yes, Dr. Bradfield?" Miss Brown spoke in a soft, friendly voice.

"Would you review your plans for Mr. Gray?"

"Yes, of course. Dr. Buchanan suggested we might combine the radium implant and heart transplant protocols. We didn't have any worked out for artificial hearts. Mr. Gray will be placed in Room Two-three-oh at the end of the hall. It's an isolation room. It'll keep the transients out and it's a single-bed room. We can get better security. Visitors will have to go past the two nursing desks. We can station a security officer in the anteroom. We have two precautions with respect to staffing. First, they'll have to limit their daily duty to eight-hour shifts to reduce their exposure to radiation. This means all the girls will have a chance to care for him except those who are pregnant. That's the second precaution. So far, the whole shift has signed up!"

"Well done, Miss Brown," Bradfield said, still thinking of the episode in the sauna, and trying to suppress a furtive smile. "Do you know Miss Chen, the patient's fiancée?"

"No."

"She's his only relative. She's outside. Try to get her in early to see Gray and then encourage her to go home and rest, will you?"

"Yes, certainly. Is there anything else?"

"There are a couple of things. The isolation environment is often hard on the patient's psyche. Everybody coming in with a cap, mask, and gown can throw off the patient's contact with reality. Each nurse assigned to Mr. Gray should wear some identifying decal on her gown. It would be a good idea for the nurses to introduce themselves every time they enter the room. Also, dim the room lights in the evening so that he'll have a notion of day and night."

"We'll do all these things right away, Dr. Bradfield."

"Be very aggressive about security. We're stopping the news media at the front desk. Some reporters can be pretty belligerent, but on the whole, I think they'll respect Gray's privacy. On the other hand, there's always the chance of some screwball running about thinking that Gray is some sort of gory medical freak."

"Right, okay. We'll be real tight. You look very tired. Would you like some hot coffee before you go?"

"Yes, thanks. I think I would. Where's the pot?"

"No, no. I'll take care of it for you. Black?"

"Yes."

Ginger Brown left the nursing station quickly, glad to be able to perform that small service for the fatigued surgeon.

His office had the only light burning when Bradfield returned to the medical school wing. He could hear a typewriter flying at a rate that always astounded him.

"Hi, Valerie. Still working?"

"Hi, Dr. B. Since I was going to be here, I thought I'd finish your correspondence. Things go all right?"

"Yes, finally. It was touch and go for a while. I'm going to stay until Don gets him out of the O.R. It'll be an hour or so." Bradfield stretched his arms and yawned. "Why don't you go on home? Is it still raining?"

"Yes. Mr. Ridley finally called a few minutes ago. He said there was a mudslide blocking the road to his home."

"Did you tell him where we got the fuel?"

"No, I didn't know at the time. Later, one of the residents told me you had a plutonium capsule removed from one of the cows. Some trick!"

"Well, I'd like to see the expression on Ridley's face when he hears about it. I've never met anyone so stubborn in my life. We would strangle in our own red tape if everybody stuck to the letter of the law. Surgery moves ahead because it has enough mavericks to act on the spur of the moment!"

" Don't be too harsh on Ridley. He's young and very idealistic."

"Since when are you on his side, Valerie?"

"I'm not. But he could create trouble for you. I just don't want to see you in any sort of trouble, that's all."

"Well, you needn't worry, Valerie. Ridley is a nobody. He's in no position to hurt anyone."

"Is plutonium as dangerous as he claims?"

"It's supposed to be. But the trick is it's encapsulated in a well-engineered container. The plutonium itself is pressed into a small disc so that even if the capsule were opened accidentally, the spill wouldn't involve inhalable particles. There might be intense local radiation. There's always that danger. But there's a danger in everything a man does. We always have to balance benefits to society against aggregate risks. Well, there'll be lots of questions on that subject tomorrow. I'm sure we'll have to hold a press conference, the phones will be ringing all day, and Dean Geld will want to keep his finger in the pie. I think you had better get on home. I suppose you never did hear from Harris?"

"No. He's disappeared. He has a deposit at the Holiday Inn and his plane landed at San Francisco at four. I can't imagine where he is."

"Well, that's because you're a sweet young innocent. Harris is a middle-aged man three thousand miles from home. I'll bet he's in San Francisco having a ball!"

Chapter 14

The bartender at the Hollow Eagle, a topless joint on Broadway, made the arrangements.

"Okay, everything's set. You have a room at this motel." He showed Harris an advertising card. The number was written in pencil on the back. "She'll be there in a half-hour. Her name's Julie. One hundred bucks, plus the room fee. For a guy like you, it's a good deal. She's good and the intellectual type. You have the bread in cash?"

"Uh, no. Traveler's checks."

"Uh, uh—won't do. Tell you what, make them out to the Hollow Eagle. I'll give you the change over your bar bill." He smiled ingratiatingly.

Harris drove his car up Broadway and turned right on Columbus. He spotted the steady neon sign of the two-story motel, three blocks from the waterfront. He pulled up under the overhang in front of the receptionist's desk. An older man sat at the desk.

"Good evening, sir. Can I help you?"

"Yes. I've got a room reserved for the night." He looked around. The motel was clean and functional.

"Oh, yes, just called in. Room One-thirteen on the main

floor. Sign in here, and this is the key. I hope you have a pleasant night."

Harris noted instantly the charge for two people. A feeling of guilt swept over him causing his stomach to churn. He hadn't realized it would be so obvious. He paid in cash and left the office, still unsure if he should go through with this first marital infidelity.

Harris put the key in the door and opened it. A warm, carpeted, softly-lit room confronted him. He removed his raincoat and sat down in front of the TV set, his eyelid twitching slightly. A soft knock came on the door. Harris opened it. A petite young woman wrapped in a blue cloth raincoat smiled up at him.

"Hi. I'm Julie. Can I come in?" She wore a plastic rain scarf over her springy, light-brown hair. A drop of rain hung on to her pert nose. Her skin was clear, her eyes brown and heavily accented in dark mascara. Harris thought, This girl is almost as young as my daughter! Aloud he said, "Come on in."

She put her overnight bag down near the door and Harris helped her off with her coat. Underneath she wore a dark-red woolknit suit, with a string of cultured pearls round her neck. Harris was uncertain as to how he should proceed, but she took the situation in hand.

"I prefer that my clients get the monetary affairs over with first," she said confidently.

Harris had the money in an envelope sitting on the dresser. He picked it up and gave it to her. She matter-of-factly opened the unglued flap and quickly counted it.

"Swell. Let me just put this somewhere safe, and I'll change into something comfortable. I'm a bit hungry. Could you order something from room service?"

"I didn't realize you hadn't eaten. Would you rather go out?"

"Why don't we? Do you like Chinese food? There's a great little place on Washington Street where the natives go. Are you game?"

Julie's enthusiasm was persuasive and out they went.

* * *

At the hospital the lights in Gray's isolation room were dimmed. Two capped, masked, and gowned nurses attended the patient. A therapist routinely checked the function of the respirator. Jack Johnson was in his eighteenth hour of continuous duty. He sat in an easy chair that Ginger Brown had appropriated from some unsuspecting office. She knew he was going to be there a long time, just looking and thinking. Sue Myers had gone home to rest. She would be back to take a split shift in the morning. The morale of the team was high. The nurses and technical assistants were eager to participate in the postimplantation care. It was an exciting time.

Johnson mulled over many factors as he saw them occur. The first two were peculiarly unique and in a way threw everybody off balance. The atomic heart had no electrical activity. There wasn't any electrocardiogram to give an idea of the quality of the beat. The observers felt uneasy. The same unease was present on the treatment side. Johnson, as others before him, had spent hours studying a group of drugs that act mainly on the heart's rhythm and contraction. Atropine blocked the vagus nerve to the heart, so it would beat faster. Propranolol blocked the excitatory effects of heart nerves so that the heartbeat would slow down. Digitalis, one of the oldest known heart drugs, improved muscle contraction. Lidocaine, also used as a local anesthetic in minor surgery, had a quieting down action on heart rhythm. These drugs were no longer applicable to the patient with the artificial heart. Indeed, if given at all, there was a chance that "peripheral effects" might be unmasked.

And there were two more immediate problems: continued bleeding and a hint of a more rapid than expected rise in Gray's temperature.

During surgery two plastic tubes were left in Gray's chest cavity to drain out seeping blood. The tubes were connected to a plastic rectangular container, the Pleurevac, which caught and measured blood loss. Gray had lost a lot of blood an hour after surgery, and midway into the second hour. The loss rate had decreased, but was still far above desirable. Pressure had dropped noticeably and urine production was low.

Johnson ordered the nurse to administer a blood transfusion to maintain a balance of plus 200, and searched for a drug to raise the pressure. In the usual patient the drug for this purpose is isoproterenol. The drug makes the heart beat faster and harder by dilating the peripheral vessels. Johnson decided he couldn't use this drug because it would have no effect on the mechanical CORA. He dug deep into his pocket manual for a list of possible agents. He came across a drug called Vasoxyl, a pure alpha stimulator, a vessel constrictor.

"Nurse, add one microgram per cc of Vasoxyl to the intravenous bottle," Johnson said.

She complied. The patient's pressure increased from an average of 65 to 75. Bleeding continued at a slow, steady rate. A half-hour later, Gray's temperature had hit 99.4°.

Johnson said, "Let's get some ice and wet towels on the surface of his body." The nurses followed his instructions, but the temperature continued to go up.

The problem which Johnson didn't realize was this: by constricting the peripheral vessels with Vasoxyl and ice, the body had become a poor heat radiator. CORA produced 45 watts of waste heat. It had to be removed from the body in some way. Johnson needed advice desperately, and he was too mentally fatigued to know it. He was managing the patient with the best of twentieth century experience—but this was twenty-first century medicine.

Midnight.

The hospital P.R. man sat in his basement office typing a draft of a press release. Jerry Cibelli had started his career as a sports writer on the student newspaper. His interest in medicine began as a result of an interview with doctors who had started out on athletic scholarships. One of them was a second-year resident named Don Buchanan.

Cibelli spent his first postgraduate year as a writer in the sports department at Aspermont, but he applied quickly when the position at the hospital opened up.

At the moment Cibelli's desk was cluttered with information for his story. He had Bradfield's government contract describing the medical techniques. He had the project's budget, a copy of Gray's biography, and a brief note about Janet Chen. On Cibelli's desk were references on atomic energy, nuclear reactors, and plutonium.

Cibelli had his procedures planned. He knew that when television decided to cover a big story, the costs of maintaining equipment and people on location were astronomical. TV reporters would be under pressure to file stories daily whether or not events warranted it. His typing was interrupted when the phone rang. It was Jim Hickman of WNTL-TV.

"Hello, Jerry? I'm checking on a tip that one of your doctors has implanted an artificial heart. What's the story?"

"Your tip is correct. It's been done. The patient is in I.C.U. The first report I have is that things are going well. I'll have a more detailed statement in a couple of hours. We'll be arranging a press conference in the morning. Will you be down?"

"You bet."

"Looks like the story is beginning to roll already. My other line's ringing."

"Okay, Jerry. Good luck on this one."

"Thanks, and goodbye."

Through the early morning hours the calls kept pouring in, after the wire services had moved a bulletin on the operation. The calls came from as far as New York, London, Tokyo, and Berlin. Jerry got his office assistant out of bed to help him cope with the calls so he could continue working on the other arrangements. Within an hour all five telephone lines in the small office were lit up. Unable to cope with so many calls, Cibelli informed the switchboard operator to implement the contingency plan. It was part of the hospital's overall scheme for handling calamities like an earthquake, explosion, or a 747 jet crash at San Francisco airport. The plan for the public relations office called for several administrators to report instantly and render assistance.

Of course, the operation itself could hardly be likened to a disaster, but it could become one if information about it were mishandled.

It was 2:00 A.M. Cibelli was tired. He hadn't been up this late since the days he had traveled with the football team.

Chapter 15

Bradfield met with Buchanan, Romanoff, and Belknap outside Gray's room. They were making their final rounds before scattering to their rooms or homes to rest.

It was peculiar to see armed guards pacing the corridors of the I.C.U. The heart transplant experience at Cape Town, Houston, and Stanford had demonstrated that the pursuit of "stories" by ambitious journalists and the invasion of individual privacy were subject to wide interpretation. In one of the hospitals a photographer had been caught scaling down the wall outside, dangling from the roof by a rope. He had been trying to get "exclusive" pictures of the patient through the window.

Bradfield and the residents removed their white coats, put on caps and masks, booties and sterile gowns, then entered en masse. Johnson was asleep in his chair. The patient was soaked in ice and wet towels. The floor was wet. The nurses were changing the cold packs frequently while inspecting and counting the inflow of fluids, blood, and vasopressor.

Buchanan glanced at the Pleurevac. The blood volume

draining out was still worrisome. He brought this point up with Bradfield.

"We're going to tough it out," Bradfield said. "It's going to be virtually impossible to reopen him to explore the bleeding site. There aren't any vessels in CORA of course. We need to keep his blood replaced. What I'm concerned about is his temperature. Wake Johnson up. Let's get the details here."

Buchanan nudged the bone-weary Johnson, who immediately woke up. His buttocks hurt from sleeping sitting up in one position. He was surrounded by the inquisitive team.

"Hi, sorry to wake you. Bill has some concerns about Mr. Gray's temperature."

"I have, too. The temperature has hit over one hundred and two."

"It's one hundred point five now. Still too hot for an adult with the ice treatment he's getting, and he doesn't look very good. He should be alert by now. Takaoka had him pretty well awake by the end of the operation. Let's look at him together, Jack."

The group moved over to the bedside. The nurse confirmed the blood pressure recording, then slipped back out of the way. She joined the other nurse a few steps away from the bed. Both remained attentive to help if they were needed. The patient's skin was cool to the touch where ice towels had covered it. Where the ice had not made contact, the skin was decidedly hot and red. His body and limbs had a checkerboard appearance and his face was hot, flushed, yet still jaundiced. He wasn't perspiring. His pulse was thready. Johnson remarked that Gray looked and felt like a patient suffering from sunstroke.

"Let's go over this step by step," Bradfield said. "His arterial pressure is low, eighty-eight over sixty. Venous pressure is low, fluctuating around four to five. Respirations twenty-two, shallow. Urine production down for the last hour. Fluids—IV fluid in the left arm—glucose. The blood is running in the CVP at plus four hundred. What's piggybacked into that other IV?"

"Vasoxyl," the nurse replied.

Bradfield said, "One doesn't normally use a pure vasoconstrictor. I wonder if that's the problem. Why don't we stop that drug and try a vasodilator like isoproterenol?"

"Won't that drop the arterial pressure even more?" Buchanan asked.

"Obviously not. There's no cardiac effect by the drug."

"Well, we can avoid the hypotension by increasing the blood into the heart. I think he needs more blood. Go plus one thousand over the next half-hour. That will fill CORA better and should increase the output. Then the vasodilator should permit a greater heat loss. Also use a fan to circulate the air over him. And give him some diazepam to reduce his shivering and to tranquilize him a little bit."

The nurses were already taking down the bottle with the Vasoxyl.

Bradfield turned to Johnson. "Stick with it, Jack, but I don't think you need to stay in here with him. I should expect the temp to fall within an hour or so. The bleeding? Well, it's not great. I think you can keep up with it. It'll stop one way or another."

"Okay," Johnson said, his eyelids heavy from lack of sleep. "I'll stay here another half-hour, then go upstairs to sleep."

"Let's make a decision about the bleeding problem at morning rounds. I think we all need some sleep," Bradfield said.

There was silent agreement. It was two o'clock in the morning. There was a feeling of renewed confidence. A course of action had been agreed upon. Surgeons were not always right, but they could never be undecided!

Harris and Julie left the restaurant and walked slowly to their wind-slapped automobile in the parking lot. Without a word, he helped her into the car for the short ride back to the motel. Harris had not done anything like this before and had second thoughts. He could say "thank you for the enjoyable evening," drop her off, and drive on down the peninsula. There was something else nagging him. How could he sleep with his wife if he caught some rare venereal disease?

He started the engine and drove slowly back down the wet pavement. The rain had stopped, but the wind and speed of the car blew enough drops of water off the hood to require use of the windshield wipers. Julie snuggled close up to him. As oncoming lights lit up the interior, he took his eyes off the roadway briefly to look at her. She returned the brief glance.

Suddenly, he said, "Where do you live? I'd like to drop you off."

Her eyes widened in surprise. "Well! Are you afraid? You shouldn't be." Seductively, she suddenly reached out her hand and firmly rubbed the bulge of his genitals through his trousers.

"Please, don't do that!" he said hoarsely. "I can't drive in this weather with that going on."

"You concentrate too much on just surviving. Enjoy yourself!" In one swift movement, she unzipped his trousers as he drove, his hand rigidly on the steering wheel. She laughed softly, contentedly, when she felt his erection. "Why did you deny it for an instant?" she whispered.

Harris decided he wasn't going to drop her off at her home. Her overnight bag was still at the motel and they would have to pick it up. Besides, the hundred dollars had been paid. Why shouldn't he get his money's worth?

"Hey, stop it, Julie. Please stop!" He feared losing control of both the automobile and himself.

"Only if you promise to stay with me tonight."

"Yes, yes. I will."

"Okay."

Julie would have called it a short profitable night and taken up his offer to drop her off but for two reasons. It piqued her pride to have this john nibble at the bait without biting. Unlike other girls in her profession, she needed to have a man's lust demonstrated for her completely. She was never sure of her power until the moment of submission and conquest, even if the satisfaction did not stay with her long. The second reason was more complex. It seemed to Julie that Harris had more influence than his title had indicated. In her client contacts, she looked routinely for inside information—secrets her clients' competitors would be willing to buy for the right price. Julie looked far ahead, thinking of security for her old age. And who knows? She might find someone along the way she could actually love. She didn't know enough about Harris yet. Nor was he sufficiently tied to her string. There's nothing like a happy surfeit of sex, she thought, to catch a man.

As Harris drove into the driveway of the motel, she pulled his zipper up halfway. Their room, the only one with lights still on, was warm and comfortable when they entered. Clumsily, he embraced her with raincoat still on. She stepped over to her night bag.

"I'll be back in a moment," she whispered and disappeared into the bathroom.

2:30 A.M.

Even Jack Johnson felt the lull that now dominated the hospital scene after the intensive effort. All the actors in the drama had moved on to seek some rest. The tall, heavy security guard walked slowly around in a circle just outside Gray's door. The patient was sleeping a normal sleep, the anesthetic having worn off. Johnson got up from his chair and stretched his lanky body.

"How are the numbers?" he asked the nurse.

Her serious eyes looked out over her mask at Johnson, then down to the tabular chart. She replied in a tired but confident voice. "The pressure has been stable. Blood loss has decreased. We could strip out only seventy ccs in the last hour."

"That's a good sign."

"His temperature has come down to ninety-nine."

"Good, good!"

"Urine volume has been increasing almost one hundred and five cc's an hour. His skin color is still yellow, but he doesn't have the blotchy look he had earlier. I can hear some crackles in his lungs but no junky stuff."

"He still needs to cough to keep his lungs from collapsing."

"I'm going to wake him up in an hour and cough him and change his position. You know, Dr. Johnson, he looks good enough to dangle on the side of the bed."

"You really think so?"

"I do."

"Wait until seven or eight. Let Dr. Bradfield decide that. He'll be pleased."

"Okay."

"I'm going out to walk around a bit. Call me if anything comes up."

"Sure, Dr. Johnson. I can take care of this. You need some exercise."

Johnson stepped out into the quiet corridor and stripped off his hot gown and face mask. The guard looked at the black surgeon.

"How's he doing, Doc?"

"Good, sergeant. Real good!"

"Great. Everything's quiet out here."

Johnson walked past the dimly lit waiting room. There were two occupants sitting up wide awake: Janet Chen and an older little man who looked like he worked with his hands. He had on an old tweed jacket, and stiff cotton pants and shirt. As Johnson walked over to speak to Janet, a nurse stopped and whispered something into his ear.

Chapter 16

Jim Hickman had been around the San Francisco TV news business for a long time. But the peninsula courthouse scene, the sheriff's offices, and fire departments were his beat, not medicine. Medicine could get too esoteric at times. In fact, Hickman wasn't really too eager to cover this story. There was a printer's strike and he had been working overtime covering news ordinarily not touched by commercial television stations. But after receiving the tip about the implantation, he did call his assignment editor at home to apprise him of the situation.

The editor was excited. "Jesus Christ, you must be kidding. Have you verified it yet?"

"Yes, but I was hoping you might want to assign someone else to do it. I'm kinda tired."

"I don't have anybody else to spare. You have to get rolling. Let's meet down at the station in an hour and let's go over it."

At the studio, there was plenty of activity as the morning news-variety show was in preparation. Hickman walked through a narrow hallway to the newsroom. The editor was at his desk with his feet up, talking into a phone. The other lines were blinking furiously.

Hickman browsed through the morgue to do a quick study on Bradfield and the artificial heart. The station's files contained nothing on the subject. He would have to get his information from the wire reports or P.R. handouts. He entered the teletype room to check. Blankly, he watched the white paper stutter out of the rollers and fall into the wire basket, and there it was, a bulletin from the Associated Press. It was brief but it told Hickman what he wanted to know.

"I've asked Elaine to go down to Aspermont with you because I figured this story will be big."

"It's all over the country already," Hickman said, handing the wire copy to the editor.

"Let's not waste any time then. Go down there right away and see if you can interview any of the doctors. If they don't want to do it, see if you can get anything from relatives, orderlies—anyone who will talk."

The editor's assistant entered and handed him a piece of paper with a note scribbled on it. "Here's a commercial angle," the editor exclaimed. "The company that makes the artificial heart is over at Berkeley. Their public relations man just called our business editor."

"What's the name of the company?"

"ATOCOR."

"But the story is at the hospital," Hickman complained.

"Okay, stick with the hospital, but tomorrow go over to ATOCOR."

"Right."

Hickman left to drive down to the medical center. He would meet with the TV news producer at about eight in the morning to go over the plans and all the shots they would need. Meanwhile, it was important for him and the cameraman to obtain the background story. As he got into his car, he was thinking hard about the visual possibilities. Perhaps he could get some footage of the operation for the evening news. That ought to get some comments. He could get the wife or kids talking about their dad, the patient. Some real heart throbbing stuff. Hey, that was pretty good! They'd start out with that old song "I left my heart in San Francisco." He wondered if that had been used before.

Julie undressed quickly after turning on the infra red heating lamp in the bathroom ceiling. She looked at herself with a critical eye. Her face was clear of blemishes, the skin fine and youthful. The brown eyes were large with a kewpie-doll shape. Her mouth was oval and her teeth white and regular. Her smile was a happy, natural one, hinting of friendship and gaiety, tempting to a man like Harris with thoughts of more than just lust. It was not, definitely not, the frozen smile of a harlot. Her breasts moved enticingly as she brushed her hair, still watching herself in the mirror. She had the attractive, firm body of a young woman who had not yet borne a child.

Julie quickly washed her face and brushed a touch of cologne on her earlobes, the very tips of her nipples, on her belly button and the inner aspects of her thighs. It was her standard operating procedure. She pulled on a filmy blue peignoir and opened the door to find Harris still clothed and staring fixedly at her. His trousers were still partially unzipped, the bulge visible even to an uninterested eye from across the room.

"You are so lovely," Harris said.

"I'm really glad you like this," she replied. She put down her purse next to the bed and walked over to him. He stood up suddenly and rushed to meet her, an uncontrollable urge building up within him. He threw his arms around her, pulling her soft buttocks against him. She thought briefly, God! He's going to crush me into pulp right away!

"Come on, Ron." She pushed at his chest. "Let's get comfortable on the bed first." With practiced fingers, she started to help him undress, but he needed no assistance. He tore his clothes off.

Harris was not a handsome specimen of manhood. He had a hairy chest and the suggestion of a paunchy abdomen. His flabbiness stemmed from years of desk work, irregular eating, and traveling. His frame was large and bony. There were a few pimples here and there, and his skin was swarthy and dry.

Julie lay down on the bed, on the side next to her purse. She held her legs together demurely, and pulled the bottom of the peignoir down over her thighs. Harris came over and looked down at her. She smiled and raised her arms to him. With that action her breasts moved seductively, riveting his attention on them. He fell on her, not at all lightly, and clasped her body to him. His hands covered her breasts, caressing them roughly. He felt the firming response of the nipples. He became bolder, and she wriggled and cried softly, a well-practiced response but not completely unfeeling. She rolled from side to side on her back and opened her slightly moistened thighs to accept him. Harris began the ancient rhythm. Her legs encompassed his buttocks, and she responded to his thrustings with tightening of her pelvic muscles. He ejaculated. No more than two minutes had passed by, but he felt elated, exhilarated.

After twenty years of marriage, he thought, he was now in bed with the only other woman in his life. The thought made him disengage from her and turn away. The physiological sadness descended upon him. In the dimly lit room, he stared into the mirror over the dresser and saw his reflection. A feeling of disorientation, of fantasy swept over him as he again looked at Julie's face, so different from that of his wife.

Sam Bacigalupe, seventy-two-year-old immigrant from southern Italy, had shared the quiet I.C.U. waiting room for a good part of the night with Janet Chen. He had been lonely as he faced another long vigil for his wife, dying of acute leukemia in a nearby room. Sam was well known to many of the old settlers of the mid-peninsula as a fruit and vegetable man and part-time gardener.

Jack Johnson approached while Janet was talking with Sam. She was sharing with him her childhood experiences in Little Italy, adjacent to Chinatown in New York City, as it was in San Francisco. Sam became animated as she talked.

"Ah, that sounds so familiar, Missus Chen! My brother, he

went to New York at the same time I came here. It was an exciting time. He worked the pushcarts. God rest his soul! He died fifteen years ago from a stroke. I visited him just once after we came over here and that was to bury him."

"I'm sorry to hear that."

"No, no, don't be so sorry. He raised seven boys and three girls. All married and one is a lawyer and one is a big man in city government. He done real good. He was a real man. Passing on is the way of life. The nurses, they all ask me why am I here now, in the middle of the night. Why don't I go home? But I'm a simple man. Certain things I know I must do. I can't know all the things you know," he said, glancing at Johnson. "Isn't that right, doctor?"

The surgical resident was tolerant of the old gnarled man. Sam made no trouble for anyone, but the nurses worried about him as they saw him continue his vigil day after day and through the nights. They tried to cajole him, they even threatened him, but to no avail. He stayed at his post. It was heart-rending when the old man with arms like a blacksmith was allowed to enter his wife's room during visiting hours. These visiting periods were short, three times a day for ten minutes each. Sam would enter slowly and smile politely to the nurses, hoping he was not interfering with the care of his beloved Nina. He would caress her hands and moist forehead and very softly sing Neapolitan love songs into her ear. Mrs. Bacigalupe, his Nina, had been unconscious now for three days, and the end was near.

She had an infection. It was in her lungs and bloodstream. The drugs she had received had no effect. Still, the doctors and nurses tried. The respirator ventilated her lungs monotonously. The intravenous drugs dripped slowly and steadily. She was fed a liquid diet by a nasogastric tube. She was tended to by a crew of young people with love and dedication.

If anyone had asked Sam, and obviously no one did, he might have told them to let her go peacefully. Passing on is the way of life, he would have said. But of all the professional people there, few understood Sam as well as Janet, who had only met him that evening. It was not so strange as it seemed. Janet's life experiences and values were similar to Sam's in many ways.

Americans refer themselves automatically to the hospital when illness strikes. Death for most of them is not a part of life, except for the violence of the street or screen. But for Janet Chen and Sam Bacigalupe, death at home was natural. When Janet's mother had died at thirty-six, Janet had been only eight. Her father knew there was no hope for Mrs. Chen in the hospital. The Bellevue doctors might not have agreed, but there was little they could do. So Janet, a third-grader, and her two older sisters had cared for their mother and cooked for their father while the Hodgkin's disease had slowly progressed over the better part of a hot summer.

In the fall of that year, Janet's mother died as Janet sat by her bed reading quietly. Janet had waited in the cramped, second-story tenement until her father and sisters returned home. Together, they had tenderly washed the remains and wrapped the body in a white shroud, then placed it on the bed. Incense was burned while visitors came and paid their respects. Janet had mourned her mother as any young child would. But the family had drawn together more closely. Death was not a stranger in the night.

Janet's life had paused again at sixteen, when her father suffered a stroke. He, too, had died at home, leaving Janet and her sisters in the care of an aunt and uncle.

As it was to Janet, first-generation Chinese-American, so it was to Sam of old Italy. Death was in the natural order of things, like the ebb and flow of the tide, like the rising and setting of the sun. In that way of life, these things were not turned over to strangers—professionals, to be sure, but strangers all the same.

"Mr. Bacigalupe," Jack Johnson interrupted, fidgeting in his rumpled surgical suit. "Your wife's doctor is not here now, and the nurses have asked me to tell you some bad news. Your wife's heart has stopped. I'm very sorry."

Although his wife's death was expected, it was still a shock to the old man. He started to sob openly, his shoulders shaking pathetically. "Well, doctor," he quavered, "you did everything you could."

"I didn't actually take care of your wife. I was just asked to relay the message. But I'm sure that your wife's doctors did all they could."

Janet embraced the old vendor. "I'm very sorry. Whatever I can do to help, please let me know. Why don't we go in her room together and say goodbye, and then you go home?"

Janet helped walk Sam into the I.C.U. room. As they passed the nursing station, she told the clerk to order a taxi. Sam was in no shape to drive home. He stood by his wife's bedside for a few minutes and looked long on the face of the woman who had been his mate for forty years. As he left, he spoke to Janet, the tears streaming down his face. "Goodbye to you, Missus Chen. I trust God will listen to your prayers and your Mr. Henry will have a full life with you, and that you'll have a lot of children. You've helped an old man very much tonight." He grasped her tightly and kissed her cheek.

She felt a surge of compassion. "I'm sure God will remember all of us in His goodness and mercy. You and Nina will meet again and love forever."

Sam nodded and shuffled out into the darkened empty hallway.

"Mr. Gray looks a lot better now," Johnson said to Janet when she returned to the waiting room. "Fever's down and the bleeding which I was so worried about has virtually stopped."

Janet was visibly relieved. "It's strange, isn't it, Dr. Johnson, that you can take an old heart out and replace it with a machine. Yet in the very next room an old woman can still die of a disease that we have known about for a long time and we still can't do anything about."

Chapter 17

Bradfield awoke at 5:00 A.M.

It was quiet except for the dripping of the rain off the drainpipes of his home. The storm had passed and, unlikely as it might seem, he felt rested.

He left the bedroom quietly to wash up, wondering how Gray was doing. The problems now facing Bradfield were of a different kind. He had to consolidate his gains and strike now while things were going his way. He would flush the graybeards at the university out of their lairs, so that his programs would receive high priority. He would make public appearances to enlist funds and support. He would get a series of cases done to bring the era of artificial heart surgery to maturity quickly. The press conference he was to hold later in the day had a singular significance. It would launch Bradfield's campaign to achieve his goals. A meeting with Cibelli would be the second order of business. The first was, of course, to check in on the patient.

Bradfield was half-dressed when the telephone rang. Instantly, he thought something had gone wrong. He hopped on one foot to answer it before his wife was wakened. He was too late. Charlotte had muttered a sleepy "hello" into the mouthpiece.

A thin quavering voice asked, "Is this the home of the doctor who just did the artificial heart operation?"

"Who's calling, please?"

Charlotte put her hand over the mouthpiece and said softly to her husband, "It's not the hospital. Someone calling about the operation."

Charlotte always tried to protect Bradfield from patient calls at home, unless it was an emergency. The number listed for Bradfield in the phone book was his office at the hospital. The home number was listed under Charlotte's name. But since there were only three Bradfields in the book, any persistent patient could try them all in a matter of minutes.

Bradfield hopped back to the dressing room, as Charlotte went on, "I'm afraid, sir, you'll have to reach him at the hospital."

"I just called the office and he's not there. Now, where is he, lady?" Charlotte detected hostility in the voice.

"I'd like to take a message for him and have him call you back. What is your name, please?"

"Never mind, you're probably as guilty as he is. You tell him this. We normal Americans are sick and tired of his brutal experiments. Why is he torturing this poor man? Is the glory worth it? The right food and vitamins could have saved him. Ask your husband how many dogs he tortured and butchered in his laboratory first. Your husband is sick, lady. God bless humanitarians who cut funds for medical research, so we taxpayers don't have to pay for it. I hope you and he roast in hell for your bestiality!"

Charlotte heard the phone click off. She lay back on her pillow dumbfounded. She had spoken with angry and excited patients, with depressed and sorrowful families of patients, but she had never had a call like this before.

"Bill!"

"What's the matter, darling?" Bradfield heard the change in

his wife's normally cool tone of voice. He moved back into the bedroom.

"That call," she said. "The man's insane!"

"Why, what happened?"

Charlotte explained.

"Probably just some crank," he said. "I'm afraid we're going to get a lot more of these as the story breaks further."

"Who are these people? Does anybody know?"

"Unfortunately, nobody knows until they surface. They're obviously disturbed, unstable, or just have a macabre sense of humor. Some of them are insane. They seem to be affected by things they see or read in the media. I should have warned you about this. I didn't realize it would upset you so much."

"Oh, Bill, what are we getting into? I sometimes think you should have gone into private practice."

"Well, in academe the money isn't that good, but when this artificial heart gets accepted, I believe things will change."

"Are you going to be home more often now that you've succeeded, or is there going to be something else?"

"I predict something a lot better, Charlie. By this time next year, you and I will be on the international circuit—Rome, Berlin, Tokyo, Paris! Every surgical group will want me to attend their meetings. Think of it, magnificent hospitality, the best accommodations, hours of the finest museums in the world. The question, my dear, is—are you ready for it?"

Charlotte considered what her husband had just said. "Well, we'll have to see about that when the time comes. Meanwhile, can't you do something about these insane phone calls?"

"If they keep coming, we'll have to get an unlisted number. Or maybe we can use your maiden name. Okay? What are you doing today?"

"I'm driving up to Woodside. Helene and Carrie are meeting me at the stables. Ride in the morning, then go to Allied Arts for lunch."

"You're going to miss the press conference on television."

"Oh, really? Is it going to be on today?" Charlotte called out from behind the dressing screen.

"It'll be televised at ten. Naturally your husband will be the star!"

"That's nice, Bill. Maybe I can convince the girls to quit early. We can have a cocktail in front of the clubhouse TV set."

Charlotte dressed in brown jodhpurs and low-heeled, hand-softened leather boots. Her long silky blond hair was done up in a severe bun. Bradfield had made the coffee and prepared cereal for both of them by the time she came to the kitchen.

"How sweet of you, Bill! You're a dear."

"I wanted to make up for the phone call. Since I'm usually gone by the time you get up, I thought it would be nice."

Breakfast was disposed of quickly and the two went off on their separate ways.

Buchanan and Company, as some called the motley group, had just finished their ward rounds when Bradfield came striding in. He wore his white coat over a dark business suit. The nurses followed his handsome figure with eyes that reflected their admiration, the kind that only young women hold for a male sex symbol.

The chief resident called out to Bradfield, "Well, he looked hopeless, so we killed him!"

"He must be pretty good," said Bradfield, recognizing Buchanan's humor.

"Yes, sir," came a chorus of voices.

"Let's see."

Buchanan said, "You can take a peek at him from the doorway."

Bradfield peered in through the partially opened door of the isolation room. He saw the emaciated man sitting up on the side of the bed supported by two nurses. The endotracheal tube through his windpipe had been removed. He was breathing shallowly but frequently. With each breath, the surgeon could see the spaces between Gray's ribs sucking in a little bit. Gray, however, was breathing without mechanical assistance for the first time in twenty-four hours. The patient's legs, weak from loss of muscle mass, looked like toothpicks. His abdomen was decidedly less protuberant than on the previous day. The catheter to his bladder was still in place. Bradfield followed its course down to the plastic container hanging from the steel bedside. It was heavy and swollen with clear, pale urine.

"He's losing a lot of his fluid," Bradfield observed.

The nurses were aware of it. One of them said, "We've had to change the bag twice during the night. The kidney circulation is terrific." It was a good sign. The artificial heart in Gray's chest was pumping enough blood to the kidneys to clear the excess fluid in his tissues. His color was better.

"His lungs sound less crackly, too," the nurse said. This was another sign of improvement. The chest drainage container, Bradfield noticed, was still in place. A thin pink fluid settled on the top of the darker blood that had drained out earlier. There was little bleeding now.

"How's he doing in general, girls?"

"Just amazing, Dr. Bradfield. Great!"

"What do you think, Mr. Gray?"

Gray nodded his head weakly. A wan smile appeared on his parched, cracked lips. He could only croak, as the breathing tube, which had been in place a long time, had irritated his vocal cords.

"Okay, keep fighting. You're the key, now. We've done our job. It's up to you and the nurses."

Gray actually looked and felt like hell. His chest hurt. His throat hurt. The thin skin had abraded wherever adhesive tape had been placed. The skin came off in sheets when the tape was removed. To nonmedical eyes, Gray did not look any different from a Dachau camp survivor. But Bradfield could see the future Henry Gray as a picture of health. And Gray was elated that he felt anything at all.

The two of them, doctor and patient, gazed at each other

across the room. Their eyes met. They looked deeply into each other and they admired the courage they saw.

Buchanan closed the door quietly. Looking at his watch, he said, "It's almost seven-thirty. Time for the first case."

Bradfield recalled, "It's the boy with the atrial septal defect, isn't it?"

"Yes," Buchanan replied.

"I'm going to be busy with Cibelli this morning, Don. Is Johnson ready to do the case?"

"Well," Buchanan drew the word out while looking at the eager young resident. "He should be pretty tired after working all night."

Johnson interjected quickly, "Not that tired, sir. I can do it."

It was going to be Johnson's first open heart case. It was Bradfield's way of rewarding him for the outstanding care he had given the patients, and especially Gray. He foresaw no increase in risk for the patient if a junior man performed the surgery.

"Don, you go ahead with Jack. Good luck."

Buchanan and company moved to the operating room talking excitedly about Johnson's good fortune.

Bradfield walked separately to the I.C.U. waiting room, where Janet Chen continued her vigil.

"Good morning, doctor," she said brightly.

"It's a good morning all around, Miss Chen. I've just come from Mr. Gray's room. I'm very pleased at his early course."

"Yes, one of the nurses told me how well he is doing. I'm going in at the next visiting period, at eight o'clock."

Janet looked strangely attractive to Bradfield just then. The warmth of concern her tired face projected, the intensity of emotion that was silently transferred, the joy that was so obviously deeply felt—these were things he didn't realize he had missed in his own personal life until now. A thought struck him that it might not be a bad idea to use Janet in his campaign.

"I was just thinking, you might want to participate in the press conference today," he said.

"Oh, dear, I think not," she answered softly. "It would be too much for me right now. I'd have thought you'd want us out of the spotlight. A bit sensational, don't you think?"

"As you wish." Bradfield backed off quickly. "If you have any problems, please get hold of me through Miss Commons. I've got to attend to some business now."

"Thank you very much for taking the time to see me, Dr. Bradfield. I know you're busy. I'm very appreciative."

Bradfield left for his office. On the way he could see that the news people were already gathering.

Chapter 18

The hospital security force was out in full strength directing several large vans containing remote control facilities for live television coverage. The parking lot was already half full.

Bradfield asked the sergeant in charge, "What's going on?"

The sergeant smiled. "I think the circus is coming to town!"

The surgeon thought, The patients coming to the clinic today will have a difficult time parking. Little groups formed and reformed in a random pattern. ABC claimed a spot next to the fountain for the equipment, cameramen, producer, and reporters. Next to the garden was CBS. NBC had the largest crew and number of reporters, one each for the *Today Show* and the *Evening News*. It also had two big color cameras and portable units to operate from any remote location.

"Watch those guys with the portable cameras," the sergeant ordered his men. "They might try to sneak into the I.C.U. Don't let them out of your sight!"

Bradfield smiled inwardly and walked to his office. The sidewalk was still puddled over with small pools of rain water, and long tracks crisscrossed over the walks, evidence of equipment being moved into place. There was a light, cold breeze picking up. The sun was breaking over the top of the hospital, sending its warm rays over the fast-shifting throng.

Jim Hickman was speaking frenetically with Elaine Whitmore, his producer. The crew in white coveralls and work-boots pulled equipment out of the van, unconcerned as usual with the activity around them.

"We've tapped the mother lode! Nobody else was down here," said Hickman. "You got a cigarette?"

"Sure." Whitmore reached in her bag and flipped a filter-tipped Marlboro to him.

"God!" Hickman said. "There's not a single cigarette machine in the whole place. 'No Smoking' signs are everywhere. What a place!" He drew deeply and exhaled contentedly. "And now, where's the conference going to be?"

"Over there in the medical school auditorium. They're expecting a huge crowd."

"I'll send the crew over now to set up the equipment."

"Tell me about the patient."

Hickman consulted his notebook. "Forty-three years old, computer man, owns software-hardware company on the peninsula, unmarried, never married."

"Not queer, is he?"

"Not by reputation. He's got a fiancée named Janet Chen."

"Chen?"

"Oriental, Chinese, or Japenese. I saw her in the I.C.U. earlier. We ought to get an exclusive with her as soon as possible, but we can't get the cameras up there. They have security guards all over the place."

"Let's get a hold of Cibelli soon."

"The patient's room number is two thirteen. I've got it pegged on the outside. Doesn't look like we can get a shot except from the ground."

"Any chance we might bribe one of the orderlies to sneak a camera into the room?"

"I doubt if he could get through the guards."

"Okay. We'll skip that stuff. What else?"

"There's a building about seven hundred yards in back of the main center. That's where the experiments were done. There's a high cyclone fence with barbed wire on top and a locked gate. I'm told they have a couple of experimental cows in there with artificial hearts working."

"Can we get in?"

"Maybe. The gate is unlocked at the moment, but it's rather muddy and sloppy."

"Did you see anyone around?"

"Not a soul."

"Okay. Let's get over there first. We have a couple of hours before the press conference."

Whitmore signaled a man with a portable camera and videotape recorder. The three of them moved off to a panel wagon with CHANNEL 13 marked in large bold letters, got in and, with squealing wheels and a splatter of water, took off rapidly.

Fred Hull, the customers' man for E. L. Gerard and Company, was also up at 5:30 A.M. The three-hour time difference between the East and West coasts meant that Fred had to be in his office at seven each morning to make the ten o'clock opening of the New York Stock Exchange. The market in general had been good to Fred. Forty thousand dollars a year in commissions alone was not unusual. In addition, there were the profits from the stocks he traded in for himself.

Fred was strong in a special field—health care technology. He had the knack of understanding the financial significance of the latest research developments in medicine. Health care was becoming something the public wanted to pay for. The drug industry, the medical instrument companies, the computer companies, the for-profit hospital corporations, the insurance companies, the small research and development companies—all were fertile fields for investment. The last were particularly good for speculative investors. The risks were high but so were the returns.

Over the years Fred had developed his system of medical

information by cultivating his doctor customers. If a particular company was supposed to be readying a new product, Fred would go down the list of doctors and ask them what impact such a product would have. This give and take of information would be matched with the research department's assessment of the company itself. He would then call the doctors back with the company's official position. For penny stocks, Fred could not and did not make any recommendations; it was against company rules. In general, he avoided them anyway. But when he got strong tips from highly placed officers of medical establishments, he thought it was his duty to his customers to mention the possibility of a windfall. So it was with ATOCOR today.

There was no mention of the heart operation in the morning *Wall Street Journal*. The radio had carried a brief announcement but, as the local printers' strike continued, there was no newspaper coverage. Fred's route from his Russian Hill apartment to the Montogomery Street office was simple. He walked four blocks to Lombard Street and caught the number eight Muni bus, which carried him across town to the California Street cable car. A longish ride down California Street deposited him a block away from his office at 6:30 A.M.

As expected, when Fred got to his desk, the phone started to ring. There were two peak periods in his day for calls from his doctor customers. From 6:30 to 7:30 A.M. the surgeons called in to discuss their positions before going into surgery. From 8:30 to 9 A.M. it was the internists' turn to check in before their first office appointments.

"Hello, Hull here."

"Hi, Fred. This is James Tucker."

"Oh, Dr. Tucker. How are you?"

"Fine, Fred. I see Syntex has closed up a point. What's your advice?"

Fred ran his fingers down over a black-and-white computer terminal. In five seconds it flashed up on a dark blue screen the summary of James Tucker's account. "You have four hundred shares at forty-six. The close yesterday was fifty-three and five-eighths. You bought four point five months ago. Doctor, we think the one pill a month contraceptive they introduced last year is now catching on in terms of sales. We believe the stock will hit the seventy to eighty range by the end of the second quarter. Also you have one point five months before the capital gains deadline. Our advice is to hold."

"You got any tips, Fred?"

"Have you heard about the artificial heart?"

"No."

"I heard yesterday that Aspermont Medical Center was putting one in. This morning it was announced on the radio. It's a bit too early to tell, but it seems the surgery was successful."

"What's the gimmick?"

"A company in Berkeley, ATOCOR, is manufacturing the heart."

"Is it public? What do you think?"

Fred became cautious. "Doctor, the company's public. I have to tell you I can't solicit purchases on this company. It's over the counter and selling at two and a half."

"I can ask you about it, can't I? Ha, ha!"

"Of course. Ask me about the company."

"Okay. Tell me about ATOCOR."

"The company was formed six years ago. It manufactured atom-powered pacemakers. Its earnings doubled every year until last year. General Electric announced a cheap ten-year chemical battery for use in pacemakers. It competed very well and eventually wiped them out. The company got support from the government when it went in on a joint venture with Aspermont on the artificial heart. The stock collapsed, of course."

"You know, Fred, I don't know that much about artificial hearts. I'm a gynecologist, but my buddy, Brad Warren, is sitting right here in the dressing room with me just chomping at the bit to talk to you. Let me have you tell him about ATOCOR. Ol' Brad is a thoracic surgeon, you know, and he might be interested. Here, Brad, here's your chance to make your second million! Talk to old Fred on the phone."

"Okay, Fred. What's this about a hot stock?"

Fred changed his computer display to Dr. Bradford Warren.

Brad Warren was well known to Fred for more than his stock dealings. Warren had burst onto the San Francisco scene ten years earlier as the society cardiac surgeon. He was competent, his mortality rates were respectable, his personality and looks devastatingly attractive to women. Through these female contacts, the middle-aged husbands afflicted with coronary heart disease were referred to Warren. He was shrewd in setting up his operations at a nonuniversity-affiliated hospital. The competition for beds was nil, and any potentially difficult complications were sent to Aspermont, the University of California, or Stanford where "the research on your problem or disease is being done."

Warren was working on his third wife in seven years and he was frequently pictured in the society pages in his foreign car, his yacht on San Francisco Bay, or in his penthouse apartment on Telegraph Hill. Once he had showed up at a dress ball in tuxedo and pearl-handled revolvers. He was Oklahoma born and bred.

In response to Fred's mention of ATOCOR, Brad Warren challenged, "What! You're selling that dog of a stock again? You know I got out of it when it was twenty. What makes you think it's any good?"

Hull outlined the information again, suggesting the source without actually naming it. "Dr. Warren, have you done any heart transplants? How will they affect the continued development of artificial hearts?"

Warren chewed on an unseen toothpick as he contemplated the questions and financial possibilities. "You say there was only radio coverage of the operation this morning?"

"As far as I know."

"And no mention has been made of ATOCOR?"

"Not yet."

"Well, here's what I think. Bradfield's going to have a tough time bucking the establishment on artificial heart transplantation. It's going as well as one might hope. So it'll take at least a year or two before somebody else picks up the procedure. I'd be wary about that. If this heart works—and that's a big if—it'll shoot the hell out of human heart transplantation because of the donor problem. There have never been enough donors and the operation so far has depended on a whim of fate, bringing the patient needing a heart and a dead person together in the same place at the same time. The government is going to have to subsidize the gadget. I know what the price of plutonium is from the last time I was in ATOCOR. It's one thousand bucks a gram. Worth more than gold and silver combined. So I don't think there's a long-term future in it at all."

Warren's Oklahoma drawl made the "at" into two syllables and the "all" into three. "On the other hand, Fred, old boy, you can't invest in a heart transplant company. How much was the asking price yesterday—two?"

"Yes."

"And I assume you'll mention this company to a select few before the news gets around?"

"That's right."

"Then I'll take five thousand at the market. How about you, Tucker?

"Fred, Tucker says he wants two hundred shares—a real conservative! Keep me informed."

Fred Hull continued similar conversations throughout the morning. The movement of the stock was noticed all over the financial district and by the satellite brokers in the smaller towns. It sent the brokers and business editors scurrying to their records to find out just what kind of a company ATOCOR was. No one understood it, except the select few, until the TV programs were interrupted by the 10:00 A.M. news conference live from the Aspermont campus. By that time the price of ATOCOR stock had climbed to four and three-quarters. It would continue climbing faster for the rest of the day.

So the stock market was good to Fred, and Fred was good to his customers. These were straight honest business deals.

Bradfield sat alone in his office. He was about to let Cibelli know that he was in the hospital. The lights were on and he suspected Valerie Rigg had already arrived. He thought she had gone down to the coffee room, then he heard a motley blend of strangely accented voices from around the bend in the corridor. Bradfield waited curiously until he realized the sounds were coming from a Japanese surgeon, Akobi Tanaka, and his entourage. Of course! This was the day the visiting team from Japan was to present itself. Bradfield smiled broadly. He certainly had something to show his visitors. Tanaka would beam at being the first on the scene of such an historic event.

Valerie appeared at the door followed by the short, outgoing Tanaka.

"Ah, Dr. Bradfield." Tanaka walked in with his hand extended, brushing Valerie aside. She was immediately engulfed by the accompanying multitude. Relieved of the burden, she waved to Bradfield happily and backed off hurriedly to her own office.

Bradfield stood up as Tanaka introduced his colleagues. "Dr. Nishimura, my second-in-command."

A short, slim, white-haired man stepped out of the crowd and bowed. Bradfield offered his hand. Nishimura took it gently, and a camera clicked in the background. Nishimura stepped forward into the office to make room for the next man.

"Dr. Todeo Suzuki, my chief anesthesiologist."

One by one each visitor stepped forward as the ritual was repeated. Tanaka seemed oblivious to the fact that there wasn't enough room in the office for all the group. But it seemed more important that each one have a photograph of himself with Tanaka and Bradfield.

Bradfield held up his hand and suggested that they move to the departmental library. He indicated he would speak with them and that perhaps Dr. Tanaka could split up the party into smaller groups. Tanaka remained close to Bradfield while Valerie once again led the group down the hallway to the library.

In the library Bradfield took the initiative. "We welcome your distinguished group to Aspermont University, Dr. Tanaka, and we hope to have a mutually educational relationship. Miss Rigg has made appointments for your administrative people to meet with the hospital director and the director of nursing. Dr. Don Buchanan, my chief resident, is operating now in Room Thirteen. Perhaps you might send a small group to the operating theater now. The chiefs might be interested in a special case I did last night," Bradfield went on with a sense of the dramatic.

"Yes, please," Tanaka said. "We would be most appreciative if you would share your case with us."

"We implanted an artificial heart."

"In a patient?" Tanaka asked, his eyebrows rising.

"Yes, sir."

The Japenese were all thunderstruck when the translator repeated the announcement for them.

"Very exciting, Dr. Bradfield. Is the patient doing well?"

"Oh, yes. We can go over to see him later."

"On what principle does the heart work?"

"The heart itself consists of two sacs with a metallic core. The sacs are driven hydraulically with a miniaturized steam engine. The excess heat is circulated through the heart and transferred to the blood. The patient then dissipates the heat."

"There are no outside power connections?"

"No, we use atomic fuel. We have a hundred grams of plutonium with a half-life of eighty-seven years in the capsule."

The audience was electrified. They spoke rapidly with each other in Japanese. A young man, about two-thirds of the way in the back, stood up and, after a brief bow, spoke to Tanaka. Even to Bradfield, it was clear that the tones of the man's voice were sharper and harsher than normal. He spoke rapidly for a minute, then sat down, his eyes narrowed, a pulse visibly beating in his neck. His face was immobile as perceived by Western eyes.

Tanaka was apologetic as he faced Bradfield. "I'm sorry for the bad interruption," he said. "I must explain that Dr. Kimura was, shall I say, quite excited about the use of atomic fuel. There is a certain segment of people in my country who do not, shall I say, like nuclear power. Dr. Kimura was born in Nagasaki. Let me say he expressed some very strong thoughts. I'm afraid, for very stupid reasons, your invention will raise great controversy among some people in Japan. Dr. Kimura also asked a question on how you propose to safeguard the fuel from hazardous use."

Bradfield described the containment design and testing that the device had been put through. Tanaka was still effusively apologetic at the behavior of one of his group. Bradfield accepted his apologies with grace, but he knew a simple little victory had slipped away. The power of nuclear fission had been introduced to the Japanese people in a horrible way. It would take more than an atomic-powered artificial heart to overcome the terrible trauma of August 1945.

Valerie Rigg interrupted the questioning by telling Bradfield that Jerry Cibelli was waiting. He asked Valerie to escort the Japanese surgeons to the operating room.

Chapter 19

The mild spring sunshine fell on the isolated temporary building. The focus of activity in Bradfield's experimental surgery was now and forever shifted to the human scene—to the hospital. The lab where the basic experiments were carried out, where young medical talent had worked long hours, would soon be abandoned. No plaque would mark the spot where the first living thing had survived for a significant time with an atomic heart.

Three people walked around the outside of the chain-link and barbed-wire fence until they reached the unlocked gate. They walked down the soft, muddy walkway. The cameraman had difficulty carrying his heavy equipment and keeping his balance.

Elaine Whitmore directed the filming to begin.

"Get a shot of the weeds, the mud, and swing over to an overall view of the two wings of the building."

They came closer and up the long ramp to the first wing entrance. They saw a cow standing peacefully in a stall chewing her cud.

"Get a close-up of that cow. It'll be pretty good."

"The light's a little low in here."

"Tim, get the lights."

"Still not enough."

"Okay, cut. Let's go into the other area."

The three came upon Richard Wheeler. He was in his surgical suit wearing a black rubber apron and red rubber overshoes. He stood in front of a 350-pound black-and-white calf, strung up with the rear hooves tied to a block and tackle attached to the ceiling. It was evident he was eviscerating the carcass with an eight-inch hunting knife. The guts were held in a large plastic garbage sack. Red congealing blood dripped on to the unprotected floor. The foul air assaulted their nostrils.

Richard looked up from his task. Hickman had seen murders and beatings but was unprepared for a sight like this. He felt nauseated and had an urge to throw up.

"Hi," said Richard.

"Hello," Whitmore said. "Is this part of the artificial heart project?"

"Yes, ma'am. This animal lived six months, but we had to kill it off last night for the fuel."

"What do you mean?"

"Well, we had to get the fuel, the plutonium, out of this animal to put in the patient."

"Why?"

"I don't know, just had to."

"Didn't you have fuel for the human case?"

"I don't know. I just take it out and put it where I'm told."

"What are you doing now?"

"I'm going to take the meat and freeze it."

"That animal?"

"Do it all the time. Tastes real good in barbecue. You can also use the hide for leather."

"Is it safe—the meat, I mean?"

"Sure—okay. Saves money, too."

"Would you like to be on TV?"

"Sure. Why not?"

"Turn the operating room lights on. That will give us enough light."

The cameraman proceeded to his picture-taking with a good view of the split-open calf in the background.

"Need some action. Go on skinning the calf."

"Skin the calf? Sure."

Wheeler deftly and expertly ripped the hide off the subcutaneous tissue with his right hand, while slicing with the exceedingly sharp knife in his left. He didn't buttonhole the leather to preserve its saleable value, but he did make a minor knick in the skin between his right thumb and forefinger. It seemed as though he was being more careful with the carcass than with his own person.

"Be careful, there!"

"Oh, it don't hurt—got myself good a couple of times already."

"Thanks, I think we've got enough here. What's your name?"

"I'm Richard Wheeler."

"Okay, Richard. You might be on TV tonight. Six-thirty on Channel Thirteen. Be watching."

"You bet. Thanks a lot."

The trio stepped back out into the now bright, cold sunlight, the sky so bright a blue it hurt their eyes.

"God!" Hickman said. "Let me have a cigareete. It was really putrid in there. I don't see how that guy stands it." To Whitmore, "We can't use that stuff. Why did you take it?"

"For two reasons. We may do a special on this some day, and we should have it for the record. You'd never be able to get it again. The second reason is the university doesn't know we won't use it, and they won't want us to use it. We can talk them into trading an exclusive interview with Bradfield, the patient, or the girl friend, or all of them. No harm trying."

"Pretty crafty, Whitmore, Pretty crafty! Let's get a hold of their flack—what's his name?"

"Cibelli?"
"Yes, Cibelli.'

Jerry Cibelli was closeted with Bradfield in the surgeon's office going over the details of a carefully worded press release:

FOR IMMEDIATE RELEASE:

Aspermont—March 24, 1976. Aspermont medical scientists Wednesday night successfully implanted for the first time an artificial heart into the chest of a 43-year-old California man.

The patient is Henry Gray, a computer specialist from Menlo Park. He received the new heart in a four-hour-and-fifteen-minute operation performed by a team led by Dr. William Bradfield.

Bradfield, also 43, is professor and chief of cardiovascular surgery at the center. He perfected the techniques which made artificial hearts possible.

He was assisted in the operation by Dr. Donald Buchanan and Dr. Jack Johnson, surgical residents; Dr. James Takaoka, associate professor of anesthesia; and Washington Belknap, a medical student.

Gray suffered from severe and irreversible heart disease.

In the operation, Gray's ailing heart was removed and replaced by a six-pound nuclear-powered engine the size of a fist.

"The artificial heart is basically a miniaturized blood pump," explained Bradfield. "Its job is to maintain the flow of blood and consequently life itself."

Bradfield stressed that the patient would have died within 24 hours if the heart had not been replaced. He had been studied elsewhere for heart transplantation, but was not considered a suitable candidate.

The surgeon said the operation is the culmination of approximately 12 years of laboratory work here at Aspermont.

The heart is totally implantable. It was designed and built

by Aspermont biomedical scientists in collaboration with two private companies. The work was supported by grants from the National Heart Institute.

Unlike earlier experimental models, the heart has no power or control lines leaving or entering the body. This is made possible by use of nuclear fuel encapsulated in the patient's body.

The nuclear fuel used to power the heart is Plutonium 238, a man-made transuranium element incorporated into the machine with a half-life of 87 years. Plutonium produces energy by nuclear fission, giving off alpha particles consisting of two neutrons and two protons. The alpha particles have a short range and do not penetrate to the outside of the body. When they collide with matter, heat is produced.

In the artificial heart, this heat is used to drive a miniature steam engine which runs on a drop of water. Heat increases the temperature to 1200 degrees Fahrenheit, but is insulated from the patient by a triple layer, vacuum-foil insulation, a technique developed for space exploration.

"The steam-type engine devised for the heart would be barely recognizable to the engineer of a locomotive or a steamboat of another era," Bradfield explained. "It produces no huge rushes of hot steam."

On signal from a computer, two magnets cause a miniature bellows to expand, pushing a drop of water from a reservoir up through a narrow column into a boiler. There the drop of water becomes steam. The steam expands and pushes down on another tiny bellows. This bellows activates a piston which forces hydraulic fluid out through a feedline. That causes other bellows to expand. The action compresses the ventricles and makes the blood move. As soon as the blood is pushed out, a sensor in the heart gives a signal, everything reverses itself, pressure drops back down again, and all is ready for the next stroke.

A big problem engineers had to face in designing the artificial heart was that hot steam could raise the temperature of the heart pump itself. The engineers had an answer to this problem: they designed a metal heat-exchanging system onto the pump. The metal transfers the pump's excess heat directly into the blood as it rushes by. Like the water in the radiator of the car, the blood dissipates the heat throughout the body, preventing any one spot from getting hot.

The body's built-in temperature control mechanisms—the most familiar of which is sweating—take over at that point to dispel the excess heat.

"The artificial heart was developed as an alternative to heart transplants," said Bradfield. "These have several drawbacks for general use, the main objection being that the organ must come from a dying patient. In addition, complications of drug treatment for rejection are still a big problem."

With the successful implant, surgeons say the chances of meeting the crisis of the epidemic of deaths from heart attacks appear brighter. A total of 50,000 Americans in the prime of life could be saved each year if artificial heart replacement were available.

Initially, artificial hearts are expected to cost more than $30,000, but eventually experts believe they can be produced economically. This will be possible when nuclear power plants using breeder-reactors will begin to produce plutonium in large quantities. Many such power plants are now under construction throughout the world.

Plutonium has been used as a power source in other projects, most notably for the Apollo space flight series. Plutonium is highly toxic. But in an accident, both the patient and others will be protected because the plutonium container has been built and tested to withstand all conceivable accidents.

A press conference is scheduled at 10:00 A.M. Thursday in Room 506.

END. For further information contact Jerry Cibelli—426-9000.

Bradfield read the release carefully.

"Fine, Jerry. If anything I'd take out the phrase 'plutonium is highly toxic.' There's no use scaring anybody. And delete the paragraph about costs. There's no point raising this issue now. Also, can you add that international attention has already been drawn to this technique by the visiting delegation of Japanese surgeons this morning?"

"I could work more things in, sure. But this is ready to be printed and distributed. It would work to your disadvantage if it wasn't ready for handing out at the conference. You'll get a chance to talk about it at the meeting."

"Okay. Just black out the toxic bit and the one about costs. You have to do that."

Valerie Rigg appeared at the door.

"Dean Geld's secretary just phoned and asked that you meet with the Dean about the events of last night. Ridley registered a formal complaint. She said if you give Dr. Geld time, he can arrange a meeting with a couple of members of the executive committee to clear up the situation."

"Okay. Tell him one o'clock."

"Right."

"Jerry," continued Valerie, "there's a message that Jim Hickman is en route to your office and would like to see you."

"Thanks, I'll be right down."

"And Dr. Bradfield, the O.R. phoned to say that your first case is on the table. By the way, Jerry, I just noticed you didn't mention how the patient was doing in your press release," Valerie said.

"Oh, yes. Just how's the patient doing, Dr. Bradfield?"

"Hey, I forgot that myself. He's doing well. Let's say condition is stable. We've got to remember not to get all excited about the device and forget the patient!"

"One more thing, Dr. Bradfield. Ronald Harris phoned in. Said he was in town and wanted to see you. I told him you would be tied up. He said he wanted to sleep in this morning, but then he got terribly excited when I mentioned the press conference. He wants to be there."

"He'd better be there!" Bradfield interjected.

" . . . and Bethesda has been on the phone. The office of the acting head of the Heart Institute called. They wanted to know if this was one of their sponsored projects. They were put out about not being contacted on publicity plans. They also asked if we knew where Harris was. At that time I didn't."

"Well, the press release isn't out yet, so they don't have a gripe," said Cibelli. "The feds are a pain in the ass when it comes down to who gets the credit, but I'll give them a call. I've got to get moving. Any last questions about the conference?"

"No, that's all," said Bradfield.

Cibelli went out the door on the run. He was visibly excited by the enormous dimensions of the response to the operation, the newsworthiness of the moment, and his awesome responsibility in reporting one of the greatest medical achievements the world had ever known.

Janet Chen was allowed into Gray's room at 8:30 A.M. The nurses said she could only stay ten minutes. They wanted to get their routine chores done. The patient's intravenous lines needed to be replaced. Blood had to be drawn for testing. They watched him carefully as they gave him a toothbrush, shaved him gently, then washed his face, combed his hair, and tucked him back under the white, sterile sheets. He was fatigued.

Janet wore a white paper cap over her hair. A paper filter mask covered her nose and mouth and a lead apron had been placed over her dress. On top of that, a nurse had helped her tie a sterile cotton gown. She had on paper booties. She entered the anteroom, washed her hands with germicidal soap, then stepped into Gray's room.

His eyes were closed and he breathed shallowly. A fine stream of oxygen flowed in through his nostrils. The vacuum still bubbled through the Pleurevac. The constant popping sounds filled the otherwise quiet room.

Janet stood at the foot of the bed. She did not wish to wake him if he needed to sleep, but she wanted so much to talk to him. He had been in a semicoma for a long time before the operation. When she had visited him the night before, he had not recovered from the anesthetic.

The nurse nodded sympathetically. "He's doing magnificently. I don't think he's fully asleep."

Janet said quietly, "Hello, Hank."

Gray's eyes opened. He had heard his name. He couldn't focus as yet on the blue-clad masked figure at the foot of the bed. But Janet's soft, familiar voice had penetrated the foggy veil. To him, the sound was unmistakable. The pieces fell into place and his eyes focused. He could now recognize the dark almond-shaped eyes smiling at him over the mask.

He croaked in a husky voice "Hi, Jan," and raised his taped right hand in a wan greeting. Yet another intravenous solution was flowing into him. The nurses had taped his hand to a solid base to immobilize it so that the needle would not accidentally fall out of the vein. He felt the warmth of Janet's hand. She touched him on his forearm in a gentle reminder not to move. The tapes, the bottles, the paraphernalia of nursing care were familiar to her from long experience and training. Indeed, she viewed the scene with a professional eye. The nurses assigned to Gray were young and eager, and quite sharp. She was thankful for that. Janet moved more confidently. She could read the signs she saw much better than the ordinary visitor. They were good. She urged him not to talk.

The visit passed all too quickly. She was reminded that the ten minutes were up. She told him that the vital signs were good, that the operation had passed quickly. She told him that Bradfield was confident of the course he had taken. Then, not able to hug or kiss him, she touched her fingers to her mask and blew him a gentle kiss.

"I'll be in my apartment for a short while. I'll see you at the next visiting period. Bye-bye, love," she said cheerily.

Janet stepped out of the door and removed the hot, moist encumbrances of isolation. She shook her coal black hair free from under the cap and breathed in the dry air of the hospital. Then, alone in the waiting room, she sat down. Tears welled up in her eyes and her body shook with sobbing as relief came from long-built-up tension.

Chapter 20

Cibelli picked up Bradfield at his office on the way to the medical school auditorium.

"Ready to go?" Jerry asked.

"Let's do it."

"By the way, Jim Hickman of WNTL-TV met me just a while ago. He said they would like to have an interview with you. Somehow, they seemed confident you wouldn't refuse. I told them I'd have to ask you—you're so busy."

"It's up to you, Jerry. You know these guys better than I do. We have to get the widest possible public exposure about the importance of this procedure and its ramifications."

"Well, I agree. I have to tell you, though, that things haven't started too well in that regard. Some exploration by Hickman and his crew led them out to your animal lab. The gates weren't locked, so they went in."

"Hmmm?" Bradfield listened as they strolled out the door to the courtyard in front of the auditorium.

"They went right into the operating room," Cibelli continued.

"Nothing wrong with that yet."

Bradfield and Cibelli went into the auditorium. It seemed as though miles of cable had been laid down. Banks of lights were strewn helter-skelter about the room. The babble of private conversation among the reporters and interested observers held constant at a moderately dull roar. Bradfield was unrecognized. There was a scattering of white coats about, interested spectators—doctors, nurses, and medical nursing students.

Cibelli went on with the conversation. "Your man, the technician—"

"Richard Wheeler."

"Yes. He was butchering a cow strung up from the ceiling. He told them a bit about the setup out there."

"Oh, for crying out loud! All the gory details, I suppose."

"Wheeler let them take pictures."

"Damn. How responsible a person is Hickman?"

"I've never worked with him. He's on the courthouse and police beat mostly. I don't know. In any event, they—Hickman and his producer, Elaine Whitmore—want to trade for an interview with you."

Bradfield shrugged off the problem. "Well, it doesn't make any difference. It's not much to hold over us, but I'd be glad to do the interview anyway, right after the press conference."

"Fine."

They reached the front of the auditorium. Cibelli stepped to the miniature forest of microphones at the podium. One after another the TV lights were turned on. An eerie brightness filled the large room and soon Cibelli felt the heat rising. A fine perspiration broke out on his face.

"Ladies and gentlemen."

The babble hushed slightly. Cibelli squinted into the blue haze of tobacco smoke. Several photographers clicked the shutters of their cameras. Many of them, laden down with multiple cameras, crowded up to the front to get shots from all conceivable angles. A chorus of "down in the front" rose as the more aggressive photographers ignored the viewing angles of those behind them. The jostling increased. A paper missile flew from out of the audience with well-practiced aim. It hit its target, the shiny bald head of a tall fellow standing just in front of the podium. Laughter and applause greeted the expletive that shot out as the man returned instantly to a kneeling position.

"Ladies and gentlemen, and I use both terms advisedly after that display," he began again. "I'm Jerry Cibelli. The press release has been distributed at the door. I will read a brief statement now for the national television audience. Dr. William Bradfield will be available to answer questions."

There was a rustling sound as the reporters looked around and camermen pointed their wheeled instruments down to the front row, where Bradfield was sitting. Very few of them knew who Bradfield was as yet.

Cibelli read the statement rapidly. Then he asked Bradfield to come to the podium. As Bradfield stepped up to the platform, another figure appeared and took up position directly in front of the podium. It was Irwin Geld. Cibelli saw him approach and quickly covered by introducing the Dean as well.

The two doctors stood together in front of the bunched microphones. Geld almost instantly broke out in a fine sweat from the heat of the TV lights. Bradfield remained cool, inured by years of tight situations under the operating room lights. Geld, rather aggressively, began to talk.

"Everyone is waiting for Dr. Bradfield, so I won't take up more time than a commercial—a minute or two. Today we are all proud of the surgical feat achieved by our dedicated team of surgeons and nurses. Their achievement offers great promise for the multitudes dying of heart disease. With this demonstration, I have faith that the Federal government will continue to generously support medical research and education. The research which led up to this historic operation could not have been carried out without the superb facilities you see around you. So I say again, the people of America will be grateful to the farsighted men and women whose vision founded and supported this medical school. Of course, we can't claim all the credit for this breakthrough into the nuclear age of medicine. We must recognize the company ATOCOR for manufacturing the heart and Zee Electronics for the control system; and of course our little sister institution to the north, the Menlo Institute, for designing some of the electronic parts. This was a venture carried out in the true spirit of free enterprise."

Geld wanted to continue when he noticed that the cameras had been turned off. "Well, I've taken enough of your time. We're glad that you're all here, and of course we're happy that the nation can view this announcement of remarkable scientific achievement. I'm sorry, but I have an important meeting now, and will not be able to answer any questions. Dr. Bradfield here will fill in most ably, I'm sure."

Looking directly into the TV cameras, which had been turned on at the mention of Bradfield's name, Geld swept his arms up in a wave and said "Goodbye."

Bradfield stepped up to the microphones.

"Good morning, ladies and gentlemen," he said, quietly and calmly. "We certainly appreciate the kind words of Dr. Geld. I've no further statement to make. Would you like to start the questions?" He pointed to a young man sitting in the front row with his hand up and waving.

"Thank you, Dr. Bradfield. I'm Tom Hammer, the *Aspermont Prowler.* In the press release you say this is a clinical trial. What do you mean? It suggests a euphemism for human experiment. Have you really worked out the details completely in animals? Isn't this more of a stunt than, as Dean Geld said, a 'remarkable achievement'?"

Bradfield thought it was astonishing that the youngest reporter in the room, and from the student paper at that, should ask the tough questions first.

"The decision to perform any operation places great responsibility on the surgeon. This responsibility weighs even more heavily when the operation is new and hasn't been performed before. I don't believe that because a patient has a fatal disease, he's fair game for any ludicrous medical plan. In this instance, however, the patient's outlook was indeed grim.

His heart stopped before we got to the operation. It was that desperate. So the need for surgery was certainly there. I won't take the time to outline fully the experimental work that preceded this implantation. You can look it up in the literature. But I can point out that many experimental operations have been successfully completed. By successful, I mean over six months of trouble-free performance after the surgery. The data from these trials have been published. And there was agreement both by the Federal government and our committee for research in human subjects that the heart was ready for human trial. I'll admit there's an element of human experimentation in the term 'clinical trial,' but I hope we won't quibble over semantics. Will we, Mr. Hammer?"

The young reporter glanced up from his notepad and agreed with a nod, realizing his rather brash attitude.

"Jack Hewitt, ABC News, Dr. Bradfield."

"Yes, sir?"

"We're interested in the comparison between the practicality of your device and the heart transplant operation. Do you think it will replace human heart transplantation?"

"Heart transplants are already an established procedure, but the success rate is still only seventy percent at one year because of rejection. In addition, despite the recognition of brain death as legal in California and other states, there aren't enough donors. Consequently, heart transplants aren't going to be of much help to the large number of people dying from heart disease. Artificial hearts, mass-produced with, shall I say, America's genius for such things, can surely solve that problem. Before I let that go, however, I should emphasize that the best way to reduce mortality and increase productivity is to prevent heart disease. But arteriosclerosis is a multifactorial disease and its prevention isn't yet within our grasp. Until that halcyon day then, we must be prepared to treat the disease. And another thing. Some of us feel that medicine should increase the numbers of healthy, productive people. For every heart transplant, another person must die. The mathematics of that situation is inescapable—it's one for one."

"But, doctor, what do you mean by multifactorial?"

"I apologize for my use of medical jargon. A multifactorial disease is one in which several factors have been shown to play some part in its development. In the case of hardening of the arteries, these include overeating, underexercising, type of person, smoking, and stressful situations. In addition, one other cause for coronary artery disease includes strep throat."

"Thank you."

"Robert Ronsard, *Paris-Match*, Dr. Bradfield."

"Yes?"

"We heard the first heart transplant patients suffered from severe psychotic reactions. Do you expect this to occur with a mechanical heart?" The questioner was a thin man with a heavy French accent.

"There was no connection between psychiatric problems and heart transplants. That was in fact an aberration of the press. Any normal patient is subject to strange behavior under stress. Open heart surgery is no picnic. I'd therefore expect some psychological stress reactions in patients undergoing heart replacement."

"But," the reporter persisted, "at least in heart transplants the heart's from a living thing, a warm human being. This thing you've put in, it's an inanimate object—a pump. Won't Mr. Gray have mental confusion, thinking of himself as an amalgam of man and machine?"

"I don't see any choice for the patient other than death. Perhaps you can worry about that point for him while he enjoys life!"

There was a smattering of laughter from the audience, but the reporter pursued his point. "How soon do you expect Mr. Gray to resume normal activities?"

"I expect him to be out of the hospital in ten days! This is in contrast to heart transplants, which require four to six weeks of intensive care to combat rejection and other complications."

"Doctor, my question meant his sex life. What about that?"

"No comment. May I have other questions, please?"

Several reporters asked for recognition simultaneously.

Bradfield scanned up and around. The crowd was now larger as more curious spectators from the medical center staff sprinkled themselves among the working press. The pall of cigarette smoke still hung in the air. The lively scene was beamed instantaneously across the country and by satellite around the world.

In Los Angeles, Jack Comstock, M.D., Chief of Surgery at California College of Medicine, was about to cross Figeroa Street to the Faculty Club, a plush, elegant California-Spanish-type building. A resident from his team came running up.

"Dr. Comstock. An artificial heart was implanted last night in a patient at Aspermont!"

Comstock looked at the thin dark-skinned man in disbelief. The resident was from India, one of many foreign medical graduates flocking to places like Comstock's for their post-graduate training. He spoke in a clipped British accent.

"Surely, you must have that wrong. Dr. Singh. Nobody's close to putting artificial hearts in yet."

"But, sir. There's a television news show going on at this very moment."

"What channel?"

"All three networks," Dr. Singh continued in his musically inflected voice. "Come and see, come and see."

"Thank you, Dr. Singh, but I'll watch it over at the club."

Comstock walked away from Singh with measured steps, but when the resident had disappeared into the hospital, he began walking as fast as possible to the game room of the Faculty Club. There, in the quiet of the oak-paneled room, he turned on the TV set and watched with envy.

Another question was directed to Bradfield. "We know an open heart operation is quite delicate surgery. Is the artificial heart also so delicate? I mean, stuffing all these parts into the chest cavity. There doesn't seem to be enough room."

"Good question! Let me explain the technique that permits us to implant this machine. When a natural heart becomes damaged and weak, it compensates by enlarging. Mr. Gray's heart was enlarged tremendously. When it was removed it left ample space for the pumping part of the new heart. I used a technique that had escaped the notice of other surgeons interested in this field. The breastbone is of structural importance only. I redesigned the pump so that the controls and power supply are in the shape of the breastbone. I attached the rib ends to this new package. This gives us considerably more room in front of the patient to fit everything in. Putting in an artificial heart doesn't have the same esthetic quality of other types of heart surgery, but it's effective. "

Roy Turner, the *Herald*'s correspondent, caught Bradfield's attention as he stood up. He was a man with graying short hair and pinched-in cheeks who looked as though he were perpetually on the brink of starvation. He was a scholarly, experienced science reporter, and had attended the news conference out of personal interest—the *Herald*'s printers were still on strike.

"Dr. Bradfield, first I would offer my apologies for the rather boorish behavior of some of my colleagues."

"Thanks, Mr. Turner. No apologies needed."

"As I understand the heart research field, the major advance is in the power source. Kolff of Utah has reported survival of calves with a plastic heart in which the driving source was compressed air."

"That is correct, Mr. Turner. Kolff showed that the pumping mechanism itself was reliable in long-term experimental animals. The system required the heart to be connected to a tank of compressed air, which weighs quite a lot. So it's patently impractical for patients to live with long connecting hoses to compressed air sources."

"So the problem really has been in developing long-term implantable power sources?"

"Yes."

"Isn't it true that plutonium is quite expensive? To me, this argues against the possibility you propose of mass-producing the artificial heart. I understand the cost for medical grade plutonium is $1,000 per gram. Given that your device requires one hundred grams of plutonium in it, I calculate that the cost for the fuel alone is $100,000 per implant. Would you please comment?"

"Your figures are correct. These are the points we considered. Medical history has shown it's far more expensive to treat disease than to prevent it. This is another example of that dictum. The human heart is simple, yet the technological problems to simulate its reliability and efficiency have been immense. Nevertheless, we can't do less than try to treat the individual patient as he comes to us."

"Do you recommend that other U.S. medical centers now do the procedure?"

"I'm glad you asked that question, Mr. Turner. I think the number of clinical trials should be limited. We believe, of course, that for the sake of good surgery, adequate followup and so on, this center should be the only one to carry out the several implants required for the initial trial period. As for the long-term results, the half-life of plutonium is eighty-seven years—longer than the expected life-span of several patients put together. Our fiscal consultants suggest the cost could be amortized over that entire period. So we're talking about $100,000 divided by eighty-seven years, or about $1,000 per year plus interest. Now I don't think this would be an outrageous price to pay and it could be distributed among several patients."

A voice came out of the crowd. "Then you expect your patients to die pretty quickly?"

"The artificial heart certainly doesn't confer immortality! But I do want to finish my response to Mr. Turner. Even that modest cost will be diminished in the near future. I'm told that the plutonium supply will increase with the construction of breeder nuclear reactors. The first ones are scheduled to go into operation in four years."

"Dr. Bradfield, are you tying the artificial heart project to the nuclear power controversy?"

"No, not at all. The breeder reactors being built to supplant the nation's electric power needs will generate plutonium. The artificial heart project can use it. That is the only tie. I see in the audience Dr. Ronald Harris, Project Manager for the National Heart Institute. He's a physicist and my close collaborator. I would like to ask him to come down here to answer some of these technical and political questions on plutonium."

Harris was sitting in the third seat from the aisle at the top of the auditorium. He had been waiting for recognition from Bradfield. His walk down the steps to the platform was surprisingly light considering his lack of sleep. His bearing was erect, his walk sprightly. He went over to the microphones with a confident smile. His nervous tic had disappeared.

Chapter 21

"Dr. Comstock, you have a telephone call from your secretary."

The well-dressed, clean-cut young man stood next to Comstock's easy chair as he sat watching the television set intently.

"Thanks. Will you bring in an extension phone, please?"

"Yes, sir."

" . . . and a gin and tonic, too."

"Yes, sir."

The faculty club of the California College of Medicine was well appointed, and had the air of an elegant, old-fashioned men's club. In a crowded urban area like Los Angeles, the club permitted a low-cost sense of exclusiveness for the more society-minded members of the faculty. Comstock, being a fifty-six-year-old bachelor, enjoyed the camaraderie among his fellow members.

"Dr. Comstock, this is Helen. We've been deluged with calls. All about the artificial heart operation at Aspermont."

"Who are the callers?"

"Well, our news service, for one. The campus newspaper for another. And *Newsweek* and the *Los Angeles Times.*

That's just in the last ten minutes. They wanted your reaction to the operation."

"All right, tell them this. This is a magnificent accomplishment in the annals of cardiac surgery. A word of caution, however, must be sounded at this time. The widest possible experience must be gained by the leaders in this field before the device can be termed therapeutic. We hope this new heart machine will be made available to the larger medical centers in the United States as quickly as possible. This is particularly applicable since the Aspermont program is funded by the American taxpayer. I am calling for a national meeting to discuss how to implement this suggestion. I have just sent Dr. Bradfield a telegram congratulating him on his work. Got all that?"

"Yes."

"All right, then send a flowery telegram of praise to Bradfield and get our news service to call me over here. Oh, yes, and in about fifteen minutes get the Senator on the phone. Okay?"

"Yes, I have it all."

"All right. I'm going to watch some more of this press conference."

When Comstock hung up, the young man slipped up to take the extension phone. Comstock waved him off.

"I expect another call."

"Yes, sir," he replied in a soft Filipino-tinged accent and glided quickly away.

It was not long before the news service did call.

"Dr. Comstock. We've been very busy flagging the calls. Do you want any other release or comment?"

"Yes. Try to emphasize the amount of collaboration involved in the development of the heart. This isn't the work of one laboratory. The problems were of such magnitude they could not be solved by a single institution or agency. Nor could they be solved by a single industry. This was a prime example of group research. The California College of Medicine has been one of the leaders in it right from the start."

Comstock spoke to give the impression that he was rather ticked off to have Bradfield, a newcomer in the field, swipe away the first case. "What I wanted to talk to you about is that we need to get more exposure for our own artificial heart program."

"Uh, I thought we didn't have any calves alive with the engine in?"

"But we were very close. I'm sure it would have run in a patient. Humans are easier to operate on than calves. Humans will tell you if something's wrong."

"I suppose you're right, Dr. Comstock. I see what you mean."

"In any event, I'll be available if you receive any requests for interviews. Do you think some of the network shows like *Today* and *Tomorrow* might be interested?"

"I don't know. If they are, I'll let you know."

"I have another call coming in, so refer anything else to my secretary."

"Okay, and thanks, Dr. Comstock."

The young man came in again.

"No, no," Comstock said. "Just leave it here, will you. I'm going to get more calls. Bring me another gin and tonic."

"Yes, sir."

Comstock returned to the TV as Harris began to talk about liquid breeder reactors.

"Why, that weasely son-of-a-bitch!" Comstock exclaimed out loud to the empty room. "So it was he who let this happen."

The phone rang again. It was the Senator.

"Hello, this is Jack Comstock, Senator."

"Oh, yes, Jack. How are you?"

"Just fine, Senator. How's your daughter?"

"Doing very well. My wife and I are quite grateful to you, you know."

"One has to be very careful about lumps in the breast. My philosophy is to take out everything. No problem in trying to make a decision. Now, of course, we know the lump was indeed benign."

"We didn't know that breast lumps in a nineteen-year-old girl could be cancerous."

"Well, it's not common, but we can't be too sure about these things."

"Well, we're thankful that you did the operation, with all your heart surgery experience. What can I do for you today?"

"Senator, do you remember when we reviewed the programs for the artificial heart?"

"Yes, we had the Director of the Heart Institute on our appropriations committee carpet just about—what was it?—about three months ago. They've spent about twenty-five million dollars on that program and all they had was a couple of live cows. Can you imagine that!"

"Well, Senator, there have been a few shenanigans going on."

"How's that, Jack?"

"A surgeon has just put one in at Aspermont Medical Center."

"A California group?"

"Yes."

"Well, it's about time!"

"We think so, too, but there's going to be a problem. I heard they want a monopoly on the device until they complete a series of cases."

"That's outrageous! We funded that program for all the fifty states, for Americans here and abroad. What do you mean a monopoly?"

"The Aspermont group wants to limit the initial trials to their center for the time being. They claim it's good science to do so. I disagree violently. I think other leading centers should now be allowed to conduct trials. We should have the heart for clinical evaluation at our own hospital. Many patients in urban areas are in dire need of this device. It would, shall I say, be good for you if the people of Southern California were to be made aware of your role in the funding of this project. The best way, I think, is to have several patients done here at CCM walking around Los Angeles. Do you see?"

"Yes, I do, Jack, I certainly do. It's an excellent idea."

"Perhaps you could pass the word to the Heart Institute Director of your deep interest in this project? There's also a lower-echelon man named Harris. He's a career Federal employee. Perhaps you might just let him know also of your desire to have this device widely tested?"

"That'll be easy to do, Jack. Next year's budget has yet to be passed. They had better toe the line or they won't have so many toys to play with."

"Of course. You're right, Senator. Those basic scientists have had their field day far too long. They really have been gratifying themselves with a lot of expensive tools. I've long thought that applied research should be getting more emphasis."

"I'm glad to hear you doctors say that. I'll see what can be done about this. Regards to your wife and family, Jack. Goodbye."

"Goodbye, Senator."

Comstock sat back in the overstuffed chair, a slight smile on his face, and watched the remainder of the show from Aspermont.

Elizabeth Browning had slept late. She saw her daughter off to school and drove off to the laboratory at nine o'clock for a quick check. When she heard from Valerie Rigg about the press conference, she sped home and picked up her portable television set. Back at the laboratory, she set it up in the middle of the operating room.

Richard Wheeler had left behind quite a mess. He had taken away the butchered calf to his mother's freezer, intending to return and clean up later. Elizabeth busied herself with routine duties. She whistled contentedly, giving an ear and an eye now and then to the announcement of their success on television. She had never before felt this kind of glow, this participation in a major nationally recognized achievement. It was an unexpected bonus in her humdrum work-a-day life.

Wheeler, back from his personal trip, saw the television set and immediately sat down to watch.

"Hi, Elizabeth. Is that Dr. Bradfield's show you have on?"

"Yes, Richard. Richard, will you please get the blood off the floor and start pitching in with the instruments. Check them over. I taught my daughter to keep working and listen at the same time. You can do the same on company time."

"Okay, okay, Elizabeth. Will do." He turned to face her. "Elizabeth, won't you ever come off your high horse with me, even today?"

"Richard, when you learn to work efficiently, I'll be much kinder to you."

"I don't think you'll be satisfied until I'm gone. Why can't you treat me like a man? I'm twenty-one now—an adult," he said and shook his head in frustration.

"Just mop up the floor, Richard. Just mop the damn floor and put on some gloves to protect those cuts on your hands."

Richard ignored her and lackadaisically began to swab down the floor. The argument had taken the edge off the morning for him. The excitement of the operation, his own role in it, being on television, had all been dashed by this tough, efficient woman who refused to acknowledge his maturity and experience.

Elizabeth continued her work, listening contentedly.

In San Francisco, in a small coffee and doughnut shop, Daniel Cooper watched the press conference in progress with intense interest.

Six months had passed since he had lost his case. After leaving Aspermont, it had been all downhill. Cooper was decidedly ill. He had no job, and employers avoided him because he was a poor insurance risk. A trick of fate so sudden and so absurd, he couldn't believe it was happening. Finally, he had found temporary work for $1.70 an hour at a private school. From a nuclear technician's job to a crummy little backwater job in several months. In rare moments, when his objectivity prevailed over his physical pain and mental anguish, he would accept his fate and try to live with his cancer as best as he could. In less objective moments, however, which were more frequent, he blamed the university and its slick city lawyers for the result. He knew he was right.

On the TV screen above the counter Harris was now answering a reporter's question. Cooper guessed the reporter had caught Harris off-guard because he leaned toward Bradfield and sought consultation. Bradfield looked back and talked quickly in Harris's ear.

"You're correct, Mr. Turner," Harris said. "Plutonium is dangerous. Inhaled accidentally it could cause lung cancer. But in the artificial heart, the plutonium is well protected against accidental opening. The fuel is pressed into a tight disclike shape. It's not a powder. So if it's opened, it won't fly into the atmosphere. The container is designed to withstand any conceivable accident. The manufacture of the capsule is subject to stringent regulation by the Atomic Energy Commission. Moreover, the AEC believes, on the basis of present data, that even if the fuel capsule were to be breached, there's little likelihood of a significant event involving numbers of people."

For a moment Cooper thought he was dreaming. So Bradfield had a patient who would soon be walking around with a plutonium-powered heart! With his training, Cooper realized the implications immediately.

Soon he had tuned out the proceeding completely. He walked to the cash register to pay the check and left the shop for his apartment to think about this some more. In his mind now revolved thoughts of retribution, money and, at last, hope.

Harris was well prepared for the questions thrown at him by the reporters. He could quote supportive affirmative data by the yard.

"Mr. Turner, the decade of the nineteen seventies is the turning point for the use of nuclear energy for power. There are two dramatic advantages in nuclear energy: the fuel supply and nonrelease of combustion products and particulate matter into the atmosphere. The most frequently asked question about power plants and nuclear fuel sources is, 'Are we subjecting the unconsenting general population to an unjustified risk from a nuclear accident?' My response with regard to nuclear power plants is 'No.' If you really analyzed what is possible, given the safety engineered into the system, the worst possible accident would be no different from the crash of a large jet. As long as we recognize that nothing in the world is one hundred percent risk-free, I think we'll find that in nuclear power the risks are trivial compared to the benefits. In the case of the artificial heart we have fifty watts of energy produced by a high grade plutonium 238. The bulk of the material is small. The risks are negligible."

Turner asked abruptly, "What about the risk of plutonium from artificial hearts falling into the hands of terrorists?"

Harris glanced at Bradfield. The surgeon bent forward attentively. Harris hesitated, and Turner knew he was skirting a real problem.

"We've been told there are immense practical difficulties in assembling plutonium in a quantity and form that could be used as an explosive," Harris said finally. "Although deliberate opening of a fuel capsule is possible with specialized tools, the only likely casualty would be the criminal. I assure you, Mr. Turner, the probability of such events as I described ranges from exceedingly remote to impossible. Now, let's see. Your final point was . . . ?"

"Well, I didn't have a chance to raise it yet, but it was this," Turner said. "The nuclear fuel of the heart, I presume, emits a certain amount of stray radiation. How dangerous is this to the recipient and to those around him?"

"The problem of low-level radiation should be negligible, except for spouses, and this depends a good deal on social habits. The biological effects of low-level radiation have been studied and debated for a long time. Except for a scare or two, no hard data have been published. Thank you."

Hickman turned to Elaine Whitmore. "What the heck did the last guy say?"

Elaine replied, "They're depending on the container to

hold together when the patient's in an accident. They don't think anybody wants the plutonium, and they're ignoring the last problem."

"Oh!"

Ridley was pacing in the tight confines of his office. It was evident to his secretary that her boss was caught in an internal conflict of such gravity that it was tearing him apart. She had tried to ease the situation with coffee and had offered to run to get some rolls from the cafeteria. His refusal had been uncharacteristically sharp. At ten o'clock he abruptly left the office to go upstairs.

"I'm going to watch the television show. Page me if there are any important disasters!"

Ridley's secretary shook her head in dismay. When she had first come to work for him, he had been a calm, considerate, and gentle man. The nuclear heart program had, from its very inception, slowly insinuated a malefic influence on his work. At every turn he had given ground, compromising his principles, and now he had been made to look a fool by Bradfield in the use of fuel from the calf. Today Ridley was a changed man, she thought. He ought to quit and seek a place where there were fewer sharks swimming in the pond!

Ridley walked first to the medical student lounge. The room was packed to the door. It was difficult to see the lone television set, so it was not until he reached the I.C.U. waiting room that he got a clear view of the TV screen. The I.C.U. staff were more concerned in making history than observing the report of it. The few visitors watching TV made room for the long-haired, bearded young man. The visitors in general were a naturally worried lot since their relatives were either in critical condition in the I.C.U. or in surgery, but they took time out from their own concerns to listen to the progress of the famous patient down the hall. They seemed fascinated as Bradfield, using charts and diagrams, demonstrated the mechanical design. He also had a color picture of the old heart, a startling sight.

Ridley sat in silence. The hair on the back of his neck bristled at the glib, but evidently convincing, dissertation on nuclear safety given by Harris. Reluctantly, Ridley had to admit the show was good in spite of Turner's heretic questions. Every heart surgeon in the world would want to have a little plutonium in his operating room for his own heart patient. But the dismaying aspect of the press conference to Ridley was the Dean's blind support of the clinical trial. It was now crystal clear that Ridley's scheduled meeting with Bradfield and Geld over the unauthorized use of plutonium would be a waste of time. Ridley thought, Why bother bucking the tide? Was it possible he could be wrong in opposing it? Could it be that this was just another of those situations where men of good will and judgment could come to different conclusions? The considerations were again weighed rapidly in Ridley's mind. The alternate arguments were those on which he had based his current actions: that it was his duty to regulate dangerous materials, that rules were being blatantly ignored or broken, that his knowledge of the risks in the use of plutonium compelled him to influence those in control, and that people like Bradfield should be exposed for taking the law into their own hands.

An elderly, anxious-looking woman sat next to Ridley. She turned to him and commented, "I think it's wonderful what you doctors can do these days."

She looked at Ridley, expecting a reply, but his mind went blank. In fact, he wanted to shout out to this eager group that there was great danger hanging over them and the world. He managed to restrain his urge and walked off abruptly.

"My goodness!" the woman said to his departing back. Another, younger woman remarked, "What I don't understand is how Dr. Bradfield can be giving this press conference when he's supposed to be operating on my boy."

Chapter 22

The three men returned to Bradfield's office in a glow of satisfaction. Today the world was their apple. Valerie brought out coffee in paper cups and sweet rolls from the cafeteria. Gaily decorated paper napkins, left over from an office party, were passed around.

"It went very well, Dr. Bradfield," said Valerie. "I saw the conference in the student lounge. Everybody was cheering—it was like a football game! But that Dean, he was awful! Oh, yes, there's a telegram in your basket from a very important alumnus in Los Angeles. It was sent to the President's office and was forwarded here."

Bradfield opened the telegram and read slowly: IT IS CERTAINLY A PLEASURE TO SEE SOMETHING GOOD ABOUT ASPERMONT IN THE LA TIMES AND ON TV. THE COVERAGE HAS BEEN FANTASTIC. FOR YOUR INFORMATION, NBC INTERRUPTED ITS LATE MOVIE TO GIVE A SPECIAL BULLETIN ABOUT THE OPERATION. THIS HAS BEEN GOING ON SINCE WEDNESDAY NIGHT AND SOMEBODY UP THERE IS DOING A FABULOUS JOB. I MIGHT ADD, DOCTOR BRADFIELD BELONGS IN THE MOVIES. HE COMES ACROSS

LIKE A MILLION BUCKS. HE HAS A GOOD SENSE OF HUMOR, IS CLEAN CUT, KNOWLEDGEABLE, AND JUST APPEARS TO BE A GOOD REGULAR GUY.

Bradfield turned to Cibelli. "How did the press conference come off from your viewpoint, Jerry?"

"I thought it was pretty convincing, too. You had those reporters eating out of your hand. We only had one difficulty. Some screwball kept trying to get in during the conference. Had no credentials and claimed to be from a Texas college newspaper. We couldn't get in touch with the editor to verify if he was legit. We caught this guy early this morning snooping around my office and going through the wastebaskets. He was quoting the Bible and all that. He harangued reporters to expose your 'sinful invention'! Eventually we had to use force. What's next now?"

"That's up to Harris here. I think we should put a couple more in at least, in case this first guy dies. What do you say, Ron?"

"Well, I think we've gotten as far as we can without official sanction."

"Wait a minute, Ron—"

"No, let me finish. What I meant was that I should get a written approval from my director to progress beyond the three you have fuel for. It's going to cost a bundle to do more. I just don't have the authority to supplement your budget until next year. Look, I'm all for you, no question!"

"It looks like we're going to get bogged down in the usual bureaucratic quagmire. I think the government should strike when the iron's hot. I mean now," Bradfield said emphatically.

"I couldn't agree with you more, Bill. You're absolutely right, but I know the Heart Institute forwards and backwards. You have stepped on their hallowed turf by forging ahead with this prototype."

"You were the one who gave me permission."

"Not in writing."

"Oh, for Christ's sake, Harris!" Bradfield shouted. "Look, I've made you—"

"Likewise, Bill, likewise . . . just calm down. It's not going to be that hard. I can get the funding through. This news coverage is terrific for the senators. They'll love it! By the way, it was well organized, Mr. Cibelli. Good job."

"Thanks."

"Jerry," Valerie interrupted. "Elaine Whitmore and Jim Hickman are outside."

Cibelli put his coffee down and looked expectantly at Bradfield.

"Why don't we meet in here to start with, Jerry?"

Harris rose from his chair. "It's going to be very crowded around here. I'd better leave."

"No, stay. They'll want more pictures."

Whitmore came in, followed by Hickman. The cameramen and the audioman remained in the hallway with their equipment.

"Hello, Dr. Bradfield." Hickman offered his hand and shook Bradfield's vigorously. "Great show, Doc. Those pictures of the heart were beautifully gruesome! This is a breakthrough, isn't it, Doc?"

"Yes, I guess you could call it that."

"Great! You got any questions, Elaine?"

"We thank you for letting us take some of your valuable time. We plan to do a half-hour special report on the artificial heart. I realize that at the press conference you gave us a lot of straight information, but we need more visual stuff. If we have your cooperation, I think we'll be helpful to Aspermont. Your accomplishment is awesome!"

"I won't argue with that, Miss Whitmore, but I'm sure you understand there's a code of ethics which we need to follow."

"This holds particularly true for Federal contracts," interjected Harris. "Public statements on research funded by the government are supposed to have clearance from Washington."

Cibelli chimed in, "I believe, Mr. Harris, that the university negotiated that clause out of this particular contract. It was basically inimical to the concept of academic freedom."

"Jerry's right," Bradfield said.

Whitmore spoke. "I understand all that, and I can assure you that we can do this in good taste. As to the need for prior government clearance, that would be tantamount to censorship. And we wouldn't tolerate it."

"We're making a mountain out of a molehill," Harris said, waving his hand sideways through the air. "That clause is usually inserted there to regulate the commercial firms that I have contracts let to. Business ethics are quite different from medical ethics."

"I'm sure of that," Whitmore replied.

"What do you mean, Mr. Harris?" asked Hickman.

"I mean that business is obviously based on financial considerations—money."

"And doctors are not?" Hickman asked.

Harris grinned wryly. "Certainly not here at Aspermont, for example!"

"Well, I doubt that, even at Aspermont." Hickman was convinced that this noble air of altruism was a facade, but he shrugged his shoulders at arguing further. He was there to get a story with Whitmore, not to debate motives, but he couldn't refrain from a last parting shot. "Hospitals and research programs need money, so . . . " and his voice trailed off.

Elaine said briskly, "Can we do an interview with you and Mr. Harris?"

"Okay."

"Let's get the crew in here and shoot, Jim. We can only get one camera in this room. So what we do is record the two of you talking to Jim, who'll be in back of the camera. Then we'll turn the camera on Jim and he'll repeat the questions. You two nod while Jim talks. We edit the questions and answers in the studio. Okay?"

"Right."

Cibelli said, "After that we can go to I.C.U. and shoot some pictures of Gray. Let's get the fiancée, too, if she's willing."

Elaine was elated at the prospect. Hickman began smoothing down his hair for the picture taking.

The night people of San Francisco, including Julie, slept silently through the live televised conference. Undoubtedly they would see it on the six o'clock news. But in the East, the one o'clock lunchers, the senators and congressmen, the government agency administrators and the special interest lobbyists followed the proceedings with startled and sometimes incredulous interest.

"Somebody really did perform an artificial heart implantation!"

For the housewife, it was an excellent replacement for the soap opera. For the thousands of dying heart patients, it was perhaps the raising of false hopes. For the bureaucrats of the government agencies, which supported academic research, it was a triumph of the ideology of the "technological fix."

In Operating Room 13, the surgical team of Buchanan and Johnson was unaware of the fact that electromagnetic waves were passing undetected through the walls. Trouble had struck out of the blue. The repair of an atrial septal defect in a child is, as heart surgery goes, relatively simple. The atrial septum is a thin wall of tissue that divides the upper chambers of the heart. In the case of Jason Nichols, the boy now on the operating table, the septum had a hole in it. Jason tired easily, had shortness of breath when he exercised, and was scrawny for his age—all as a result of the hole inside his heart.

The area of the defect contains no critical structures. A surgeon with ordinary skill can repair the lesion permanently with a mortality rate close to zero.

It was with this knowledge that Bradfield had delegated the case to Johnson, under Buchanan's guidance. The operation had proceeded smoothly. The boy was on the heart-lung machine and the atrium was open. The heart was put into a quivering nonbeating state. Nervously, but with extreme concentration, Johnson started to close the well-defined defect—

one stitch, then another. Then, suddenly, there was a blackout in the operating room. The emergency lights came on and then, just as suddenly, the power was restored. They presumed it was a random thing, most likely related to the heavy rain of the past week, which had caused a short in some distant power transformer. The power shortage appeared to have done no harm until Buchanan saw with horror that the boy's heart was beating. A foamy froth of blood and air was being ejected from the heart with each damaging beat. An electric current was required to keep the heart fibrillating while Johnson operated with the heart open. With the power failure, the current had ceased briefly, and the heart had resumed its beat spontaneously in the semidarkness. When full power resumed, the heart fibrillated again, but the telltale lucencies in the coronary vessels were visible. No one knew, for certain, how much air had penetrated into the brain or kidneys. That would not be known until later.

"A big bucket of warm saline!" Buchanan rapped out. "Fill the heart cavity up, Jack! Flush out all the trapped air in the left ventricle!"

"Yes!"

Johnson took the liter container of saline and poured it in rapidly.

"Another!"

Instantly, a second container was placed in his hand. Buchanan massaged the heart slowly. The bubbles gratifyingly escaped back into the operating field through the partially closed defect. The aortic valve, the outlet from the left ventricle, was held tightly shut by the high pressure of the heart-lung machine.

"Okay, Jack. Sew that hole shut fast."

"Empty needleholder, please."

Johnson took the needleholder and reattached the needle and suture. With three final stitches the defect was closed.

"Okay. Now repair the atriotomy and let's get out of here."

Johnson used the same fine, smooth Dacron-coated Teflon

suture on a curved needle. With a dozen deft maneuvers, he had the opening into the right atrium completely sutured.

Johnson said, "Turn off the fibrillator."

This time the current was deliberately switched off. Again, the once wriggling heart spontaneously resumed its own beat.

"Damn it, Don, that heart looks a little blue."

"We'll give it a little longer ride on the heart-lung machine. It'll clear up. I'm more worried about air embolism. How does he look to you, Dr. Stearns?"

"Can't tell now, Don," the anesthesiologist replied. "I have him pretty well zonked."

"Let's wait just a little while."

At that point, Mrs. Donald, the O.R. director came in. She wanted to know if everything was all right.

"By the way, Helen, what caused the power failure?"

Helen Donald looked straight at Buchanan. Then she shook her head. "You won't believe it. The television lights at the press conference drained more power from the hospital than the system was designed for."

It was 11:30 when Ridley returned to his office. The solid, natural birch door labeled HEALTH PHYSICS was closed and locked. His secretary had gone to lunch. Ridley entered with his key. The lights had been left on. As he sat down to consider his future, there on his desk top he saw a delightful stuffed lion. It stared at him with large black-and-white linen eyes and a large, ferocious smile. On red stationery, attached to the lion's neck like a bib, was a note in a feminine hand:

There's no use cryin'
Said the lion.
I'd rather roar
than be a bore!
Stick to your creed,
in all your deed(s),
and life will give you more!

YOUR FAITHFUL SECRETARY

* * *

P.S. Sorry, it's the best I could do on short notice.

P.P.S. What's done is done. Why don't you make sure the nurses and patients are safe?

Ridley looked at the vacant secretarial desk and shook his head smilingly. "I should have done that without her suggesting it, of course," he said aloud. He found his portable Geiger Muller counter and a copy of the red radiation safety practices manual, and briskly went about his assigned job.

Chapter 23

Ridley, on his way out of the I.C.U. after completing his radiation check, passed Bradfield entering. They did not speak to each other. Bradfield was engrossed in pointing out the facilities to Hickman and Whitmore. In the computer room the data from thirty patients were displayed on oscilloscope screens. The boring, repetitive job of counting each heartbeat was performed tirelessly by the black and gold electronic devices. Bright dots shone on the television monitors, as they related analyzed data to the two specially trained nurses who sat in semidarkness watching the performances of the machines, and thus the patients.

The kidney dialysis unit was adjacent to the rear entrance to the I.C.U. The area was quiet and isolated. Four patients were in the hospital beds, their arms dressed in white bandages. Plastic tubes dropped from them down to the metal and plastic artificial kidney. Soft, relaxing music pervaded the air. About every three days these patients came into the unit, undressed, got into a gown, and lay down to have their blood cleansed.

Bradfield, in his sharply stiff white coat, paused to describe the complicated system to Whitmore and Hickman. The patients were always a bit discomfited at being put on display like this to strangers, but it was part of the game of public relations. The staff gave little thought to privacy rights here.

"Thanks a lot," Bradfield said to the unprotesting patients.

"No trouble, doctor, you're welcome. I'm just glad I'm here to get this treatment."

As he ushered the group into the I.C.U., Bradfield continued, "Medical care has become exceedingly complex. It's generally not too well understood that for a small amount of money you can get a good level of care, but to improve it just fifty percent in some specific units, the cost may double or even triple. We must learn to accept slight improvements at high cost. The bureaucrats can use cost-benefit ratios in allocating funds, but we can't. It seems strange to me that the public fails to grasp this fact."

They approached Gray's room. Johnson and Stearns entered the I.C.U. from the other end, pushing the bed with the child, Jason Nichols, on it. Five of the visiting Japanese surgeons, with Tanaka in front, followed a few paces behind. Tanaka saw Bradfield and continued down to the end of the hall with his group. It suddenly became very crowded and noisy in that corner of the hospital. Bradfield was about to open the door of Gray's room when the head nurse, alerted by the commotion, caught his attention by shouting above the din.

"Dr. Bradfield, you can't go in there like that! That room is isolated at your request. Everyone will have to put on a cap, mask, and gown. Mr. Ridley has placed the patient on radiation safety precautions." She spoke in firm, exasperated tones. Well-experienced in I.C.U. management, she knew that physicians frequently applied their own orders to everyone but themselves. A firm hand was called for in this situation.

Ridley had instituted appropriate warning signs and safety clothing. He had not detected any unwarranted levels of radioactivity in the area or from the patient. The patient's own tissues were most likely absorbing any stray radiation. However, a yellow sticker had been plastered on the outside of the door warning of a radiation biohazard.

"We'll let one cameraman in with me," Bradfield said. "The rest of you will have to stay outside the I.C.U. I'm sorry, Dr. Tanaka, our rules don't allow so many people in the area at once."

"Yes, yes, Dr. Bradfield. Perhaps we can take picture, please?"

"I don't see any harm in that. Let's open the door and you just step inside and take your picture from the doorway."

"Dr. Bradfield!" The head nurse expostulated again. "That is out of the question!"

Bradfield saw no future in continuing to press his wishes. "Well, I'm sorry, Dr. Tanaka. I'm afraid that's out, too."

"I see, Dr. Bradfield. Can we take a picture of you in front of door? Is that okay?"

Bradfield shrugged and nodded his head, inwardly amused that his photograph in front of the patient's door satisfied the Japanese.

He posed for a minute, and then the visitors went off happily.

Whitmore and one cameraman changed along with Bradfield to enter the room. As Hickman and the rest of the crew started to walk out of the unit, Whitmore said, "Jim, get a gurney and put a camera on it, then wait outside. I want a dolly shot of Bradfield as he leaves the I.C.U."

"Right," Jim shouted back, oblivious to the disruption he and the group were causing in the unit.

The head nurse protested. "Please, remember you're in a hospital."

"Okay, lady. Everybody else is pretty noisy. Why don't you tell the others to shut up? I thought that was the way it was in this hospital!"

The head nurse had not finished with Bradfield. "Dr. Bradfield, I really thought better of you than to bring this mob into my unit. We've gone to considerable lengths to have security guards posted and personnel alerted just to keep newsmen out. And now you bring them in, and other visitors, too. My unit is beginning to look like Grand Central Station."

Bradfield was appropriately contrite. "Yes, I *am* sorry. I see I've put you and your staff in an awkward position. It won't happen again."

"It certainly won't," she interjected.

"On the other hand, these people have persuaded me that the tax-paying public has a right to know just what its dollars are buying. So I thought it would be appropriate to film the patient. I've cut the number down to three. Under the circumstances, I hope you and I can compromise."

The head nurse nodded. She was wise and understood that, unless a smooth give-and-take situation occurred between surgeon and nurse, it was the patient who eventually suffered. She realized, too, the spectacular feat this determined surgeon had pulled off. He was entitled to his moment of glory.

Gray was resting quietly. His nurse sat watching as the ungainly trio in their safety clothing entered.

"Is he awake, nurse?"

"Yes, Dr. Bradfield."

"Mr. Gray, if it won't bother you too much, we have a TV reporter here for just a brief interview. It would help our program of heart replacement a lot if you would consent."

Gray looked at the strangely clad figures and nodded in agreement. Elaine Whitmore stuck the microphone in front of the patient's sunken cheeks and thin lips. She was a little flustered, as the man was so obviously ill. For the first time, she felt she was an intruder.

"Mr. Gray, how are you feeling?"

Gray lifted his head with difficulty off the pillow and began speaking. His voice came out in a croak.

"Not bad at all considering the circumstances."

Whitmore spoke into the microphone herself. "How do you react to the charge that you're a menace to society as a possible walking atomic bomb?"

"I don't react at all, except to wonder at the stupidity of the thought. I know enough physics to be reassured there's no danger. Now, do you mind, Dr. Bradfield? I feel rather worn out."

"Thank you very much, Mr. Gray," said Bradfield. "I think that's enough, Miss Whitmore."

"Yes, okay. Thank you very much, Mr. Gray, and good luck to you."

Outside the room, Whitmore asked what to do about the gowns and headgear she was wearing.

"Just take them off and put them in that sack over there. The patient is in reverse isolation. We wear sterile overgarments to protect him from us. If he were an infectious case, we would leave the garments in a bag in the patient's room. Now, let's finish up your filming. The hospital routine has been disrupted enough by all this."

"We're very pleased with your cooperation, Dr. Bradfield. We probably need only one last shot of Hickman interviewing you for a couple of minutes. Would that be all right?"

They started to walk slowly down the hallway.

"Certainly, but let me give you a hint. I hope you'll all quit harping on the explosion theme. On the basis of what we know, there will never be an atomic explosion. If you push that notion on the air, some nut might get ideas. Don't you see?"

"If the artificial heart places this patient and society at risk, that's news, doctor. What you suggest is close to censorship. Nobody wants that, not even you."

"No, but there's a point where a line must be drawn. What about airplane hijackings? Didn't they start as a result of some television movie?"

"Nobody has proved any connection, but in the world we live in someone would have thought about it sooner or later."

"But in this case, the point is negative, negative!" Bradfield said sharply. "It can't be a bomb, so don't suggest it."

They were interrupted by Johnson, who had come out of Jason Nichols's room.

"Dr. Bradfield, I need to have a word with you about Jason." Johnson's voice held a note of urgency.

"Yes, Jack. Can't it wait until I'm through with Miss Whitmore here?"

"No, sir."

Bradfield said to Whitmore, "Wait for me outside. I shouldn't be long."

"Okay."

"What's the problem, Jack?"

"There was a power failure during the atriotomy. The heart defibrillated spontaneously. It came back nicely after the repair, but I've watched him now for about an hour. He's not waking up. He still needs the respirator, and his limbs are flaccid. Dr. Stearns says the anesthesia effect has gone by now. He and I are concerned about brain damage."

"Damn it! On a simple ASD?"

"The fibrillator was not hooked to the emergency power."

"Well, it's not your fault. Could have happened to me just as easily. You're sure it wasn't due to cerebral ischemia when the pump was running?"

"I'm sure. The pump technician was right on it, moving the pumps by hand until power was restored. There was good flow all the time."

"Then he's a little slow in recovering. I've never seen a kid fail to regain cerebral function in this situation. Kids' brains are tough. If it were a thromboembolus, then it would be a different story. Hang in there. He'll be okay. No lateralizing signs?"

"No."

"Okay, I'm finishing this TV stuff and then we'll start on the second case."

"What should I tell the mother? She's in the waiting room."

"Don't worry, I'll talk to her. She won't understand it was an unavoidable accident, nor will she believe that he'll be all right, so why get her all upset? I'll be positive. Help her get her spirits up and all that. As the pediatricians do, we have to treat the patient's mother, too," Bradfield added with a wry smile.

Johnson shook his head. "Things seem to be getting out of hand around here. Too much going on. The artificial heart case is still critical, news people all over the place, Japanese doctors visiting, this kid's gorked, and we still have another case to do!"

Bradfield's eyes gleamed and his mouth twisted in a lopsided grin. "Keep cool, Jack. This is what cardiac surgery is all about. Keep busy. When things look like they're going to hell, plug away until you're absolutely exhausted. In the end, it'll all turn out great. Glory in it now! These are the situations which separate the real cardiac surgeon from the dilettante, the surgeon who advances his art from the surgeon who embellishes what's already known with gimmicks!"

Bradfield's voice took on a note of elation. His face shone as if he had seen a vision. It was an aura that inspired the young residents in his training program to performances beyond their endurance. It was the secret of Bradfield's success: a complete dedication to his profession. His curious attitudes toward marriage, his contempt for rules and bureaucracy were indications that nothing else in life mattered. Hobbies, sports, or any other interests were expendable in his book. His profession was everything.

"Jack, I've said it before, and I'll keep on saying it: a surgeon may not always be right, but he's never in doubt!" He hurried away at a brisk pace, radiating the energy of supreme confidence.

As Bradfield came out of the I.C.U., the conference between Whitmore and Hickman broke up. The cameraman and the crew suddenly came to life.

"Lights!" Whitmore shouted. A curious crowd began to gather immediately. Hickman came up with his slender microphone in hand.

"Well, doctor, this is about it. We don't need much else except some long shots of you walking down the corridor. We'll just follow the camera on the gurney. It gives a sense of movement and urgency. Perhaps you can make one or two general comments, if you will."

"All right."

They started to walk and Hickman said, "Dr. William Bradfield, Chief of Cardiovascular Surgery at Aspermont Hospital.

Dr. Bradfield, this has been an exciting day for you, hasn't it?"

"Yes, indeed."

"Dr. Bradfield, how sick does one have to be before you recommend heart replacement?"

"Very, very sick!"

"Ha, ha, yes." Hickman turned to Elaine, "Is that enough?"

"Yes, I guess so. Okay, let's go home."

"Pardon me, Dr. Bradfield?" A young, well-dressed woman had come up to stand beside him.

"Yes."

"I'm Mrs. Nichols, Jason's mother."

"Oh, yes. Jason is doing as well as can be expected. There may be a few problems, but he's in no immediate danger."

"I'm relieved to hear you say that, doctor. But Jason doesn't look as I had been led to believe he would look at this stage. The pediatrician told me that in this hospital, it was just like having your tonsils out."

"Yes, well, just leave the worrying to us. We do a good job of that, too. We'll let you know if something drastic happens."

"One other thing, Dr. Bradfield. I saw you on television at the time you were supposed to be operating on my boy. I thought you were going to do the operation? We're not a charity case, you know."

"We operate as a team, Mrs. Nichols. I know that for this particular lesion little Jason had Dr. Buchanan, who is exceptionally well qualified. In fact, being younger and all that, he would take even more care than I would."

"I'm still not happy about it, doctor."

"I really think that's just a reflection of your concern. Everything will seem rosier in just a few days. Excuse me now. I see Dr. Stearns and I have to talk to him."

Bradfield moved away from Mrs. Nichols and hailed Stearns, who was about to reenter the I.C.U. When he was clear of the anxious mother, he spoke in low tones to Stearns.

"Thanks for the help on both the ASD and the cardiac arrest, Isaac."

"I'm worried about the boy," Stearns replied. "I believe he got a good dose of air during the operation. Your residents have told you about it?"

"Yes. As you know, if he doesn't aspirate at this point, the chances are for full recovery."

"Damn shame! Your boys were doing a great job. How did the mother take it?"

"Oh, I told her not to worry."

"But it's more serious than that. She deserves to know more."

"Well, that's going to be the official line for the time being."

Stearns nodded reluctantly. The anesthesiologist was not the primary physician in this case, and there was no more psychologically destructive act than to have parents receive conflicting reports from multiple sources.

Stearns diplomatically changed the subject. "How's Mr. Gray?"

"Really surprisingly well. Yes, I believe the damn thing is going to work."

"Bill, I admire your work tremendously. That fellow was at death's door yesterday."

"Well, he's up today, and he's diuresing fabulously. We all have our fingers crossed!"

"Oh, you do that, too, eh?"

"Someone said, I'd rather be lucky than talented."

"Well, Bill, you're both. Going in to see your patients?"

"No, I'm heading for the Dean's office. I've a little administrative matter to clear up. See you later."

Chapter 24

Dean Geld asked everyone to sit down when they gathered in his office. The people at the early afternoon meeting were Ridley, Bradfield, Harris, and Frances Holborn. Ridley, feeling uncomfortable, fidgeted in his chair, while Harris sat heavily, slumping a little. He had still not caught up on his sleep. Professor Garret Miller walked in. He had been asked by the Dean to sit in as an unbiased observer.

"Gentlemen, I'm sure we can settle this entire question amicably," Geld began. "There's no need for tension in this school. Allen, you explained to me that the plutonium in Dr. Bradfield's patient was not released formally by you for this purpose. You also stated that safety precautions for the welfare of the nursing staff and physicians were not taken in the Intensive Care Unit until this morning. And finally, you were unaware that the human trial of the artificial heart had been approved. Am I correct so far?"

"Yes," Ridley said.

"These are points well taken," Geld continued. "But it's most important to clarify, adjust, and rectify any matters in dispute. I'm serious when I commend you on the attention you've given to the letter and spirit of the regulations involved. It's the conscience of the watchdog that is all too often overlooked."

Geld glanced at Bradfield. "Bill and I had a meeting yesterday in Dr. Holborn's presence. I must say I honestly didn't know that Bill did not have the go-ahead from the AEC to implant the fuel. Now, in Bill's favor, of course, is the decision of the Human Experimentation Committee. I'll vouch for that. This was one of those situations when critical judgment had to come into play. We had a heart ready and a dying man. It was quite appropriate to cut through the red tape with some vigor."

Geld blanked out temporarily on how to proceed, so he asked, "How's the patient?"

Bradfield replied that the patient's progress was quite exceptional. "Indeed, better than I had dared to hope for."

Geld beamed as if he, too, had been a participant in the operation.

Bradfield had wanted to settle the questions with a concise decision, made as cleanly as a surgeon's scalpel. But it was not to be. Geld was going to waffle along, he thought, until he could read clearly which way the wind was blowing.

Harris spoke up. "The root issue here is whether or not plutonium should be used in this form in patients. Mr. Ridley's argument deals only with form. Should Dr. Bradfield have the formal permission of the radiation safety officer?"

Ridley interrupted. "That's the legal point of my complaint, but it's not the most important issue." He paused as he felt the concentrated gaze of the assembly on him. He felt he was out of his league. He fought down the feeling and continued. "The real issue is the distribution of a strategic material like plutonium. There's no way on this earth to ensure that it won't be used by some terrorist group to blackmail or even to destroy whole cities without warning. Perhaps it won't happen tomorrow, or next month, or even next year, but it'll happen!"

Only the expression on Geld's face altered. He looked grim and a little perturbed. The rest of the group remained impassive.

Harris asked pointedly, "How does one carry out this hypothetical threat with one hundred grams of plutonium, and how does one get it?"

Ridley replied, "If you have one hundred grams in each patient and you have fifty thousand patients, then you'll have five million grams of plutonium circulating in an open society. That's five thousand kilos of the stuff."

Harris responded quickly and sharply. "The smallest amount you need to make one bomb is three and a half kilos of plutonium. To get that amount you would have to get hold of thirty-five patients. You'd have to kill thirty-five people!" Harris sat back rather satisfied. It was a mind-boggling figure, and he knew he had scored a direct hit on Ridley.

But Ridley hadn't given up. "I've a different scenario entirely . . . "

Holborn interrupted. "I'm sorry, but this discussion is wandering considerably. In my view, the issue of this meeting should be restricted to the charges as summarized by you and Dean Geld, and not to the various scenarios, plots, or threats that one might dream up if you had one too many 'joints!' "

Ridley flared visibly. "Now, wait just a minute . . . "

Geld thought immediately, Holborn, you may be a good surgeon, but you certainly lack tact. You also like to get to the heart of a problem and bite hard and ferociously. Diplomatically, he turned to the man who up to now had sat quietly observing the exchange. "Dr. Miller, do you have any-thoughts on the subject?"

It always surprised people when Professor Miller spoke with a British-German accent. The tall, white-haired physiologist had been born in Germany, but had done his early work in England after the Second World War. He was another of the coterie of famous established people Aspermont had hired away from other institutions for their reputations' sake, rather than for what the scientist might accomplish in the future. Miller spoke in his soft, well-modulated voice. "Well, let me summarize what I think, Irwin. Young Mr. Ridley has objections to the plutonium in the artificial heart, but he had no control over that. So he registers a complaint about the manner in which the operation was carried out. I see no harm in asking Dr. Bradfield to tell us what happened."

Geld listened carefully to Miller's words, trying to determine by the inflections of his voice which side the Professor was on. He decided Miller was against Ridley. The clue was the use of the word "young" in describing Ridley. In present company, it could only imply inexperience, brashness, and ignorance.

Bradfield thought the discussion was entirely typical of academic committees. Each participant viewed the questions on his own, ignoring both the issues and the evidence. Men of achievement, having risen to high places, no longer listen, he thought, they talk.

"The situation was desperate," Bradfield said, responding to Miller's inquiry. "The heart had been exposed. The patient was sinking fast in terms of the physiological life-support parameters." He looked hard at Geld as one who might understand the fear a physician has when his patient is dying because of a wrong medical decision.

Bradfield continued. "We were in voice contact with Mr. Ridley when the phone went dead. I later learned that a mudslide had washed out the telephone lines to his home. The idea of using the plutonium from the calf came, to my chagrin, from one of my technicians. In my best professional judgment the action I took was fully justified by the situation, and has been confirmed by the course of events since the operation."

"It seems to me, Irv," Miller said, "we'll have to be practical in this case. We'll accomplish nothing by chastizing Dr. Bradfield. It's all over and done with. With regard to future incidents, we must make certain that the proper safeguards are built solidly into the system. All of us in this room can cooperate in applying these safeguards."

Ridley objected immediately. "Can't you of all people understand that this device should have never been implanted? At least not without a study of the risks to society at large. Now it's too late. If Gray survives, we'll never be able to hold the line against broader use."

"But we could restrict its use," Professor Miller said.

"Do you know what might happen if you restricted a cure for heart disease? You'd have the biggest political issue since the Civil War!"

"Perhaps Allen would care to be a little more specific about the nature of the threat he sees in the artificial heart," said Geld.

"Yes, sir," Ridley took a deep breath. He knew he was putting a whole career and his reputation nakedly on the line. There was a good chance that before the meeting was over he would be without a job. "One hundred grams of plutonium in resourceful hands," he said slowly, "could be used to contaminate an area as vast as the entire state."

Geld looked around the table, his silence inviting comment.

"According to the data such an accident is impossible," said Miller.

"Nothing is impossible!"

"I'm sure any accident can be contained. Dr. Harris has assured us the risks are calculable and negligible.

"Yes, but suppose some terrorist gets hold of the material?"

"How? It's implanted in the patient's body."

"By killing him!"

"What?" Professor Miller was incredulous. "That's most unlikely. I think, Mr. Ridley, you've seen too many horror movies lately."

Ridley was flabbergasted. Miller, this supposedly brilliant man, must really be naive, he thought. Another scientist locked up in his ivory tower. He looked around the group. It was obvious they were all in agreement with Miller. He was persona non grata. Ridley stood up.

"Thank you, gentlemen and Dr. Holborn. I see there's nothing more to discuss. You're skirting the real problem. I shall tender my resignation in two weeks."

Geld spoke up carefully. "Perhaps you'll reconsider and speak to me tomorrow or the next day?"

Ridley looked at Bradfield. "Before I go, I wanted to tell you how deeply concerned I am about your project and its implications. I understand how much it means to you. I'm not arguing about the need for it—it certainly exists. But the nuclear heart represents a new attitude which I question seriously. To gamble on this one piece of technology means you're convinced that heart disease is an insoluble biological problem. It assumes that the best you can do, within the next ten years anyway, is to wait until the disease has had its free run, until the organ has been demolished, and then replace it with this hideous machine."

Bradfield listened to Ridley without moving a muscle. "I don't agree with your outlook," he said forcefully. "Who are you to make these predictions?"

"It's common sense," resumed Ridley. "Once you've started on the notion that heart disease is an insoluble problem, there's no turning back. Every patient will have a plutonium heart. I'm not sure we have a collective intelligence to deal with the troubles this would create."

"The artificial heart is nothing more than just another prosthesis."

"That's plain wrong. If some check is not put on this development, we're going to see an incredible fiasco!"

Ridley suddenly whirled about and left the office abruptly. When he was gone, Miller spoke up first. "Well, Bill, I sympathize with you. It must have been difficult working with that queer duck for all these years!"

Bradfield felt a sense of contempt for the young man questioning his authority. There was no doubt Aspermont would be better off without him.

Professor Miller continued. "Personally, I don't think plutonium fuel is really the way to go. Do you really believe it, Dr. Harris?"

Harris was brought up short. "What? Oh, yes, I do."

"My feeling is," Miller said, "that Ridley has some good points. Plutonium is dangerous stuff. But I assume this is the only way to go for a while. The money is there to complete the research, Dr. Harris?"

"It's my opinion that if Dr. Bradfield can get a couple of patients through, we can swing the Congress without a whimper. It really is too good to pass up, as you suggest."

Geld asked, "How much do you think is in the realm of possibility?"

Harris replied, "Enough, I should hope, for a new laboratory, a hospital floor, and supporting funds for operational aspects."

Geld asked Bradfield, "Bill, what are you going to ask for?"

"I hadn't thought about it yet."

"From my viewpoint as Dean, I'd guess about one and a half million dollars a year for five years would do it."

"At least that much." Harris thought out loud.

"No surgeon's fees, of course, for taking care of the patient."

"No, of course not. That'll look good to the committee—Aspermont's contribution."

"Yes."

Holborn summed up, "Well, that's it? We're all agreed that the official positions of the department and the School of Medicine are as follows: we regard this a tremendous breakthrough, we congratulate Dr. Bradfield and his surgical team, and we see nothing wrong with his actions except a slight bending of the regulations in the emergency that existed?"

Geld nodded and Miller said yes. Holborn then continued. "I'll contact Cibelli and tell him to prepare a statement in the event there are any press questions. It'll cover the first two points. The third point is an internal matter and doesn't concern anybody but us. I hope Dr. Harris here will add the official blessing of the Federal government."

"Yes, of course."

"And we can expect appropriate funding to continue the venture?"

"Yes, I'm sure."

Bradfield looked at his watch. It was late. "Hate to sound like a broken record, but I've got to run to my second operation."

"Congratulations!"

"Yes, congratulations, Bill."

"Okay, see you later."

Bradfield left with an increased sense of power within the councils of the school. He also felt he had found the measure of Irwin Geld. Harris left with him. "Bill, I'm heading back after a nap. Give me a call about the patient tomorrow, will you?"

"Sure and thanks."

"There will be hell to pay in D.C. but not out loud as long as that patient is alive!"

"I understand."

Miller had been left alone with Geld. Miller had a wry smile on his narrow face. His head was bouncing up and down. "Well, Irv, I'd like to get some of that money for my research. What about it?"

"Look, we'll put your lab and office in Bradfield's new space. That should help out."

"I was on the same wavelength!"

"Have you considered investing in ATOCOR? It's the company building the heart."

Miller looked at Geld suspiciously. "No, Irv. I wouldn't invest in that company. A bit of conflict of interest, and I can't use the money anyway. My Chevrolet runs like a top, even though it is eight years old. . . . "

"Okay, just wanted to know."

"I'd get the money for that thing, but in the long run I'd look for a better power source—maybe a different type of battery. Plutonium is really not the final solution."

"I agree with you."

"Yes, well, if there's nothing else . . . "

"No, and thanks a lot."

"Okay, goodbye."

Geld sat alone in his office. Yes, indeed, he thought, Aspermont is now on the world map!

Chapter 25

The day began to turn gray as evening approached. An interim quiet had settled on the hospital, but the I.C.U. was as busy as ever. The heavy birch door opened. A nurse peeked out, a sly smile on her face. The corridor was crowded, but no one noticed as Janet Chen came out followed by a thin, pale man in a nightgown and bathrobe. He walked slowly, almost tottered, out of the entrance. He was supported on one side by a nurse. With his other hand he held onto the chromium pole on wheels which carried the intravenous bottles. The bottles dripped very slowly, just enough to keep the tubes clear of blood and to prevent clotting. His chest tubes were clamped. He did not need oxygen, but he breathed heavily with each step. The grin on his face was modified by the frown of studied exertion.

"I can do it, I can do it," he repeated with just a smidgeon of snappishness.

"Okay, okay, Mr. Gray," said the nurse. "Just take it easy. You've got lots of time. How're you feeling?"

"Not bad, so far, but I feel a bit unsteady," Gray said.

"Of course! That's going to take a while yet."

A maid mopping the floor looked up and exclaimed as she saw Gray, "Oh, Lord! Look at that!"

Gradually, one by one, the busy nurses and technical staff paused and watched the first human with an artificial heart move about on his own. The head nurse looked down the hall at the sudden quietness and saw Gray resolutely trying to walk his way toward her. Happily and unconsciously she clapped her hands. This triggered a brief ripple of applause from the staff. Smiles broke out on their faces. Gray waved his free hand in acknowledgment.

"Just wait until tomorrow," he said hoarsely to a young woman with a huge grin on her face. "I'll run fast enough to catch you!"

A bystander quipped, "That's no test—to catch her!"

A ripple of laughter rolled over the group.

"Okay, everybody! Hate to be a spoilsport, but let's get back to work. Each of you will have your chance to work with Mr. Gray. Let him walk in peace."

A murmur acknowledged the command from the head nurse. Gray waved his arm again as well as he could. He continued his walk, the first small but difficult steps into history.

The hubbub resumed as Gray walked past Jason Nichols's room. He could see it was a child, and wanted simply to turn in and say hello, but the nurse shook her head.

"Why not?"

"Well, he's not doing so well."

"Oh, I'm sorry to hear that."

"It's a sad story," said the nurse. "There was a power failure during the operation. I don't know how it happened exactly, but some air bubbles went to his brain and he's not waking up normally."

"Oh, that's awful! I'm very sorry. Can we go in and pray for him?"

"Well, Mr. Gray, there's a second problem, you know."

"Oh, what's that?"

"The radiation safety officer has asked that we limit working with you to four hours. That's just a precaution because of the plutonium in the heart. The doctors aren't sure of the low-level radiation effects on people. I don't mind in the least, of course. I'm sure the whole thing is exaggerated, and . . ." she said, with a slight quirk in her lip, "I know I'm not pregnant. But even minuscule radiation exposure to children should be avoided. Thirty years ago, it was common for doctors to give low doses of radiation to the tonsils of children with frequent colds and adenoids. Five years ago doctors found that adults who received this treatment when they were kids often develop slow-growing thyroid cancer. Most medical centers are now asking such patients to come in for thyroid examination. Looks like we can't be too careful."

"Yes, I see what you mean. We just stay away. I do hope he gets better."

A deep voice came from behind him. "Mr. Gray, please don't be startled." It was the sergeant who was assigned to him. "Look along to the end of the hall."

"Yes?"

"See that man in the white coat?"

"Yes."

"He's fishy." The sergeant turned to the nurse at Gray's side. "Please take Mr. Gray back to his room."

"Okay."

The man the sergeant had pointed out wore an open shirt and a white coat. He put his right hand in his pocket and simultaneously picked up his stride while looking nonchalantly from side to side.

"Do you think he's a doc, nurse?"

"No, I don't."

"Hey, you there!" The sergeant called out.

The man walked quickly toward the policeman. "Who? Me?" He was now ten feet from Gray. He suddenly broke around the burly sergeant and started to run while pulling a small 35mm camera from his pocket. After running past the group for twelve feet, he planted his feet solidly for a base, and began shooting pictures of the patient, his IV bottles, and Janet. Then he turned around and took off again. But the maid quickly stuck her mop out. He tripped over it, falling heavily and with a sickening thud. The sergeant was on him at once, grabbing his arms with controlled force.

"Okay, fella. What are you up to?"

"Easy, easy, officer. I'm just trying to make a living, same as you."

"Stand up. Lean against the wall, hands up and feet out. Nurse, get your patient into his room." The sergeant had taken command swiftly and competently.

Gray just made it on his own volition to his room. Funny, he thought, my heart isn't pounding with all this excitement! He still could walk only ponderously.

The sergeant pressed a button on the brown and white emergency in-house transmitter strapped to his belt. A second guard would show up within two minutes. Then he did a one-hand frisk, while holding a cold, menacing 38-caliber pistol on the intruder. He threw the Nikon camera on a nearby sofa after looking at the identification.

The young man risked a comment. "You can't blame me for trying, eh, Sarge?"

"No lip, fella."

"Yes, sir."

"What are you doing here?"

"I'm a freelance photographer. You've probably seen my work in the movie magazines."

"Not me! You have anybody who knows you around here?"

"Oh, yes, the newspapers."

"Huh! They're out on strike."

"Oh, yes. I forgot."

"I'm sending you to the station for trespassing and confiscating your camera. You go with this other officer."

In the room, Gray fell heavily into bed. "Oh," he said, "that feels awfully good!"

Janet helped him with his bathrobe and slippers. The nurse adjusted the rate of the IV and reconnected the suction to remove any remaining blood from the chest cavity.

* * *

Johnson entered the room after pausing briefly to put on the required sterile gown, cap, and mask. "You all right, Mr. Gray?" he asked with a touch of breathlessness.

"Yes, fine. What's the matter?"

"I had a stat call for this room. I thought something had happened. The cops were escorting away a shaggy-haired guy in a white coat as I came up. Some bird posing as a doctor, I suppose, and trying to make a buck or two on the artificial heart story—real bloodsucking leech!"

The junior resident was visibly relieved that two disasters had not happened to him in one day. He had slept heavily for two hours in the on-call quarters, utterly exhausted. He awoke for dinner and was watching the evening news with the other residents when the stat page had jerked him into a mad dash down the stairwell to the I.C.U. "Stat" in hospital parlance, meant crash emergency, and Johnson was aware of the page as never before in these past twenty-four hours because it had literally not stopped.

Don Buchanan and Sasha Romanoff also arrived in Gray's room.

"Well," Gray said. "All my doctors are here. We can hold a postmortem on the day's events."

"We're here to start our evening rounds, Mr. Gray." Buchanan looked at the patient, now resting comfortably. "Let's look at your chart."

"I'll step outside," Janet said. She kissed her fiancé quickly and left. Buchanan abstractedly acknowledged her departure while looking systematically at the data of the vital signs the relays of nurses had written.

"Humph, up out of bed already! Pretty quick!"

"We thought he had so much drive that we should try it," a nurse said.

"I agree. Good! Look here—the heart rate increased when he got out of bed. That control system is pretty good! No dip in pressure all day. The bleeding has stopped. Temperature? Well, just a bit elevated from the excess bleeding in the chest cavity."

Buchanan looked up at the patient. The edema, or fluid in the tissues, had noticeably decreased. His breathing was still more rapid than normal, but distinctly less strained. The lungs were less stiff. His urine was still pale and voluminous.

"You look good on paper, Mr. Gray. Let's see how you sound. Please sit up."

The nurse gave Gray a lift to a sitting position and dropped off his gown. Buchanan bent over with his stethoscope plugged into his ears. Methodically he listened over the patient's exposed back. He compared the left lung sounds to the right lung, listening for any telltale crackles of wet, heavy lungs. The presence of sounds would have meant that the heart was not pumping well enough, that plasma was filling up the lungs' tiny air sacs. He heard only a rare crackle. He was delighted. He also listened for the absence of sounds in any area. That would have been a telltale indication of lung disease—atelectasis—in which the lung had collapsed and the hissing sounds of breathing were not passed through.

"You need to cough and deep-breathe a little more. This area on the left lung is slightly collapsed. The nurse will help you work on it. Now, let's listen in the front."

The nurse removed the first layer of bandages to expose the wound. This was already sealed by the natural processes in the eighteen hours since closure. The plasma had seeped out between the fine, strong nylon monofilament suture and had clotted. The healing had started, although the tensile strength would be negligible for the next few days. The now familiar and remarkable whistling, wooshing sounds of the steam engine were almost audible without the stethoscope.

Buchanan stood up. He was satisfied, actually pleased, at the progress Gray had made, since his condition had been so touch and go during the night.

Out of bed on the first postoperative evening was remarkable.

Gray said, "You know it hurts less than I thought it would to cough, Dr. Buchanan. I can cough more now."

"This incision, down through the breastbone, cuts little

muscle and few nerves. An incision through here"—Buchanan indicated a line across the chest—"of necessity cuts through muscle. When you breathe or move your arms, tension is placed on the cut inflamed muscle, and it hurts. Most of the pain you feel is probably caused by those remaining chest tubes. They rub inside against the sensitive lining of the lungs, the pleura. We'll have them out in the morning. Just deep-breathe and cough when the nurse wants you to. It'll help your lungs expand. The chances of getting pneumonia are reduced then, you see, and the gas exchange in the blood is immediately improved."

"Sure, anything you say. So far, it's been great advice. What do you really think?"

"Couldn't be better, Mr. Gray, couldn't be better. By the way, you were on TV news this evening. Maybe you can catch the eleven o'clock replay. Lots of interest. They gave the story almost five minutes on the networks and ten minutes locally."

"I don't want the attention. I'm only doing it because it might help somebody else make the right decision."

"Fine. And thanks—it should help Dr. Bradfield's research fund raising at the very least."

"Will Dr. Bradfield be in tonight?"

"No, unless things go bad, so consider it a good sign."

"Hmmm . . . "

The troop of surgeons left the room and walked to the next one, where their mood changed from cheerfulness to gravity. Bradfield had been in to see Jason Nichols immediately after the second case was over. He left by the back door to avoid facing the boy's mother again.

Buchanan went through the almost computerlike routine of the evening: he looked at the written data on the patient, spoke to the nurse, and then examined the patient as his juniors looked on.

"Jack," he said to Johnson, "what do you think? How does he look to you?" There were no recriminations, no breast-beating. "Ginger, did Dr. Bradfield have any comments when he was in?"

Nurse Brown replied, "He just said 'too bad' and 'make sure he doesn't aspirate.'"

"Is he apneic?"

"No, we can stop the respirator and he'll breathe."

"Oh, good, good."

"Don, I'm going to check his reflexes."

Johnson ran his fingernail along the bottom of the patient's foot. Jason's toe curled downward. "Ah, a negative Babinski."

The knee jerk and biceps reflexes were normal, perhaps a little increased. The pupil constricted normally to a flash of light and the neck was not stiff.

One could see that Johnson was groping hard for every positive sign of brain recovery, and he was finding them. He stepped back and let a sigh of relief escape him. "He looks better, Don."

"I think so, too. Just a matter of time."

"Just a matter of time."

"We're going to squeak by."

"Squeak by."

Buchanan looked at Johnson. It struck him as peculiar to hear his remarks repeated. The strain and insecurity often experienced by young residents had taken their toll. Perhaps in the years to come, after much experience, and after seeing death and life pass under his own hands, Johnson would react differently. For the moment he was on the verge of emotional collapse. Doing his first open heart case, having it almost come to an operative death, assisting in a historic operation—it was all too much. The signs of improvement in Jason's condition had brought his mental defenses crashing down. Now he just stared off into space.

"Sasha," Buchanan said gently. "Take Jack upstairs and let him sleep it off. I'll finish rounds with Belknap."

Once again the only sounds cutting the atmosphere were those of the respirator hissing in and out at a precise fourteen breaths per minute. Buchanan and Belknap walked out to the hallway and watched the two residents leave the I.C.U.

"He'll be all right," Buchanan said.

"All right," repeated Belknap in a robotlike manner.

Buchanan looked at the medical student quizzically.

Belknap giggled. "No, no! I'm okay, just agreeing with you."

They both laughed, breaking the tension.

"Dr. Buchanan." The ward clerk held the phone. "The emergency room is looking for you."

"Don, this is Tim Harrison, resident in the E.R."

"What've you got?" Buchanan asked, staring intently at the wall.

"Trouble," the resident said unhappily. "Forty-three-year-old female. Was well until this morning when she experienced severe chest pain that had stabbing quality all the way to her back. She's tall, thin, and looks like a Marfan's syndrome. Left radial pulse is diminished . . . "

"Sounds like a dissecting aneurysm," Buchanan interrupted.

"The aorta is widened on the plain X ray. I think it's dissecting."

"Okay. Is she stable?"

"Pressure's good. Gave her some morphine."

"Okay. We'll start the ball rolling in the O.R. Admit the patient to Bradfield's service and have the radiologist do an angiogram. We should be ready to cut at about midnight."

"Fine, thanks."

"I'll see her in about a half-hour. Let me know if there's any deterioration."

Buchanan hung up and said to Belknap, "We've got another good case for tonight. You ready?"

"Of course."

Wheeler's hand was swollen at the places where he had nicked himself while skinning the calf. This was unusual, as was the throbbing pain. The inflammation was not easily visible because of his dark skin. He drove along Bayshore Freeway, commuting the fifteen miles each way from East Palo Alto to Aspermont. Palo Alto was a predominantly white university town, heavily planted with trees and grass, the show town of Santa Clara County. East Palo Alto was divided from Palo Alto by the six-lane freeway. It was also in a different county, San Mateo. It was unincorporated, predominantly black, and without the landscaped amenities of its neighboring suburban communities.

Richard drove with one hand into the driveway in his red-and-white Toyota, the only new car on the block. He was a man with a job, one of the few on his street. His mother, forty-five years of age, worked as a laboratory dishwasher at Stanford University.

"Hello there, brothers and sisters," Wheeler said to the half-dozen neighborhood children playing in the neat, unfenced front yard.

"Hello, Mr. Wheeler," they said in unison. "Wanna play some basketball?"

"Can't sister, hurt my hand today. Maybe tomorrow."

Wheeler left the group playing with the wooden basketball backboard he had put over the garage.

"Mama, I'm home. We really had a time today. TV men all over the place."

He sat down in the kitchen, where Mrs. Wheeler was putting together the evening meal. Richard was to eat and head for night school. Their home was warm and comfortable but frugal.

"Last night we put in that heart, the one we've been working on so long. I went into the operating room and gave them the atomic fuel from the calf to put in a patient. It was my idea. Then, this morning, some TV people came by and took my picture. How about that, Mama?"

"Oh, Richard, that's just great, real fine."

"Maybe I can learn to run the heart-lung machine for the patients. I really want to do that."

"You worked for Dr. Bradfield for all these years now. He should let you learn. How about that woman who's always picking on you?"

"Oh, Ma, she's not so bad. Anyway, I can handle her now. Dr. Bradfield is real happy with what I've been doing."

"Black people haven't got it good yet, so I won't be surprised if you don't get the job. Keep on trying though, Richard. You're the best that I know around here."

"Thanks, Ma."

"But you stay away from all those rowdies at the corner. Remember the last pay check you got, they borrowed seventy-five dollars and never gave it back. You're the only one out of that bunch that's got a job."

"You're right, Ma."

"How come you're eating with your other hand?"

"This one is all puffed up. I cut it this morning. It'll get better, don't worry."

"You gonna see a doctor—your Dr. Bradfield?"

"Naw, costs too much. Besides he's a heart doctor—doesn't do anything else."

"Well, you take care of that hand, you hear?"

When Wheeler drove to class that evening, his hand was too painful to move. He felt feverish, and he did not pay much attention to his classwork. The early inflammation multiplied rapidly in the now deeply infected hand. The mixed bacteria off the cowhide were not meeting his normal immune body defenses.

In a way, Wheeler was right in brushing off his cuts. Normal, healthy men could handle showers of bacteria—from the mouth or from cuts. But Wheeler was unaware of the radiation dose he had received as he transported the plutonium from the laboratory to the hospital. The radiation dose wasn't large, but it was enough to compromise his normal body defenses against infection. The radiation had impaired the white cells in his body just enough to allow the bacteria to grow unchecked. Wheeler was now a culture medium, seeding his blood with staphylococcus aureus, a virulent bacterium.

Chapter 26

A week later.

Harris sat at his desk in Bethesda talking on the telephone to Jack Comstock in Los Angeles.

"I've received word that you favor a general clinical trial on the new artificial heart. Let me say we fully agree. I've sent a letter inviting you to serve on a panel to establish guidelines by which centers may be chosen to do future implantations."

"You're just putting me off, Harris. I'm going to be perfectly frank, and—"

Harris interrupted with a confidence born of success, "Not at all, sir."

Comstock continued, "—and I won't stand for it. The attention this gadget has received is almost unethical. It gives Aspermont an unfair advantage. The device must be made available to all qualified groups now."

Harris recognized the problem, and it wasn't what one would normally call "ethics." One consequence of medical publicity is that it creates a disequilibrium in patient referral patterns. The institution receiving publicity is flooded with letters, cables, and telephone calls from patients seeking the new cure. The considerations were really territorial and financial, but surgeons rationalized the situation by calling it "unethical."

"We're trying hard to do just that, Jack," Harris said. "But as you know, it'll be very expensive to carry out a good program. We must persuade the budget people and Congress that Bradfield didn't just pull off a publicity stunt. That's where you come in. If we get the experts to write a report and a protocol, I believe I can grease the wheels and get it through. It'll take time and effort and, particularly, it'll take the names of important surgeons like yourself to convince the powers that be. I'm sure you realize that. Also, being on the panel will put your group in a leading position to respond to the request for a proposal that will be carried."

"What level of funding will these centers have?"

"I expect there will be building funds and on top of that we've figured operational costs of one and a half to two million per year for five years. I project twelve centers, three in each geographic area—East and West coasts, Midwest and South."

"How soon?"

"Depends on how fast your panel works—maybe six months."

"And Bradfield, is he continuing?"

"He has permission for just two more."

"Then?"

"Well, he has to apply for a renewal, but you know he'll get it. So my best efforts will be to get the other programs started. Do you see?"

"Yes. Okay, I'll do that."

Harris hung up and dialed the next number on his list. Comstock was not the only one putting pressure on him through his congressman. There were fifteen names, so there was no problem whatsoever in making the panel selection. It was already complete.

"Hello, Dr. Smith? I understand you are in favor of . . . " Harris would go on like this for the next two days. He had planned ten artificial hearts for each center per year, after the first year's warmup. The numbers were 12, then 132, then 252, and so on up to 600 hearts. His branch alone would control more than $30 million annually, with the concurrence of the institute heirarchy and Congress. More important, the new era of the artificial heart would be solidly established. People otherwise marked for death would be alive, socially and vocationally rehabilitated. It was, on the face of it, a worthy goal and within reach in a matter of a few years.

"Well, now. How is Jason today, Mrs. Nichols?"

Buchanan, Romanoff, and Belknap stood in the playroom of the seventh-floor pediatrics surgery ward. Jason sat cuddled in his mother's arms while she rocked on an Eames-designed plastic rocker with birch legs. The boy wore only underpants and a short, child-size patient gown that barely covered him.

"Looking very well today, Dr. Buchanan," Mrs. Nichols beamed up at the chief surgical resident.

"Let's take a listen. Huh, Jason?"

Jason flipped the front of his gown over his head exposing the small, cherubic chest with the thin, fine incision. They had used a suture material that was absorbed by the body and a stitching technique that hid the suture under the cut edge. There was no appearance of a disfiguring, cross-hatched, zipperlike wound.

The boy automatically breathed deeply in and out as Buchanan listened.

"Okay, big fella."

Jason pulled his gown down and hopped out of his mother's grasp. She stood up and watched him disappear gaily into the giant log playhouse.

"It's amazing how resilient kids are," Buchanan said.

"We were pretty worried last week," said Mrs. Nichols. "I must admit I had lost my faith in you all."

"Well, Mrs. Nichols, it all turned out well. He's fine. Let's send him home with you in the morning. All right?"

"That's wonderful news. Simply wonderful. I haven't seen

Dr. Bradfield. Will I get a chance to see him before we leave? I want to apologize for what I said to him."

"I'll remind him to try to see you before Jason goes."

"There won't be any more problems, will there?"

"Don't worry about it. Okay?"

The young mother smiled and nodded as Buchanan's entourage flowed out of the pleasant children's ward and headed for Gray's room.

Aspermont's P.R. man looked haggard, lines of fatigue etching his pleasant face. Ever since Gray's operation he had been working an average of eighteen hours a day. The word was out, however, that the famous patient would soon be leaving. Cibelli's ordeal, which he had accepted with such initial enthusiam, was about to come to an end. He sat tiredly on the couch in Bradfield's office. Valerie Rigg brought in a couple of paper cups of hot coffee for the two of them and tea for herself. She took a sip as she listened to the unfolding story.

"I've such a list, you wouldn't believe it," Cibelli said to Bradfield in a mock New York accent and rolled up his eyes. Bradfield was amused. Every day about this time, Cibelli came in with the names of news organizations, schools, societies, associations, and just single individuals who had called to interview Bradfield or Gray, or both. Cibelli had been accused of being both an utter dictator for rejecting these requests, and a publicity hound for allowing some interviews. It was a no-win situation, but he had done a good job serving as an umbrella for Bradfield.

"Here's one for you. The Chinese-American Alliance of Milpitas says they have an opening for a ten-minute talk at their annual picnic in July! So, if you like barbecued Chinese food, you might take that in!"

"Nope, sorry, Jerry," Bradfield laughed. "Got to have more incentive than that."

"How about Belgian TV?"

"How many stations in the network?"

"One."

"Not enough clout. Tell them I can't speak Flemish!"

"Well, don't say I didn't try! I have booked you, though, for the Mike Douglas and the Johnny Carson shows. And two weeks from now you're scheduled to be on *Meet the Press*. The Heart Institute arranged that and asked me to make sure you're on it."

"Fine, Jerry. I realize some of this is necessary, but sooner or later I'll have to start turning requests down so I can get back to work."

Liz Browning came in. "Am I interrupting?"

"No, not at all. We were almost finished. What's on your mind? You know Jerry Cibelli, don't you? Jerry, Liz Browning, my right arm in the laboratory."

They exchanged greetings. Then Elizabeth said, "It's about Wheeler."

"Oh, yes. The bane of your existence."

"Well, he hasn't been in for five days now. He just calls in and leaves a message with Valerie for me that he's sick."

"We're not doing anything in the laboratory now anyway, are we?"

"It's the principle of the thing. He thinks he can get away with murder because he's black and on the affirmative action program, so we can't fire him. He's really not that good, anyway."

"If you think he's goofing off, Liz, document it. Get him to bring in a written doctor's excuse. That's in the union contract, you know. If that doesn't work, then we'll see. All right?"

"Okay. If you say so."

The phone rang and Valerie answered it. "It's the Dean."

Bradfield grabbed his phone. "Okay, Irv. How can I help you?"

"Bill, how's our patient today?"

"Very good. Thought I'd send him home soon."

"Really? This soon, eh? Seems like only yesterday you did the operation."

"It's been eight days."

"Then this call is timely. I understand people have been

trying to interview you and you've been referring them to our P.R. guy, who acts like the Swiss Guards in the Vatican!"

"As a matter of fact, he's sitting right here with me now."

"I have a big favor to ask of you both then. I have contact with a possible donor—money that is, not heart—who would like very much to meet you. He's just a lay person, but you know how it is, don't you?"

"Sure, Irv. Anything to help out the Dean's office."

"Maybe you could show him around your lab and introduce your patient?"

"Sure, Irv."

"You should meet him today at the faculty dining room for lunch."

"All right, Irv. See you then."

Bradfield hung up and said to Valerie and Jerry, "Nothing mysterious. Geld has a client on the hook and wants me to put on a show for him."

Cibelli said, "What I came up here for is to check out the discharge time for Gray. Do you want to have another press conference with the patient as he leaves the hospital?"

"No, no more. I think he should leave quietly without fanfare. He ought to go straight home and not give any interviews for a month at least."

"Okay. Will he be in for checkups?"

"Yes, he will. First, twice a week for a month, then weekly for six months, then monthly."

"When's he leaving?"

"I'd like him to leave Saturday, when no reporters are around."

"Okay. Well, that's all. Thanks for your time."

Bradfield sat back in his swivel chair and looked out of the window. His thoughts were very simple. He had implanted the first human artificial heart and the patient was going home. The magnitude of his satisfaction was incalculable.

"Hey, Don!"

"Hi, man. How are you?"

Ridley, in a white coat and Geiger counter in hand, caught

up with Buchanan. "I just left the patient. He really looks sharp. No radiation problems."

"Okay, Allen. Have you changed your position yet? I haven't seen you for a week."

"Not really. I'm glad for the patient, but he represents a danger that neither you nor he really understands. I stopped you mainly to say that I'm leaving today."

"I'm really sorry to hear that, Allen."

"It's a week earlier than I intended, but an offer came through yesterday and I've got some vacation coming."

"What are you going to do?"

"I'm going to be on the staff of the Society of Concerned Atomic Scientists."

"Sounds rather argumentative. Ominous, anyway."

"It's a group that has taken an adversary position on the use of atomic energy. It's just that. From the safety records I've seen, it's clear man is not quite in command of the technology yet. I realize one person can't buck the trend. It'll be one organization against another. But I feel I must do it. So long and good luck."

"Okay, Al. I'm sure we'll be hearing from you," Buchanan said, smiling.

"You can bet on it!"

Gray looked out from the eighth floor of the hospital, where he had been moved three days after the operation. From the windows the burgeoning Santa Clara Valley could be seen, the southern tip of San Francisco Bay, and the flat marshes filled with large salt evaporation ponds. The ward consisted of private, single rooms, and the ever-present guard was standing watch.

Buchanan entered the room. Janet and Reverend Milton Kastenmeyer were visiting with the patient. All three sat in chairs, as Gray was now completely mobile.

"Your doctor is here to see you," the Reverend said, "and I must be going."

"We'll see you then tonight, pastor?"

"Yes. I'll be here at eight o'clock."

"Janet and I are so grateful for your attention and support."

"Well, goodbye again."

"Goodbye, pastor."

Buchanan drew up a chair. "I've reviewed the nurses' notes on you. Everything seems to be in good order. Are you ready to leave?"

"By all means. I've nothing against your hospitality, but home is where I want to be right now."

"Any questions?"

"Just a few on caring for myself."

"Fire away."

"How about the wounds. Can I bathe?"

"Yes, everything is well sealed, though not completely healed yet. So you must still be careful about injury for about, say, six months."

"What about exercise then?"

"Rest up for another week or two, then gradually bring up your walking—say around the block, as fast as you can tolerate it."

"I'm to be back to see you twice a week in the clinic?"

"No, we think you ought to come to Dr. Bradfield's office—to keep away from the other patients."

"Okay. So what else is there, Jan?"

"I can't think of anything."

"Has Miss Commons made arrangements for a private duty nurse and so on?"

Sly smiles appeared on their faces.

"As a matter of fact," Gray said, "Miss Commons has not had much to do with these arrangements. I'm going to have a permanent private duty nurse. Janet is moving in with me tonight."

"Yes, but it'll be all legal and moral," she interrupted, blushing a little.

"We can't think of a better time and place to celebrate the joy of life and its continuity than here. We've decided to get married this evening in the hospital chapel."

"Hey!" Buchanan's big face lit up. "That's just swell. I'm really happy for you. What a great idea!"

"I can't thank you all enough," Gray went on, "but I'll be seeing you regularly, so we won't get maudlin in our farewells."

"You're a great patient. You have a lot of courage. We shall miss you."

"Oh, one more thing. I haven't seen Dr. Johnson for quite a while. I wanted to say goodbye and thanks to him, too."

"Dr. Johnson? Oh, yes. He needed a vacation. He'll be back to work in a couple of weeks, and I'll tell him about the wedding."

"I'm sorry to hear he's been ill, but it's a wonder to me that you don't all break down completely with all your comings and goings."

"It's part of the trade, Mr. Gray, just part of the trade. Take care of yourself and goodbye now."

At Stanford Hospital, just ten miles north of Aspermont Medical Center, a white ambulance drew up to the emergency room entrance. The crash-helmeted driver and attendant got out quickly to open the rear door. The black man on the stretcher was in a coma, and breathing rapidly and shallowly. An oxygen mask was loosely applied to his face. It was evident Wheeler was very sick. His mother accompanied the brisk, efficient men into the E.R. A nurse stopped them at the reception desk and took a quick look at Wheeler.

"He'd better be seen right away. Take him to Room Four. The doctor will be in right away. Jenny," she called a license vocational nurse. "Take this patient's vital signs right away." She turned to the worried woman in front of her. "Are you a relative?"

Mrs. Wheeler's eyes were thick with tears, her voice almost inaudible. "Yes, I'm his mother. I told him to see a doctor, every day I told him to see a doctor, and he kept on saying it cost too much, he wasn't ten dollars' sick."

"What's that?" the nurse asked, "ten dollars' sick?"

"Not sick enough for a ten-dollar taxi ride to Aspermont where he works."

"Oh."

"He kept on saying he would get better."

"Then what happened?"

"This morning he started breathing funny and foam came out of his mouth. He shook like he was in a fit. Oh, my, it was terrible. His face broke out in little spots and he's got the fever."

"Well, Mrs. Wheeler, go into the room with your son and give the history to the doctor when he comes in."

The resident on duty came in promptly when Wheeler's condition was brought to his attention. The history was taken simultaneously with the physical examination. The pulse was weak and collapsing, the skin hot, with many, many pustules. His arm was swollen up to the elbow.

As the doctor listened to the heart, he heard the telltale murmurs of valvular insufficiency in both the left-sided valves. Richard had endocarditis. Bacteria were growing on the valves; they had burst out in the little pustules that were carried all over the body by the bloodstream. In his mind's eye, the resident could see little holes in the delicate valves, permitting them to leak as he listened. The heart strained to push out blood, half of which would fall back in, backing the blood up. The lungs were full of edema fluid. It was a common picture in mainline drug addicts who had used unsterile needles and syringes.

"Your boy on drugs, ma'am?" the resident asked dispassionately.

"Lord, no. He's a good boy, had a good job. He works all day and goes to school at night."

"He's very sick. Are you sure?"

"Oh, yes."

"His hand is all puffed up. Did he injure it then?"

"He said he cut it."

"Doing?"

"Butchering a calf."

"When?"

"A week ago."

"Mrs. Wheeler, I'm sure your boy has an infection of the heart valves. I'm going to start treatment—antibiotics and a heart stimulant right now. He should be admitted to the Intensive Care Unit. Do you understand?"

"Yes, doctor. Help him, won't you. He's all I got."

"We'll try to do our best. Jenny, here's a list of stat orders on this patient."

An X ray was taken. The lungs were indeed congested, the heart shadow grossly enlarged. The resident reported to the consultant by telephone. "The only puzzle in the diagnosis is the low white-cell count. I don't know why. It looks almost like he was suppressed."

The consultant replied, "Don't let that lead you astray. The important thing is to start treatment right away. We can defer the academic exercises until the situation is controlled."

"I agree. Oh, oh! It may be too late. The red light is on over Room Four. Got to go."

The resident moved quickly to the patient's room. In the pale, sterile light, an intern was hunched over the patient applying closed chest massage. The anesthesiologist was placing the breathing tube for artificial respiration. A nurse stood by the defibrillator.

"Where's the mother?"

"In the waiting room."

"I wouldn't try too hard. The fellow is septic. Be careful and certainly not heroic."

The intern stopped the massage and listened for a heartbeat. The chest was deathly quiet. He lifted up an eyelid. The pupils were fixed and dilated.

"I think it's all over."

"Okay, stop the resuscitation measures. I'll tell his mother. Too bad he didn't get in here earlier. He was undoubtedly curable. I'll be interested in the postmortem if we can get one."

The nurse said, "He's a coroner's case. Died unattended by

a physician within twenty-four hours. We'll ship the body to the morgue at San Jose."

"A coroner's case, eh? Well, I guess we'll never know. Their autopsy procedures are designed for forensic medicine, not scientific inquiry."

The resident nonchalantly slapped the thigh of the body. "Well, fella, I guess we'll never know why your white-cell blood count was so low. Too bad. Okay, ship him out. Let's wash up."

At approximately the same time at Aspermont Hospital, not far from the place where Wheeler had died, Gray and Janet became husband and wife. The Reverend Milton Kastenmeyer prayed for a long, happy, and fruitful marriage. Gray, the bearer of the deadly plutonium, stood steadily in the candlelit chapel of the hospital with Janet at his side. Bradfield, Buchanan, Belknap, Romanoff, and several nurses sat quietly in the very silent audience as the marriage vows were completed.

Reverend Kastenmeyer said, "Let us give thanks once more to a loving God, who bestowed upon you the gift of life, who has blessed you with the companionship of Janet, and the skills of this hospital and its dedicated men and women."

As the simple ceremony ended, the party murmured quiet, heartfelt congratulations.

A few minutes later, the couple emerged from the hospital and walked toward a waiting car. The Grays had begun a truly new life together.

Chapter 27

A Sunday morning in June.

Daniel Cooper sat in his apartment, staring at the fog rolling high and low through the straits of the Golden Gate.

The apartment was located at the top of the Marina Towers, a residential high-rise made of steel-reinforced concrete. The door to the flat was of thick, natural oak. A plate-glass sliding door led to the balcony. When it was closed, it isolated him completely from noise and neighbors. The apartment was spacious, but its contents somehow looked as though they had been hastily assembled. There was a second-hand plastic overstuffed chair, a dinette, a divan. In the corner of the living room sat a large fan and apparatus that more properly belonged in a laboratory. The apartment had only been rented for a brief time. He had picked the spot deliberately.

For some months now, Cooper had grown perceptibly weaker. His weight was down, his cheeks distinctly hollow. In the stillness a wheeze was heard with every breath. Frequently, there was a painful, hacking cough. The cancer had grown so large, it almost blocked a bronchus. As air streamed through the narrow passageway, it sounded like a pennywhistle.

In an hour, Cooper figured, the coastal breezes would clear away the fog. They would expose the Bay below him and the multiangular buildings of Sausalito, the artist colony eight miles away. It would be a typical summer day: cool, with early morning and evening fog; the winds would come and go with regularity. This condition would be repeated all summer.

Cooper lit a cigarette and inhaled deeply. He got up to pace about, as he went over in his mind the plan and sequence of events. It was a start, his chance at last, though it would entail grave risk and enterprise. And it was a step to raise money for the controversial cancer remedy, Laetrile.

In California, Laetrile was banned as a quack remedy. The FDA had pronounced it ineffective. But people spoke about it. Cooper heard discussions on radio talk shows. The newspapers carried articles about disciplinary actions against doctors who prescribed it.

He traveled to Mexico, where one could get the drug legally. He listened to patients testifying to miracles. He visited the factory clinic where apricot pits were ground into powder, passed through extraction and precipitation steps to emerge as tablets and serum. And he saw patients, tears in their eyes, as the material was confiscated by border guards. Incensed that U.S. authorities had seen fit to deprive cancer patients of their last hope, Cooper was convinced there was a conspiracy from those who profited from cancer. This thought he held firmly in his mind as he thrashed about for a means of getting the forbidden substance for himself. Now it was within his grasp.

He would call the Mexican clinic to make an appointment. Then he would contact the airline to book his reservation. He walked as he had done many times before to a locked door off the kitchen. Unlatching the double locks, he entered, closing the door behind him. The room with automatic temperature controls had been used by a previous tenant for wine storage.

Rows of wine racks, now empty, lined the walls. The room had the musty smell of any underground cellar.

In the stark artificial lighting, Cooper threw back his head and, at the top of his voice, let loose with a piercing scream like a wounded animal, "Help! Help! Murder!"

He waited in the resounding silence that followed. As before, there was no response from anywhere, and he was satisfied.

1:00 P.M., Logan Airport, Boston.

Cynthia Ridley looked at the large clock above the rows of ticket and baggage counters. She checked her watch. TWA Flight 761 to Portland was boarding, but Allen was nowhere in sight. She scanned the busy streams of travelers, trying to spot him. Her thoughts turned to her children. Sadly, she visualized their small faces with large teary drops welling up in their eyes as they were comforted in the ample bosom of the new babysitter.

"Mrs. Ridley, you just relax. The children and I will have a great time. I haven't been a grandmother sixteen times for nothing!"

Cynthia was indeed glad to have found her to look after the children. For the first time, she and Allen had been able to get away together.

"The phone numbers are here," she said, pointing to the black book next to the kitchen phone. "Everything's listed—the doctor, my sister, and Timberline Lodge."

Perched at 6,000 feet on the south slope of Mount Hood, the lodge is off U.S. Highway 26. The mountain, perpetually snowcapped, rises more than 11,000 feet, the highest elevation in Oregon. Glaciers extend to near the timberline on all sides. Snow cats and tractors transport visitors to the 10,000-foot level, and it was from there the Ridleys had planned to climb the last thousand or so feet to the summit. It was not a difficult challenge as mountaineering feats went, but Cynthia was excited. Allen had worked long hours, becoming deeply involved in his job. She, more than he, had planned this quick outing.

The Society of Concerned Scientists was a small public interest group organized by a nucleus of dissidents, mostly from atomic physics. It was incorporated in Massachusetts for the purpose of educating the public on issues arising from scientific discoveries. The executive council made policy, and hired experts with the necessary knowledge and dedication required for this type of endeavor. Ridley specialized in the biological effects of radiation. He had just presented his message at an ecology conference on UHF Channel 14 in Boston.

As Cynthia waited, Ridley was in the studio talking with an attractive young woman. She carried a small, bundled-up infant in a wool sling that held the child comfortably to her bosom.

"Mr. Ridley," she spoke in a soft voice. "I was fascinated by your talk. I'm overwhelmed at the terrible costs we are willing to pay to exploit nuclear energy."

Ridley glanced at her. She radiated a youthful charm. He thought she couldn't be older than twenty-two.

"Thanks. That's the point we overlook," said Ridley. "We've been conditioned to believe technology can fix anything. Let me give you an example. This one happened in a processing plant in the Midwest. A worker was handling plutonium dust in an isolated box. He was using rubber gloves, but there was a pinhole leak. He inhaled the dust, which was deposited in his ribs and lungs. Radioactivity from these deposits is two and a half times greater than the body will tolerate. It's damaging his tissues. The stuff will remain there for a while because it's excreted slowly. Now place yourself in this man's position. Imagine his anguish, how he feels knowing he's been contaminated!"

"What happened to him?"

"He became obsessed by the fear that he was getting cancer. They had to put him in a mental hospital."

"Wow!"

"There are few scientists today who are comfortable knowing how plutonium behaves in man," said Ridley. He was aware now he might be late for his plane, but the girl kept talking.

"Well, how can I help?"

"I'm not too embarrassed to ask for a donation. Any amount would be helpful. Volunteer work is important, too. We're up against well-financed, experienced medical and industrial experts. Are you still going to school?"

"Oh, no. I could volunteer full time."

"Well, that's good, but now I really must go. I have a plane to catch. Perhaps we could meet again some other time."

Ridley was impressed with the girl's obvious sincerity. But how little she really knew about the sweat it took to get the public to listen. He thought of the three meetings he had attended in the last two days. This young woman was one of only a hundred people who had bothered to come. Ridley put up a brave front, but he was deeply disappointed. One hundred people were nothing; they were worse than nothing, because they were evidence of the apathy of the vast masses of the public.

He kept smiling and said, "It'll take more than just the two of us, I'm afraid. It might take a calamity to reach the public. Perhaps we should stop trying to prevent it and let it happen. . . . " His voice trailed off on a note of despair. Then, realizing he had to go, he left the girl abruptly. The pressures of his job had kept him constantly away from his wife and children, but the trip to Oregon was more than just a pleasure trip. It was also an action to save his faltering marriage.

"I see you've been talking to our unconventional nature mother." It was the voice of the TV panel moderator.

"Nice kid," said Ridley. "But I've got to get out of here and call a cab. I must get to the airport at once."

"I'll drive you. It will be faster."

"Thanks, thanks a lot."

The two men rushed out of the building. As the car sped through Boston, Ridley sat in deep thought, oblivious to the screeching of brakes, the wild cornering, and the roar of the car's acceleration. His mind wandered back over recent events. It was obvious from the results of his conferences that he had no leverage. Bradfield had all the advantage; the might of industry and government were on his side. He had a successful lifesaving device and a patient for all to see. And he reached millions of TV viewers whenever he appeared. Ridley and his organization had no influence. Moreover, they talked of a conjectural risk that the public could not see or feel. It would take a stroke of luck or some unexpected calamity for Ridley's society to break into the ballgame.

The car screeched to a halt at the airport concourse. Ridley hopped out with a shout of thanks over his shoulder. He headed for the departure gate at a fast run after a quick glance at the TV screen. As he reached the boarding area, the accordion loading ramp was still in place. He shouted, "Hey, wait." Then he saw his wife. Her worried eyes met his.

"Let's go to Oregon, sweetheart," said Ridley and took her arm.

Gray collected the newspaper and brought it into the kitchen where he and Janet were having breakfast. He tasted a spoonful of cereal, then pushed the bowl gently away. The motion caused Janet to look at him with concern.

"Something wrong?"

"No, I'm just not hungry."

"Are you sure?"

"Yes, my dear."

Gray's eyes met hers and he leaned over and caressed her face. She kissed his hand. "I'm just fine, darling. Nothing to worry about."

At times, he thought, Janet pampered him a bit too much. But, as usual, her intuition this morning was right. There was something troubling him, something he had avoided discussing for fear of upsetting her.

For Janet and Gray, the first months of their married life could not have been happier. His health and strength had returned. After a brief honeymoon, they had moved to a new home and Gray had resumed work at the office. Their days passed in joy and warmth. She knew he could be relied upon. When doubts and fears troubled him, Janet would dispel them just by her presence.

Gray's speaking engagements had become frequent after his recovery, even though other patients had now received artificial hears at Aspermont, Los Angeles, Houston, Cleveland, and New York. Still, he was the most sought after because he had been the first. He gladly accepted invitations to speak without reimbursement, and his speeches were eloquent. "Straight from the heart," he would say, with a wry smile at the bad pun, and he won his audiences wherever he went. His activities made the columns from New York to California and newspapers all over the world.

The artificial heart worked almost perfectly. The soft, whooshing sounds from the miniature engine were faintly heard, the plastic valves clicking reassuringly in quadruple cadence. The only side effect was the discomfort Gray experienced after physical exertion. When he and Janet made love, or he did more than walk, his temperature would rise, the result of dissipation of stored heat from the nuclear fuel. Winter and spring were the best seasons for him. In a stiff wind he would run and exercise in comfort. When the cooling rains came, he would romp in the wet like a child and feel simply great.

The problem that preoccupied Gray all morning had begun the day before with the receipt of a certain letter. It was not unusual to receive letters from strangers, but there was something unsettling about this one, and Gray had thought about it most of the night.

Excusing himself from the breakfast table, he returned to his study to take another look at the letter. A manual typewriter, he thought, as he held it in his hand. The impressions were uneven, the O's blocked in solidly with ink. The paper was good bond but off a pad, probably some EZE-AZE. The letter had no return address and the name of the writer meant nothing to him. There was something else peculiar, too—the quality of the ink impression of the signature was different but, more importantly, the horizontal alignment was a fraction off. The writer had apparently taken the letter out, then rerolled it through to type his name.

Gray was scheduled to speak at the Heart Association meeting in the Mark Hopkins Hotel. The evening talk had been well advertised. The stranger wanted to meet him there, and this, too, bothered Gray. Not that making appointments at meetings was out of the ordinary; it was the curt and unvarnished way the writer had put his request that piqued Gray.

Chapter 28

It was late afternoon and shadows extended along the rocky terrain as a man got out of his car at the Visitors' Center on the San Francisco side of the Golden Gate Bridge. The brisk, cool ocean wind whipped through his cotton summer suit, catching him by surprise.

Ron Harris squinted into the wind and sunlight. A Grayline bus was unloading passengers, the female tourists placing hasty hands on blowing skirts and hairdos. Tourists and bicyclists gathered here before crossing the two-mile span to Sausalito. Below the bridge was Fort Point.

Harris was tempted to return to the warmth of his car, but he waited, hands in his pockets, shoulders hunched up, his back turned to the wind. Julie was to meet him at four o'clock, and desire overrode his discomfort.

Their meetings had become frequent. Harris had used virtually every excuse to arrange business in San Francisco, now that the artifical heart program was in full swing. On this occasion, however, he had veered off course. His present mission concerned the troubled heart-program at the California College of Medicine in Los Angeles. It had, as Bradfield had warned, caused the deaths of several patients, presumably from surgical failures. It was going to be Harris's task to shut that school out unless changes were made. It was not clear just what these would be, other than sacking the incompetent surgeon. But that Los Angeles visit would be made tomorrow. This afternoon was a time for other things.

In his late middle years, Harris was trying to achieve a manhood he had never had. One would assume that a man of his intelligence would not be so gullible as to think that women like Julie could be faithful to one man; but Harris did believe this, at least to the extent of never challenging her directly. Only rarely did they not meet when he was in the area. He thought, rather tenuously, that she liked him. He never asked about her clients, and her fees were charged to his accounts as "secretarial services."

Harris was early for the rendezvous, but so was Julie. She walked up quickly behind him and said in a low, teasing voice, "Need some help, Dr. Harris?"

He turned, startled that anyone here would recognize him, but smiled in relief as he saw her.

"Hi," she said, laughing.

"Julie, don't do that to me, please!"

"Oh," she mocked. "Do you think the eyes of the world are upon you?"

"Come on, lay off, Julie. It *is* risky for me."

"Well, you certainly do look conspicuous in that blue suit. Nobody here is dressed like that."

"How was I to know it would be cold? It was ninety-eight degrees when I left D.C."

Julie was dressed in faded blue jeans, a wool shirt, a nylon quilted parka. Horn-rimmed dark glasses topped off her outfit. She was playfully happy. Harris, she thought, was certainly the easiest guy to tease and play practical jokes on she had ever met. She felt a bit guilty, however, about bringing him here, because she intended to end their relationship. He was getting serious, and that situation could be awkward. Moreover, she had all the information about his work she would ever need. A fair sum of money had been speculated in ATO-COR, and handsome profits realized, with more to come. Her silver Porsche 614 had been bought outright a month after she had met him. Municipal bonds worth thousands of dollars were paying seven percent tax-free interest. The time had come to bow out.

"Let's get into your car and drive to the Fort," Julie said. "I guess it's about the last attraction in town I can show you."

The roadbed of the Golden Gate Bridge arches five hundred feet above the venerable stone structure of Fort Point. Constructed by master stonemasons in 1861, the fort was made a national historic monument in 1970, and restoration work by the Park Service was evident. Harris and Julie joined up with a group of sightseers gathered on the main floor of the three-story structure. A ranger held a bullhorn close to his mouth.

"A tour of this fort will now begin, if you'll follow me." Over his uniform the ranger wore a heavy wool jacket. On his hands were thick leather gloves. In a well-practiced style, he began his spiel and time-honored jokes, which varied not one syllable as he gave his talk every hour.

"This fort was built for defense against ships entering the Bay. There was fear the British would enter the Civil War on the side of the South. The fort contained one hundred and seventy-seven muzzle-loading cannon in three tiers of gunports. Any invading ship would have to run the gauntlet of these guns on this side, then face the batteries on Alcatraz Island over there." He pointed out through the portholes on the northeast wall to the barren former penitentiary in the middle of the Bay.

The guide took his flock up into the shadowy, stone stairway, some not so attentive now that they felt the biting wind knifing through the open casements.

"Look at this stonework," the guide droned on. "It has never been duplicated. You can't even place a thin knifeblade between the stones."

Feet shuffled and stamped, figures huddled together to

keep warm as they reached the top. None of the visitors could stand still except the guide and Julie.

"Why the hell is it so cold here?" asked Harris.

The guide smiled. "Four o'clock is the worst time to visit. The sun is low. The only gap in the coast range is right here at the bridge. Sea-cooled air rushes through the Golden Gate every afternoon. It hits its peak just about now. Any dust or smog generated by bridge traffic takes sixteen minutes to reach Oakland and Berkeley."

Julie and Harris quickly walked about the barbette area. He was chilled to his blue fingertips, and had the unsettling feeling she had brought him to this place deliberately. Indeed, he remembered her telling him on the phone to come dressed as he was. He couldn't figure out what she was up to. His old eye tic flared up again.

It was five o'clock. Harris would have to get what he wanted from Julie in a hurry to make an early flight back to L.A. Once back in his hotel, he would phone his wife to establish his location and time. It would then appear to all concerned that he had never left Los Angeles.

In a studio of WNTL-TV Jim Hickman was preparing his three-minute segment of the Sunday night and Monday weather. Since his TV coverage of the artificial heart story, Hickman's partner, Elaine Whitmore, had left for the New York scene and national prominence. Hickman himself was given what is best described as the "lateral arabesque." He did not have the good looks to become an anchorman nor the administrative talent to become a bureau chief. But no one faulted his delivery, so he covered the weekend weather.

The studio contained the paraphernalia of meteorology—the standard mercury barometer, gauges connected to a weather station on the roof for monitoring wind and temperature, maps of the Bay area, the Pacific Basin, and the United States. To Hickman, the most useful instrument was the steel-gray receiver which printed satellite pictures obtained by telephone wire from the Weather Bureau.

"What's the forecast, Jim? asked the anchorman during a break in the preparations. Hickman was going through the routine of placing temperatures on the map: a high 65° in downtown San Francisco, 58° in Pacifica, 80° in Oakland.

"It will be cool along the coast, early morning and afternoon fog with westerly winds fifteen to twenty miles per hour; hot in the inland valleys."

"Same old San Francisco weather!"

"Funny you should say that. Look at the jetstream map. The stream normally travels at seventy knots eastward at thirty-seven thousand feet over Alaska and the Pacific Northwest. There's a disturbance out there by Guam. It could force the stream in a different direction."

"What's that mean?"

Hickman pointed to the northern Central Valley, an area two hundred by four hundred miles, protected by coastal range mountains bounded on the east by the Sierra Nevada. "In a day or two a high pressure ridge can form in the Sacramento Valley. If that happens, there'll be a balance of air pressure between the ocean and the valleys. The winds will drop to zero. It will be clear and hot for a couple of days, maybe three. Then the old pattern will resume."

"Hell! The hot spell will be in the beginning of the week. It should happen on the weekend, when I can go out to the beach."

"I'll be off Monday and Tuesday. I plan to go for a dip or two," smiled Hickman. "What stories do you have?"

"A couple of good features. One has to do with radioactivity from drums containing atomic wastes near the Faralones. The wastes were dumped into the ocean near these islands off San Francisco because they thought it safe. Now the steel drums have corroded. The stuff is seeping out slowly, and the authorities are concerned.

"The other story comes out of Japan. It seems that four decades after we dropped the A-bomb on Hiroshima and Nagasaki, some Japanese are still dying of radiation effects. The cancer incidence in these two cities is three times higher than the rest of Japan."

"Scary, isn't it? To have such effects after an exposure that lasts only seconds."

"Say, are you going to mention anything about the weather change on the air? About the high pressure ridge, that is?"

"I see no reason not to."

Cooper listened to the six o'clock news. The predicted change in the jetstream was unexpected. It could interfere with his strategy. But if he hurried, he might make it before the hot spell arrived. Precisely at 6:45 he left the apartment and drove off to the Mark Hopkins Hotel.

He drove slowly through the city. A fine mist was falling. He turned on his windshield wipers, as it was hard to see the road ahead. He reached Nob Hill and found a parking space on Taylor, a street so steep the sidewalk was actually in the form of steps.

He got out of the car into the darkening gray fog. The moisture bothered him. He coughed profusely. He walked up perhaps fifteen steps to reach California Street. The Standard service-station neon sign shone red, white, and blue on him as he passed the large public parking garage. The sidewalks were turning dark with moisture deposited by the blowing fog. The passing traffic coming over the hill sent beams of light up through the white stuff as it climbed the heights, then abruptly would flash level on Cooper and others as they reached the flat surface.

With the changing of the traffic signal, Cooper walked on past Cadillacs, Rollses, and Bentleys into the warm, stately Mark Hopkins foyer. He would wait in the public rooms. Cooper had carefully dressed for this evening—a freshly drycleaned suit, polished shoes, a blue tie, a white shirt with French cuffs. He carried only his driver's license and some small bills in his wallet. His car keys were in his pants pocket. He had no weapons, except several tablets of a common hypnotic.

He depended now on guile, cunning, and the unsuspecting nature of his victim.

Chapter 29

The Mark Hopkins Hotel was a hive of activity—from Iowan tourists to Arabian millionaires, from high school couples on dates to suburbanites spending a night on the town.

Some recognized Gray. To others he was just another dinner guest in black jacket and white tie.

Bradfield and Charlotte entered a few minutes later. Gray greeted them and they all walked through the lobby to the banquet room. The P.R. director came up to them quickly. "You know," she said enthusiastically, "we're going to get a large crowd, thanks to you two. We're grateful you could come. Go on in, pick up your name tags. Although that's silly, really! Everybody knows who you are!"

With a flutter of her hands, she was off to make arrangements for the postbanquet press conference.

The Heart Association, San Francisco Chapter, was a mélange of factions and interests: some altruistic, some naive, some political and economic. In the thirties, heart clubs were made up of doctors who met informally to share new thoughts and treatments about heart disease. After the Second World War, laymen developed a serious interest in disease-oriented movements, so, like the March of Dimes, the heart clubs gradually evolved into sprawling scientific, social, fund-raising, educational enterprises with something for everyone. There were the scientists who received support for their research, volunteers who took to the streets on Valentine's Day to solicit funds, and the contributors, people who gave cash on the barrelhead and organized gala affairs—mostly for their entertainment, with a little extra thrown in for the movement.

Tonight was such an occasion. It was an event for the society physician who was not really interested in the latest scientific discovery. It was for the wealthy who needed a cause to give to—cancer was "too deadly" and polio had been conquered. The heart seemed just the right cause, and the excitement of it was grand.

Dr. Brad Warren was a prominent member, as was Fred Hull of E. L. Gerard and, of course, Mayor Delmonico of San Francisco, who had just walked in. The more stuffy academics boycotted these affairs, indicating their disapproval of the Madison Avenue tactics, but the directors knew that raising money for a cause had to be attractive to be effective.

Bradfield expected to receive funds for his training and research. To him, how the money was raised was of little concern. Every dollar counted, and he was never too proud to bend down and pick one up. There was another reason he had come. He wanted to be in head-to-head competition with Brad Warren. Bradfield sensed that publicity about the artificial heart had had degrading effects on his regular surgical program. There were subtle indications that surgeons like Warren, for profitable motives, were spreading nasty rumors. One of them had it that if you were admitted with ordinary heart disease to Aspermont Hospital, you would be lucky to escape without an artificial heart. So as he and Charlotte circulated through the crowd, Bradfield would drop hints about this interesting case or that remarkable operation to any and all of the cardiologists present who might send him patients. Charlotte smiled, complimented the wives, and looked radiantly happy. Operating on the heart was still the basis of Bradfield's existence. He needed referrals to keep growing.

Gray walked through the crowd, oblivious to the medical politics behind the scenes. He relished these glimpses of opulence, but he was glad that Janet had not accompanied him. She would not have enjoyed this evening at all, or being stuck with Warren. Warren had come up and asked Charlotte if she had heard the one about the lady whose pet cats had died. The lady wanted them remembered and brought them to the taxidermist, who had asked "Do you want them mounted?". "No," the lady had replied, "just nose to nose will be all right!"

While Warren's fourth wife had managed a giggle, Charlotte had merely smiled politely and said, "How clever! I see they're waving us to be seated. I hope we shall meet again, Dr. Warren." And she had walked to the head table with Bradfield and Gray.

Ten o'clock.

The press conference following the speeches had ended. Bradfield and Charlotte were getting ready to leave. In the press room the iodine lamps were dimmed, the reporters departing to file their dispatches for the morning editions.

Gray was opposite the doorway, about to cross into the foyer, when he saw a man standing just up inside the exit. Trying to be casually unhurried, Gray headed toward the door, undecided if he should confront him. He passed by and headed out into the foyer. Immediately he sensed he was being followed, then heard quick, small steps closing in on him. Gray stopped abruptly, turned around and faced the man, who was surprised and breathless.

"Excuse me, sir," Gray said in a soft voice. "Are you the man who wanted to see me?"

"Yes." he said, catching his breath in slightly labored gasps. "I'm Daniel Cooper."

The chandelier above them gave off a dim light, accentuating the man's pale complexion. Gray was shocked by the cold hand thrust into his, and recoiled involuntarily. This man is sick, Gray thought, probably very sick.

"I've been trying to get your attention for some time," said Cooper. "At these meetings you're hard to reach. There are serious issues you obviously aren't aware of—about the artificial heart, I mean. I've got to talk to you."

"Oh, yes? What do you want to talk about?"

"I know a great deal about the artificial heart. I've worked in nuclear physics. What I have to tell you is very important."

"Well, why don't we sit down over there in the corner. It's secluded."

Without looking where Gray was pointing, Cooper said, "We've got to get away from here. I've got some stuff in my apartment you ought to see."

"It's a bit late," said Gray. "Where do you live?"

"On the Marina, but perhaps we could talk at the Buena Vista. That's near my place."

It occurred to Gray that he could simply make some excuse and go home. But, on the other hand, he was now really curious to hear Cooper's information.

"All right. I'll go back to my car and drive to the Buena Vista. I'll meet you there in about twenty minutes."

Cooper nodded and hastened away.

Gray's automobile rattled over cable-car tracks as he looked for a place to park. He could find only one, and a tight one it was, on Northpoint Street, two blocks away from the Buena Vista Cafe. Street construction had just been completed and new parking signs were going up. He locked his car, then hurried through Ghirardelli Square and down the steps to Beach Street.

The Buena Vista was at the bottom of the hill on the flat facing the Bay. A singles bar, it was known for its snacks and Irish coffee–potstill Irish whiskey topped with whipped cream in a heavy brown mug.

Miguel Calderon, the young man behind the bar, was tired. It was getting close to shift change. Cooper entered the bar first and elbowed his way to the counter. The bartender stood back, polishing up the last glass in the stack, ready for another round.

"Two Irish coffees," Cooper wheezed out. He took up a position well down the bar from Calderon and cocked his head at the bartender. Calderon continued about his business, putting the glasses onto the stack. Perhaps it was his seeming indifference that prompted Cooper to rasp out in a louder voice, "I want them now!"

"Okay, okay!" Calderon's eyes flashed in anger. "You're next! What's the rush?" With deliberately exaggerated slowness, he brought the two heavy mugs over to the bar for the coffee while watching the grim-faced man out of the corner of his eye. Cooper brought up some thick phlegm into his mouth and spat it out onto a tissue. An inebriated customer next to him moved away in a rocking motion. "Phew, lot of germs around here!" he muttered, too drunk to care if he was offensive or not.

Cooper took the drinks over to the only empty table near a window. He looked out of the window into the dark and saw the bartender's reflection. As soon as he felt he was not observed, Cooper reached for the soft gelatin capsule in his coat pocket. He palmed it as he glanced around him quickly, his eyes darting from one table to another. With the capsule in his palm, he passed his hand down over one of the mugs and dropped the drug into it as he watched the door. He caught sight of Gray just entering, and began to rise to catch Gray's attention. As he did so he glanced down at the mug. To his dismay, the orange capsule floated in plain sight on top of the whipped cream. He quickly stuck his bony index finger down and dunked the chloral hydrate under the cream. The coffee was hot. He jerked his finger out, carrying a ring of cream with it. Quickly he stuck the finger in his mouth. Now one cup had a hole in the bed of cream; the other did not. Cooper was getting panicky as Gray worked his way through the crowded tables. He stuck his finger into the other mug and again licked off the cream. Now the two mugs looked exactly the same.

Calderon, wiping yet another glass, observed this odd sequence of events in the mirror behind the bar. He was puzzled by the weird behavior. Some pretty sloppy habits this guy had. See all kinds of nuts in this joint, he thought. He also saw the vaguely familiar man sit down at the same table. It occurred to the bartender the two men were an odd contrast. One was healthy-looking, cheerful, the other hollow-cheeked, depressed-looking. The eyes of the latter reminded Calderon of a trapped animal, filled with pain and fear. He kept glancing intermittently toward the odd couple, trying to place the second man. The bartender prided himself on his ability to judge people. So it came as a shock when he saw Gray get up a few minutes later. It was Gray, not the weird guy, who had a staggering gait and glazed eyes. The bartender kept his eyes fixed on the two men as they made for the exit, the short skinny one supporting the tall, heavier man.

Gray felt as if his head was spinning in space. He must be drunk, he thought. He vaguely heard Cooper's voice suggesting that he should stay at his apartment for a while until he felt well enough to drive. They headed slowly south on Hyde. Behind them the lighted cable car squealed to a stop to pick up passengers. Those well bundled in heavy coats jostled to sit on the outside benches; the thinly clad out-of-towners moved to the central enclosed portion of the car. The carman gripped the humming, slapping underground cable and the car lurched off, swaying side-to-side up the hill at a steady pace.

The Northpoint movie theater disgorged its audience as Cooper and Gray passed. It was a silent crowd, heading for the shelter of their automobiles.

Cooper tried desperately to keep Gray from falling down. He had misjudged the dose. The coffee was supposed to have kept Gray awake until they had reached the apartment. The alcohol in the whiskey, however, had accelerated the process. Gray, at first, had been higher than a kite, but now he was crashing fast.

The street was emptying quickly. A Muni bus roared past the pair, enveloping them with noxious diesel fumes. Cooper stopped, leaning against the lamppost, still supporting Gray, and had the dry heaves. Out of the Bay a foghorn sounded distantly, the sound carrying for miles. Church bells for midnight Mass were also tolling, but the wind carried the sound off in another direction. When they reached the Marina Towers, Cooper looked even more haggard, and he was sweating heavily. The two men entered and walked over to the elevators slowly.

There was only one other person in the deserted main floor foyer. A young, well-dressed woman, carrying a brown leather overnight case, was on her way out. It was Julie. Cooper did not know the woman, but her presence at this hour startled him. His heart jumped into his throat. The woman stared at the odd couple as she went past them. Then she turned around and looked again before going out of the main door.

Cooper hurriedly pressed the elevator button. The door opened. Gray was pushed roughly into the interior, his feet stumbling on the cushioned carpet. Suddenly all was quiet and still, and he was falling into deep blackness as he lost consciousness.

Chapter 30

Monday.

Janet opened her eyes with a sense of foreboding. The clock registered 8:00 A.M. She had been awake until 3:00 A.M., expecting every minute to hear her husband returning, and becoming more and more concerned as the time went by. She had dropped into an exhausted sleep, finally, and now she had overslept an hour past her usual time. After throwing on her robe, she searched the house rapidly. The living room was empty. In the kitchen the coffee pot had not been plugged in. The garage was cold and empty. On the driveway the newspaper sat mutely. As she picked it up, she saw a single child on the way to summer school. Otherwise the street was deserted.

She sat down heavily at the kitchen table. If there had been an accident, she should have received word by now. Gray carried several identifications. One was the silver MEDIC-ALERT bracelet around his wrist. Round his neck he wore a dog-tag necklace made of pyroceram; fire- and shock-proof, the tag displayed the familiar three-bladed warning emblem of the radioactive material he carried within his body.

Janet riffled quickly through the newspaper. The Heart Association meeting had been written up in a routine fashion; nothing unusual. She found no other news item that could involve Gray. Picking up the telephone, she started to place a series of calls—to Bradfield, the police, the highway patrol, various hospitals.

Cooper roused himself early that morning, for he had much to do. Gray lay sprawled on the floor of the wine cellar, now converted into a makeshift cell. He was still drugged and unaware of his surroundings.

Cooper bathed his face with cold water and read the morning paper that had been thrown against the apartment door. He dressed, ate two soft-boiled eggs, and drank a cup of coffee. Precisely at 9:00 A.M. he left the apartment and rode the elevator down to the lobby. He caught a taxi at the corner to the bus depot on Market and Seventh.

"Let's get a newspaper, Allen."

"The *Oregonian*? Have you got twenty cents?"

"Where's the forecast?"

"On the back page. Let's see."

The bus moved out onto Interstate 80 North as Allen checked the forecast. "Snow line at 5,000 feet. . . . cloudy and occasional showers through Wednesday."

They settled down on the coach seats as they watched the darkness start to turn gray. The flat lands and fertile farms soon gave way to twists and tunnels along the Columbia River Gorge, pathway of early northwest explorers. Ridley could see neither the river nor the lofty cliffs and mountains, but on a clear day the waterfalls could be seen cascading down the basaltic walls to the roadside. With a groan, the bus turned right onto a two-lane asphalt road which led upward from orchards to bare alpine crests forming the end of the timberline.

"Mount Hood Meadows up ahead."

"What's that sign we just passed, Cyn?"

"Population one hundred." Cynthia smiled. "Quite a metropolis!"

"There's a tow lift." Allen peered into the snow to see what lay ahead at the rest stop. "And an open service station . . . a cafe . . . a Forest Service guard station."

"Yes, and over there I can just barely make out a couple of state police helicopters. Probably for rescue work."

The warmly-lit diner advertised itself as "LUCY'S CAFE REST STOP." The passengers dropped down from the high bus platform, carefully helped by the driver. Stepping gingerly into the newly fallen snow, they padded onto the walk and in single file entered the cafe. The place was brightly painted, the tablecloths plastic, the floor linoleum covered. It was tacky but warm and friendly.

"Hey, look at this!" exclaimed Allen as he opened the newspaper. "Bradfield has made the headlines again on page two—'GOVERNMENT REGULATIONS ARE KILLING PATIENTS!'" he read slowly. "Speaking at a Heart Association meeting last night, Dr. William Bradfield, artificial heart pioneer, accused the Federal government of slowing down the application of the atomic heart. He estimated that up to 50,000 deaths a year could be prevented by artificial hearts. . . ." Ridley's voice trailed off on a note of indignation.

"What's wrong, Allen?"

"Well, Bradfield is now a nuclear power expert. You get famous in one field, the media blows you up, and hey presto! you're a genius with knowledge in all human endeavor! God, it makes me so mad!"

"Please, Allen. Remember, we're on vacation. Forget Bradfield, forget plutonium and nuclear reactors. You're becoming one-dimensional. It's not right. . . ." She gulped as she tried to fight back her tears.

"Okay, Cyn. You're right. I know it's not fair to you. Let's get back on the bus."

They slipped outside. It was snowing lightly, a wet snow, just the kind that would last a day. The silence was broken as a single car, with tire chains slapping against the asphalt, came down the highway heading away from Mount Hood. Their bus moved off slowly with a roar from the diesel engine. Ridley put out his hand and touched hers.

"Hey, I'm sorry, Cyn."

She turned away from the increasingly indistinct window scene.

"I promise, Cyn. No shop talk for the rest of the week."

The tears still shone on her cheeks, but a little smile struggled through.

Far to the south on the coast, the yellow-brown nitrous oxide hung as usual like a thick suffocating blanket over the Los Angeles basin. Industrial and auto exhaust fumes had been trapped by an inversion level.

The men were closeted in a darkened room, deep in the air-conditioned administration wing of the California College of Medicine. The four, all physicians, sat along one side of a large teak conference table. They were consultants to the Heart Institute, selected to review developments on the artificial heart. Briefcases were placed next to their chairs, papers and tablets in front of them. They were listening to a speaker standing in front of a reflecting screen. The bright light of a 35 mm projector cut through the semidarkness. The ninth autopsy of a dismal total of ten was being discussed by the stern, white-haired surgeon. An intern, a resident, a cardiologist, and Jack Comstock sat opposite the four. At the head of the table was the Dean of the school. Seated behind the group at the table was Ronald Harris.

Harris had selected the consultants, had set the investigation rules and determined the number of participants. He would strongly influence the written report, and he already knew it would be negative. At the meeting, however, he simply served as secretary. The objective of this exercise was to give the outward appearance that decision-making in medicine was done by the physicians.

"Will you show that last slide again, please." One of the visitors spoke up. "It appears that the last two stitches in the pulmonary artery anastomosis . . . Yes, that's it. There's a hugh tear on the recipient side. Could that be the site of the massive hemorrhage?" He looked around the table and the others nodded in agreement. "I'd say the suture was knotted too tightly. . . . The transverse placement pulls against the line of tissue."

He glanced at Comstock with a questioning look. He thought, You incompetent fool! A first-year resident would have looked for the site of bleeding instead of closing and hoping for coagulation to plug the hole. Instead he muttered, "That's tough luck, Jack!"

Comstock nodded appreciatively. Listening to the discussion of the ten postoperative deaths gave him pause. He desperately wished that the damned program had less public attention. He was sure that with twenty more patients the tide would have turned. When Harris had queried him worriedly after the fourth death, he had replied this was normal. "Surgeons take at least four or five to get their team together." After the eighth death, Comstock had convinced himself that his patients were sicker than most. And now the grim results were paraded before the select group, the pathologist pointing out one technical error after another. He wished he had never gotten involved in this experiment. And so did the Dean who sat next to him.

"Let's have a break and complete the last presentation later," someone said.

"No, let's march ahead. We can all catch earlier flights home."

The intern got up to present the final case before the autopsy surgeon summed up his findings.

Harris was not feeling well. His stomach was upset at the unending slides depicting human organs in one surgical disaster after another. It was drafty in the air-conditioned room and he was seated directly under the louvres of the outlet duct. This did not help at all. He was certain he was coming down with a cold, presumably from yesterday's meeting with Julie. Harris was still angry and he quickly tuned out the intern's presentation. Julie had played him for a fool and given him the brushoff. Harris had gained some insight into human behavior over the past year. Prostitutes do not give the brushoff, he thought. It's strictly a cash deal. He unobtrusively tapped the Dean on the shoulder, and with permission, left the proceedings to use the Dean's private telephone. He called San Francisco.

It was only a coincidence that the police ledger in San Francisco contained these two consecutive entries on Monday morning:

10:30 A.M. Caller—Mrs. Henry Gray, Menlo Park, California
Object: To report husband, 43 y.o., failed to return home following meeting in San Francisco.
Identifying characteristics: heart recipient, artificial, nuclear-fueled heart.
Action: Canvas of S.F. hospitals. To Missing Persons in 24 hours.

10:34 A.M. Caller—anonymous.
Object: Prostitution.
Action: Description and phone number to Vice Squad.

Chapter 31

Bradfield's office was being renovated. A door space had been hacked out of the steel mesh and plaster wall separating him from his secretary. On the other side an entire wall had been removed. Walnut paneling was going up and the shower head that Bradfield liked had been sawed out, capped, and concealed by a false ceiling. Geld had suggested a more elegant look to give visitors a good impression. Valerie Rigg thought her boss had long deserved it, and Bradfield had allowed it, reflecting a change in his tastes.

Bradfield had just returned from the operating room. Hearing his step, Valerie quickly came through the gap in the wall to see him.

"Hi! I've got five calls this morning. These first three concern patient referrals. None of them seems urgent, but the doctors wanted to get their patients on the schedule."

"When do we have some open dates?"

"You're filled to mid-August, except for the slots I've left open for case shuffling and emergencies."

"All right. We'll start filling in those openings. What else?" He sat down in his comfortable rocker chair and put his feet up on the desk.

"Janet Gray called. She's concerned about Mr. Gray. She wouldn't tell me just what it was. She wanted you to call her."

"Wonder what that's about. I saw him last night and he looked great."

Valerie shrugged her shoulders. "And finally, there's a call from a Mr. Smith." She giggled, "I doubt if that's his real name."

"What did he want?"

"He wouldn't say except that it was very important. He gave this number."

"Salesman, maybe?"

"I don't think so, more like a crank. He has called a couple of times. He's persistent."

"Okay, put a call into him first. Then we'll get Mrs. Gray and find out what's up."

Cooper sat at the bus depot facing the bank of telephones. He had left the number of the pay phone with Bradfield's secretary over an hour ago.

The depot was in the slum district of downtown San Francisco, surrounded by cheap bars, pawn shops, and two-dollar-a-night flophouses. Steady streams of travelers passed through, and winos shuffled up well-worn stairs to the mezzanine restrooms. The acrid odors of humanity, mixed with diesel fumes from the waiting buses, permeated the air. The roar of engines joined with the babble of voices in the waiting room.

The phone rang in the telephone booth. Startled, Cooper jumped up and answered, his voice nervous and raspy. Turning his face into the wall, he placed a linen handkerchief over the mouthpiece.

"Hello?"

"Mr. Smith?"

"Yes."

"Dr. Bradfield is returning your call."

"Okay."

There was a click, a brief silence, and then a crisp, businesslike voice. "Yes?"

"Dr. Bradfield?"

"Yes. Can you speak louder, please. Your voice seems muffled."

"Well, Dr. Bradfield, you just listen very carefully. We need some money. In fact, we need a lot of money!"

Bradfield signaled to Valerie through the gap in the wall, making circles around his temple with his finger. It was the sign he had often used to indicate a "nut" call. Once, a fellow had phoned him wanting to know where he should shoot himself so that his body parts could be used for transplants. "Carefully, outside the hospital!" had been Bradfield's reply. Eventually he had transferred the call to the Psychiatry Department, knowing that the staff there would be more sympathetic.

"Mr. Smith, I'm really very short of time. Just what is it that you want of me?"

"Two million dollars!"

Bradfield laughed. This was a real, live one! "We all want money, Mr. Smith. I could use a couple of million myself for a new hospital wing, a research program, some needy patients without insurance . . . maybe *you* could help *me*!" He looked out the window. It was bright and warm outside, but by afternoon it would be stiflingly hot.

Cooper was taken aback. He had not expected his demand to be taken lightly. He felt a twinge of panic.

"Listen, doctor, I'm dead serious. If you don't believe me, things will be very bad for you and Gray."

"If this is a threat, Smith, you will be reported to the police."

"Listen, carefully," Cooper said again. "I'm not going to repeat this. One, I want two million dollars delivered in small bills. Two, when I get the money, Gray gets off with his life. If I don't get it, he dies and we get the plutonium. Three, don't call the cops or the deal is off. Four, at 6:00 P.M. this evening go to a public phone booth on El Camino and Oakwood. Wait there for further instructions."

"You're crazier than a hoot owl if you think anyone is going to pay attention to all that!"

"If you want to find out about Gray, you better be at the phone booth at six o'clock sharp, or else!"

The telephone went dead.

Bradfield was tempted to ignore the whole thing. The man was obviously crazy. But, on the other hand, crazy people do crazy things. He placed the return call to Janet himself. Her news that Gray had not yet come home from the meeting was a shock. But even more shocking was his own instinctive denial when Janet asked if he had any information about Gray. Without hesitation, the blatant lie came tumbling from his lips.

"No, nothing at all. We left the hotel separately last night. Have you checked with the hospitals?"

"Yes, and I've called the police and the highway patrol."

"Don't worry, Mrs. Gray. He'll turn up soon. Keep in touch, though, will you please?"

Now Bradfield placed a third call to Geld's office. A secretary said Geld was in conference.

"It's urgent. Who's there with the Dean?"

"Mr. Workman."

"Perfect. Keep them there. I need them both."

Northpoint Avenue was a narrow, busy street. San Francisco merchants had lobbied for better traffic flow so that tourists and shoppers could move quickly, and signs proclaiming that the avenue was a one-way street had gone up in the morning. A car, apparently parked there the night before, was now facing in the wrong direction. It did not take long to catch the attention of the meter maid. The officer had delayed ticketing the illegally parked car for two hours to give the owner the benefit of the doubt, but by 9:00 A.M., on a busy day with commuter traffic building up, the officer decided it was a tow-away time.

The young man with the big yellow truck pushed the leaver forward, lifting the abandoned car's rear end up with a grinding sound. Almost recklessly, he pulled out into the traffic and towed the car ten blocks to the public garage—another lucrative job done.

The officer had written down the make and license number of the car, but the registration was not visible.

Cooper arrived by taxi an hour later and walked cautiously toward Ghirardelli Square.

The night before Gray had told him where he had parked his car. Cooper had his keys. Cooper's next step was to remove Gray's automobile from the scene one way or another.

As he approached the spot near the square, his heart leaped into his throat. The car was gone. This was completely unforeseen. It wouldn't be long, he thought, before the auto registration showed up on a central police computer. Under the circumstances, he would have to sacrifice some precautions to expedite delivery of the ransom. As long as Bradfield didn't screw up, no one would have time to connect the location of the car with Cooper.

Geld reminded himself he should remain calm to consider every bit of information Bradfield had just given him. He was aware, too, that very soon Bradfield should be persuaded to call the police, after which the FBI would probably get involved. As for the ransom, Geld had no intention of paying it. Bradfield, he reasoned, was the target of the alleged extortion, not the university. And Gray, as far as Geld was concerned, was just another citizen, with no university connection whatsoever. Their meeting began calmly, but as it progressed, the temperature soared.

"If you maintain a tough stand, refusing to be bluffed or intimidated," Geld declared, "this entire hoax will fizzle tomorrow."

Bradfield pursed his lips doubtfully. "*If* it is a hoax, Irv. But what if you're wrong and Gray dies? There's something else, too. I resent the implication that I, somehow, bear the sole responsibility for this man and the university does not."

"Well, frankly, I'd like to help. But two million dollars! The President, trustees, no one would stand for it. What you're asking is just impossible."

"I'm not asking," snapped Bradfield, his voice tight with anger. "I'm telling you—go to the President if you have to and get the money."

"I won't!" Geld's voice rose. "Besides, what the devil is this? Who do you think you are, storming into my office, giving orders?"

Bradfield glanced over his shoulder. The office door was ajar. He got up, closed the door, then returned.

"I'll tell you who I am, Irv. I'm the guy who made you. I am the guy who put Aspermont on the world map, who attracted the money to keep your enterprises going. Now, everything you and I have worked for could cave in if we don't handle this right." Bradfield leaned across the desk and slammed his fist down hard. His face came close to Geld's. "If this kidnapping gets out, patients will lose confidence in the heart. The entire project will fold, along with ATOCOR. We've got to get Gray back alive."

Bradfield emphasized the ATOCOR point. He knew that Geld served on Aspermont's investment committee, and that it was at Geld's suggestion that the university itself held a hundred thousand shares of precious ATOCOR stock.

"There's something else you must consider," Bradfield continued. "Publicity. If the patient dies, there will be investigations. But even before that, the press will probe this thing on its own. When the questioning starts, it's unlikely that the university will escape attention."

Geld's smooth face creased. He was shocked by the sudden realization that they were in trouble. Never a decisive leader, he reacted to situations rather than created them. Strong faculty members frequently influenced his decisions, as Bradfield was doing now.

"So what do you suggest?"

"We should negotiate with this fellow, try to feel him out," Bradfield said. "If we find he means business, we act accordingly."

Geld turned to Workman. "Andy?"

"Bill, what about the plutonium?" It was the first time Workman had spoken. "We hear a lot of talk these days about nuclear diversion. It is possible that someone might—"

"Not possible," Bradfield interrupted. "Impossible as it can be. But the kidnaper may think he can use it, act on the notion, and kill Gray. That's what I'm afraid of."

Geld said, "Okay. We'll do it your way for now. Go on, talk to this fellow, Bill. Negotiate. But don't make any commitments without consulting me. Understood?"

"Of course."

After Bradfield left, Workman said to the Dean, "Do you trust him?"

"I don't know."

Geld opened a small black notebook and dialed the university President's number.

Chapter 32

Simus Twomey made his way to the central communications office. He lit up a cigar, one of his addictions, as he passed through the swinging doors into the large glass-and-chrome room where officers sat answering telephones and entering incoming calls for dispatch.

Two men passing in the hall outside the office caught Twomey's attention. They looked familiar, both husky and rugged in appearance, one black, the other white. They were dressed in business suits. They saw Twomey through the glass doors and both hastened their steps, obviously eager to avoid him. Twomey acted almost reflexly.

"You two!" he called out as he pushed the swing doors outward.

The men stopped and turned to face him as he barked, "Do you have identification?"

"Yes, sir. We're patrolmen, sir."

"Let's see."

The white man opened his suit jacket and brought out a wallet. A photo and the gold-and-blue star confirmed the statement. Twomey relaxed. "Where have I seen you before?"

"You saw us two years ago in Narco," said the white cop. "We were cadets. You were leaving then for the Anti-terror Detail."

"Oh, yes. I remember. What are you doing in civilian clothes? You're pretty late for roll call."

"We're on Vice. Already got our assignment and we're on our way out. We got a good one tonight!"

The black cop grinned. "We're going out on a date, sir. Going to get the goods on a high-priced hustler who's had somebody protecting her for a long time. Yeah, probably a whole bunch of somebodies!"

The cops sobered quickly as Twomey looked at them with steely eyes. "Look," he said, "I'm not your superior officer, but you listen as if I were. You two screw up this job by fooling around, and I'll call it to the attention of the promotion board, by God!"

"Yessir!" The men turned abruptly and went.

Twomey slammed his way back into the communications room, muttering to himself at the decreasing quality of officer candidates the force was getting.

Twomey was a good Irish cop. Tall, husky, with red hair and fair-freckled skin, he was known in police circles as methodical, ambitious, quick-tempered. He had been a solid, plodding winner in everything he did. He began his career on the beat, rotating through all the specialties—traffic, narcotics, bunco, bombsquad, vice, robbery, and homicide. He did the tour again as a sergeant. Now he was a lieutenant on the newest unit of them all—the awkwardly named Anti-terrorist Detail. The word around the hall was that Twomey was to be respected but not liked. He made the other officers look like slackers. This explained why he was still in the Hall of Justice on this particular evening after the day shift had long gone home.

The desk sergeant said, "Sir, can I help you?"

"Let's see the day's ledger."

The officer handed Twomey a stack of computer printouts, a dozen pages thick. They summarized the incoming calls for the first eight hours of the day. Twomey reviewed the ledger daily to keep in touch with the department's work. His eyes soon came upon an item which caused him to pause. It concerned the disappearance of a man with an atomic heart.

Bradfield arrived at the telephone booth early. He drove past it cautiously before parking one block south. The booth, located on the corner of a vacant lot, was exposed to the sun. A well-marked beaten path ran diagonally across the lot, a shortcut worn through the arid vegetation by pedestrians. El Camino Real was heavy with traffic as the late afternoon exodus built up.

He sat in his car in the scant shade of a small tree and reconsidered his position. The conviction that he could rely on Geld to help him out of this awkward situation was now not so definite. Moreover, Bradfield was less sure about the attitude of the university President. A man who prided himself on his social status and friendships in high places would behave predictably under the circumstances and summon the law on the scene. So, Bradfield reasoned, he would have to make it difficult for them to circumvent his decisions. Bradfield had always been proud of his ability to make good spur-of-the-moment judgments; it was one of the reasons for his success. Surgery was full of opportunities for quick decisions, and it was obvious his track record had been excellent.

Intuitively, Bradfield now made a decision that was contrary to what he had promised Geld. That decision, he believed, was the safest. He would go along completely with Smith's demands, promise to give him the money and trust Gray would be freed. The university, presented with a *fait accompli,* would have no alternative but to come up with the ransom on his terms.

Bradfield left the car and walked along the pavement to the booth. The tarred walk was slightly soft under the hot sun, cushioning his step. A sweat broke out on his face and neck, and the collar of his shirt became confining. The phone was ringing as he approached the booth, and he hurriedly picked up the receiver. It was hot to the touch, having been baked mercilessly in the exposed location.

"Hello?"

"Who's this?"

"Bradfield here."

"Right, okay."

"Listen, Smith. We're ready to put up the money."

"Good, very wise of you."

"I assume you're ready to give assurances for Gray's safe release?"

"No doubt about it. Police not in it?"

"I can unequivocally say they don't know a thing."

"You're smarter than I thought, doctor."

"How and when do I get the money to you?"

The conversation might well have been between broker and client.

"Tomorrow night—at Candlestick Park—look in locker 3150."

"But two million is a lot of money! That's not enough time."

"That's your problem, Doc."

The line shut off with a click. Bradfield hung up. He felt he had made the right decision. Now, however, he had to sell his plan to Geld and the President, and time was limited.

Thump! Thump! Thump!

Only these muffled sounds could be heard from the makeshift prison cell in Cooper's apartment. Inside the cell Gray felt disoriented. The effect of the drug had worn off hours ago, but profound darkness enveloped him oppressively, as if he had become blind. There were no clues as to the entrance or exit, and he bumped into wooden partitions in every direction. He was confident only of the position of the floor. At first he had crawled about, feeling ahead and letting his hands see for him. His wristwatch with its luminous dial was missing, but he could count the beats of his mechanical heart; every sixty beats equaled a minute. At intervals he would count the passage of three hundred beats, or five minutes, but it gave him little comfort. He had no idea how long he had been unconscious. Was it hours or days? Was it morning or night? And just where was he? He thumped on the wall regularly, hoping to be heard. He shouted, but there was no response.

Gray could not hear Cooper padding around the kitchen or the sound of the door as Cooper came and went. Indeed, he was not sure if there was an outside. He could be underground. He recalled reading about a woman, kidnaped and buried in a coffinlike chamber with only a thin pipe leading to the world above. Was he also entombed beneath the earth? If so, the carbon dioxide would build up as oxygen was consumed. He would get short of breath, inhale more deeply, then sweat profusely. As yet, nothing of this sort had occurred, but he could not be confident that he was not about to suffocate horribly.

He sat huddled on the floor and waited.

Chapter 33

They were in the President's office that Monday evening. Bradfield had come in following his rendezvous with "Smith." What Bradfield told them had angered and frustrated them.

Geld's face was troubled. He paced the room, trying to explain to a vexed President what had occurred.

"He told me," Geld said, pointing at Bradfield, "that he was making contact with Smith just to feel him out. At first I was skeptical, then gave in because his arguments seemed convincing. But I swear to you no ransom agreement was ever discussed."

Geld glanced at Workman. "Isn't that right, Andy?"

Workman nodded.

"I believe you, Irv," said the President. "Bradfield didn't tell you about his plan because he figured you'd disapprove of it. The question now is what to do."

Bradfield sensed his gambit, with its practical emphasis, had captured their attention. In an adroit way, he managed in the next few minutes to move the problem off dead center. He convinced them that "Smith" was clearly immovable, possibly very dangerous, and his demand had to be met. They had no reason to suspect that Bradfield had not made a maximum effort to negotiate. To believe that a person of Bradfield's caliber would lie outright was unthinkable. Even Bradfield, now faced with the harsh reality, had convinced himself he was telling the truth.

At the end Bradfield asked the President the sixty-four-dollar question, Would he authorize the ransom payment?

"Absolutely not."

There was no indecision in the President's voice. "University funds cannot be used to pay extortion. There are rules."

"You can bend them."

"It would establish a dangerous precedent."

"That's not the point."

"What is it then?"

"We're talking about a human life."

"I sympathize, but the fact is . . ."

Geld closed his eyes and lowered his head into his hands for a moment. "Look," he said, "this discussion isn't getting us anywhere. I've been thinking that we might just be able to raise the money outside. Get a few of our wealthy donors and ATOCOR investors to back a bank loan."

"That's not a bad idea," Workman said.

"Well, I doubt that you'll get any support under the circumstances," said the President, "but if you all feel strongly about it, I won't stop you."

There was a discussion about how it could be done. The President made it clear he was not to be associated with the scheme. If Geld agreed to assume the role of money-raiser, he would be on his own. "And don't expect me to help you with the budget or to repay the loan some time down the line."

"That's very one-sided," muttered Geld.

"You're damn right. Bur remember, you got yourselves into this mess. You don't have any choice apparently. That atomic heart should never have been developed," said the President with all the authority of hindsight.

Workman stood up. "We're wasting time. We should get started right away."

The President shook his head. "From my experience with fund raising, I know the people Geld has in mind. You can't interrupt their lives at this time of night. Tomorrow morning will be soon enough."

Bradfield stared at the President in disbelief. It was a look of contempt, but the President ignored it.

"When should we notify the FBI?" asked Workman.

"Let's wait until morning," Geld said. "We don't have to make the drop until tomorrow night."

"How will we explain the delay in calling them?"

"We'll tell them we thought it was a crank call at first and ignored it."

"We shouldn't call the FBI at all," protested Bradfield. "At least, not until we get Gray back."

"*If* we get him back."

"I understand your feelings, Bill," the President said. "But I think this operation should be coordinated by one man. Irv Geld will take charge."

As the meeting broke up, Bradfield was angered by the zigzag of events. They had lost a lot of time since Smith's call. They were losing more by deferring action until tomorrow morning. Clowns! he thought.

6-14-76

TWX NICI, FBI HEADQUARTERS, WASHINGTON, D.C.

TO: SFPD, ANTI-TERROR DETAIL (ATTN: TWOMEY)

SUBJECT: MISSING ARTIFICIAL HEART

YOUR QUERY EVALUATED BY THIS DIVISION. AS PER ROUTINE WE ARE REPORTING THAT PRODUCT IN QUESTION IS PU 238. CAUTION - HIGHLY RADIOTOXIC. LOSS SHOULD BE CLASSIFIED AS MUF (MATERIAL UNACCOUNTED FOR) REQUIRING IMMEDIATE INVESTIGATION. SAN FRANCISCO-LOS ANGELES FIELD OFFICERS HAVE BEEN ADVISED. PU 238 IS FEDERAL PROPERTY.

Twomey read the teletyped message from the National Crime Information Center. He had initiated the inquiry based on the report he had spotted in the log. He still hoped it would be routine, but he did not want to take chances either in waiting to begin his investigation in the morning. He went home for dinner, took a quick shower to cool off, and drove to the peninsula.

It was dark when Twomey arrived at the Gray home. Janet opened the door. She looked concerned. It was a scene all too familiar in the cop's career.

She invited Twomey in. They sat down around the coffee table where cups, a pot of green tea, and cookies had been spread.

"Have you any information?" asked Janet.

"No, ma'am. I made a quick check of all hospitals."

"Do you think he could have been in some sort of accident?"

"It's possible. If it was a minor accident, there would be no record of any hospital admission. But I should clarify something right now. Missing persons isn't my detail."

"You said on the phone, you're with a special investigative unit."

"That's right. My group is concerned with the missing nuclear material."

"I assume, lieutenant, this is routine. You don't really think . . ."

"Well—" Twomey was blunt—"we don't know, ma'am. There could be a link."

"Who would want to do that? Hurt, my husband, I mean."

"That I don't know, ma'am. That's why I'm here to find out."

Twomey's tone was odd, and she turned to look at him. A knot within her tightened.

"We had assurances there was no risk," said Janet. "The heart was studied completely before it was released."

"I suppose so, ma'am. I certainly hope so. But the fact is the fuel is missing as long as Mr. Gray's whereabouts are unknown. The heart in proper working condition in his chest is undoubtedly safe, but I have to think of a wide range of possibilities. It seems to me government people can often overlook something or other."

"Of course. But what can I do to help?"

"I'd like you to tell me anything you can about your husband—anything that will help us find him." He looked at her with a questioning look.

Twomey did not leave until 1:00 A.M. The moon was high, the crickets sounding off sporadically. It had cooled off considerably. It took Twomey fifty minutes of freeway driving to get to the city. He entered the Hall of Justice and walked into his office. He opened his file drawer. It rolled out loudly in the empty office building. He thumbed through the records until he reached a file marked PLUTONIUM. It was thick with information. He examined the contents until his eyes were stinging with fatigue.

He pulled up his tilt-back swivel chair, put his feet up on the desk, and caught a nap for several hours.

Shortly after midnight, the unlisted phone rang in Bradfield's study. It was the hospital telephone operator.

"Dr. Bradfield, Dr. Harris is on the line from Los Angeles, returning your call. Shall we transfer or have him dial direct?"

"Transfer it, thank you. . . ."

"Hello, Bill. I just got in from watching a Dodgers' ball game, or I'd have called sooner. Something wrong?"

"Ron, we've got a problem. I don't want to talk about it over the phone. You'll have to come up here and in a hurry."

"Why can't you tell me now?"

"Can't be discussed over the phone."

"Damn! Let me check the flight schedule."

"I know the last plane is at 1:00 A.M. from L.A. International."

"You want me to take that one?"

"You must."

"I suppose I can make it if I hurry. I'll stay at the Holiday Inn. Should be there about 3:00 A.M."

"I'll meet you there."

Julie sat in the uncomfortable, brightly-lit interview room in the Hall of Justice. This was her first encounter with vice-squad bullies. Her body showed a bruise here and there. They had been rough when she had resisted arrest, but they had not touched her face. She wore a drab, formless prison gown, and spoke bitterly to her lawyer.

"I'm going to get those guys, if it's the last thing I ever do."

"Listen, Julie," said the lawyer. "We've known each other for a long time. I'm going to give it to you straight from the shoulder. There's no chance. Testimony of two officers, the money in your purse, refusing a physical examination."

"I wouldn't let those bums touch me. Ugh! Not on your life."

"It will cost you plenty in court costs. Legal fees will be high, because it will take time."

"I've got the money."

"How about the newspapers? None of your clients can be caught in your company once your picture is in the papers. You'd be off limits."

Julie shrugged. "I've been thinking for some time now that it was time to quit, get out while I still have my looks."

"Well, okay, great, but still take the rap and then get out. I'll handle your investments and you can live a comfortable life."

"You really don't understand, do you? I'm going to get those two jerks *and* the one who turned me in."

"How, Julie, how?" the lawyer said in exasperation.

"I'll plead entrapment."

"I couldn't prove that for you in a month of Sundays!"

"All they had to do was to pay me—then I was soliciting for an immoral act. But they went further than that—both of them completed the act. I want specimens taken from me by an independent doctor, do you understand?"

"What does that prove? They'll just claim it was two other guys before them."

Julie allowed herself a little smile. "Sperm cells live about twenty-four hours. They can be typed just like red cells in the blood. The blood bank can do it. It can match the results with the blood types of those two cops. If they refuse the test, and you know they will, they'll have to drop the charges."

Julie moved gingerly. Her body still hurt. "When can you spring me?"

"Sometime in the morning. I've got to get a gynecologist down here to take the samples first. It will take a few hours. Can you wait?"

"Going to have to."

As a matron led Julie away, Twomey came down from his office. He passed them in the hall and flashed a smile of recognition to the matron. She responded. "Lieutenant Twomey! Haven't seen you in a coon's age. What are you doing here so early in the morning?"

The lieutenant cast an appreciative eye at Julie, sizing her up astutely. Good-looking hooker, he thought, then pointedly ignored her and turned to the matron. "Well, Sal, nothing definite yet, but could be something big."

"Secret?"

"No, just nothing concrete yet. Remember that fellow with the artificial heart?"

"Oh, yes. It was big news last year."

"He's missing."

"So?"

"He may have been kidnaped."

"Oh, really?"

"The fuel in his heart—it's nuclear. Could be that someone wants it to make something of it."

"Wow!"

"Then again, it could be nothing. He could show up today, bright and happy as a daisy."

"Could that stuff be made into a bomb?"

"I've just been refreshing my memory, reviewing notes I took last year. At the moment, I just don't know."

"Well, tell me more sometime."

"How about breakfast with me? I'll be free in a few minutes."

"Well, thanks. I'd like to, but I've got to get home right early. Perhaps another time?"

Julie's heart raced as she overheard the conversation. She had to get to a telephone quickly.

"Listen," she said to the matron as Twomey ambled off. "I've just got to make a call. It's terribly important."

"Sorry, dearie. You've had your constitutional limit."

"Can't I call my lawyer again?"

"No, you can't. Come on now, no more talking."

"Please, please!"

"Don't pull that sweet innocent stuff on me, kid. I know what you're here for."

"Goddamnit, I've got to get out of here. Can't you understand?"

The matron was unmoved. She propelled her charge along the hallway to the cells without another word.

Both men were weary and bleary-eyed when they met in the Holiday Inn room in the early morning hours.

Bradfield briefed Harris. After a pause, when they had both brooded silently over the dilemma, Harris spoke up. "Has the FBI been notified?"

"Workman is going to call them in the morning."

"Well, thank God for that." Harris's tics and twitches, his feeling of confusion, the gripping tightness in the pit of his stomach were all back to plague him. He had expected to hear of a sudden malfunction in one of the hearts, a death perhaps, caused by a freak accident or associated disease, a surgical error. But kidnaping! He was dumbfounded, shocked almost to the extent of being anesthetized. "Are you going to get the money?" he asked Bradfield finally.

"We'll try."

"Christ, get it—get it, somehow, anyhow! The government isn't going to get it, and I can't get it, that's for sure."

Bradfield looked at Harris, who was disintegrating before his eyes. The physicist's response seemed out of scale, too emotional. "Geld wants reassurances that the stuff can't be of use to anyone with criminal intent," he said. "I explained it was virtually impossible. You agree, of course."

Harris hedged. "Well . . . in principle that's not quite correct."

"What do you mean, 'in principle'?"

"Well, we're dealing with strategic material. In the wrong hands it could be . . ." Harris hesitated.

"Could be what? Out with it, man. Could it be made into a bomb?"

"No! But there are other things."

"Good Lord, Harris," Bradfield gasped. "Now you tell me! Why didn't this come up before?"

"It did, but we thought it wouldn't happen. The idea of terrorists seizing patients with atomic hearts seemed so far-fetched it wasn't worth discussing."

Bradfield looked disgusted. "What else have you been holding back?"

Harris did not reply. He just stared at Bradfield.

It was 4:00 A.M. when Bradfield left the hotel. The question of how a dribble of plutonium could be used by a deranged criminal was still unresolved. In Harris's confused state of mind anything short of a bomb was possible if the stuff was in the wrong hands.

Harris, still dressed, lay down on top of the double bed. He was unable to sleep, conjuring up visions of what could happen. Even if the plutonium amount was small, the propaganda value of the kidnaping to the environmentalists would be enormous. That damn Ridley would have a field day!

As the time crept slowly by, Harris decided that Gray's rescue was not the issue. The FBI had to get the plutonium back. He had to make it clear to them and Geld that they had to get the stuff back even if it took a big payoff or an armed assault. Gray was dispensable.

Rising from the bed, Harris caught a glimpse of himself in the mirror. He looked at his sunken eyes, beard, rumpled suit. "Too many damned one-night stands in motels," he muttered to himself. And now this, threatening his career, everything he had worked for. He called Geld to convey the sense of urgency. Then, as soon as he hung up, he thought of Julie. Should he warn her to get out of town—just in case? Maybe not. She had played him for all she could get. And even as the thought came into his head, he took up the phone again and dialed her number. He heard the blank, distant ringing buzz. He hung up, then redialed. He let the phone ring for another long minute. She's out, he thought. Deep hatred welled up inside him. He banged the phone back on its hook muttering, "Damn whore!"

He flopped back on the bed, closed his eyes, and waited for full daylight.

Chapter 34

Tuesday.

Security in the Federal Building in San Francisco was routinely tight. A reception alcove on the main floor was manned by uniformed guards. Ropes and stanchions guided the flow of visitors and staff past the inspection point. All were required to wear ID's—photos pinned to lapels or tags with the bold lettering VISITOR hung around their necks.

On the seventh floor, in the offices of the FBI, the agent in charge was in conference with Twomey. Both had been briefed about the ransom by Workman and were annoyed at the university for not reporting the kidnaping promptly.

"I think we're on to something big," Twomey said. "Using Gray as a hostage represents a high level of sophistication. Somebody understood that the plutonium was there for the taking. That's a clue to the player."

The buzzer rang and Harris was shown in.

Twomey looked at the fatigued Harris and said, "Sit down, please."

The FBI man began the interrogation. "If you wouldn't mind, sir, I'd like to ask a few questions about plutonium. Just to get some understanding of what we're dealing with."

"Sure. What do you want to know?"

"Start with the stuff itself. Can you make a bomb with it and quickly?"

"Not really. If one could, it wouldn't be terribly efficient. The amount of plutonium in one artificial heart is small and in the form of an oxide. You'd have to convert it into metal first."

"How's that done?"

"The chemical theory is easy. But practically, after you convert it, you have to be very careful. It can ignite spontaneously. It can go critical, and if there's any dust, you can inhale it."

"Dangerous for the person fooling around with it?"

"Oh, God, yes! Making the stuff into a bomb involves steps extremely dangerous to the builder."

"Any special equipment needed?"

"It was done in Los Alamos with standard equipment. All you need is a furnace which costs a couple of grand, and a safety box for maybe six hundred. You could get those things from any scientific supply house. It's not complicated."

Harris went on to explain how, if someone could steal enough plutonium, and if he were able to convert the material, he still would not have a bomb. To make a bomb, properly sized pieces had to be brought together quickly and held in the presence of a source of neutrons while the fission reaction proceeded. Carefully shaped charges of plastic explosive were needed to accomplish this.

"The technology of bomb-making is complex even if one has the right kind of nuclear material," Harris said.

"How long would it take once the stuff was obtained?" It was Twomey now asking the questions.

"Perhaps a couple of weeks of concentrated effort, given absolutely no hitches."

"I gather the heart contains one hundred grams. It would take, then, a very experienced bomb-maker to put one together?"

"Not only one very experienced bomb-maker, but more plutonium and an entire team—tool-maker, explosives expert, electronics engineer, actually."

"The more plutonium, the easier it would be?"

"Yes."

"What is a nice round figure?"

"About three kilos."

"And how many artificial hearts have been installed?"

"Exactly fourteen."

"That added up amounts to almost half of your round figure. Are all the patients accounted for?"

"I don't know," said Harris. He felt a stab of pain in his stomach. Was the cop implying that this one kidnaping was part of some grand conspiracy? "Nobody could kidnap all of them at once, could they?"

"Where are these patients, Mr. Harris?" The FBI man jotted down a few notes.

"In Dallas, New York, Boise . . . I have a complete list."

"Scattered all over? We're going to have to protect them, aren't we? Round the clock!"

"That could generate attention. Don't you want to put a news lid on the kidnap to avoid panic?"

"Look, we're caught between a rock and a hard spot. We can appeal to the news media for cooperation until we know what's happened. But it would be foolish to leave other patients without protection."

The FBI man continued. "If you give me your list, our field offices will arrange protection. We'll need four agents per patient—a total of fifty-six men."

"Only fifty-two. One of the fourteen is Gray."

"All right, fifty-two. We need some clues about the kind of people who could pull this off. Obviously they have to be knowledgeable in nuclear technology."

"Yes."

"Can't it be narrowed down?"

"The workers in Los Alamos, Oakridge, Livermore, Batelle,

nuclear generating plants—it could be a good number."

"How about terrorist organizations? Have you heard of underground units with this expertise?"

"No."

"Well, that will be all for now. Stay in the area where we can contact you."

"But I've got to get back to Bethesda."

"Oh, I think you had better stick around here for a while. In fact, I insist on it!"

That statement piqued Harris. He started to protest, then capitulated. His shoulders drooped as he stood up to leave. He realized he was losing the numbers game. It came to him when the FBI man had calculated the number of men needed to guard one heart patient. Four men per day at $25,000 a year equaled $100,000—a total of $1.4 million for the current patients. Sooner or later, Harris knew, one of those congressional watchdog committees would start asking questions. But wait a minute! That's it!

"Maybe it's all a hoax!" Harris said abruptly.

"How's that?"

"Yes, a calculated attempt to discredit the project. By God, Ridley and his crusading outfit. They might have arranged the disappearance to generate publicity!"

"Who's Ridley?"

"A health physicist. He quit Aspermont in a huff after the heart implantation. Been working out of Boston for some antinuclear outfit, a rather aggressive bunch, I would say. Get him and I bet you'll find Gray." Harris was close to incoherency with excitement.

"Okay, we'll check him out first."

The FBI man called out as Harris went through the door. "Mr. Harris, it seems you had better give a few second thoughts to your artificial heart. Even if this turns out to be a hoax, the next one might not be!"

Harris felt the chilling words skip through his head like a knife, and he increased his pace.

The agent looked out over the unusually warm city. Below,

the flags of the Civic Center Plaza hung limply. A brown haze, filled with noxious pollutants, had built up. He could no longer see the Oakland end of the Bay Bridge.

"What's your assessment?" asked Twomey.

"Harris is probably right. Fabricating a nuclear bomb is not that simple. Certainly not a basement bomb factory item. It would take someone weeks or months, and he would have to get more plutonium from somewhere."

"Where does that leave us? Straight kidnaping for ransom?"

"Maybe, or sale of the stuff in the black market, on top of the ransom."

"Your guess, then, is that he'll go through with the killing?"

"Can't tell. A psycho would."

"I suppose you're right. But I can't help feeling there's something more here. It's just too much of a coincidence that the kidnaper would pick out this particular man!"

On this Tuesday morning the standard turnoff to anyone who tried to contact Bradfield was: "I'm sorry, Dr. Bradfield is operating. He cannot be disturbed."

Bradfield had deliberately set up the day's schedule to overlap. As he finished one operation, the next patient was anesthetized and ready to go. The cardiologists were under orders to find a case to follow the preceding one—from anywhere.

After talking to Harris in the hotel room, Bradfield had driven home, thinking furiously in an attempt to sort things out. He had decided, The hell with it all! If he was not going to be in control of the situation, he would bow out of the negotiations completely. He'd let the university President, Geld, Workman, and the rest of them shoulder the responsibility. He would retreat to his citadel, the operating room, to do what he knew best—save lives. Nobody could criticize him for that. He would remain in the operating room, incommunicado, until the crisis had been resolved one way or the other.

Chapter 35

Meanwhile, in the wine cellar, a threatening situation was about to arise. Gray had not been warned about it. The makers of the artificial heart knew it could happen but had ignored it.

When animal life crawled out of the oceans eons ago, it carried with it the salt and water of the sea. Early life forms were cold-blooded, their body temperature varying with the environment. In cold, the animals moved sluggishly, their defenses slowed, and food-gathering powers were limited. In warmth, reactions speeded up, permitting greater mobility. This was also true of the brain, cells made up of electrically active membranes, polarizing and depolarizing in milliseconds. Later species evolved a mechanism for stabilizing their body heat, thereby increasing their mobility and range. This ability imposed a new limit, however. Water in body cells had to be conserved, and so skin evolved, to reduce evaporation, and kidneys, for removal of wastes. Man developed even more complex systems at the automatic level—hormones, glands, and organs helping to maintain temperature at 98.6°F and a water content of 92 percent of total body weight.

Harris had had the scientific problem of waste body heat studied. His files were filled with reports and memoranda from a certain researcher, who had now retired.

Memorandum to: James Tiller, Ph.D. June 18, 1967
Professor of Physiology
Mojave State University
From: Ronald Harris, Ph.D.
Sir: I am empowered to seek consultation concerning the waste heat effects of a proposed artificial heart system in the human body. Your name has been suggested to me on the basis of your research on the effects of heat and water deprivation on the human body.
The standard fee is $75 per day. R.H.

To: R. Harris June 25, 1967
From: J. Tiller
Thank you for your memo of June 18, 1967. My current work is in the area of the effects of environmental heat such as the desert and tropics, not endogenous heat. However, please send further information. I may be able to fit the problem into my research schedule. J.T.

To: Tiller July 4, 1967
From: Harris
We are pleased to hear of your acceptance. The program will be enormously benefited by a man of your stature.
I might summarize the key questions raised by the Physicians' Consultant Panel: "Given that the plutonium power source will generate 50 watts of energy and given that the heart will use 5 watts as mechanical energy, what will be the physiological effects of the excess 45 watts?" R.H.

To: Harris Aug. 1, 1967
From: Tiller
The questions asked cannot be answered by extrapolating from previous experience. Rather, it requires a direct experimental approach. J.T.

To: Tiller Sept. 3, 1967
From: Harris
Our panel feels that it is not necessary to have a large-scale trial for the purposes of this subsegment of the program. Please give estimate of total direct and indirect costs and the scientific protocol. I can assure you personally it will receive the highest priority possible. R.H.

To: Harris Sept. 21, 1967
From: Tiller
I propose to implant an artificial heat source of 45 watts in the abdomen of 25 experimental animals and maintain them at the Mojave State animal colony. Multiple laboratory tests will be carried out as outlined in the attached protocol. J.T.

To: Tiller Oct. 1, 1967
From: Harris
Your proposal has been found to be acceptable. The program will be funded in full, beginning Jan. 1, 1968. Monthly letters stating current progress will be required.

The university must file a statement indicating that it is an Equal Opportunity Employer. R.H.

To: Harris Feb. 1, 1968
From: Tiller
Animals have been delivered. Supplies have been ordered. Implantation begun Jan. 29. J.T.

To: Harris March 1, 1968
From: Tiller
Twenty heat sources have been implanted. Two animals died of technical error. These will be replaced. J.T.

To: Harris April 1, 1968
From: Tiller
A total of 25 living animals are now in the colony. Animals are healthy, eating and drinking well. Weight stable. All animals have a fever of 1° C in line with new stable point for heat loss. J.T.

To: Harris May 1, 1968
From: Tiller
All animals doing well. One female, now known to be pregnant, delivered healthy offspring! Mother doing fine! Request permission to suspend monthly report until final summary in September. I am going on vacation. J.T.

To: Tiller May 14, 1968
From: Harris
Congratulations on becoming a father! Delay of monthly reports granted but must be written on return from vacation. R.H.

To: Harris Aug. 1, 1968
From: Tiller
Twenty-one animals still doing well. A problem has arisen. During summer weekend, automatic watering facilities were inoperative in four cages. Animals were found dead with severe dehydration. The disturbing feature is not that the watering failed, but that the animals succumbed so quickly. I will advise you further. J.T.

To: Harris Sept. 1, 1968
From: Tiller
The deaths of four animals during the summer have been examined closely. We have simulated the body fluid components on an IBM 7094 digital computer. The tentative results are probably the most fascinating to arise from this study.

The mechanisms of heat loss are as follows: 1) convection, 2) radiation, 3) evaporation of sweat excretory, and 4) calories carried in respiratory water. The physiological adjustments made by the normally hydrated animal obscured the fact that, although the body temperature was raised only one degree at the balance point, this was achieved by a remarkable increase in water turnover. Thus, we noted a rapid breathing, an increase in fluid ingestion, and urinary volume.

The accidental interruption, on a warm day, of the water supply indicated what a delicate balance these animals had achieved. They died in about half the time expected when totally deprived of water. It is a positive feedback situation. The less hydrated the animal, the hotter patient/animal becomes; the hotter the patient/animal, the more water lost through the saturated breath and sweat. Thus, there is less cooling water, and the cycle continues on to a form of heat exhaustion. We suspect this may be a dangerous situation, i.e., in an abnormal setting, for a patient with such an endogenous heat source.

I believe further studies should be carried out on this aspect of your heart program. J.T.

To: Tiller Sept. 10, 1968
From: Harris
We are in receipt of your communication of Sept. 1, 1968. You did not mention the fate of the living animals. Please follow protocol originally submitted: what is your conclusion re artificial heat in normal conditions? R.H.

To: Harris Sept. 15, 1968
From: Tiller
Under normal conditions, 21 animals survived the experiments well, but as I have written, there seems to be too slim a line between safety and disaster. We have the administrative aspects all lined up to carry on the studies suggested. These remain the most interesting data we have achieved. It is important to continue the experiments as four animals are not a significant number from a statistical point of view. J.T.

To: Artificial Heart Advisory Group Nov. 4, 1968
From: Harris
We are in receipt of the final report from Prof. James Tiller of Mojave State University. It is accepted and on file in the offices of the Section on Artificial Hearts for those of you who have the time to review it.

In summary, I quote directly from his last memorandum: "Under normal conditions 21 animals survived the experiments well." Four animals did die and this was related to an accident with the water supply. In any event, and I quote again, "Four animals are not a significant number from the statistical point of view." I recommend we move on to other aspects of the development program. R.H.

To: Tiller Jan. 5, 1969
From: Harris
Your final report has been accepted by the Advisory Committee.

Your distinguished work has aided the program and undoubtedly thereby thousands of Americans suffering from heart disease. The committee did not recommend any further studies. R.H.

The westerly breezes were gone as Cooper waited for nightfall. He turned off the thermostat and opened the windows and balcony door to let the hot air in. Hot weather comforted him. The cancer had wasted much of his natural fat and with the insulation gone, he always felt cold and clammy.

It was not too long before the temperature in Gray's cell started to rise. Gray's body, already working overtime to rid itself of the atomic heat, began to burn with fever.

Chapter 36

"Brad Warren!" James Tucker, gynecologist, called out over the rush of water. "I was hoping to find you here."

The heart surgeon stood ritually scrubbing his hands and arms with iodinized soap. Since medical school, Warren had washed his hands literally thousands of times in scrub rooms. The light in this particular one was bright, the walls hard-tiled. The sink was stainless steel and water temperature tepid.

"You've got a case today?" asked Warren.

"Yes, but not for a little while. Heard something mighty strange this morning. Wanted to talk to you about it."

"Fire away, but you'd better be quick. Got a three-thousand-dollar case just dyin' to meet me in there." He nodded toward the operating room beyond the swinging doors.

"I was down at the city jail today."

"Things getting that tough, old boy? Or did some society gal get busted for a little whatchamacallit?"

"Hang on, Brad, just wait a minute. Got called by a good lawyer friend of mine about a hooker who claimed she was entrapped by a couple of cops."

Warren smacked his lips at the prospect of a juicy story. He loved to hear of the peccadilloes of others, and not infrequently Tucker shared them with him.

"Man alive! That would be hard to prove." Warren chuckled.

"Maybe, but I've got some tests that might help identify the man."

"Whee! You got to stop this science crap, Tucker. Can't have fun without being called into court—even with a hooker? What's the world coming to?"

Warren turned away from the sink, shutting off the water with his knee. Holding his arms up in the traditional fashion, he allowed his hands to drip toward his elbows. His surgical trousers were wet.

"So some cops got caught with their hands in the cookie jar, so to speak."

Tucker had to change to surgical clothes to get into the scrub area. His cases were not scheduled until later, so Warren knew that the story had to be of some importance. He waited for the rest of the tale.

"This gal . . ."

"Good-looking?"

"Baby doll, but underneath as tough as nails—pretty experienced. After my exam, she came up and asked me to relay a message to her lawyer. She said there was evidence from inside the police that Gray, the man with the artificial heart, was missing and that an explosion was possible. She wanted me to tell her lawyer to sell all the stock in ATOCOR right away. She emphasized that in no uncertain terms. Now last March I dabbled in that stock with you, if you remember."

"Yep, sure do, Tucker, sure do. Did you pass the message on?"

"Yes."

"What happened?"

"He just said thanks."

"Not going to take payment out in trade, are you, you devil?"

"Of course not."
"Tucker, it looks like we're all going to make a pretty penny. Yes, sir. I knew something was terribly fishy this morning when I got called by the university about making a donation."
"You knew already?"
"Just some bull. My name was on their donors' list, so they called. Wanted me to contribute to an emergency contingency fund. Just collateral, mind you. I didn't have to give. They said there was a possible malfunction in one of the hearts which needed something or other. They really didn't spell it out. Man! They didn't know who they were trying to con with that stuff. Wanted 25K! This Okie knows an empty till when he sees one!"
"Well, any fund-raiser would do that. Best foot forward ol' chap! What did you tell them?"
"To bug off."
"Not like that?"
"No, worse. But it all makes sense now."
"Want to sell short?"
"Tucker, you're learning! Learning from me."
Warren pushed open the operating room door with his washed hands and called into the waiting team. "Just keep him asleep a little longer. I have a brief emergency to take care of."
"He's already intubated!" protested the anesthetist.
"You start cutting if you want." Warren turned back to Tucker. "Damn fool gas passers anyway. Let's get to a phone."
"Aren't you worried that someone might actually blow up San Francisco?"
"That would really depress the price of ATOCOR, wouldn't it?" said Warren, his eyes sparkling with greed. "Don't worry, friend. Our little asses are safe tonight—take it from me."
"But the public can be panicked and ATOCOR is going to get the old crash treatment. I'm just surprised it didn't collapse earlier. You predicted the pump wouldn't fly, if I remember correctly."
"Not a bad memory, Tucker, my boy, but a little bit off. I

predicted it would be too expensive from the plutonium standpoint. I didn't know the level at which Uncle Sam was subsidizing it. But when this news gets out, it will be the living end for sure. Now there's a beautiful phone."

Tucker stood anxiously by while Warren called his broker.

"Fred? Brad Warren. I want to sell short my entire credit line of ATOCOR on margin. That's 50K, right?"

"Yes. What's the reason?"

"I can't talk—just starting another operation. I'll have to go."

"The New York Exchange is closed."

"Sell on the Pacific Coast—anything. Just get going. Here's my friend, Tucker."

"Hello, Tucker here. How about selling five hundred shares?"

"Okay. Still a secret?"

Tucker looked at Warren, who shook his head.

"Not really, but a little complex. Hope to hear from you soon."

Tucker hung up and both men grinned broadly.

"That's old-fashioned wheelin' and dealin'! Just like my old dad," smiled Warren. "'Course, he lost more than he made and died in the poorhouse, but he was a millionaire a couple of times! We'll just wait until the news gets out. Let the market simmer a bit."

Warren moved off back to the operating room and Tucker followed him.

"Notice the heat?" said Tucker.

"The O.R. was a little warm this morning, but I haven't been out. Air conditioners probably working right up to the limit."

"Hotter than a pistol when I came in. Must be about ninety degrees now at least."

"Glad I'm workin' inside. Got a customer that might cool off permanently if I don't get to him soon. Glad to do business with you, Tucker."

"Any time, Warren. Any time."

* * *

In Oregon the remnants of the weather front blew small, gray-white clouds rapidly across the high mountain tops. The air was crisp, the snow hung in the shadowed areas of the hills, but it was fast disappearing. The U.S. weather station issued the 2:00 P.M. forecast, indicating return to stable conditions for the Pacific Coast.

Cynthia Ridley, dressed warmly in gray wool slacks and a pullover, walked hand-in-hand with Allen into the darkly natural, wood-sculptured lobby. Timberline Lodge reflected the craft of the thirties, as it had been constructed by the artisans of the Roosevelt Civilian Conversation Corps. Doors were made of metal, hand-tooled and joined without welding. Murals depicting the legend of Paul Bunyan were blasted out of opaque glass. Elaborate mosaics of wood and stone caressed appreciative eyes wherever one turned. Save for electric lighting and the telephone, the lodge left high technology to the crowded city masses.

Cynthia's wind-bitten cheeks were rosy, her laughter gay and infectious.

"Would you care for a glass of sherry, Cyn?"

"I feel more like hot apple cider or rum."

"Swell."

Allen guided her by the hand into the tranquil lounge and sat her by the crackling cedar fire, then kissed her on the cheek. Her hair had the fragrance of pine and fir. She sat and watched the dancing fire while he went off to get the drinks.

Cynthia Ridley was a modern, well-educated woman. She had chosen marriage deliberately after a brief career and a living-together existence in college. The early years of marriage had been idyllic with the give-and-take shared equally and with normal day-to-day problems. Until last year, she thought, when the atomic heart problem struck suddenly and without warning. The strains on the marriage were real and threatening, and she knew she could continue to give only a little bit more on the one-way street it had become.

Allen appeared suddenly with two spicy apple ciders in old-fashioned mugs. "Here's to you, Cyn!"

She smiled and blew him a kiss. "How long will this last?" she asked.

He knew what she was talking about. "How much more can you stand?"

"Not fair! I asked first," she giggled.

"What's really wrong with us, Cyn?" Allen's voice was serious.

"You really want to know?"

"Yes, of course I do."

"Well, it's hard to put into words. You've cloaked yourself with an all-consuming moral authority which puts you out of step with all the rest of us. I admire you for it, but I can't live on that alone, raising the children by myself. While I respect the need for people like you in the world, I don't want you to carry the whole burden on your shoulders."

"It's been that bad?"

"Yes, I'm afraid it has."

"I'm only doing this for the children, so they can grow up in a world with a rational future."

"And I agree with that, but it would be nicer if they knew their father a little better."

They sat silently for a few minutes. He understood quite clearly his wife's distress.

"Okay," he said finally.

"Okay, what?"

"It won't be long now."

"You're going to look for another job?"

"In a few months."

"Is that a promise?"

"Yes. When we get to Boston I'll pass the word that I'm available."

"Oh, Allen. I'm happy that you see it my way." She moved her face upward until her lips touched his.

"You know, Cyn," said Allen," when I first met you, I thought you were the most beautiful woman I'd ever seen. I still think so."

She held his hand, and joy welled up in her heart. The love

and intimacy that had long been absent from their relationship had returned.

"Let's go to the cabin," Allen whispered.

"Like yesterday after lunch . . . ?"

"Yep."

She laughed and scooted quickly out of the door with Allen after her.

Chapter 37

Twomey's squad had been alerted. He had extra men transferred from other duty stations, and leaves had been cancelled. The lieutenant was walking toward the squad room when he saw the two officers. Though now in uniform, Twomey recognized them. This time there were no smirks or grins on their faces, just obvious tension. They flinched when they saw him.

"What are your names?" Twomey barked.

"Washington, sir," said the black.

"Murphy," said the other.

Twomey bore into them, nose to nose. "The pinch you were supposed to haul in caught *you* two like a couple of poor fish."

"Yes, sir."

"The word is she decided not to press charges. You don't deserve to be that lucky."

"No, sir."

"And now you've been assigned to me. If I didn't need the bodies, I'd not have the likes of you near me. If you screw up again, you're out. Now get in there and listen."

"Thank you, sir."

They moved into the squad room. Twomey stood on a small dais looking over the men assembled in front of him. He felt their grim mood percolating below the surface and saw the fatigue lining the faces of some. It mattered hardly at all to Twomey. There was a job to be done and that was all there was to it. Still, uniformed police officers do not act like automatons. The psychology of leadership had to be exercised, and he began the briefing.

"Okay, you men. Come to attention. Officer Washington, close the door. A white male has been kidnaped by persons unknown within SFPD jurisdiction. The FBI has information that a ransom demand has been made. The overall investigation therefore rests with the bureau."

A soft "Boo" wafted down from the back of the crowded room, followed by tension-breaking laughter.

"They have legal jurisdiction," said Twomey, "but the small force of their field office is thinly spread over the Bay area. They'll need a lot of help."

There were a few cheers and claps.

"This is no ordinary kidnaping, as you can see by the size of the task force," continued Twomey. "The victim's name is Gray. Many of you may remember him. He's the first man to get a successful artificial heart. The ransom is two million dollars."

There were whistles of surprise and excitement. "What makes him so special?"

"His heart is powered by an atomic battery made of plutonium. As you know, the stuff is used in nuclear power plants. But it's also a key component of atomic bombs. Obviously, the source is quite limited on the commercial market. It could be traded to other countries, or it could be used to build an explosive right here in the city."

A murmur of discussion swept through the audience.

"Now, before everyone gets all hot and bothered, the experts feel that making a bomb with this small amount of plutonium is next to impossible."

Twomey spoke emphatically. "But we do not rule it out. There might be some other tack we don't know about. So we must be prepared. Other jurisdictions have been alerted, but we are the prime force.

"The size of this group is dictated by the need to act as a protection force. Terrorist activity against public and industrial property has been at a low point recently. This may be the lull before the storm. So there must be intensive surveillance of all major buildings round the clock until further notice."

"Oh, for crying out loud! Statue of Liberty duty!"

Twomey ignored the sally. "The physical size of a crude atomic explosive is such that it's difficult to conceal. Watch the delivery entrances, trucks, station wagons—that type of activity.

"As for the hostage, the drop is to be made tonight. He might be freed or he might not. M.O. not standard. We have several clues. The victim is a public figure. His face is well known to many. We've found a letter indicating he was to meet someone at the Mark Hopkins. His car hasn't been located, but we're looking. We have photos of Gray to show you later."

"Lieutenant, any clues with respect to the perpetrator?"

"It doesn't look like the work of radicals. No communiqués, nobody claiming credit. Possibly a random incident, but the FBI isn't taking chances. It's contacting all artificial heart patients to offer them protection. The kidnaper seems to have knowledge of nuclear physics. That's too unusual to be a coincidence, and we want to be prepared for any eventuality. Okay, now break it up. There's a lot of work—physical evidence to track down. Take a look at the photos over there and get your assignments."

The men dispersed to the bulletin board and regrouped to get instructions. For most of them, it would be a long, warm, dull night.

Washington peered at the list: taxi duty followed by reassignment at headquarters. Pick up a Mr. Allen Ridley at San

Francisco airport arriving by air taxi and rush to the command post. "What do you have, Murphy?"

"Damn, I'll be pounding the beat at the Marina Towers."

"Well, it's cooler out there by the bridge."

"Yeah. Should be thankful for small mercies!"

Even before agents had been dispatched to Oregon to find Ridley, the FBI had set in motion a wide-ranging network of activity in cities where artificial heart patients lived.

Just before noon, a gray, unmarked sedan drove up in front of the Sunland Apartments in Dallas. The buildings were white with touches of yellow and lined a narrow, rather bleak frontage road. The Texas sun made the steps hot for the two men who walked cautiously toward the entrance.

"That's the one."

He knocked on the door while the other man surveyed the area. The door opened. A woman answered. A cool breeze spilled through the closed screen door.

"Mrs. Seguira?"

"Yes."

"We're from the FBI. May we come in?"

They displayed their open, badge-studded billfolds with their identification. They peered through the screen into the dark living room. It was empty and quiet.

"Well, all right," said the middle-aged, slightly obese woman.

The two big men entered, both wiping the heat-generated sweat off their foreheads with their handkerchiefs.

"Is Mr. Seguira at work?"

"No, he's home. He works evening shift. Juan!"

Seguira appeared from the kitchen dressed in Levis and an undershirt with a can of beer in his hand. "Yes?" He looked impassive, while the wife's eyes darted between the two men and the husband with growing anxiety.

A sheet-metal worker, Seguira was pleasantly anonymous until he suffered his first and only heart attack. This was not unusual, there being some 600,000 heart attacks suffered by

Americans each year. But the timing of his misfortune coincided with the local heart research institute's receiving its permit to begin implanting artificial hearts. Seguira followed the Big Doctor's advice and the heart was implanted. It was the fourteenth in the world, and Seguira returned to work a minor celebrity. Then he had been left alone until this day.

"We're from the FBI, sir," said one of the men. "There's a bit of a problem with another patient. Something to do with the nuclear fuel. We have orders to give all patients with the heart round-the-clock protection."

"Jeez! From what?"

"We're not at liberty to say."

"Okay, I suppose. Anything the government wants to do. I'm a good citizen. Sit down, won't you?"

"We'll just look around first, if you don't mind."

"Okay, sure. Go right ahead. I don't have a big place. How long do you think you'll be here?"

"It's indefinite, I'm afraid."

"That long, huh? I don't have to pay for this, do I? I can't really afford this on my pay?"

"Of course not."

"How about my job?" He followed them as they began to inspect the apartment."

"Someone will go along with you—unobtrusively of course."

"It must be really serious!"

"It is, Mr. Seguira, it is. But you've got nothing to worry about as long as we're around."

"Call me Juan. We're going to get pretty close, I expect, for a while. Want a beer? Or how about a Coke?"

"A Coke would be fine."

"Elvira, get these boys a Coke."

Other artificial heart patients were approached in the same way by the FBI. Within two hours all the patients in seven cities had been located.

Chapter 38

The chartered jet plane carrying Ridley approached San Francisco. Ridley had been located at the lodge after one telephone call by the FBI to Boston. Within an hour a state police helicopter dropped out of the sky at the lodge and two field agents from the Portland office interrogated him. It was not difficult to persuade them he knew nothing of the kidnaping. But it became clear, as he discussed the situation with the agents, that the FBI was underestimating the potential dangers associated with 100 grams of plutonium in the wrong hands. A nuclear bomb was low on his own list of possibilities. In a call to San Francisco, Ridley could not explain fully the ramifications and he asked, almost demanded, that he be flown south immediately. They had finally agreed.

"Well," Ridley said to Cynthia, "the problem has finally surfaced."

She looked at him with stricken eyes. "Will it be dangerous for you?"

"It could be dangerous for many people."

Cynthia did not try to dissuade him. It would have been useless anyway, she knew. She would just pack up and go home to Boston.

The lights of the bridges and the streams of cars passing along the freeways beneath were soon in view. Beads of lights outlined the streets with large dark areas indicating the parks and peaks. Then, quickly, with priority clearance from the control tower, they were down on a narrow runway taxiing to a remote airport hangar.

A black-and-white police car was already waiting for him. As soon as the ramp was down, Ridley bounded off the jet.

While he carried many details about the toxic properties of fissile material in his memory, Ridley knew documentation of some kind would be needed to convince some very skeptical cops who might probably take him as just another "nutty" environmentalist with a scare story. He needed to produce concrete evidence, so a short side trip on the way to San Francisco was justified.

"Officer Washington, take me to a technical library first."

"Will the public library do? It's about ten blocks from the hall."

"No, not good enough. It would have to be Stanford or U.C."

"I'm supposed to take you right to headquarters."

"Stanford is close. It wouldn't take long to find what I need."

"Well, okay, but they could have my rear end on the deck fast!"

"No, they won't. I'll see to that," Ridley said with a false assurance.

The cop spun the car around, turned on the red lights, and took off, sprawling Ridley backwards into the seat trying to maintain his equilibrium.

It was near closing time when they arrived at the main library on the Stanford campus. It was an old building dating back to the twenties, near the large modern Meyer Undergraduate Library. The physics subsection was on the first floor.

Ridley walked rapidly over the floors of well-worn wood. The windowsills were thick with coats of black paint applied over the years. Incandescent lights illuminated the room.

Stacks of books lined the walls, and heavy oak reading tables were centered in two rows of three each. It was a quiet, old-fashioned place with a single prim-looking woman seated at the entrance, watchful over her silent, stationary charges.

"Miss," said Ridley. "I need to get some references to the San Francisco police very urgently. This officer will testify he will be taking me there as soon as I leave here."

She appeared dubious.

"I have identification, as does this officer. We can get the materials back to you in an hour or two."

"Well, this is highly irregular . . . but the San Francisco police. I guess it will be all right. Can I help you find what you need? Do you have a list?"

"I know the references by heart. One, the *Plutonium Handbook*; two, "Science,' volume one-eighty-three, pages seven-hundred-fifteen to seven-hundred-twenty-two; three, 'Radiation Standards for Hot Particles,' NRDC, nineteen-seventy-four; four, *Physics in Medicine and Biology*, nineteen-seventy-five; five, 'British Journal of Industrial Medicine'; six, 'Health Physics,' volume twenty-two, nineteen-seventy-two."

"Gosh!" said the librarian. "What do you want them for?"

"If I told you, you wouldn't believe me."

The intern on Bradfield's service sat slouched in the doctors' dressing room, the standard paper cup of coffee balanced on the arm of the chair.

"Damn, something's really screwy!"

It was 6:00 P.M., the routine operations had finished, and most of the staff had gone on rounds and then home. A lone medical student, fresh and anxious, had joined him. An intern in a hospital was the lowest in the pecking order of M.D.'s, but to a student—well, he was virtually the ultimate because he had decision-making authority.

"What's going on?" asked the student.

"The old man has doubled the schedule throughout his entire day. As one case is finishing in the O.R., he's had another start in the adjacent room so that he doesn't rescrub! Just slips into a fresh gown and gloves, and bingo! next case. I don't know about him, but I've had it!"

"Are you going to walk out?"

"I've half a mind to. It may get too dangerous for the patients."

"Gee! Really walk out on Bradfield?"

The intern raised a weary eyebrow. "You know, that guy would give the anesthesia himself if the anesthesiologist refused to do the case. He'd turn the heart-lung machine on to autopilot if the technician did not show up! If *I* failed to show up, he'd rig up an instrument holder from the ceiling to hold the retractors and I'd be fired, but he'd still operate! I tell you, something crazy is going on."

The hurried schedule was having its impact elsewhere, in a ward where another patient was being prepped for surgery. An intern was finishing the history and physical examination.

"How come I didn't get any dinner tonight?" the patient said plaintively.

"Your stomach must be empty before the operation."

"But my operation isn't till tomorrow afternoon. That's what I was told."

"Dr. Bradfield has rescheduled your operation for tonight. Maybe he thinks you need it in a hurry."

"What do you think, doctor?"

"Well, I haven't seen your X-ray studies. I can't say for sure."

"My angina hasn't changed. I told my family it would be tomorrow. They won't be in to visit until eight or nine in the morning."

"Well, it will be all over by then. That will be a nice surprise for them."

"Are you sure I'm going to have surgery tonight? My name is Bob Jones!"

The intern smiled. "Yes, sir. We don't have any other patient by that name on the ward."

Bob Jones lay back on the bed, perplexed. "Strangest thing I've ever heard of."

* * *

"Is that the last one?" Geld asked.

"Yes," Workman answered, his voice low and tired.

Outside, the unmarked police car that had brought the last delivery of cash drove away. The banks were closed. Several offices at Aspermont's administration building were still lit up. It was getting close to the time to make the drop, but only $700,000 in cash had been raised—far short of the demanded two million.

Two uniformed police stood guard in a room adjacent to the office. The cash was placed in a large, leather suitcase equipped with a false bottom containing a low-frequency transmitter.

Geld and Workman had worked furiously throughout the day making every contact possible. They had wheedled and whined, had used Bradfield's magic name liberally. They had used the ATOCOR shareholders' list, too, although they had not mentioned the specific problem.

The instructions said that Bradfield was to be at a certain locker at the Giants' baseball stadium at ten o'clock. There were still a couple of hours to go.

As Workman closed the suitcase, an FBI agent came in from the outer office. He looked dispassionately at the two harassed administrators. "Well, at about ten tonight the ballgame at the stadium will be just about over. This kidnaper is clever. I should think there will be further instructions to go on to some remote spot. He'll probably be in the crowd, watching to see if our man shows up. No chance of our being able to spot him there. Then, with all the cars leaving the stadium, we'd have a tough time tailing him."

"What are you going to do?"

"We'll still keep track through Bradfield."

Geld was relieved. He had been told that putting up the ransom was still a sort of private deal. Officially the FBI would have no part of it. Now, however, they had plans to follow the go-between. There was a chance they might nab the suspect and get the victim and the money back.

"Shouldn't we put in a note saying we couldn't get all the money and that we'll get the rest tomorrow?" asked Workman.

The FBI man shook his head. "No, let him count it himself."

They planned to track the suitcase with mobile radiodirection finders. The baseball stadium was on the east side of the peninsula. There was one north-south freeway on the east, and a parallel one on the west. Police cars would be stationed on several peaks in the area so that the radio signal from the suitcase would be triangulated. It was a routine method. After determining the direction of the delivery car, police would then track the suitcase to the dropoff spot. The main precaution was to be sure not to spook the pickup man.

Cibelli, the P.R. man, came into the room after Geld had reached him by phone. "Well, I'm ready, though frankly, I feel scared."

Geld said, "We appreciate your agreeing to take Bradfield's place if we have to use a substitute. That son-of-a-bitch got us all into this mess and now he's hiding out in his lair." Geld was uncharacteristically heated and outspoken.

The FBI man said, "You know you may queer the drop by sending a sub."

"Damnit, I didn't know what else to do. Bradfield is holed up in the O.R. It's difficult to haul him away from there."

The agent shrugged. "It's your money."

The phone buzzer rang, startling them. Geld answered, then handed the instrument over to the agent. "It's your chief from San Francisco. Wants to talk to you."

Chapter 39

Mario Delmonico, Mayor of San Francisco, had received an urgent message to report to the Hall of Justice. A sudden contingency had arisen. Worried and wondering, he had hurried out the side door of his home into a waiting limousine.

The limousine entered the basement garage of the building and the Mayor took the express elevator to the third floor, breathing fast as he stepped out. Indulgence at family dinners and political banquets, plus a lack of exercise, had taken their toll. His rimless glasses perched precariously on his wide nose, engulfed by a full, round face.

A shaft of light pierced the darkness of the hallway as Delmonico opened the door. In front of him he saw a large wall-sized map of the city. It was made of a light-blue transparent plastic. Streets stood out clear and colorless. Fire houses, police stations, hospitals, defense shelters, staging areas—all were clearly marked. Two men stood beneath the map. Their job was to move markers indicating mobile units to preassigned locations. A bank of yellow battery-operated telephones was spread along a row of desks. Teletypes, their clatter confined within a glass box, were placed off to the left. Consoles of radio communication equipment were next to the teletypes. These included a DEC computer-driven network, a high-speed teleprinter, monitors tuned to network and closed-circuit TV. Tall cabinets, filled with neatly organized binders, were set against the walls.

Here was the operations room, the brain center, of San Francisco's Office of Emergency Services. From here coded orders to field units could be sent automatically and be instantly translated into action. The people who ran this command post thought of the unthinkable and were prepared to act when it struck. Alerts could be activated in a disaster when normal systems became overloaded or inoperative, when there was a threat to life and property, when coordination of forces required special arrangements.

Key officials from police, fire, medical services, public works, and the Red Cross were on their way in.

"Now, what's this all about?" asked Delmonico after looking around at the orderly commotion. "This isn't another practice alert, is it?"

"No, sir, not at all. We have a very bad situation," Twomey replied and then introduced Ridley. Delmonico offered his hand in a brisk shake. They moved into a glass-partitioned office at the end of the command post, and the Mayor was briefed. At the end, Twomey said, "Allen, tell the Mayor what you told us about the plutonium."

Ridley began slowly by explaining that the heart-makers had chosen plutonium because it was an ideal fuel. A small amount could generate power for a long time. On the moon and Mars were five plutonium capsules powering instruments of the Apollo and Viking missions. Heart pacers, containing only a fraction of a gram, controlled heart rhythm in over a thousand patients around the world. And of course the artificial heart had 100 grams.

Twomey, listening, thumbed through one of Ridley's reference books. One section on the toxicity of plutonium contained four hundred and twenty-one pages of single-spaced type and complex tables and figures. It was "the source" but too technical for lay readers.

"Back in the forties," Ridley said, "Seaborg at the University of California pointed out that plutonium was potentially hazardous. Studies followed showing that plutonium was radiotoxic in small doses injected into experimental animals."

"How toxic?" asked Delmonico and looked at both men.

"About ten times more toxic than radium," said Ridley. He took the volume from Twomey and held it out before Delmonico.

"This book reports the studies of animals which have inhaled plutonium, trying to simulate conditions humans might encounter."

Ridley paused and looked directly at Delmonico, trying to size him up.

"Radiation from medical grade plutonium will not penetrate the skin," Ridley continued. "The stuff is insoluble. If swallowed, almost all of it will pass through the digestive tract and on out of the body. But if one breathes it—well, that's a different story. The inhaled particles will be carried to the air sacs and stay there in intimate contact with lung cells."

Ridley opened the book to show the mayor a graph of experiments. "On page eight hundred and three, here, is the crucial figure. It tells the whole story. It plots survival of the animals in days after inhaling plutonium."

Delmonico shook his head. "Yes, I see it, but I don't really understand it. What's this Curie?"

"A Curie is a unit of radioactivity. An artificial heart has seventeen hundred Curies. These data indicate that if one hundred millionth of one Curie were inhaled by the animal, it would die of direct lung damage in twenty days. If the particle were even smaller, say, ten millionth of one Curie, the immediate damage to the lungs would be less, but the animals would still die of lung insufficiency in a year. Here, the process is slow death of the lung cell, which is replaced by scar tissue. Scar tissue is ineffective in transporting oxygen, and gradually more of the lung is replaced by scar tissue; so death occurs in about a year.

"Now, there is enough plutonium in one artificial heart to kill seventeen million animals in twenty days or a hundred and seventy million animals in one year!"

The Mayor blanched as the enormity of the figures sunk into his consciousness.

"Unfortunately, there's more," the somber Ridley continued. He pointed back to the mute graphs that told the awful story. With his finger he indicated on one graph black dots (• • • • • •) rather than a line of open dots (o o o o o o) that filled the intersection of time and dose.

"Must mean something different, I suppose. Those dots are different," said the Mayor,

"Right, sir. They do mean something entirely different. If the plutonium dust is made even finer, there's a qualitative difference in the result. The lungs still scar, but more slowly, and the animals survive four or five years. Now they die with lung cancer. The mechanism is not clear. But we do know that low levels of long-term radiation are associated with cancer. In the lungs the plutonium cannot be dissolved or excreted by the body. It remains trapped in the site, giving off radiation. There's enough plutonium in one heart for one billion, seven hundred million animals. . . . "

Ridley handed the book back to Twomey. He stood up and stretched, waiting for Delmonico to grasp the horrific content of his remarks. The Mayor was only just beginning to comprehend the size of the problem. "What," he asked Ridley, "does all this mean in terms of human lives? You're talking about small animals."

"Okay. Assume the human lung is five times bigger and retains less plutonium, say fifty percent. All it means is that the number of doses is cut down by a factor of ten. So there would be one point seven million human doses instead of seventeen million. That's not a comforting figure. And as far as we know, man would respond in about the same way as an animal.

"Now, I'll give you an example of the physical dimensions of the problem. California has set up a so-called safe standard of plutonium. It's described in the State Code of Industrial Safety. If the amount of plutonium in one heart was perfectly diluted in the air to State Code level, it would take up a volume of air two meters high by eight hundred fifty million square kilometers. The surface of the earth is seventeen hundred million square kilometers!"

Delmonico understood that Ridley spoke of hypothetical possibilities. But even at that theoretical level, the Mayor could only gasp in recognition of the numbers involved. It was certainly no formula for comfort.

"But how does the artificial heart patient avoid getting contaminated with the plutonium inside him?" Delmonico asked. "That's something I've never been able to understand."

"The plutonium in the heart is separated from living tissue by the capsule. The range of the alpha rays from the radioactive decay is very short and absorbed by the insulation layers. The fuel itself is specially processed. It's not a powder, but a glass-hard disc. The container of the fuel section was designed to withstand any credible accident, and has been proven in tests of high temperature similar to accidental cremation, by shooting bullets at it and so on."

"Then what is the concern? What's the danger if it's so well protected?"

"The danger is that we don't have an accident situation in our hands. We've got a nut, a criminal, maybe an insane criminal, a terrorist, and the container can be opened and used by someone with minimal technical knowhow. If he can convert the fuel disc to a dust and, say, explode it, it could be very dangerous for many people."

"But won't it be dangerous to the manipulator, too?"

"That is, so far, the only good point in the whole situation. I don't know just how it could be done, but the potential is there. If he has figured a safe way to do it—well, then, we're in a no-win position."

Twomey led the Mayor back into the command post. The emergency director and his assistants were waiting before the big illuminated map.

"It's the real thing, all right," Delmonico said bluntly. "We hope the kidnaper is only after the ransom. But in the meantime we have to plan for the worst. We have to be ready for him or whatever he is after." He felt a small twinge of pain start somewhere in his gut, born, he knew, of nervous panic.

The coordinator of emergency services spoke. He seemed confident and calm. "This is how I see the various options. First, I agree we have a potentially serious problem. But I see some possibilities to work with. There are always ways to deal with a situation if one looks at it carefully. The choice of Gray was not accidental, or just related to his being famous. It's clear that San Francisco is peculiarly vulnerable."

"The Golden Gate?" said Ridley.

"Exactly!"

Delmonico rolled his eyes up to the ceiling in silent supplication.

The Director went on. "We all know the wind whips right through there like clockwork—west to east. You get the dust out there, and we'll have all of the East Bay and most of the populace of San Francisco contaminated by the stuff."

Ridley nodded. "No doubt—minutes—an hour at the most."

"The particles will rise, fall back to the ground, then recirculate into the air for days."

"A good thundershower would take care of the problem."

"When was the last time we had a thunderstorm in June in San Francisco? Brother, it won't happen," and Delmonico shook his head despairingly.

The Director interrupted. "The danger lies in wind dispersion of plutonium dust. The present heat wave is a godsend. I guess it will be a day or two before the breezes return. That means we have time to prepare. Now, if we could force his hand and disperse the plutonium before the weather breaks, we have a chance. Radioactivity will be confined to a few square blocks around the site. In that case the countermeasures will be to wash the stuff down into the sewers, keep it from refluxing into the air. Also, we must advise people to shut all windows, turn off fans and air conditioners and remain indoors."

"Why not evacuate everybody?" asked Delmonico.

"It could be done," said the man from traffic control, "but it would take more than a day. We can empty the baseball park of fifty thousand people in thirty minutes. To move seven hundred and fifty thousand people is a giant undertaking."

"Then, we'd need housing," said the man from the Red Cross. "In the north, there are the abandoned air bases. In the south we could use Moffett Field and school buildings all the way to San Jose. But evacuation isn't that simple. Looting should be expected without people around to protect their homes."

The Emergency Director spoke again. "I like to think of my approach as being the most practical. It's the least expensive and would protect the maximum number of people. If we asked the State and the AEC now, we'll have the radiation monitors here in twenty-four hours."

"What if we discover the kidnaper's location? Should we negotiate?" a voice broke in.

"The police chief answered. "We've a top-notch weapons and tactics squad. They can handle any situation."

"And the hostage?"

"He's expendable, I'm afraid. We have to get the heart."

Delmonico glanced at his watch. It was late. He thought of all the people living peacefully in the city. What a horror if massive radiation damage were inflicted on them. It was unfair! A mayor was not supposed to have this kind of responsibility. A president, a general, the leaders who had guided the nation along the path of nuclear future—they should be sitting here now. He was definitely no maker of grand decisions on death and destruction.

The Mayor pulled out a handkerchief from his pocket to dab the sweat off the top of his forehead. He said to the men, "Get on with assembling all the supplies and equipment you need. I want you to begin plans to establish triage centers for potential casualties. I want the medical facilities available ready for emergency operation. I want the police ready to restrict property loss from looting or damage. Everything that can be done to be in a state of readiness must be done. That's all, gentlemen."

Twomey said, "We'd better inform Aspermont of the new potential here so they don't drop the ball."

"Yeah, and get more people on the surveillance."

Delmonico sat still for a moment, his eyes closed. Then he rose and looked at the Director. "Get me the Governor on the phone," he said quietly. "I'll take his call in Twomey's office."

The FBI man took the phone and listened. There were a couple of "yessirs" and "nosirs" but Geld, Workman, and Cibelli could not piece together the gist of the conversation. The agent hung up.

"Well, well, well. This is going to be more interesting than I thought." He looked over at Geld and pointed at Cibelli. "This guy isn't going. You get Bradfield out of the operating room now and down here pronto. I don't care if you have to turn off the electricity or something, just get him here."

Geld said, "Well, you guys are finally getting on the ball."

"Doctor, a fellow named Ridley says this mess could blow up into a catastrophe. The whole Bay area could be poisoned with that device of yours. They think it's more than a run-of-the-mill kidnaping, and they aren't taking chances. Come on, we don't have time to explain. Let's get going."

The Dean dialed the O.R. "This is Geld. I'd like to speak to Dr. Bradfield. It's urgent!"

A feminine voice said, "I'm sorry, sir. He's operating and can't be disturbed. Is there a message?"

"Yes. You go in and tell him I need to see him right away."

"Sorry, sir. I can't do that. Dr. Bradfield gave explicit orders . . . "

"The hell with orders. Go in and fetch him."

The woman still hesitated.

"What's your name?" snapped Geld.

"I'm Nurse Bollinger."

"Well, Miss Bollinger . . . " Geld paused. It was of no use. This woman was immovable. "Never mind, I'm coming up to get him myself."

He walked to the hospital wing. It was the end of visiting hours and the elevators were crowded. He walked up the stairs and arrived panting on the third floor. He hadn't run like this for years and thought he was having a heart attack. He pressed the door button and the automatic double doors of the O.R. opened.

"Doctor," a nurse yelled, "you can't go in there. You have to put on a mask and gown."

"Well, get me some."

In the operating theater, Bradfield peered above the surgical mask. "What the hell is this?" he said to Geld.

"We need you right away to make the drop."

"Have you got the money?"

"Only a part."

"I won't do it," he shouted at Geld. "This fund raising was your stupid idea. Without all of the cash and the police in on it, my patient will get killed for sure. I won't have any part in this."

Geld flared up. Tempers in the O.R. mounted. The argument rose to a high pitch, and then Geld told him about Ridley.

"That son-of-a-bitch, I knew it," said Bradfield. "So he's in on it."

"No, no," said Geld. "He's helping the police. He's determined that we're dealing with a nuclear blackmailer . . . something you told us couldn't happen."

Suddenly Bradfield shivered, cold, his mind shrinking from the possibility that confronted him. He knew he could not evade the truth any longer. He turned to his assistant and said, "Jack, finish up."

He signaled Geld to follow him and they walked out.

"God, what a terrible thing to happen! Are we responsible, do you think?" Workman asked Geld after Bradfield had departed for Candlestick Park.

The question summed up their dismal position. They had come upon the university scene when things were getting difficult. The endowment had shrunk, tuition had reached prohibitive levels, and competition for funds was fierce. To provide the best education possible as they saw it, their prestige university had been drawn increasingly into large technological developments. The source of money was inevitably the Federal government: the National Institutes of Health supported the medical school; the AEC provided for the high energy physics programs; the Defense Department and the National Science Foundation supported engineering; and NASA helped in aeronautics and astronautics. In seeking and using all this support, the once private, liberal education university had been transformed. Now there was no escaping the description—the university had become an advanced Federal technical research unit. The transformation had taken place not unthinkingly, but with full internal debate. They knew they were riding the tiger and there was no getting off.

Ridley and the Mayor walked slowly back downstairs. The hallways were silent, despite the increasing activity in the squad room, the laboratories, the command post.

In his public life Delmonico had made good use of the little hypocrisies considered essential for a politician. Under the smiling, gregarious style, however, he was a different man. He could concern himself with grander strategy if the need arose. He had to now. The Mayor wanted more information from the young man at his side, who seemed so knowledgeable on the crisis at hand.

"Ridley, how come we are in this fix?"

They seated themselves in Twomey's empty office.

"Well, sir. I wouldn't know where to begin."

"Start at the beginning," said Delmonico leaning forward in his chair.

"Some years back doctors recognized they had to do something for patients who suffered heart muscle damage."

"Nothing wrong with that," said Delmonico.

"One line of thought revolved around the notion of replacing the natural heart with a machine. Studies were commissioned, committees debated the feasibility and costs. They decided the shortest route to that goal was through the nuclear fuel approach, and so they went that route. There was the assumption of course that university scientists who evaluated this were unbiased."

"Well, the public expects that," remarked Delmonico. "If the professors aren't objective, who is? Academic freedom is based on the philosophy that they are engaged in the search for truth and knowledge to benefit mankind!"

"Right, Mayor, but that's not always the case," said Ridley. "University research today is really government research. If a professor can't get a grant, there's nothing much to work with. Scientists aren't paid to prove something *cannot* be done. They must demonstrate practicality and applicability of their results. When the government decided to build an artificial heart, all applicants tried to show why their way was the best to attain that goal."

"So the experts can't be trusted?"

"No. Take the doctors. We used to think of physicians as being different from other professionals. It's not that way at all. Some have just as many prejudices as the next guy.

"They saw in the information from the technologists that the heart was safe for individual patients. That had been their main worry, not what it might do to society. Once they had hurdled that obstacle, their objective was to apply it, and the more patients, the better. They're used to taking life-and-death risks for the individual patient, but they're poor judges when it comes to the big picture."

"I get it," said Delmonico. "If we ever get out of this, we've got to make sure it doesn't happen again."

"But how do you change things?"

"That's what politics is all about."

Ridley excused himself and left to freshen up. He had to consider how the kidnaper, obviously a clever individual, could carry out his terrible plan if indeed he intended to use the fuel disc as Ridley suspected. To Ridley, it was a difficult problem. One normally does not dream up ways to kill millions of people.

The phone rang and Delmonico picked it up. While he waited for the connection, he thought that Ridley would fit well on his staff next year when he declared his candidacy for the U.S. Senate. He would remember him. A deep voice came through on the line.

"Hello, Governor? Delmonico speaking." His voice was quiet and firm. "I'm sorry to bother you at this hour, but an emergency has come up. We need to have you alert the National Guard. . . . "

Chapter 40

The bright arc lights shone into the warm night sky, dust particles reflecting back pockets of light above the moving crowds. The Giants had won in the bottom of the tenth, 1–0. Twenty thousand fans cheered and waved signs in the air. The noise they made, like sunshine, lit the scene.

Bradfield had arrived on time, but the game had gone into extra innings. He stood near the lockers, waiting until he was surrounded by the departing fans. He felt quite self-conscious. Here he was, a talented heart surgeon, now a bagman, a messenger boy. He had no control of the situation. The roar of the crowd died away as the fans started to move out of the gates. He knew that several pairs of eyes in that sea of faces were trained on him. It came to him that this was dangerous. He had assured "Smith" he would be alone. Now his tension mounted.

He opened the locker and retrieved a message. It was enclosed in a plain envelope and typed neatly. It gave long, complicated instructions. He was to put the money in a duffel bag he would find in the locker. He was to drive by a circuitous route down the San Francisco peninsula and crisscross

Skyline Boulevard and Junipero Serra Freeway. The drop point would be marked by a flashing red light. He was to fold the message and put it in with the money, then return to Aspermont.

Good maneuver with the message, Bradfield thought. He couldn't just drop the message for a cop to pick up. He had to deliver it back to the kidnaper. "Smith" was smart, no doubt about it.

Bradfield looked up and around, tucking the bag under his arm, the note into his shirt pocket. Then he blended into the stragglers descending the hill against which the stadium was nestled.

Back at his car, he unlocked the trunk and removed the suitcase. Headlights picked him up momentarily, shining brightly into his eyes and throwing his shadow against the car. The other car passed on, the passengers noisily concerned with the next agenda item in San Francisco's North Beach.

Bradfield began to fall into the swing of events. He carried the suitcase with its small fortune and hidden guide device around to the front seat as if he were carrying a change of socks and a toothbrush. Handful after handful of paper, colorless gray in the dark car interior, was stashed into the duffel bag, the note on top of the pile. Then he drove off to the rendezvous.

Above the traffic, police technicians noted the changes in direction of the signals.

"He's heading south onto Two-eighty!"

The tracking process had begun.

It was 11:00 P.M. The communicator at Emergency Headquarters called out to Twomey and Ridley, "The auto is now on Skyline Boulevard in San Mateo County."

Skyline Boulevard was a wide two-lane highway along the spine of the Santa Cruz Mountains that ran the length of the San Francisco peninsula. The coordinator had been directing unmarked police cars to swing up from the south as Bradfield's car crossed through the various jurisdictional areas.

The triangulations progressively became less precise. Traffic was light and the cars trailing Bradfield would be obvious if someone were watching. Deliberately the tails dropped further and further behind.

"He's going down King's Mountain Road. He's off Skyline!"

"Hmmm. That road is very narrow. I've been there on a bicycle," Ridley said. "Maximum speed is about twenty miles and most of it is twisting and turning at five to ten miles per hour."

Twomey looked at the map silently. "What do you think the next turn will be, Allen?"

"Skyline runs along the top and Junipero Serra parallels the bottom of the slopes. King's Mountain runs from the summit to the bottom, and Page Mill further south does the same trek. He could have Bradfield drive down to Junipero Serra, then back to Page Mill. On a night like this, you could see a tailing auto for several miles."

"A drop could be made on those roads."

"It looks that way. He has to come out by road. The mountains are too steep, full of scrub oak with thorns and so on."

"Let's take a chance. We position two cars on each of the crossroads before Bradfield gets there. One could be near the top, the other near the bottom."

"I see. It won't look like a tail."

"Right. We'll have them drive slowly and exchange positions, then block the road so that no one can get out. There are no other side roads."

"How will you know whether the drop has been made on Page Mill or King's Mountain?"

"The bug in the suitcase will no longer move."

"Lieutenant," an aide called. "Here's some information on the interlibrary loans."

"Allen, you'll be interested in this," Twomey said, his voice rising in excitement.

Ridley looked at the list. He noted that one of his Stanford volumes had been checked out from a San Francisco branch library in the Noriega district. It was the only request this

branch library had processed for scientific technical material.
"Which volume?" said Twomey.
"'British Journal of Industrial Medicine.'"
"And here's a record from the library—a request to provide a photocopy of an article in that journal. Oh, those dear, sweet, compulsive librarians! Keeping all these records!"
"Article?"
"Page four-seventy-six."
"I'll look it up. It's one of those books I picked up. You cops amaze me! It was very clever of you to think about checking in the library, lieutenant!"
"Thank you, Allen," Twomey said simply.
Ridley rapidly turned the pages of the volume. "It's about reclaiming plutonium from the oxide."
It didn't take Ridley long to catch the significance. "Of course—hydrosulfanyl acid!" He looked up at Twomey. "No dust!"
"No dust?" said Twomey, bewildered.
"Solution!"
"What?"
"They don't use a dust. They put it into a solution. They get the plutonium into a solution. That's the way to do it. Then it could be blown out—like a hair spray!"
Ridley's thought processes ran on unchecked. "No. Even better! As a fog! San Francisco's fog machine!"
"Holy smoke!"
"That's it. Dissolve the plutonium in solvent in a closed container. Get a commercial fog maker, put it on the bridge or in any tall western building, open the window. Set a timer to start the fog hours after you've long gone! There won't be a flash in the sky, no thunderclap, no odor. Just a silent, deadly, invisible, radioactive cloud of plutonium particles whipping through the city in a matter of minutes, carried by the prevailing winds. . . . "
"Diabolical!"
"Somebody out there has asked the right questions and gotten the right answers. You've got to get him!"

"Sir," the aide interrupted again. "We've got the borrower's name."

Ridley looked at the message. "Cooper, Daniel Cooper. My God!"

He felt as if his head was going to blow up. It was full of revelations. It all fitted together. Motive—Cooper done in by Aspermont, or so he thought. Intelligent—Cooper was very bright. Method—Cooper had worked in the cyclotron lab. It fitted all too well.

There was a further break in the case. A bartender in the Marina was shown Gray's photo and remembered him in the company of a man with a trigger temper and rather odd behavior Sunday night. "We've got him coming in," the aide said.

Ridley looked at Twomey. "You've got two leads now—lab equipment companies and industrial chemical companies."

"How?"

"We could try to find out who bought one or the other in the last six months and where it went. The acid is the best bet."

"Let's get on that right now."

It was midnight.

Julie awoke with a start. After her release earlier that day she consulted her lawyer and went on home, where she had collapsed in bed. Her night in jail had bruised her mentally and physically. She had planned to take a nap and then leave, get out from this place as far as she could.

She had a headache. Her mouth was dry and stale. She felt very stiff. She would have slept longer, but up from her subconscious had emerged a disturbing memory to wake her. The man she had seen in the elevator on the way up Sunday night. She had thought his face was familiar, but she hadn't been able to recall where she had seen him. Now she remembered. That was the man with the atomic heart! That was Gray. She had seen his picture in the newspapers. He must be here in this same building somewhere!

"Damn! I'm not staying around here any longer," Julie murmured. Quickly, she threw the bed cover aside and leaped upright. She dragged out some suitcases from the closet and commenced packing.

"Lieutenant Twomey, the hostage's vehicle has been located."

"Where?"

"It was impounded for illegal parking at Northpoint."

"Abandoned?"

"It looks that way."

"Have a crew going over it?"

"They're on their way from central lab. The auto is intact, no signs of violence. The trunk was empty—no clue of any sort in it. Nothing to indicate that a body had been in it."

"Northpoint?" said Ridley. "That's northwest San Francisco. He may not be far from there."

Chapter 41

Bradfield reached the Page Mill Road turnoff from the freeway at thirty minutes after midnight. He pulled over to the side of the road, stopped, and noted the mileage on the odometer. He felt tired. Pouring a cup of hot coffee from a thermos flask provided by his secretary, he sat back and relaxed for a few minutes. He had expected the drop to have been made on King's Mountain, but there had been no signal. The son-of-a-bitch! He's playing games, he thought. The coffee gave him a lift but Bradfield's eyes still burned with fatigue and lack of sleep. It was a familiar feeling, he reflected, recalling his days in training.

He started up the engine and resumed his journey. The road from here on was winding but fairly wide for the first three miles. His headlights lit up briefly scenes on each side of the road—a narrow footbridge over a dry creek, a turn past the last home with a corral and a horse standing quietly at the fence; then the first deep curve to the left as the car started to climb toward the mountains, dimly silhouetted in the moonlight. As he looked up he saw a pair of headlights weaving down the mountain side, but he lost them as the car passed around a bend.

Now down to five miles per hour, the engine purred in low gear, shifting automatically over the crest as the road curved down and to the right. The road was narrowing as it entered thick groves of redwood trees. Around the curve, Bradfield saw the headlights of the descending car, flicking up and down. He honked his horn. The two cars met, both traveling slowly. Bradfield, on the outside of the road, almost came to a stop to allow the other car to pass. He looked intently and saw two men silhouetted in the front seat. The other car had no insignia. It moved slowly but continuously. The men looked over.

Bradfield breathed deeply. He hoped they had not lost him. He hoped those were police. His hands were slippery with sweat and he wiped them off on his pants, one by one. He continued upward, peering carefully onto the left side of the road for the red signal light.

The two cops became tense and alert. They were in the right place at the right time. "Was that the doctor?" said the cop.

"I'm pretty sure it was."

"It's possible we've got the kidnaper in between us and the patrol at the summit," one of them said. "If it's true, he can only drive out by this road, I reckon. He'd be a fool to try to walk through the scrub."

"Should we set up a block here?"

"Let's turn around and face upward. There's a wide spot about half a mile down from here to turn around."

When they reached the spot to turn they saw an old car with a flat tire taking up the space.

"Wouldn't you know it?"

"We've got to drive down, turn around, and get back up in a hurry."

They drove down the road another mile and a half. Finding the first convenient spot, they turned around and roared back up again. They stopped in the middle of the paving at a point where the road ran straight for a short distance.

"There. No car will be able to make it past us."

They got out to look around. The road was narrow. They were risking a rear-end collision parked as they were.

"Shouldn't I put flares out?"

"Can't. It will warn them."

They spoke in loud whispers.

"If anything comes, we'll turn on our headlights at the right time."

"Okay."

They reentered the car and waited.

Cooper had driven from Candlestick Park immediately after spotting Bradfield. His route was direct down Skyline Boulevard to Page Mill Road. Halfway down the road he stopped and dropped off a bicycle and a red flashlight. Concealing them behind some bushes, he drove the car farther down the road to an area wide enough to have a decent shoulder. He parked. He worked with one of the tires. A long hissing sound penetrated the quiet. The auto sank crazily to one side. He trudged up the steep road to the location of the bicycle.

From his vantage point he could see the first stretch of Page Mill before it started curving upward. As he waited there three cars had passed going downhill, but he had noted only two on the lower stretch. There was one car somewhere on the road below him. Two other cars had come up the road and were far beyond him. None of them had stopped when he blinked the red flashlight.

But now there was a third car coming up and this could be it. He felt his plans were reaching a climax. In the chill of air at 2,000 feet, he waited.

Bradfield drove slowly, virtually crawling when he spotted it. There it was, an unmistakable blinking red light. He looked at his odometer to mark the distance from the last reading. He slowed to a stop and reached for the bag of money. Leaning out of the window, he pendulumed the duffel bag for a couple of swings, then let it fly off the road into a shallow gully. Without bothering to look around, he stepped quickly on the accelerator and took off. He thought, I hope that does the trick and he lets Gray go.

Half a mile beyond the drop, Bradfield reached back for the suitcase and threw it out into the brush at the side of the road.

"I hope they catch that clue," he said to himself and continued on.

The direction finder was no longer sensitive to small changes in location because of the distance and the rough terrain. It took some time before police technicians were confident of their observations.

"It's been in the same place for six minutes now. Tell headquarters the drop has been made."

Cooper's heart beat quickly as the solitary car crawled up the winding road and vanished beyond him. He waited a few minutes, leaning quietly against a tree. Then he stretched his muscles and pushed himself away from the trunk. Walking heavily through the soft forest floor, he paused at the edge of the pavement and looked both ways. All was quiet. It did not take long to locate the duffel bag, only a short distance from the road in a hollow. He picked it up, hefting it experimentally. It was heavy. As he stepped onto the shoulder of the road, his foot twisted on a small rock. He fell heavily and rolled down the bank onto the earth and dry leaves below.

"Shit!" he blurted out when the prickly leaves scratched his face. He lay cheek down for a minute, panting harshly, then rolled over to look upward. Getting up, finally, he stumbled up the bank back to his hiding post. For a moment, he bent over trying to control his breathing.

In the police car the two men had just heard over the radio that the drop had been made. They were ordered to move slowly up the mountain road. Other patrol cars would converge on the scene from both directions.

Cooper had placed the duffel bag onto the sturdy bicycle, and had started downhill around the bend, pedaling furiously.

The police car engine started and the headlights came on as Cooper came flying around the bend. The lights almost blinded him, and he swerved to the inner side of the road between the police car and the rockface. He flew by with barely enough room to spare.

The cops were startled into immobility as the unexpected apparition came flying out of the darkness at them and then hurtled past in an instant.

"Call control," the driver barked. "It won't be possible to catch him if we go up the hill to turn around." In an instant judgment, he started to back the car down the road. He used as his marker the side of the pavement, but he moved too quickly. The pavement disappeared. He turned sharply, but too late. The car slipped over the edge, partly in space, partly against a tree. They were stuck until help arrived.

Cooper moved fast downhill. He desperately braked with both hands as he approached his car. The brakes finally locked the wheels and the bicycle skidded sideways into the car. Cooper felt a sharp pain in his side when he hit and fell off the bike onto the abrasive shoulder of the road. He crawled on his hands and knees toward the rear of the car and unlocked the trunk. From it he produced a bottle of compressed air to reinflate the deliberately deflated tire. He drew gasping breaths as he sat with his head propped against the side of the car. The entire effort had reduced him to total exhaustion. He pulled the duffel bag off the bike and dropped it into the trunk of the car. Then he pushed the bike off the road down the bank.

With a last maximum mental effort to overcome his fatigue, he fell into the driver's seat. He recovered sufficiently to run the car over the shoulder and drove off hoping to cover the short distance to the freeway before the cops arrived. In fact, they just missed him. All the reinforcements saw was a rapidly disappearing tail light in the distance.

En route to the apartment, he felt pressure deep within his chest. The strain of the last few hours was taking its toll and he hurried to get back. His last cough had produced a salty taste in his mouth. He knew it was blood. He could not afford to stop now. He thought he had it made when he drove into the basement garage at the Marina Towers, but his car lights picked the figure of a uniformed cop.

Officer Murphy was looking directly at him!

Chapter 42

Mayor Delmonico called a meeting with executives of the broadcast and print media. The room was stuffy and filled with tobacco smoke. The tightly packed crowd was curious, some of them anxious. At 1:00 A.M. a meeting with the Mayor was certainly not routine. Everybody who was anybody had been awakened and taken by police escort to the hall.

The Mayor's eyelids were beginning to puff up from lack of sleep. His face was drawn. He was not the hail-fellow-well-met guy, his usual demeanor with which the press was familiar. He was about to lie in his teeth to the members of the fourth estate.

"I've asked you all here because we're facing a desperate situation," said Delmonico. "I want it clearly understood that my comments about the problem I shall describe are off the record for at least twenty-four hours. I trust I can depend on your full cooperation."

There was a stir in the room as Delmonico explained the situation. Everybody started talking simultaneously and a few hands went up. The Mayor cut in.

"Please, gentlemen! Let me finish. We're urging a news blackout until the situation is clarified. We must have your cooperation. This gentleman beside me is from the FBI. He'll give you all the information you need when it's appropriate. We understand it's a big story from your standpoint, but we've got to protect the victim."

"But," someone shouted, "this is nuclear blackmail!"

"Our experts don't think there's any danger of a nuclear explosion. You can check that with independent physicists if you like. But if you publish the story, there will be panic, fatalities, property damage—even anarchy! You wouldn't want to be responsible for that, would you?"

Twomey entered, waved his arm to attract the Mayor's attention, and jerked his thumb toward the door. The Mayor turned the meeting over to the FBI man, and stepped outside.

"Fortunately, they didn't ask about the possible distribution of the plutonium by aerosol," Delmonico said to Twomey. "Those guys were about to eat me alive. But I think they'll cooperate. These news executives are businessmen. They understand what's at stake. What did you want to see me about?"

"Ridley has located a distributor of materials that can be used in dissolving plutonium," said Twomey. "It's Van Eckstein-Horner in the warehouse district. The manager will open his records if we get a court order or approval from the company owner."

"Christ!" shouted the mayor. "What the hell is going on! Can't you get a judge to issue one?"

"It will take time to get the judge going. Would you consider talking to the company president? His name is James Coulson. He lives in Pacific Heights."

"Good! I know him. His house is right down the block from mine. Let's get to a phone."

It took just under an hour to make the arrangements. Twomey and Ridley entered the deserted office building with the company manager. They went immediately to the records, stored on a small desktop IBM computer.

"Here," said the manager. "Put the tape in, hit the program key for search, then type in your defining parameters."

Ridley did so, and the characters flashed onto an eight-by-ten oscilloscope screen. Despite the computer's speed, Ridley thought the scan was moving too slowly. All of the deliveries in the first six tapes went to addresses in the Portrero and Waterfront districts. It was on the seventh tape that this information showed up:

Two 50-gallon drums of organic solvent, April 19.
1 Northpoint Avenue, Apt. #3001: 2 gallons of HSA acid.

"That's it," said Ridley. "Who would order industrial-grade acid in the Marina Towers!"

"There's a fix on the location."

The dispatcher's voice came through to the command center. In the squad car Twomey started talking into the radio, ordering a mass movement of men and equipment into the Marina Towers area. Radiation monitor teams were also mobilized. They were vans and station wagons equipped with shovels, axes, fire rakes, and Geiger counters. The fire engine companies were alerted. Two SWAT teams, fully and heavily armed, were on their way. Alerted also were several units of national guardsmen. They were standing by at the armory, ready to move if needed.

It was now 3:30 A.M.

Officer Murphy was more than a little surprised. At that hour he had been catching a little sleep when the sound of the car engine had shattered the calm and made him sit bolt upright. Cooper screeched his tires as he brought the car to a sudden halt in front of Murphy. The cop shone a flashlight directly into Cooper's eyes. "Roll down your window, please, sir."

Cooper complied nervously. Because he had to look up at the tall, heavily built cop, his stretched neck muscles in front tugged on his windpipe. This position irritated the raw sensory nerves, and he began to cough helplessly. Phlegm popped out with the coughing. Murphy jerked back, repelled, but the clot of phlegm landed on his shoe.

"Oh, I'm sorry, officer," Cooper said feebly. "I'm a sick man, you know. Here, let me wipe that off."

Cooper opened the door and reached over to wipe off Murphy's shoe. Bending over forced his diaphragm up, and the air space in his lungs was decreased. He gasped for breath, causing yet another fit of interminable coughing. The tumor in his lung wore off a little more of the pulmonary artery wall under the continued pressure. Cooper sat back on the seat of the car. He looked up at the cop wordlessly, trying to catch his breath.

"Jeez, man! Have you seen a doctor?" was all Murphy could say.

The coughing finally eased up so that Cooper was able to draw a decent breath of air. "Oh, I'm sorry," he stuttered. "I'll be all right, officer."

"You live here?"

"Yes. Is there a problem of some kind?"

Murphy kept his distance. "Well, let's look at your car."

"What for?"

"I've been assigned to guard this place."

"From what?"

"Terrorists."

"Well, I'm not a terrorist. This is my residence."

Murphy's eyes narrowed as he looked at Cooper. "Okay, you live here, but that cuts no ice with me. I have my orders. Now open up your trunk."

"Just what are you looking for, may I ask?"

"A very large package—one that could just fit in your trunk!"

"You have a search warrant?"

"You got something to hide?"

"No, no."

"How about a little voluntary cooperation with your local police then?"

Cooper, intimidated by the cop's commanding presence, got out of the car and opened the trunk. Murphy's flashlight spun about the interior, outlining the duffel bag. Cooper tried not to look at it and kept his eyes on Murphy.

"Okay," said the cop. "You can go on in. You'd better get yourself a doctor."

And with that, Murphy pointedly polished the tip of his shoe by running it up and down the back of his leg.

Julie had finished packing. All the drawers were out, the closets wide open. Jewel boxes had been emptied. Five suitcases were stuffed full. Her furniture, the paintings, the stereo, a baby grand piano were to be left behind.

She picked up the phone and dialed her lawyer's home number.

A sleepy voice answered, "Yeah. Who? Julie! Do you know it's after three o'clock in the morning?"

"I'm all done," Julie said. "The apartment is cleaned out."

"Couldn't you wait to tell me in the morning."

"No. I'm leaving now. I want you to look after things."

"Sure, I'll rent it out for you."

"Did you liquidate my holdings in ATOCOR?"

"Is the Pope Catholic? You have a tidy little sum on a thousand shares. The price was down a bit from yesterday's close."

"It will come down with a bang once the story gets out. The company is done for!"

"Where do you want the funds transferred to?"

"I'll check back with you soon. You can get me at Mendocino General Delivery."

"Fine, fine, and lots of luck! Keep in touch."

"Okay, and thanks a lot. Goodbye."

Julie had parked her Porsche on the main floor driveway. She moved the last two suitcases quickly into it. Her light Givenchy suede dress rustled with each movement. Her hair was severely secured in place with a silk kerchief. Everything taken care of, she thought. Now back up to her apartment for the last time to make a telephone call to the San Francisco police about Gray. And she could go off with an easy mind.

The elevator was at the basement garage level. She pressed the button and in a few seconds the door slid open. She stepped in and pressed her floor button. It was then that she looked at the other occupant of the elevator, and her eyes widened first in recognition, then in fright. It was the man she had seen with Gray. His face was bruised and his eyes had a wild look. On the floor at his side was a bulkily packed duffel bag.

The gasp of recognition and look of fear on her face betrayed her. Cooper was on to her.

"Not a sound," he said. "I know what you're going to do. Turn me into the cops."

"No, no. Not me, I promise. I can help you. I'll give you money. Anything you want—anything."

Say anything, she thought. She was in a tight spot.

"Liar! I know your kind."

"No, you're wrong. I'm getting out myself."

"Shut up!" Cooper said, his voice rough.

It was too late, she thought. She had to get out. She reached over to the emergency button. Almost automatically, Cooper leaped over and, with the side of his hand, chopped at her neck just below the ear. She fell, off-balance, and her head hit the side of the elevator wall with a sharp crack. She slumped to the floor, unconscious. The desperate Cooper fell on his knees beside her body. He grabbed the soft, fragile neck in his hands and, as the elevator climbed quietly upward, tightened his fingers. She had stopped breathing by the time they had reached the thirtieth floor.

The doors slid open and Cooper looked out cautiously. The hallway was empty. He started to haul the body out, his breath coming in gasps. The body was halfway out when the doors started to close. When they hit Julie's body, they automatically opened again. Cooper stepped over her and put the door switch on lock. He resumed dragging the body along the hallway, fumbled with his key and opened the door. Now, almost exhausted, he dragged the body into his apartment and let it slip down to rest awkwardly along the wall of the living room. Then, leaving the outer door open, he stumbled back to the elevator, picked up Julie's purse, gathered up the strings of the duffel bag, and hauled it out. He leaned into the elevator and turned the lock switch off. The doors slid to.

When Cooper returned to the apartment, dragging the duffel bag behind him, he was hot and sweaty. The pressure in his chest was building up again. The events of the last few hours, the exertion on the mountainside, the shock of seeing the cop in the basement, and now the murder of this woman had tipped him over into madness.

He searched Julie's purse, found and removed a small caliber gun inside, and slipped it into his pocket. Then he dug into the bag. The note was there, he noticed with satisfaction, but the money in it—it didn't seem as much as it should have been. He tipped the bundles out on the floor. After a quick estimate he could see it was far short of the full amount he had demanded.

Well, he thought, that's it. No reason to hold back now. He'd fix them all for good. Taking the gun out of his pocket, he strode over to the cellar prison, flicked the outside light switch, and opened the door. Gray, weak himself from fever, stared at the gun pointing directly at him.

"Out! Get over there!"

Cooper, backing out slowly, jerked the gun in the direction of the living room.

Gray shuffled out, shielding his eyes from the glare. Once accustomed to the light, he recognized the man he had met at the hotel. He now remembered their conversation just before he had passed out. This man had told him that one could poison the whole city with the fuel content of one artificial heart. He looked at Cooper now, dazed and speechless.

Gray stopped in the center of the room and saw the two drums and a smaller container in one corner. He saw the body of a woman slumped down awkwardly on the floor. He turned around to face Cooper, now just a few yards away and holding the gun pointed at Gray's heart.

Cooper spoke, his voice querulous. "I asked for two million dollars and no interference from cops in return for . . . " Again and again came deep hacks as he tried to go on speaking. " . . . in return for the plutonium and you. They didn't take me seriously, or they think you're worth less! Okay, I'll make the trade less, too. I'll take the plutonium and give you back."

"You're crazy. You're not going to make it. You're going to die, too, and you'll die for nothing. I can help you. I can get you a doctor and put you in a hospital to help you get well."

"You mean, you're going to put me in an asylum." Cooper's eyes had a hard, fixed stare. He was mad, crazy.

Gray tried to step toward Cooper, but he stumbled, weak from heat exhaustion. Cooper retreated a step, but Gray came on again. Cooper fired. The blast rang in their ears and Gray was driven back by a terrible transfixing pressure that spread all over his chest. He lost his balance momentarily but felt no pain. He braced himself against the wall and drew a deep breath. Cooper still stood there where he had fired, his eyes wide with fear as Gray remained upright. The bullet had smashed against the impenetrable fuel capsule which formed the front of Gray's chest.

A second blast came from the gun as Cooper desperately pumped another shot into Gray's chest with the same effect. Cooper's hand holding the gun began to shake.

Gray, had he known, might have overcome the armed man quite easily at that moment, but his thoughts had now concentrated on something else. He had to keep the fuel in his heart machine away from Cooper. The next shot, wild or not, might immobilize him, hitting his head or leg. It took only a second for Gray to make his decision.

He had gauged the distance between himself and the open glass door to the balcony as no more than fifteen feet. He dodged sideways, away from Cooper. He was through the door in seconds. He climbed onto the balustrade and, without any hesitation, launched himself out into space. Dear God, he thought, let the capsule hold! The seconds passed into an eternity.

As Gray had dodged sideways, Cooper had fired two more shots, one plowing into the smaller drum, the other hitting the glass door, shattering it into a thousand splinters. From the small drum, a stream of acid started to spill out onto the floor, eating great holes in the carpet and oozing toward the clips of money strewn about in its path.

Chapter 43

Cooper, shocked momentarily to immobility, recovered and ran out to the balcony. He looked and could just make out the body in the dim phosphorescence of the water below. That's over, he thought numbly and returned to the room.

He saw the spilling acid spreading over the bundles of notes. Frantically, he went about throwing the bundles out of range of the flowing acid. Carpeting and underpadding were converted into blocks of black-and-brown char, and the concrete was now showing through. The duffel bag was untouched. He grabbed it, stuffing as much clean money as he could into its depths. Some of the money was eaten up beyond retrieval. He took out his wallet, removed all identification cards, and threw them into the boiling acid.

Over by the outer door, he paid no attention to the scene left behind him. There was no time to do anything more. The woman's body would have to be left where it was. He swung the duffel bag over his shoulder and left.

"Hey! Officer! There's a body at the bottom of the building on the Bayside!

Murphy saw the robed man standing at the elevator door at the end of the garage. The two men pushed through the fire exit and ran around the outside of the north wing.

Murphy's companion spoke as they went. "I heard a sharp noise, then two more, then I saw something fly past my balcony. I couldn't sleep and was just going into the kitchen for a glass of milk. I knew you were in the building. It's okay that I called you, isn't it?"

"It certainly is." They panted around the last corner.

Gray's body had landed on a narrow rocky ledge between the foundation of the building and the gently lapping waters of the Bay.

"What floor are you on?" asked Murphy.

"The twenty-eighth."

"And he came from above you?"

"Yes," said the man, recoiling as he looked down at the broken, bloody corpse.

"He has to be dead. No doubt about that. Don't touch the body and get back into the building. We'll be talking to you later."

The man withdrew thankfully, and hurried back along the path to the garage.

Twomey and Ridley sirened their way along Van Ness Avenue. Other cars, lights flashing, sirens screaming, were converging on the high-rise apartment complex known as the Marina Towers. Roadblocks were being set up in a great semicircle.

Cooper, before leaving the shelter of the elevator, poked his head cautiously out the door to take a quick look round the garage. Was that cop still prowling around? But Officer Murphy was at that moment at a street police phone, talking to headquarters. Cooper heard the approaching sirens as he turned the ignition key in his car. His heart paused. The engine turned over and over and finally caught. He drove circumspectly out of the garage to evade attention. It was to no avail.

Twomey and Ridley had left their car and were running towards the front entrance as Cooper was leaving.

"Hey!" Ridley shouted as the car drove past the well-lighted entrance. "That's him. That's Cooper!"

Cooper saw them. He gunned the accelerator and swerved onto the street, rebounding off a parked car as he sped toward Russian Hill.

Ridley and Twomey raced back to their car to give chase. They radioed an alert for the escaping Cooper. At that moment Cooper's car came over the top of the hill, bouncing on the cable car tracks. He pushed the accelerator to the floor and the car again surged forward. But two level blocks ahead of him, there were police cars parked diagonally across the road bed, blocking one escape route. Cooper could vaguely make out figures of cops standing behind one of the cars. One was waving his arms; the other stood stark still.

Suddenly his own windshield had a hole in it, followed by a sharp sound. Some glass bit sharply into his face. The wind whistled by his ear. He could barely see through the shattered glass. They were shooting at him.

He hit the brakes sharply. The car skidded, the rear end swinging around wildly. Cooper mounted a curb, but then regained control. He swung the car hard to the right and headed down a side street. At the bottom of the hill were more police setting up yet another roadblock. He thought he could get through. He did not know that Twomey and Ridley were hard after him.

Then it happened. He felt a sharp pain. His cancer-weakened pulmonary artery began to leak black liquid blood into his windpipe. He coughed out sputum and blood. Each heartbeat poured out more blood. He spat out desperately with rasping coughs. Clots formed and spilled over into his good lung. He hungered for air. His diaphragm went down, the spaces between his ribs indented, but no air entered. He tried again. His windpipe was blocked. His heart beat faster, his face turned blue. He lost consciousness, then slumped forward on to the wheel.

The car careened down the hill, its speed accelerating toward the roadblock. It smashed through the first barrier, throwing wood around like kindling, and came to rest against a concrete abutment. The hot engine ignited leaking gas with a *whoosh.*

Officer Washington, manning the barricade, saw the driver's door burst open as the car hit the concrete. Cooper was hanging limply over the wheel. His suffering had ended.

"Get that guy out of there before he becomes a crispy critter!" another cop shouted.

Twomey and Ridley arrived. As they got out of their car, they saw Washington pull Cooper's body out of the burning vehicle. In the light of the flames they saw money scattered all over the interior. Washington picked a handful out of the front seat, then the heat drove him back. As he moved out of range, the car exploded. In a matter of minutes it was burned to a blackened, charred heap.

Ridley and Twomey stood behind the squad car, shielding their faces from the hot conflagration. Ridley's shoulders were slumped, his taut face now relaxed. The two men looked at each other. It was over. Cooper had lost. But nobody won.

Gray's body was in the same position when a foggy dawn came. Twomey had ordered the air conditioning in the building to be turned off. The occupants were roused and moved out, windows and doors closed off. The Bayside, upwind, was soon ringed with police and fireboats about one hundred yards offshore. Ridley and the Emergency Director supervised the operations from one of the tugboats. He watched through powerful binoculars as two figures, clothed in heavy lead-lined suits, approached the body. The men carried self-containing breathing systems on their backs to protect themselves from possible contamination. They communicated with the Director on the tugboat through walkie-talkies. The two "space" men examined the grounds minutely with ultrasensitive radiation counters. Their approach was systematic, their movements slow and deliberate.

"Sir"—the eerie, reverberating voice was heard by Ridley and the Director—"there's no contamination in the area."

"Approach the body and examine it."

The two figures knelt beside Gray's body. The darkened area where blood had escaped and congealed on the chest came under close scrutiny from the counters.

"No radiation was in the bloodstream before death. Hey! The heart's still beating!"

"My God, is he still alive?"

Ridley said softly, "No, the machine's beating, but he's dead. That beat isn't life, it's just mechanical action. It means the fuel capsule is intact."

"Okay," said the Director. "Let the crime lab people in to inspect the body and take their pictures. Let's move him out of there. Isolation procedures are now cancelled. Resume routine operations."

Chapter 44

As Bradfield was changing for the day's operating schedule, he was called to the telephone. He had slept deeply but not long enough to make up fully for the lost hours.

"Dr. Bradfield?"

"Yes."

"This is Lieutenant Twomey."

"Yes."

"We found Gray. He's dead, I'm afraid."

Bradfield listened in dazed silence. A patient lost, and the responsibility his. *His* mistake in judgment. Yet in looking back, he could not see how he could have judged differently. It was a conflict of values—values learned and inculcated subconsciously in the tenets of his profession. A surgeon deals with individual human lives. He pledges himself to do the very best he can for that individual. Bradfield believed that in implanting the heart he had done the best for Gray; he had given hope to many others like him. But perhaps this hadn't been enough.

"And the plutonium? Was it retrieved?" he asked.

"The capsule was intact."

"The money?"

"Most of it destroyed."

"Geld isn't going to like that! Has Mrs. Gray been informed?"

"I was going to call her next."

"I'll do that. It's my responsibility. When is the autopsy?"

"In a few hours."

"I'll be there."

"Okay. It will be at the Coroner's Office at San Francisco General."

Bradfield hung up and redialed.

"Mrs. Gray?"

"Yes."

"Dr. Bradfield here. I'm very sorry to have to tell you that we've lost Mr. Gray. I want to say we all regret deeply this turn of events. We tried very hard, but I fear our artificial heart is not right for the times we live in."

Janet had tried to prepare herself over the past terrible hours for such an eventuality. She had feared it was almost inevitable. Nevertheless, she still felt the shock. Her emotions hit bottom. Her husband dead, and she was carrying his child. Gray had known nothing about it because it was to be her big surprise at some just right moment.

"Are you all right, Mrs. Gray?" Bradfield asked anxiously as her silence lengthened.

"Yes, I'm all right, as well as I can be under the circumstances. What about the plutonium?"

"Safe."

"And the kidnaper?"

"I'm afraid I didn't ask."

"Dr. Bradfield, there's something you can do for me."

"Anything at all."

"Can you arrange for me to see an obstetrician as soon as possible?"

"Yes, of course. I didn't know."

"I thought it best to take a chance on getting pregnant. Now, I know it was the right thing. I want to protect the only thing I've got left."

"Yes, I'll see to it right away."

Bradfield made the arrangements for Janet's appointment, then finished dressing for surgery. Once again, he stood before the running water, undergoing the ritual washing of hands before resuming the process of saving life.

The air was still and humid. The room was brilliantly lit with fluorescent lights. A microphone hung down over each autopsy table so that the pathologist could dictate his findings.

The autopsy had just been completed. The heart had been removed, still functioning until it had been disconnected from the fuel capsule and control unit. The surgeon said to Twomey, "Curious! Two holes were found in the anterior chest wall which penetrated the skin. Fragments of lead were found adjacent to the dense fibrous tissue surrounding the power supply. In the normal situation the cause of death would have been the heart wounds. In this case the wounds were definitely not fatal. All other injuries were compatible with the fall from a great height."

Twomey said, "There were two sets of footprints on the carpet. One set of dusty footprints, presumably from the wine cellar, led directly to the center of the room, then at right angles onto the balcony. The other set—very clear prints due to the acid—did not touch or even come close to the first set."

"So Gray jumped—wasn't pushed—you think?"

"Yes, that's the conclusion. It ties in with your findings."

"Well, stress can do strange things to people."

"In this case, Doc, I don't think it was just stress. It was a well-thought out, deliberate move."

The pathologist was puzzled but asked no more of the exhausted cop. He walked to the next table and began the autopsy of the second body, the female.

Harris arrived at the Hall of Justice to pick up the artificial heart. The heart and its plutonium power supply had been placed in a large sealed container. It was guarded by two uniformed policemen outside Twomey's office.

Harris's eyes suddenly glittered with excitement when he

saw the heart. "You know, lieutenant," he said brightly, "this incident verifies that all design criteria for the artificial heart have not only been met but greatly exceeded. Bullets hit it at close range with only external wounds. Perfect containment after a thirty-story fall!"

"Three people are dead, *Mister* Harris. A city has been threatened. Is that all you can say?"

Harris took no notice of Twomey's statement. His eyes blinked once, then turned to examine the container.

Twomey said in a tightly controlled voice, "Why don't you just take that thing and get the hell out of here, Harris!"

He turned and left. The next thing he feared was tomorrow's news. As he passed the newsstands, the headlines of the afternoon papers told just the bare factual details. Undoubtedly, tomorrow and for weeks thereafter the editorials would follow: "Can the experts be trusted?" "An indictment of the integrity of science," and so on.

He had lost.

Twomey looked out of his office window and saw Bradfield walking up the marble steps of City Hall. Bradfield's step was brisk. The typical San Francisco breezes had returned and whipped at his clothes and hair. Ridley had just left Twomey's office on his way back to Boston. The cop observed them as the two men spoke briefly, their appearance awkward and restrained.

"Hello, Allen."

"Bill."

"I heard that you put it all together. You don't know how much I appreciate that."

"I did what I could."

"You should also know that I assume full responsibility for the problems that arose. It was a mistake—starting a long time ago."

"You did what you thought was right. The problems are not simple. A lot of individual moral values are involved. You and I have learned from this, but it will happen again. Each superspecialist wants to learn his own lesson. The trouble is, the stakes get higher every time."

"If there's a chance, any chance at all, that problems caused by technology could outweigh the benefits, we should stop. Trouble is, I hardly know any scientists who will dare say, 'Stop.'"

"Yes, Bill. But it's time that we tried."

Bradfield nodded and put out his hand. Ridley shook it briefly, then turned and went off down the steps.

Epilogue

A congressional committee investigated the events. It recommended curtailment of the Artificial Heart Program and legislation to regulate medical technological developments.

Harris left the Heart Institute. He is now a registered lobbyist in Washington, D.C.

Mayor Delmonico became a U.S. Senator. Ridley joined his staff as a consultant on nuclear energy.

Bradfield remained at Aspermont.

Janet Gray gave birth to a healthy baby girl. Fears that stray radiation from the father's heart may have caused congenital defects failed to materialize.

Lieutenant Twomey was promoted to Chief Inspector.

There are thirteen artificial heart patients in the United States. They live under assumed identities and constant protection. Only their physicians and the FBI know their whereabouts.